Praise for

Wunderland

"The title of this searing account of life in Nazi Germany alludes to *Alice's Adventures*—and the surreal feeling of watching what you thought was true exposed as false. . . . Inspired by the memoir of a Hitler Youth member, it's a heartbreaking page-turner."

—*People* (Book of the Week)

"Engrossing . . . Epstein reveals the devastating choices these women make."

—*Real Simple*

"[An] intimate, unflinching saga of friendship, womanhood, and the awful legacy of Nazi Germany."

—*USA Today*

"*Wunderland* is both an engrossing family drama and a foray into a dark period of history . . . a wholly original angle to the WWII novel. You'll read it in one shivered sitting."

—*Refinery29*

"A vividly written and stark chronicle of Nazism and its legacies."

—*Kirkus Reviews* (starred review)

"A wealth of history turns *Wunderland* into a novel that's both beautiful and devastating. . . . Epstein taps into the 1930s prewar era, laying out an unsparing narrative that details tragic events and horrifying legacies . . . opening a new door that may lead to redemption and joy for future generations."

—*BookPage* (starred review)

"[A] heartbreaking historical tour de force . . . Man's inhumanity to man—and the redemptive power of forgiveness—is on stark and effective display in Epstein's gripping novel, a devastating tale bound for bestseller lists."

—*Publishers Weekly* (starred review)

"[An] absorbing exploration of friendship, betrayal, and coming to terms with the past."

—*Booklist* (starred review)

"*Wunderland* is a compelling, well-crafted story that also provides insights into the daily life of history."

—*New York Journal of Books*

"Take a fascinating inside look at the twisted world of Nazi Germany in *Wunderland*, Jennifer Cody Epstein's wonderful new novel. Both heartbreaking and hopeful, this story of a daughter searching for the truth about her mother's secret past, tangled up in old secrets and terrible lies, kept me up late turning pages."

—Martha Hall Kelly, bestselling author of *Lilac Girls*

"E.L. Doctorow once said, 'The historian will tell you what happened. The novelist will tell you how it felt.' This is one of those magnificent books that will make you feel everything—love, loss, betrayal, redemption, and how everyday citizens could be swept up in the manic fervor of Nazi Germany. The unintended parallels to today's political climate are haunting. Reading this book is like reading tea leaves, foretelling a future we desperately want to avoid."

—Jamie Ford, bestselling author
of *Hotel on the Corner of Bitter and Sweet*
and *Songs of Willow Frost*

"*Wunderland* is a beautiful and haunting and utterly magnificent novel: a wrenching tale of friendship and betrayal in Nazi Germany. It's also a page-turner that kept me reading until two in the morning one night and three in the morning the next. It's that good."

—Chris Bohjalian, bestselling author
of *The Flight Attendant*

"*Wunderland* is a sweeping, heart-stopping story. Jennifer Cody Epstein has a singular gift for bringing bygone worlds like 1930s Berlin blazingly to life, but lucky for her readers, she digs deeper. This is an unforgettable portrait of friendship and betrayal, mothers and daughters, the political forces beyond our control and the personal histories we can't shake. A rich, gripping novel."

—Ellen Umansky, author of *The Fortunate Ones*

"Not only an original and searing investigation into the seductive and terrifying world of Hitler's national socialist movement and its aftermath, but also a suspenseful and profoundly moving story of love, hate, passion, and devotion."

—Joanna Hershon, author of *Swimming*

"Through the friendship of two teenaged girls in 1930s Germany, *Wunderland* depicts, in intimate and chilling detail, how fascism, racism, and xenophobia are made normal and acceptable; how ordinary people, beguiled by the siren call of nationalism, are led willingly into acts of inhumanity—and could be again, if we ignore the lessons of the past. But this novel is more than a history lesson; it's a heart-in-your-mouth page-turner that leaves you thinking about its characters and imagining how things might have gone for them in a different world, long afterward."

—Hillary Jordan, author of *Mudbound*

Wunderland

Wunderland

A Novel

JENNIFER CODY EPSTEIN

BALLANTINE BOOKS

NEW YORK

A Ballantine Books Trade Paperback Edition

Copyright © 2019 by Jennifer Cody Epstein
Reading group guide copyright © 2019 by Penguin Random House LLC

Published in the United States by Ballantine Books, an imprint
of Random House, a division of Penguin Random House LLC, New York.

BALLANTINE and the HOUSE colophon are registered trademarks
of Penguin Random House LLC.
RANDOM HOUSE READER'S CIRCLE & Design is a registered trademark
of Penguin Random House LLC.

Originally published in hardcover in the United States by Crown, an imprint of
Random House, a division of Penguin Random House LLC, in 2019.

Grateful acknowledgment is made to the following for permission to reprint
previously published material:

Johannes Beilharz: Excerpt from *To the Prince of the Grail* by Else Lasker,
translated by Johannes Beilharz. Reprinted by Johannes Beilharz.

Dutton Children's Books: "The Dormouse and the Doctor" from *When We Were
Very Young* by A. A. Milne, copyright © 1924 by Penguin Random House LLC,
copyright renewed 1952 by A. A. Milne. Reprinted by permission of
Dutton Children's Books, an imprint of Penguin Young Readers Group,
a division of Penguin Random House LLC. All rights reserved.

ISBN 978-0-525-57691-4
Ebook ISBN 978-0525576921

Printed in the United States of America on acid-free paper

randomhousebooks.com
randomhousereaderscircle.com

2 4 6 8 9 7 5 3 1

Book design by Elina Nudelman

FOR JOAN AND TOM, WHO KEPT ME LOVINGLY STOCKED
IN PENS, PAPER, AND LITERARY PRAISE

"But I don't want to go among mad people," Alice remarked.

"Oh, you can't help that," said the Cat: "we're all mad here. I'm mad. You're mad."

"How do you know I'm mad?" said Alice.

"You must be," said the Cat, "or you wouldn't have come here."

—Lewis Carroll (Alice's Adventures in Wonderland)

Wunderland

1.

Ava

1989

She sits in a sea of tangled sheets and blankets, amid the white crests of packing peanuts and age-curled pages of letters pried from their envelopes with increasing feverishness. The bed is solid: the same heavy oaken headboard, same stained, sloping mattress upon which she has slept and breastfed and read and sketched for more than a decade; the one place she comes to truly be at rest. And yet at this moment, she's somehow both floating off it and falling right through it, is both untethered and sinking like a stone.

Perching her reading glasses atop her head, Ava Fischer clasps her knees to her chest. Her face tight and hot with tears shed, dried, and shed again, she tosses the last of the letters onto the bed. She feels shaken and uprooted; as though over the past hour she's been violently hurtled back in time, her understanding of her own life brusquely turned on its head page by page, memory by memory.

Surveying the sun-challenged domain that serves as both drawing studio and master bedroom, she finds herself amazed that it looks exactly as it did when she'd sat down to open the package. And yet the illustration she's been working on still sits atop her drafting table, anchored at one corner by an untouched plate of marmalade toast and another by a cold coffee mug inscribed with *Drink Me*. A few peanuts that escaped in her initial frenzy of unpacking the box still lie strewn on the shag carpet, air-puffed stars in eccentric and porous constellations against a worn, dun-colored sky.

But it's the bed that holds the full evidence of Ava's emotional undoing. The bed, with its wrinkled sheets and mismatched cushions, its dusty bedskirt and moth-eaten coverlet, its stale tobacco tang that somehow lingers on four full years after she stopped smoking. The bed, with the now-empty Luftpost carton her daughter had signed for earlier and carried in to Ava with mild curiosity (*It's from Bremen. Isn't that where you grew up?*).

The bed upon which Ava had then waited for what felt like hours, box in her lap, for Sophie to leave to meet her friends. Upon finally hearing her daughter's plastic-soled flats patter down four flights of stairs before exiting onto Second Avenue, she'd dropped the package long enough to lunge toward the window to watch the thirteen-year-old stroll off, her hands in the pockets of her checked menswear vest, Walkman headphones glinting silver in the sun.

The bed, where she'd read the lawyer's curtly formal note less with shock than a sinking sense of acceptance:

Sehr geehrte Frau von Fischer:

As your mother's lawyer and designated executor of her estate, I regret to inform you that your mother—Ilse Maria von Fischer—passed away on the twelfth of April, after a long battle with uterine cancer.

In accordance with her wishes, I enclose her remains for your disposal and request that you confirm delivery by fax or phone at the numbers listed on our letterhead. Once we have your confirmation we will be able to release the remainder of your inheritance, roughly 71,000 mark. If you do not confirm receipt in person, I've been instructed to donate this amount to The Blue Card, a charity of your late mother's choosing.

I also include some letters that your mother asked be forwarded to you, and request that you confirm receipt of these as well.

With condolences and best regards:
Bernard Frankel, LLP

Leaning stiffly against the headboard, Ava again forces herself to make these impossible-seeming connections: between the idea of *remains* and the Tupperware-style container she'd pulled from beneath the peanuts an hour earlier. Between *Mama*—that inevitably fraught and painful thought—and the gritty powder Ava had discovered upon prying off the container's lid. It hadn't smelled like Ilse, that disquietingly familiar blend of facial soap, 4711 cologne, and faint perspiration. It certainly hadn't looked like her; in Ava's mind's eye her mother was eternally milk-skinned and muscular, golden-haired and silver-eyed. Above all, overwhelmingly *dense.*

And yet staring into the ashy depths, she'd registered the truth of the lawyer's assertion: this was now quite literally all that was left of Ilse von Fischer, the evasive, icy parent who had abandoned Ava physically during the war and emotionally in its wake; who'd left her in this very apartment twelve years earlier, while Sophie wailed from her crib. And while it saddened Ava to realize that the woman herself no longer walked and breathed, in the end it hadn't really shocked her; for Ava, Ilse had effectively ceased to exist the moment she walked out the door that hot summer of 1977. Yes, for a few years there'd been the occasional long-distance call that Ava cut short after hearing Ilse's curt *Hallo.* There'd been the slow trickle of cards and letters and the occasional small package, all of which Ava returned to Bremen unopened. But once Sophie grew old enough to answer the phone and read the return addresses on envelopes, Ava changed their number and sent a telegraphed ultimatum through Western Union:

KONTAKTIERE UNS NICHT (STOPP) FÜR UNS BIST DU GESTORBEN (STOPP)
DO NOT CONTACT (STOP) FOR US YOU ARE DEAD (STOP)

No, it wasn't so much Ilse's physical remnants that had launched Ava into this vertiginous journey back through all those fraught moments with her mother. It was the words she had left behind: detailed, careful accounts sealed into over a dozen envelopes. *I also include some letters that your mother asked be forwarded to you*, the lawyer had written, almost in a casual aside. Could he have known all that they encompassed: the crushing truths and bereft confessions? Though to be sure, some of these had merely confirmed Ava's own long-held suspicions. *I actually began writing you*, one divulged, *from an old jail in Heidelberg, where the Americans had hoped to de-Nazify me.*

Entnazifizieren! She'd blinked at that unfamiliar and faintly absurd verb (as though moral rot could be extracted like a burst appendix!). But her shiver had been less one of surprise than vindication. *Everyone joined*, Ilse would say, shrugging, but Ava had always sensed a darker story shadowing this particular deflection.

Tossing the lawyer's note aside, Ava once more takes in her epistolary inheritance. Yellowing with age and of various thicknesses, the letters lie strewn over the coverlet. None of them seemingly sent; all of them addressed to the same woman:

Renate Bauer
163 Eldridge St
New York, New York 10002
USA

It's the first time Ava has encountered this name: *Renate Bauer.* But that Ilse wrote the woman obsessively is clear: the letters are all in her old-fashioned, slightly Gothic hand. And the return address is quite definitively the Schwachhausen row house that Ava still dreams of in startling detail: the lemon yellow her mother had painted Ava's bedroom wall as a child. The green chipped mug in which they'd kept their two toothbrushes. The dark circular stain on the wooden desk in Ilse's bedroom, the legacy of some slopped coffee, wine, or water.

Reaching for the nearest one—dated August 1976—Ava smooths the two thin sheets against the wrinkled linen of her pajama pants, catching a whiff of must and mothballs, a whispered vanilla hint. Like the others, this one is written in the informal *"Du"* form, as her mother would have addressed a close friend:

> *My dearest Reni!*
>
> *Last night I had a dream. It began the day that we first met in middle school; when you—late as always—rushed into me on your way into our classroom and dropped the books you were carrying. Strange, how so much from more recent years has become vague for me. And yet I still recall small details of our first encounter with such clarity: the golden brown of your eyes. The red bow in your hair. The worn book I handed back to you, with the comment that for some reason I'd only read the sequel, but had loved it.*
>
> *Then, somehow, it was later—much, much later, and I was walking down Unter den Linden, by the newsstands and the U-Bahn station, on the route we always took coming back to your house after school. I had the book, and I knew that returning it (not to you but to Franz for some reason) was of utmost, nearly crushing importance. The street was clean and gray and so crowded I could barely breathe. But it was also completely silent. I was aware of feeling very alone, and very worried that I wouldn't accomplish my task.*
>
> *Then I saw you only a few meters ahead, hurrying in the opposite direction. You were wearing your green coat and your little black hat, and Franz had on one of those tweed newsboys he used to favor. I felt such enormous joy and relief! I tried to catch up to you but the crowd kept pushing, pushing against me, pushing me back. I tried to call out to you, but though you seemed close enough you didn't hear me. The two of you just kept walking. And eventually, you both disappeared.*
>
> *I woke up in tears, but also strangely resigned. I don't know much about dreams—certainly not as much as your mother did (I still remember talking with her for hours about what ours were, what they meant). But it seemed to me that this one was perhaps a sign that it was finally time to realize the truth: that while I continually fantasize about*

reaching out to you and Franz, perhaps even coming to New York and hand-delivering my letters to you, the truth is that for the moment at least I lack the courage to even drop them into the post. I should therefore probably just stop writing them altogether. Indeed, if I were a less obstinate person I likely would have stopped a long time ago.

But we both know how I hold on to things.

Reni. If there were just one thing in all these writings I could communicate to you, it would be this: that if I could go back and change everything, I would. Everything. I would even change the fact of my own existence, my own birth, if it meant that I could undo what was done—to you, and to your family. That I can't is a fact that pains me every single day.

In the end, perhaps that is my true prison.

Ilse

Ava shuts her eyes. For a moment the old panic threatens: the suffocating certainty that the ceiling and walls are about to collapse, choking out all air and light. To counter the attack, she summons the comforting image suggested by her last therapist: the golden Montauk shoreline, captured breezily in midsummer.

But what comes instead is another beachside memory entirely.

In it Ava is perhaps six, on a rare mother-daughter outing to the Großer Wannsee shortly after their postwar reunion. The sand is wet and grainy, the day bone-bright and raw in the way very early spring days can be. At some point Ava sees Ilse striding away from her briskly, her braid-wrapped head a shrinking spot of brightness in the chill morning light. The sight pries open a black, panicked hole in Ava's center: *Come back*, she wails. *Don't leave me.* Leaping to her bare feet, she charges after the retreating figure—only to feel a pair of strong arms sweep her up from behind. For a moment she writhes and kicks before recognizing the still-unfamiliar form, the sturdy torso and round breasts pressed into her small back.

Dummes Mädchen, murmurs Ilse, who has been behind her the whole time. *What on earth is the matter with you now?*

The recollection carries the heft and hurt of a physical blow. What pulls her from it is a sudden pounding on the door, violent enough to rattle the ancient air conditioner in its frame.

"Mom!" Sophie shouts, with that spontaneous and implacable outrage peculiar to teenage girls. "I totally forgot I promised to bring Erica back her Lou Reed sweatshirt. Did you wash it? You said you were going to wash it."

Sophie? *Why was she back?* And how had she gotten in without Ava hearing her?

After a moment of blank paralysis she leaps to her knees and begins scrabbling the letters together. "Just a moment," she calls, thinking: *Scheisse, Scheisse,* Sophie. Her daughter fully believes that Ilse has been dead now for over a decade. *What am I going to tell her?*

"Mom! Do you have it?" The doorknob chatters in its fixture. "Oh my God—why is this *locked*?"

"Hold on! Just hold on a minute!" A desperate look around the unkempt bedroom: the sweatshirt's nowhere in sight.

Shoving the urn inside the box, Ava showers it with a handful of peanuts and sweeps the letters into an untidy pile beside it. Then she makes her way to the door, her knees as weak as a New York City Marathon runner's, her heart beating like a living creature in her mouth.

"Mom! *Jesus!"* (*Bang-bang-bang.*) "Erica's waiting! What the hell is going on in there?"

"Nothing," says Ava shakily.

And with a deep breath, she reaches for the doorknob.

2.

Renate

1933

A rush of despair washes over Renate, so potent it's almost liberating. She'll just have to own up to it, she decides. Her life will be over now. Over before anything real even happens in it: before she visits Paris or sees Elisabeth Schumann sing at the Vienna Opera. Before she experiences being tipsy or moodily smoking a cigarette that sketches languid ghostly images in the air. Before she experiences her first kiss—on her lips, or anywhere else.

It's a little past two, and the low-ceilinged school library is suffused with milky late-afternoon light. Her eyes are fixed on the wooden floor, on the black-and-white picture postcard that just flew from her opened notebook. She has no idea how it managed to get *into* the notebook, since she distinctly recalls putting it in a different section of her school satchel. But it now lies directly in the pacing path of the library proctor, Herr Steinberg. Herr Steinberg, who when not haranguing his meek-mouthed assistant (young Frau Bernhardt, who always looks as though she's about to cry) likes to stride between the long oaken library tables like the Kaiser inspecting his troops. Herr Steinberg, who has already sent two notes home to Renate's parents for "inappropriate comportment": the first for whispering with Ilse, the second for sneaking snacks.

Herr Steinberg, who—as Renate watches, as immobile as Galatea before Pygmalion's life-giving kiss—is about to step right on the Book Lady's placid face. Though actually, given the card's size, not just her face. On her face, and her breasts, and her belly, and her . . . in short, on every part of her completely unclothed physiognomy.

Schau nicht nach unten! Renate prays in silence to an unspecified Almighty (though nominally Lutheran, she considers herself agnostic). *Schau nicht nach unten! Schau nicht nach unten! Please, please don't look down. . . .*

And for a moment it seems as though her wordless prayer has been answered. For after landing his polished oxford squarely atop the damning image, the reedy proctor takes two more steps. Renate has just begun considering a possible exhale when, quite abruptly, he comes to a halt.

Very slowly, he turns back a half rotation. Renate watches with her lungs gripped in some inner iron vise as he takes two very long, very quick steps back. Kneeling on his knobby knee, he picks the cardboard square up and swivels his face toward her like an owl.

"Was," he says, *"ist das?"*

Renate's brain works furiously. This will be far, far worse than the last curt note to her father. It could result in a telephone call, and suspension, or even (her mouth goes dry) full expulsion. Surely Schuldirektor Heintz has ejected students for less. She tries to picture her family receiving this news—her *Doktor* mother and *Professor* father, who both earned nothing but top marks in their many, many years of combined study. Her brother, Franz, who soared through both *Mittelschule* and *Gymnasium* like an academic meteor, with nothing sent home but breathless praise and commendation.

"I'm waiting," says the librarian, tapping his foot. "I expect someone to take responsibility for this. Otherwise—" He clears his throat again. "Otherwise the punishment will have to be far more severe."

Punishment, Renate thinks, the word lodging in her brain with the grainy stubbornness of a half-swallowed pill. Is there a punishment beyond expulsion—beyond, of course, the humiliation of having everyone in the school think she's some sort of a sex addict?

Beside her, her best friend, Ilse, chooses the moment to elbow Renate in the ribs.

"Autsch," Renate hisses. "Stop."

And with that one, suppressed protest, that faintest hint of a sway, the librarian is over them like Death over two maidens.

"Fräulein Bauer!" he cries. "I hear you speaking up. Is that because you wish to explain this to me?"

He dangles the picture before her, the Book Lady and her kneeling lover inches from Renate's eyes. She averts her gaze.

"It's—it appears to be a postcard." Her voice sounds strange to her: nasal and distant. Someone somewhere near the back windows titters.

"Yes, but what kind of postcard?"

"A blank one?"

Another ripple of laughter. "Well," he says, "yes. But what I really want to know is to whom it belongs. And how it got here. Perhaps you can give me the answer."

Renate swallows again, miserably. Because of course, of course she can.

She can give him the answer, and then her life will be over.

❧

It had started the prior Friday: an afternoon that Renate, as on most afternoons, spent almost entirely with Ilse. Renate and Ilse: study partners during class, huddle-whisperers in hallways; giggle-riders on the U-Bahn together. At three they'd set out for Renate's house on the Bismarckstraße as usual, elbows linked and gaits matched, ambling past Unter den Linden's budding lime and chestnut trees, making their usual stops along the way: the perfume store, where they eyed gem-toned glass bottles and gleaming diffusers but didn't enter (the French perfumer openly dislikes children). Then Gerstel's Hat Store, with its felted berets and smart fedoras and the draped purple turban that Herr Gerstel (who does like children) let them try on. They lingered by the window of the travel office, arguing which country they will visit together first. Ilse wants to go somewhere hot and exotic: the Sahara, the Nile. Or maybe Indochina. Renate wants to go to New York or Hollywood, though lately, based on her reading, she's become increasingly intrigued by the Orient as well—which is why on Friday they also paused in the open doorway of the Chinese tea shop to breathe in the dry, mossy scent. Ilse disliked it, but Renate found it transporting. Standing there with closed eyes, breathing in deeply, she could have been on a Peking or Shanghai street, instead of in the middle of Berlin's unexotic-but-bustling Tiergarten district. She'd tried to picture it: the scurrying Chinamen, their docile wives tripping behind them on tiny little feet, until Ilse—who has no time for dream-induced delays—cried *"Mach schon!"* and pulled her away.

When they reached the Konditorei Schloss they pooled their change for a buttery piece of poppyseed cake, which Herr Schloss—a red-cheeked man who, once a year, transforms into a fairly convincing Sankt Nikolaus—dispensed with his usual distracted grin. Their remaining two *Pfennige* got dropped in the Winter Relief collection can of a pimpled youth in a khaki shirt and white knee socks. He wasn't bad-looking, but his *dankeschön* came out in a two-toned bleat that made him sound like a pubescent billy goat. The girls barely made it another block before falling on each other, shrieking with laughter and prompting looks of startled censure from adult pedestrians.

"It was your fault," Ilse managed finally, when she'd regained her composure. "He was so beguiled by your beauty that his poor voice just dried up in his throat!"

"Me?" Renate wiped her eyes with her handkerchief. "He was staring at *you*! And thank goodness. I hate it when boys stare."

"You wouldn't hate it if you-know-who stared."

"No," Renate agreed. "I would not. But he won't."

"You never know."

"Maybe not. But he won't."

Mirth exhausted, the two resumed their walk, at Potsdamer Platz passing another rattling can. This one was held by Fritz the war veteran, in his yellow badge with the three black dots that signal blindness. Sometimes Renate buys one of his wares; not because she actually needs pencils, but because she likes the seamed smile that appears on his face as her coins clink into his cup. It makes her feel benevolent. Also, comradely, since her father fought in the war too, as a *Frontkämpfer*. And while he wasn't blinded like Fritz, he came close enough to death that (in his own deep-toned, rumbling words) he *spürte seinen Atem an meinem Nacken*: felt its hot breath right on his neck.

On this particular Friday, however, they were all out of money, and so they passed by the old soldier without pausing, Ilse meticulously licking the last cake crumbs from her sticky fingers and Renate lost in thought about you-know-who. For a moment his face seemed to hang in the air before her, so close that she might have touched a high, perfect cheekbone. The mirage melted just in time for a snatched glimpse of a blond head, bobbing several meters before them.

"Guck mal!" she gasped, gripping her friend's elbow. "Look."

"At what?"

"Up ahead. To the right."

Ilse shaded her eyes with her hand. "Who am I looking for?"

"Who do you think?"

Ilse squinted, rising briefly onto tiptoe before shaking her head and falling back. "I don't see him."

"There," said Renate. "He's just passing the U-Bahn." But her voice was more tentative now, her pointing finger less assured as she scanned the crowd, left to right, right to left. "He was just there. I swear."

Ilse grinned. "Now you're starting to see things. You should have your mother examine you."

"Ach! Stop." Her heart pounding, Renate cast one last glance down the broad greening avenue with its churning currents of late-day pedestrians. But the only face she recognized was the chiseled visage of Frederick the Great outside the Brandenburg Gate, bestowing his steely gaze on his fleshly descendants while riding his stone steed to nowhere.

Later they lay sprawled on the worn carpet in Renate's room, their bodies at loosely intersecting angles, socked feet tapping in time to Ethel Waters, bewailing her loss of diamonds and dough.

"Can you keep a secret?" Renate stage-whispered.

"Can you really be asking that?" countered Ilse. In the three years of their friendship they'd shared hundreds of secrets. Secrets about boys and girls, parents and teachers. Secrets about school struggles and bodily secretions; about budding breasts and bad grades, and how to hide one or both from one's parents in order to escape commentary on them. Secrets about what, exactly, comprises *that time of the month*, and when that time comes or does not come. And secrets about other secrets they've overheard from the grown-ups, who always seem to assume that they're not listening.

"I found something," Renate murmured. "Underneath Franz's bed."

Ilse looked up, immediately interested. "A love letter? His diary?"

"Worse. Postcards."

Ilse snorted. "How's that worse?"

Renate took a deep breath. "Not the usual postcards. Think. Remember the dirty ones we saw in Nolli?"

"Oooooh!" Ilse's pale blue-gray eyes widened. "He bought those things? When? How?"

Renate shrugged: "No idea. But he's got them. A full dozen. In a cigar box."

Ilse giggled, a little shrilly. From the Victrola came the sound of *clippity-clop-clippity-clop*, which they'd both initially thought was the sound of trotting horses until Franz explained tap dancing to them. "That's probably what he and his group do during their secret meetings," she said. "Ogle nude ladies. They only call it a 'Socialist discussion group' for cover."

"They actually call it a 'Schiller discussion group' now. So as not to attract attention." In fact, given recent laws about leftist parties and rumors of midnight *Sicherheitsdienst* visits, Renate isn't supposed to discuss her brother's politics, or any politics, really, with anyone outside the family. But of course, she considers Ilse family. "But this card . . . this woman, Ilsi," she said, shaking her head.

"What about her? What's she doing?"

"She's . . . reading."

"Reading?" Ilse looked nonplussed. "Reading what? Chatterley? De Sade?"

"It's not *what* she's reading." Renate tucked a dark curl behind her ear. "It's what's happening while she's doing it."

"And that is . . ."

Renate opened her mouth, then snapped it shut and covered it with both hands. "I can't."

"Reni!" Pushing herself up to hands and knees, Ilse crawled toward her and peeled her friend's hands from her face. "What is it? What's happening?"

Renate shook her head, pulling back, laughing breathlessly. Finally blurting: "There's a man." Eyes sparkling, she pointed toward her navel.

"A man at her belly?"

Another head shake. "Further down."

"Is he reading too?"

"No. He's . . . he's . . . you know." Renate hugged her thin calves, buried her face in her knees. *"E's fiffingfer."*

"What?" Ilse pried her friend's knobby knees apart and leaned between them, her pale face just inches from her best friend's flushed one.

"He's kissing her," Renate said breathlessly. "Down there."

"In her . . . in her *Scheide*?" Ilse's milk-pale face turned faintly pink. "You're lying."

"I'm not. I swear. I swear on my dead *Großvater*'s grave." Renate had actually never seen her dead grandfather's grave, and in fact never met the man herself, both of her father's parents having died before her birth. But it was the only oath that came to mind at the moment. And apparently it was enough: in a heartbeat the blond girl was on her feet, sprinting toward the door.

"Wait," said Renate, leaping to her own feet as Ilse's hand hit the doorknob. "Where are you going?"

"Where do you think, *Dummerchen*? To his room!"

"But he's studying!"

"We'll distract him."

"But I'm not supposed to even *knock* on exam nights!"

"*You're* not," said Ilse. "He never said anything about me, though, did he?" Without waiting for an answer she yanked open the door, nearly tripping over the wiry-haired Schnauzer who had been lying in wait just outside. Ecstatic at his sudden access (Ilse is his favorite non-Bauer), he hurled himself against her shins, whining his adoration.

"Not *now*, Sigmund," Ilse said, pushing past to resume her short march down the hallway. "Well, did he?" she demanded, over her shoulder.

"No," admitted Renate, hurrying breathlessly after her friend. "Still, you can't just *walk in* there. You must at least have a plan."

"I have a plan," Ilse snapped back. "You'll see."

Reaching Franz's room, she rapped three times sharply, just above the scrawled *Bitte nicht stören* sign (helpfully embellished with a scrawled skull and crossbones) tacked to the door. When there was no audible response she knocked a second time, louder. She was about to commence a third time when the door swung abruptly open.

"For God's *sake*." Her best friend's brother stood in the door frame, his dark hair rumpled, his expression aggrieved. "Can't you read?"

"Oh—sorry." Ilse took a step back, her bravado briefly flagging. Sigi took the opportunity to dart between them and launch himself onto the bed.

"Sorry," she said again, collecting herself slightly. "We just need your help for a moment."

"Help? With what? Sigi, *raus*." Franz threw an exasperated look back at the pet. "These aren't visiting hours," he added pointedly.

"An insect," said Ilse, improvising quickly. "There's a big insect on the wall in Reni's room. We need someone to kill it."

"An insect." Leaning against the door frame, her best friend's brother looked down at her in bemusement. "Fräulein von Fischer—who famously beat a would-be purse-snatcher off the U-Bahn—is now asking a cripple to kill her an insect."

"You know I didn't *beat* him." Ilse's cheeks were flushed again, though whether at the mention of the word *cripple* or the anecdote (which she loathes) it was hard to tell. "I lost my balance and fell into him and he . . . he simply ran off. And—" She darted a gaze past him to the book-strewn desk, against which Franz's silver-handled cane leaned in its usual spot. "And we actually need you *because* of your cane. The thing is high up enough that neither of us can reach it."

Franz just gazed at her a moment, then back at his sister standing mutely behind Ilse's left shoulder. Sigi, still lying defiantly on the bed (and in theory just above the titillating material that had sparked the interruption), began chewing noisily on his left hind leg.

"Also gut," Franz sighed finally.

Turning on his good heel, he limped back to the desk and picked up his cane, while Ilse flashed a victorious grin back at Renate. When Franz returned, however, he did not continue past to Renate's room. Stopping short of the threshold, he extended the glossy walking stick. "Your weapon," he announced, pointing at the raven-shaped handle, a tribute to his passion for Poe. "Use that big end. Just clean the guts off after. You can leave it in the hallway when you're done. Sigi, *raus!*"

And waiting only long enough for Sigi to thump off the bed and trot dutifully back into the hallway, he shut the door.

"I told you," Renate said, once they were safely back in her room, Ilse sulking, Renate disappointed if vindicated. "Just come tomorrow. He's gone until dinner."

"Can't. We're driving to Oma's." Ilse's paternal grandparents have a house in Wiesbaden; the maternal set's in Spandau. That she has four living grandparents is one of the few things Renate envies her. Her own, lone surviving grandparent (her mother's powder-pale, fussy mother) lives in a stuffy apartment just outside the Hirschgarten. After visiting, the smell of the place—like lavender oil gone rancid—stays with Renate for days.

"Come Monday, then," she said.

"Piano."

"Tuesday?"

"Seeing Dr. Stein for my checkup."

Renate groaned: Wednesday seemed years and years away. Then Ilse brightened. "Bring it to school."

Renate stared at her. "Are you crazy?"

"Why not? If you're caught you can just say you found it somewhere." Ilse smiled craftily. "Or tell the truth. It's about time Franz caught grief for something."

Renate still wasn't convinced. "You'll back me up if I do get caught?"

"Of course."

"I mean, really back me up?"

"Natürlich," Ilse sniffed, and held up her right hand. On its middle finger twinkled the ring Renate had given her eighteen months earlier, in exchange for one Ilse gave to her: simple silvery bands both, with small outstretched hands in the place where stones usually were. Each had a single letter etched on the inside: an I on Renate's, an R on Ilse's. When lined up, the little hands fit together like a shining knot.

And now here they are three days later, at two in the afternoon, in the low-ceilinged library of Bismarck Gymnasium, where Renate's short, unkissed life is about to end.

"I'm waiting," booms Herr Steinberg.

He leans closer; close enough that Renate inhales the dank smell of old cigarettes and stale coffee. Renate squeezes her eyes shut in a last-ditch effort to faint so that he'll at least feel a little sorry for her. When her body won't comply (it never does, certainly not at useful moments like this one) she swallows, hard.

"I . . ."

"Herr Steinberg?"

The teacher spins on his heel toward the interruption. "Yes, Gerhardt?"

(*Gerhardt?* Renate's eyes fly open.)

"The card is mine."

It takes Renate a moment to confirm it, and when she does she really does almost faint.

For it's true. It's him—Rudolph Gerhardt. The boy with the perfect mole and the perfect cleft chin and the perfect eyes of shifting sea glass. She has no idea at all how he got here without her knowing; her awareness of his presence is so hyper-attuned she can practically pick out his tread from one floor down. And yet here he is, a table back, with all eyes on him as though he were Gary Cooper in *A Farewell to Arms*.

Rudi, as always, wears the attention like a becoming accessory: a fedora. A fancy wristwatch. Wiry and blond in his neatly pressed khaki uniform, he looks like he's just in from a brisk hike. He's one of those students for whom the shuffling sea of pubescent bodies parts unthinkingly, and upon whom even the grumpiest teachers seem to dote. Even Herr Steinberg, whose face might as well have been carved from granite, has been known to crack a smile in his presence.

"This is yours?" the librarian asks now, adjusting his round-rimmed spectacles.

"Yes, sir." Rudi ducks his head in sincere-seeming humility. "I'm very sorry. I found it on the Königsstraße, just outside Israel's this morning. It was just lying there, face up, on the street."

Renate darts a glance at Ilse, who returns it, frowning. They both know exactly where Rudi lives. And that Israel's—one of the biggest department stores in the city—is not on his way to school.

"And you picked it up," the proctor posits. He's moving away from Renate now, and she exhales the breath she's been holding long enough that her lungs ache. "You picked it up," he continues, "and then—it would seem—deemed it suitable to bring into our school."

"Yes, sir."

Rudi gazes up at him brightly. The teacher pushes his glasses further up the bridge of his nose. "And why would you do that?"

The boy leans forward, resting his flawless chin in his palm. "Well, for one thing, I of course didn't want anyone else stumbling over this sort of degenerate image. But I also wanted to share it with my fellow students."

Gasps erupt throughout the room like gas hissing from multiple pipe cracks. Even Herr Steinberg looks taken aback. "You didn't want strangers on the street to see it, but wanted to show it off at school?"

"That's correct."

"May I ask why?"

Rudi smiles. "As a warning. About the kinds of depths to which some types can sometimes sink."

"And what kinds of 'types' and 'depths' would those be?"

Renate twists her hands together beneath the polished top of the oaken table, feeling Ilse's friendship ring digging into her palm.

"The depths of the baser races," Rudi says. "Jews, for instance. I'm certain that it's no coincidence at all that the card was outside a Jew business."

Discernibly, at least, nothing in Herr Steinberg's expression changes. But it seems to Renate that it compresses, tightening all over without a single feature actually shifting or moving.

"Yes," he says. "Yes. Of course." His Adam's apple moves up, moves down. "And what do you propose I do with this now?"

"Why, give it back to me, of course," says Rudi. "So I can warn my other classrooms."

The answer breaks the room's tension, the stuffy air rippling with barely suppressed snorts and giggles. Renate holds her breath, half expecting the teacher to explode as he famously does sometimes—as when, for instance, he intercepted Martin Beidryzcki's caricature of Frau Bernhardt, endowed with a beard and enormous *Titten*. But to her astonishment, he merely drops the postcard onto Rudi's textbook.

"Personally," he says, "I'd suggest that you dispose of it properly, rather than springing it on other instructors who may not be as understanding as I am. Either way, my young man, I don't want to see it—or anything like it—in my library again. Understood?"

The words themselves are authoritative enough. But the delivery is strangely thin, like a weak recitation in a play. Rudi seems to sense this too; as he slides the card into his satchel he actually smirks. Then, catching Renate staring, he gives her a very slow, deliberate wink. Her stomach clenches as though he's punched her in the gut.

Next to her, Ilse manufactures a cough. "What just happened?" she murmurs beneath its cover.

"I'm not sure," Renate whispers back. Her heart's still pounding, but the shock of his wink has melted into a honeylike warmth in her stomach. For actually, she is sure. Or at least, sure of one thing: Rudolph Gerhardt has just saved her life.

"He's sweet on you," Ilse says later, as they walk past the yodeling youth, dropping in *Pfennige* and collecting yet more Winter Relief pins. "He must be. Why else would he take the fall?"

"Who knows?" Renate examines her lapel pin before tucking it into her coat collar next to the other three she has stuck there, carefully keeping her tone even. Secretly, however, she's still thrumming with excitement. *Let it be true*, she thinks. *Please, let it be true.*

"And did you see Steinberg's expression?" Ilse continues, sticking her own pin in her pocket. "It was just too funny. Martin drew a cartoon of it for me afterward."

"I was too afraid to look at him. I honestly thought he was going to strangle me. Right on the spot. And by the way, you still haven't apologized."

"For what?"

"For making me draw his attention! Why did you punch me like that?"

"I didn't *punch* you. I nudged you. A little. I barely moved at all."

"If you didn't move, then why did I almost fall off my chair?"

"Because you're dizzy and clumsy," retorts Ilse. "Everyone knows that."

Renate groans. "You're impossible."

"Better than being easy," Ilse quips, and they laugh.

As they approach the perfumery they pause out of habit; Renate notes a new bottle—Nuit de Chine—in the showcase. She wonders fleetingly what a Chinese night smells like.

"You know he's Jewish, don't you?" Ilse is asking.

"Who, Martin?" Renate shrugs, lifts her voice in mimicry: *"Everyone knows that."* As they resume walking she checks her pockets to make sure she's got enough for their daily after-school snack cake. "I was afraid he'd be upset, actually. About what Rudi said. But he said it was all in good fun."

"No. Steinberg. Steinberg's a Jew too."

"Really?" Renate frowns; she hadn't known this.

Ilse nods. "If you look carefully you can tell. Something about the nose." She pinches her own snub button in demonstration. "My mother saw him coming out of that big synagogue on Oranienburger Straße last Saturday. He had that hat thing on and everything."

"The big furry thing the Jewish men wear in the Scheunenviertel?" Aptly enough, they're now passing Herr Gerstel's hat store, though for some reason it's closed today. And the purple turban has disappeared from the window. Renate wonders if it sold, and if so, who might have bought it. A movie star? A wealthy sultan? A magician's exotic assistant? Maybe they spent so much on it that Herr Gerstel has already retired. Though (selfishly) Renate hopes not. She loves his shop.

"No," Ilse is saying. "The little one. The kind that looks like a tea cozy."

The thought of Herr Steinberg with a tea cozy capping his combover sends them both into another brief gale of laughter. That subsides, however, as they approach the Konditorei Schloss.

As usual, Herr Schloss's doorway is open to the sidewalk, allowing a wafted hint of the yeasty delights inside. What isn't usual is the sign that someone's taped on the store window, where it obscures the carefully constructed tiers and towers of shortbread, donuts, and tarts; of fruit pies, stollen, and glistening, glazed apple cakes. *Deutsche!* the sign reads in cryptic-looking Gothic script: *Wehrt Euch! Kauft nicht bei Juden!*

To further the point two stocky men flank the door, each holding a sign bearing the same warning. Their brown shirts and crisp red armbands identify them as Sturmabteilung, the self-appointed militia that goose-steps down Berlin's streets, belting out songs of blood and soil and country. As the two girls hesitate, one glowers at them in silence while the other adopts a patronizing smile.

"Sorry, girls," he says. "No sweeties here for you today."

"Why not?"

"A kike owns this business."

"Really?" Renate asks, once more surprised. The Konditorei is famed for its holiday displays. Not just at Christmas, when the window fills with brightly wrapped boxes, glittering evergreens, and a festive little red train set. But also at Easter, when lamb-shaped cakes and painted eggs take their turn. And of course there's Herr Schloss's yearly costume; the big red suit, the bishop's hat. The sack filled with nuts and candy for visiting children. What sort of Jew dresses up as Sankt Nikolaus?

"Are you sure he's Jewish?" Ilse asks.

"As Jewish as Jesus," says the trooper. "So be careful. They like pretty young girls." He licks his lips pointedly, lewdly; then he adds, sotto voce: "But don't worry. I'll protect you."

"We don't need protecting, thank you," Ilse retorts stiffly. She hates being belittled.

Renate says nothing but peers past the man's shoulder. The bakery is indeed empty of customers, and Herr Schloss is also nowhere to be seen. But Frau Schloss—his pink-cheeked wife who is almost as round and fat as he is—stands at silent attention at the counter. She usually smiles so much that her small blue eyes disappear in a surging tide of rosy flesh. Now, though, her face is sober, her eyes fully visible. When they meet Renate's she offers with the faintest hint of a shrug: *What can one do?* Is she Jewish as well? Renate wonders. Can Jews be that blond and that pink?

"I heard this was going to happen." Ilse looks thoughtful. "I didn't realize it was today."

"Heard what was happening?"

"The boycott of Jewish businesses." Ilse's cook, Britta, has a son who's a stormtrooper. She often regales Ilse with tales of his feats and distinctions.

"So it's not just Schloss?"

"I don't think so. Look over there."

Renate shades her eyes and looks down Unter den Linden. Sure enough, she sees more white signs—including one on the closed hat store that she'd failed to notice as they passed. The stores that are still open are manned by more SA men. Some also have confused-looking consumers standing outside them.

"What a bother! How long is it supposed to last?" Renate is both peeved and somewhat peckish, having forgotten to bring her lunch to school again.

"Just today," says Ilse. "But it's not like it's a law. They can't actually stop us from going in."

"We shouldn't have to stop you," says the sullen-faced trooper. "You should be proud to support your country."

"I can support my country in any way that I wish," Ilse snaps.

Renate lays a hand on her friend's arm. She normally loves Ilse's *Dreistigkeit,* the way so little ever seems to truly scare her. But she doesn't always know when to stop.

Uneasy now, she looks over the two men in their tall boots. The standard-issue SA dagger each wears strapped to his belt is, she knows, supposedly just for show. But the black-handled billy club each one carries isn't. A few weeks earlier she'd been having a coffee and cake with her grandmother on Potsdamer Straße when a group of SA troopers trundled past their window, bawling a song about Führer, nation, and pride. "It might help if they took voice lessons," her *Oma* quipped (she is an amateur opera singer; it's become her standard joke).

But what had shocked Renate was what happened next: as the troop paused at an intersection, one of its members leapt apart to grab a passing pedestrian by the collar. Bellowing something in the man's face, the trooper shook him several times, hard enough that the man's head flopped atop his neck like Renate's rag doll Alice. Then—so quickly that at first Renate thought she'd imagined it—the militiaman cracked the pedestrian on the head with his club. The blow was hard enough that the latter, when finally released, slumped to the ground, his head was bleeding profusely.

His task accomplished, the trooper had returned to formation, falling back into line as the victim's female companion frantically screamed for help.

Renate tugs on Ilse's cardigan. "I think we've cake at home anyway. And besides. It's getting late."

But Ilse remains where she is, chewing on her lip.

"Ilse."

"Listen to her," says the first trooper. "You seem like nice girls. Go home and have cake with your *Mutti*."

Oh no, thinks Renate, as Ilse's jaw tightens.

"I'm going in," her friend announces. "Herr Schloss is a good baker. I don't really care if he's Jewish." She turns back to Renate, her hand extended. "If you want to wait for me here, you are welcome. But can I have the cake money?"

Renate hesitates for just a moment, torn: if she hands over the money she's also challenging the boycott. But if she doesn't, she's challenging her best friend.

For a moment she stands motionless, her hand in her pocket, her eye on her friend's upturned palm, the underside of the friendship ring glimmering. She starts to withdraw her little handful of coins. Then she stops.

"No," she says. "I'll go too."

❧

"One of these days," Renate tells Ilse later, "you're really going to get into trouble." She rolls onto her stomach. "Or worse, get *me* into trouble."

"One of these days you'll learn to stand up for yourself," retorts Ilse, and picks a poppyseed from her teeth.

Renate sighs. "What I don't understand is that I thought you and your parents liked the NSDAP. I thought you thought they were doing good things." Renate's own parents loathe Hitler and his National Socialist cohorts, seeing them as brutish bigots and oafs. Ilse's parents—who suffered far more after the Defeat and the Inflation—fully believe Hitler's promise to return Germany to greatness and credit him personally with their improving fortunes.

"I like the Party," says Ilse. "That doesn't mean I like Brownshirts. They're overgrown thugs half the time. And all this stuff about Jews . . . *pfft*." She waves a hand dismissively. "You get extremists with every movement. My grandfather says they'll grow past it."

"Hmm," says Renate, wondering whether her parents are in agreement. Somehow she doubts it. She's heard them talking tensely in their bedroom, their exchanges peppered with words like *laws* and *retirement* and *Juden*—many of their friends and colleagues are Jewish.

"And actually," Ilse continues, "I think I'm going to join the BDM."

"Really?" Renate turns to look at her. They ridiculed the new group in the past: the mindless marching, the silly songs. "Is that your mother's suggestion?"

"Mine, actually. Mama wants me to join the League of Louise. She believes it's got more class. Or something."

"Ugh." Renate pulls a sour face. The Louise Leaguers are even worse than the Bund Deutscher Mädel. They dress in cornflower blue—supposedly Queen Louise's favorite color—and gather weekly, supposedly in memory of her reign. But from what Ilse and Renate have discerned after spying on the group for several days, the members do little more than discuss French fashion and American swing dance steps. "Pampered daughters of bankers and lawyers," she sniffs now.

Ilse shakes her head. "Can you imagine spending six whole hours a week with them?"

"Not even for one second."

"But the BDM might be all right. I hear the camping and sports meets and the crafts part are all supposed to be great fun. And they do loads of joint activities with the Hitlerjugend." She folds her arms behind her head. "Besides. I'm curious."

"What about?"

"About what it would be like to be part of something . . . bigger."

"Bigger than what?"

Ilse waves a hand at the scattered shoes, pages, and books around them. "All this. This endless cycle. School, studies, sleep. Broken up only by the occasional silly birthday party. It all feels—I don't know. Weightless, somehow. Like I'm not changing anything."

Renate frowns. "What is it you want to change?"

"I don't know. Something. Oh. And guess what." She lowers her voice. "Erika says last summer they went camping with the Hitler Youth and she snuck out of her tent and went swimming with Rudi and three others." She lowers her voice further. "In their *underthings*."

Something sour stirs in Renate's stomach. She tells herself that it's not just because Erika went swimming—nearly naked!—with Rudi, but that she got to go camping at all. Renate's own parents wouldn't in a million years take her overnight in the woods. For one thing, her mother can't stand nature walks ("boring, pointless"). She also can't cook to save her life—and that's in the kitchen; never mind on a campfire. There is also Franz's limp, left by childhood polio. He already has to walk with a cane, even on flat surfaces. As for Renate's father: he claims to have spent enough time in tents along the Russian Front to last him for the next several lifetimes.

"Well?"

"Well, what?"

"Would you join if I did?"

"You know how my parents are."

"You wouldn't have to tell them!"

"Don't I need their approval?"

"You know what your father's signature looks like, don't you?"

"Seriously?" Renate gapes at her. "And what about all the records? I can't get those by myself."

"I've heard they'll order them from the Census Department for you if you need. You just need to give them enough notice."

Stretching, Renate cracks her neck: first one side, then the other. She is trying to imagine herself following Ilse's suggestion: Lying. Forging Vati's signature. Making up excuses twice weekly and on Saturdays as to why she needs to be out. The thought alone makes her queasy. Her most rebellious act so far has been sticking her tongue out at the back of her mother's head five years ago, really just to see whether she could. Apparently she could not: *Renate*, Lisbet Bauer snapped. *Your tongue belongs in your mouth.* She hadn't even bothered to turn around.

She decides to deflect. "The real question is how I get that stupid postcard back. Franz will kill me if he finds out I took it."

"How would he know it's you?"

"Who else would it be? My mother?"

"Maybe it was Raina." Ilse pokes Renate in the shoulder. "It sounds like something she'd do."

"Raina wouldn't just steal the postcard. She'd re-create it." Renate eyes Ilse sidelong. "But with a manatee instead of a man."

"Oh, horrid." Ilse pretends to retch. "Raina Bachmeier" is the name of the evil alternate personality Renate invented for herself after the girls saw *Dr. Jekyll and Mr. Hyde* together at the Concordia. Ilse's is "Ida Fuchs." They have an ongoing competition regarding whose conscience-free alter ego is more theoretically depraved: in past weeks Raina Bachmeier has burned down the Bismarck School, robbed a jewelry store, and borne Herr Steinberg's love child, while Ida Fuchs has stolen all the city street signs, hijacked the number 8 tram to Paris, and eaten a Dachshund puppy for lunch.

"I'll just have to ask Rudi for it whenever I see him next." Renate sighs. "It will be unbearably embarrassing. He probably thinks I'm the worst sort of girl on earth."

"If he thought that, he wouldn't have come galloping to your aid," says Ilse tartly. "Rescuing the beautiful damsel."

"Beautiful?" Renate snorts. If she's registered the way that people—boys in particular—have begun looking at her differently over the past months, it's in the same vague way that she's registered the changes in her own body. The lengthening of her pale, slim legs; the subtle broadening of her hips and narrowing of her waist. The way her former boyish tangle of brown curls has almost magically relaxed into a rich waterfall of waves down her back. And while she hears the soft whistles and comments—*Hallo, meine Schöne!*—she has a hard time connecting them to herself. Much less responding.

"He would have done it for you, too," she tells Ilse, uncomfortably aware that this isn't true. It's not that she doesn't find Ilse beautiful, in a golden, Amazonian sort of way. But she recognizes that there is something staunch and unyielding, something almost ungirlish about her friend that keeps boys at bay. It was that same steely instinct that had led Ilse to hurl herself at the schoolbag-snatcher that day on the U-Bahn—in a move that was not accidental in the least, though of course Renate would never say as much. Indeed, Ilse had responded to the mugger's tug with a fury as raw as it was instantaneous; as though she'd been waiting her whole life for precisely this opportunity to inflict outrage and injury on an opponent. Even remembering it—and the look on the startled thief's face as he fled—is enough to catch Renate's breath in her throat.

"No, he wouldn't have," Ilse is saying now. "None of the boys would." She stares up moodily at the stars they've painstakingly cut out and arranged on both their bedroom ceilings, in constellations of their own design ("so we'll go to sleep under the same sky," Renate said). Then she sighs.

"The irony," Renate says, changing the subject, "is you didn't even get a good look at the thing. Even after all that."

Ilse smirks. "I saw enough of it when Herr Steinberg was waving it around like a flyswatter. It looked to me like he was French-kissing her." She sticks out her tongue.

"Oh, Ilsi—disgusting!" Renate covers her head with a pillow.

Undaunted, Ilse crawls over on all fours. She pulls the pillow from her friend's face. "Maybe," she whispers, "Franz has done that to a girl. Maybe it was even him in the picture—you said you can't see the man's face, right? What color was his hair?" She laughs triumphantly. "You see, *that's* where he could have gotten them. Straight from the source."

There's an added glow to her cheeks, a thrilled tremor to her voice. But if Renate notices this she doesn't comment on it.

"You're awful!" is all she says. Grabbing the pillow back, she swings it directly at Ilse's hairline, though being Renate (weak and clumsy), she misses. Laughing, Ilse grabs it back. Then they are rolling together on the floor, laughing and panting and somehow fitting perfectly, like always, like interlocking parts in a two-piece puzzle.

3

Ava

1977

$\mathcal{T}$he 747 looked like a huge land-bound whale, beshimmered by mid-summer heat. As it taxied toward the jet bridge, the old Bob Hope line started circling in her head: *I just flew in from the West Coast, and boy, are my arms tired!* When Ava first heard the joke she'd been new to America, and duly mystified: why would someone's arms hurt from sitting in an airplane?

Now, however, it was her own arms that were aching. She'd been holding Sophie up to the window to watch landing jets and trundling baggage carts for what felt like forever, though she had just intended for it to be a few moments. Like so much else with her daughter these days, though, the exercise escalated into a battle of wills: once lifted, the toddler refused to be lowered.

"Baby," Ava tried again, reresting Sophie against her hip. Despite the overconditioned air, perspiration dripped down her spine and soaked the waistline of her Wranglers. "Look," she said. "You can still see it from here. And if I hold you here we can dance!" She bounced a little on the balls of her feet, singing under her breath in German (since she didn't know any American baby songs): *"Alle Vögel sind schon da, alle Vögel, alle . . ."*

"Noooooooooo!" shrieked her daughter. "Uppuh! Uppuh!" A chubby palm planted itself on Ava's cheek, hard enough that Ava's neck twinged in pain. She suppressed the impulse to just drop the child on the floor.

"Mummy's arms aren't so strong," she said instead, shuffling Sophie's damp weight to her other hip and noting the ammonial whiff of an overdue diaper change. "I need to rest them so that you and I can give Oma a *big, big* hug when she comes out—right through that door. See? That's where she'll be."

She pointed to the arrivals gate, where an air hostess was finally taking up position. Sophie directed a suspicious gaze at the woman, who— *God bless her*—obliged them with a white-gloved finger-flutter. Sophie generally distrusted strangers. But something about the stewardess— possibly the jaunty little red hat—had sparked the infant's interest. She lifted a chubby fist in a gesture closer to the Black Power salute than a wave, but the scowl on her face softened into something closer to a smile than her mother had been able to elicit from her for hours.

Sighing, Ava turned her attention to passengers disembarking, most of whom looked overdressed for the city's Sahara-like heat wave. Searching their wan faces, it struck her that she didn't altogether know what she was looking for. After all, she hadn't seen her mother for nearly a decade. What if Ilse had changed, had gained or lost twenty kilos? Dyed her hair black, or blue? What if she wasn't even on board?

This last possibility sparked a nervous quiver that wasn't entirely unpleasant. Ava had complained frequently to friends, lovers, and therapists about the fact that since her move to the States in 1968, Ilse had not once made the trip to visit. She hadn't come for Ava's art school graduation, nor for her first Bowery art exhibition, nor when the death of her best friend and former lover sent Ava spiraling into a monthlong depression, one that had concerned her then-roommate Livi enough to actually call Ilse about it herself ("I don't believe I'd be any help," her mother had reportedly responded). Ilse hadn't even come after Sophie was born, though she claimed to have both made reservations and secured time off at the magazine. As usual, though, something had interfered. In this case it was the sudden onset of the flu: "I certainly wouldn't want to get you or the baby sick," her mother said when she called with the news. "It's hard enough to care for a healthy newborn."

Not that you'd know, Ava had wanted to retort. But of course she did not.

So when Ilse called again shortly after Sophie's first birthday to announce she'd paid for not only a Lufthansa ticket but a hotel room in Greenwich Village, Ava's reaction had been decidedly mixed. Naturally, there was skepticism. But there was also a stubborn stirring of anticipation: a curling tendril of hope that maybe, at long last, Ilse was ready to be the loving, supportive, and (most important) open mother Ava had always wanted her to be.

Released from the stewardess's spell, Sophie resumed chanting: *"Up-up-up-up-up!"* She began to twist and buck.

"Wait, wait," hushed Ava. "A minute more. We are still looking for Oma. If she doesn't come I'll lift . . ." But before she'd finished the sentence there, in fact, was Ilse, wearing a plaid dress and matching cardigan and looking as though she'd just strolled off the Bremen underground.

"Mama!" Ava called.

As Ilse snapped her braid-wrapped head back toward them, Ava grasped Sophie's soft wrist to make her wave. The baby, whose strength was truly astonishing, arm-wrestled the gesture into a sticky slap to Ava's left cheek, just as Ilse's and Ava's eyes met. It struck Ava that her mother seemed both confused and just the faintest bit pained, a look that evoked a startlingly clear memory of the day three decades earlier when Ilse had appeared unannounced at the Bremen orphanage where Ava spent the war's end. And for just an instant, Ava felt the same queasy emotional mix she had felt locking eyes with her mother for what had felt to her like the very first time: incandescent joy at Ilse's long-awaited return. Heart-stabbing fear she'd walk right back out the door.

Instead, Ilse picked up her carry-on and strode over to where Ava and Sophie stood, walking her familiar shoulders-back soldierly walk. *"Da bist du ja!"* she said, as though she were the one who'd been waiting. "My God, I thought they'd never let us off."

As she spoke she was looking not at Ava but at Sophie, who stared back with a look of round-eyed consternation that Ava fully understood: seeing them up close for the first time, the likeness between her mother and her daughter was not just confirmed but almost confounding. Not only were their eyes mirror images of one another in shape and in color, but their noses and chins matched as well. Even their expressions— sternly fascinated, slightly wary—looked as though they'd come off the same assembly line, albeit five decades apart.

"Isn't she lovely!" Ilse was saying, with a warmth so genuine it caught Ava off-guard. "Will she come to me?"

Setting her bag down again, she held out her arms.

"She's a little shy around . . ." Ava started. Then she stopped. Not just because she'd been about to say *strangers*, but because Sophie was actually lunging toward her grandmother, chubby arms outstretched. As though she'd been waiting for just this moment for the entirety of her short life.

"She isn't walking yet?" her mother asked, as their taxi jerked onto the steaming expressway.

Ava wiped her brow with the bottom of her T-shirt. "The doctor says girls often start later. Especially if they don't crawl first."

"She doesn't *crawl*?" Ilse sounded aghast, as though Ava had just revealed to her that her granddaughter didn't breathe.

"I didn't either, remember?"

"It was a long time ago," her mother said vaguely.

Ava studied her sidelong. Though she hadn't noticed it as much in the airport, Ilse had changed over the last decade. Her body seemed stockier, her posture slightly more stooped. She still had the smooth pale skin of a Bavarian milkmaid, but close up the lines above her eyebrows and bracketing her lips appeared more deeply etched. Her hair had changed too, ceding some of its gold to silver. Overall, the effect wasn't so much aging as softening.

Indeed, her mother's behavior seemed softer too; she laughed and babbled with her infant granddaughter with an unguarded silliness Ava had no recollection of having ever experienced herself. Then again (she reflected) her own grandparents had seemed entirely different beings with her than the staid, stern duo Ilse had curtly depicted on the few occasions she'd deigned to discuss them. For Ava, the years with her *Oma* and *Opa* had been the happiest and safest period of her childhood. Even thinking about them now brought a lump of loss to her throat.

She buried her nose in Sophie's soft, sweat-damp hair. "Aren't we happy Oma is here?" she murmured.

"NO," said Sophie, and kicked her hard little heels into Ava's thighs.

"Don't hurt Mommy," Ava chided, stilling the rogue ankles with one hand.

"Don't you ever speak German to her?" Ilse pressed a handkerchief to her forehead.

"I don't want to confuse her," Ava lied. The truth was that she wanted as little connection to her old homeland as possible. She often didn't even tell people she was German.

"Haven't you read that early years are the best time to learn languages?" Ilse asked.

"I don't have much time to read anything," said Ava wearily. "This one takes up a lot of energy."

"You took energy," Ilse pointed out. "But I somehow managed to both work and read."

You had help, Ava wanted to respond, though she did not.

"Well," she said instead, carefully diplomatic. "Maybe you can give me a few tips. God knows I could use them."

It was precisely the sort of opening that the Ilse Ava remembered would have used as a springboard for further disparagement. *I can see that*, she would have said. Or, *You'll need more than a few.*

Now, though, she just smiled and touched one of the baby's white-blond curls.

"You seem to be doing well enough," she said.

In *Ilse-Sprache*, it was the highest of praise.

"What do you call your neighborhood again?" Ilse asked a half hour later, her gaze fixed on a wall caked with band posters, escort offerings, and graffiti: a peace sign scrawled over a swastika; the spray-painted suggestion to *Kill a Yuppie*; another to *Vote for Cuomo, Not the Homo*.

"The East Village."

"Didn't you live in another Village before?"

"That was Greenwich. With Livi. But then Mark and I found the rent-controlled place here, and it seemed too good a deal to pass up. It's only $150 a month."

"Mark being the father."

Der Vater. It sounded so clinical and clean; so completely at odds with the gleefully self-destructive man with whom Ava had so fleetingly shared a life. Their affair had been a white dwarf in the chaotic universe of her love life: blindingly bright, impossibly dense, heartbreakingly brief; unmatched in intensity before or since. He'd fled when she got pregnant, a mere three months after he'd convinced her to move in with him. All he'd left was a battered Martin guitar, a check for six months' rent, and a hastily scrawled note: *Sorry babe.*

"He is Sophie's father, yes," Ava told Ilse, glancing back down at her daughter, who now felt like a limp rag doll in her lap, having plummeted precariously into sleep as only small children can.

"He's American?"

"Yes." Ava sighed; she was fairly sure she'd covered at least that much in her letters.

"And is he still in New York?"

Actually, the last Ava had heard Mark was in LA, sharing an apartment (and possibly a bed) with the transvestite drummer of a glitter band called the Bobbie Cocks.

"We've lost touch," she said tightly.

Her mother studied her face, her gaze opaque. "You don't seem very bothered by it."

"By what?"

"The fact that Sophie won't know her father."

Ava actually gaped at her.

For as long as she could remember, the topic of her own paternity had been both implicitly and explicitly off-limits. As a child, she'd known only that her father had been a German soldier who had died on the Eastern Front. As a teen she'd tried to learn about him on her own, forging her mother's signature to order a copy of her birth certificate and then researching the name on it at Berlin's Wehrmacht Archives. Her findings, however, had merely confirmed Ava's darkest fears about the man, while pushing Ilse further into her sullen secrecy.

"Who knows," she said now, carefully. "Maybe he'll come back into the picture someday."

Wiping her forehead again, Ilse began rolling down her window, covering her mouth and nose as the city's signature stench of moldering garbage, melting street tar, and slow-baking dog excretion wafted in. "This was really the only place you could find to live?" she asked, her voice faintly ducklike behind her palm. "I can see why my travel agent warned me not to stay here."

"It's not as bad as it looks," said Ava defensively. "If I had money, I'd look into buying in this neighborhood."

"A job might help, no?"

"I have a job, Mama. A few, actually. There's the book proposal I'm working on with a well-known children's author. My agent says Scribner's interested. There's the play group I run on Mondays and Wednesdays; that pays something. And I still tutor high school German on weekend afternoons while Livi or Jakob watches Sophie."

"*Unglaublich,*" her mother murmured. *Unbelievable.*

Ava stiffened before realizing the comment wasn't meant for her. They'd stopped at an intersection, and Ilse was looking out the window, her gaze locked on a crumbling tenement that looked as though it hadn't been inhabited in several decades. Stripped-down car frames intersected in the rubble below at odd angles, like skeletal remains from some primordial urban derby.

"How can they just leave it like that?" Ilse said, as the cab resumed its jerky journey. "It looks like Berlin after the war."

Ava looked at her quickly again. Her mother's whereabouts at the war's end and the first year in its wake were another thing Ilse refused to discuss. Ava was half tempted to press the point now: *Is that where you were then? In Berlin?* But she knew from experience that pushing Ilse on topics she didn't want to be pushed on only led to Ilse pushing away.

So she simply shrugged. "Germany recovered well enough."

"It seems the Amis put more effort into Germany," said Ilse tartly.

For a moment they fell back into hot, sticky silence. Then her mother seemed to brighten again. "I ran into Doktor Bergen last week."

Ava felt her stomach contract hollowly. "Oh?"

"*Ja.*" Her mother nodded. "Ulrich's widow came to Bremen last month. With the children."

That's nice. Or, *How did she seem?* Or, *How old are the children now?* These were the things people normally said in such cases. But the wound of Ulrich's death felt as fresh as it had when Ava first received the telegram over a year earlier: *Ulrich confirmed killed Golan Heights sniper funeral Tel Aviv June 28.*

Ava shifted her gaze out the window, struggling desperately to think of a way to change the subject. Before she had, however, she felt a hand on her shoulder.

"It gets better," Ilse said, quietly.

And before Ava could ask what *it* was, they'd reached her apartment.

❧

Two days later, Ava found herself humming *Eine kleine Nachtmusik* as she stirred semolina on the stove. The heat still hadn't broken, and Sophie was crankier than ever thanks to a diaper rash and two emerging new teeth. After her third attempt to put her daughter down for her nap, Ava had finally resorted to the Snugli again, though this was normally some-thing she avoided doing at home. Now, though, it seemed the only way to keep the baby from screeching while Ava bustled around the kitchen.

The project at hand was her first-ever formal German meal, with recipes drawn from her formerly untouched *Joys of German Cuisine* and ingredients paid for by pawning Mark's guitar. It was an ambitious plan, given the fact that these days her culinary aspirations rarely extended beyond Jiffy Pop and Swanson's TV dinners. But it had struck her as the most apt way to express her feelings to Ilse. Her (and could she really be thinking this?) *gratitude*.

For there it was: she was actually *happy* her mother was here. Very happy. Improbably, preposterously happy. And she knew Sophie felt the same way: after two days of listening intently to Ilse chattering in Ger-man, her new favorite word had become *Oma*. *Oma Oma Oma*, she'd sung sleepily last night, as Ilse rocked her in her bedroom while Ava indulged in the tepid luxury of a bath. And Ilse, whom Ava had only rarely heard sing, had sung it right back to her, following it up with a mournful ditty Ava vaguely felt she should know but did not:

Holla-hidi hollala,
Holla-hidi ho.

Putting Sophie to sleep was no mean feat in itself, but it was only one of the many miracles Ilse had wrought. Barely an hour after landing in Ava's stuffy little flat she had proceeded to apply the legendary Ger-man *Hausfrau* energy to it, scrubbing the kitchen and its bathtub free of splattered baby food and grime. She'd returned the fungal garden that had been Ava's bathroom to something like its original state, and she'd clambered onto the unit's two fire escapes to Windex all the windows. When she was done, the apartment was so noticeably brighter that she might have whisked a stubborn storm cloud from over the building.

Yesterday, however, had been the motherly coup de grace. When Ilse showed up late in the morning, she'd had in tow a lanky youth in a Macy's apron. The latter stood huffing and panting behind her, having just hauled two large boxes up the four flights of stairs. Inside each was a shining Friedrich air-conditioning unit. "One for the kitchen, one for the bedroom," said Ilse, as Ava gaped at the appliances, speechless.

Then: "*Was ist los?* Did I buy the wrong kind?"

But Ava could only shake her head, overwhelmed not just by the gift but by the stark realization that for all her self-declared independence and self-sufficiency, for all her written protestations to her friends that she'd been "managing just fine" alone, she hadn't been. Not at all.

Ilse had the deliveryman install the units then and there, supervising with the same brisk pragmatism with which she'd supervised homework and camping trips in years past. She'd refused the reimbursement that Ava offered (purely reflexively, as she actually had no money). "I'm spending time with my granddaughter," her mother said, bouncing Sophie on her knee. "That's payment in and of itself."

And then, as if to finalize her new role as flawed-mother-turned-fairy-godmother, she took the baby out for a walk, leaving Ava to nap in the blissful, rumbling chill.

Bending carefully now at the waist, Ava set down the cooking spoon with its shiny coating of pudding batter, and opened the oven door. The *Schweinebraten*, in its crackling coat of paprika, mustard, and caraway seeds, appeared to be browning nicely, and the smell was nothing short of heavenly. Above it, a cake of Camembert bubbled merrily on a cookie sheet, its red currant sauce at the ready next to the pudding. Feeling more creatively satisfied than she'd felt in over a year, Ava shut the oven again, then leaned against the counter to wipe the heat-fog from her glasses. Sophie, who had been damply drowsing against her stomach, woke enough to take a sleepy swipe, knocking them to the floor.

"*Scheisse!* Sophie!" Holding the kitchen counter for balance, Ava performed an awkward plié as the baby kicked her heels into her groin, then tried for the glasses again. Ava gave her the pudding spoon to gnaw on instead. Opening the refrigerator, she pulled out the white Zinfandel she'd been steadily working her way through, realizing only after she'd poured her third (or fifth) pinkish splash that over half of the bottle was gone.

"*Ba-ba-ba-ba,*" Sophie sang.

"It's all right," Ava told her. "We have another one for when Oma comes."

"*Oma Oma,*" Sophie warbled.

"Yes. Oma. Do you think she'll be happy with all this *köstliches* food?"

Her daughter shook the spoon tambourine-style, barely missing Ava's nose. "*Nein,*" she said, her face and tone both so grimly Ilse's that Ava had to burst out laughing.

At eight forty-five the kitchen table was set with silverware, bodega daisies of salmon pink, and the two unchipped plates Ava still possessed. Sophie was at last in her crib, curled stomach down on freshly laundered bedsheets with the cooking spoon clutched in her plump, determined fist. To try to distract herself from her annoyance, Ava was sketching her now-congealing pork roast on an overdue phone bill. Because Ilse—pragmatic, proprietary, Teutonically punctual Ilse—was over an hour late.

Ava had called the Jane twice, to no avail; "Madame" was not answering her line. She'd manned her fire escape for a full half hour after putting Sophie down, finishing off the last of the Paul Masson and two Parliaments from her emergency pack. She'd even called the Chock full o'Nuts across the street, though given Ilse's critique of its coffee ("They should call it 'Chock Full of Nothing'") it seemed an unlikely destination. Sure enough, the manager reported that no, she hadn't seen the "nice older lady" to whom Ava had introduced her yesterday at breakfast.

Propping the window open, Ava combed her memory for hints her mother might have dropped about her intended destination. But in retrospect, Ilse had been almost pointedly vague about her plans, simply saying she'd be "doing some exploring in the city." When Ava offered to accompany her, she'd snapped, "I'll be fine," with a familiar crispness that meant *This is not up for discussion.* As usual, Ava had not pushed her for detail.

Now she stared down at the darkening sidewalk with its desultory lovers, its blowsy pilings of garbage and Jackson Pollock splashes of spilled liquids, food, and canine waste. What if Ilse had taken it upon herself to "explore" the Bronx or Harlem on her own? As omnipotent as she'd always seemed to Ava, she was still a middle-aged German woman, used to German order and courtesy, German efficiency and punctiliousness. She was about as prepared for nighttime New York as she would have been for a solo safari in the Serengeti.

Her thoughts were interrupted by a low, lingering croak from the bedroom, a cross between a cough and a squeaky door hinge. Ava held a lungful of smoke, praying it was just one of Sophie's sleep sounds. But it grew steadily into a wail that was weak, but most definitely awake.

Exhaling in annoyance, she stubbed the cigarette out in her wilting spider plant and set her glass down on the counter. So it had now officially closed: that brief window within which she and her mother might have enjoyed the dinner she'd worked so hard on all day.

God damn her.

By the time she'd reached the crib Sophie had pulled herself to her feet and was shaking the railing like a tiny asylum inmate. This in and of itself wasn't unusual. As Ava drew close, though, she immediately sensed something was wrong. The infant's scream was weak and husky, more a plea than a protest. Her face was pale, her eyes red and swollen. Picking her up, Ava pressed her lips against her daughter's forehead and her fingertips to her delicate ear. Both were burning.

"What's happened, *Liebling*?" Cradling the baby against her chest, Ava hurried to the bathroom, praying the thermometer was where she'd last left it. She hadn't had to use it very often, since Sophie was unusually hardy for a baby (another trait she'd inherited from her grandmother). Now Ava had to fumble for a few seconds—in the medicine cabinet, in the toothbrush jar—before locating the device under the sink, mixed into a broken set of Clairol curlers. She shook the mercury down and cleaned the bulb before wrestling Sophie onto her stomach back on the bed.

By now the baby's screams had faded into whimpers: rhythmic yelps that were actually harder to hear than full-on howls. As she inserted the thermometer, Ava resisted a violent urge to wail along with her daughter as she waited for the reading:

103.4 degrees Fahrenheit.

A moment of panicked paralysis: the highest Sophie had ever hit was 102, about a year ago. Luckily Livi had been there and was able to call a fellow psychology student who also happened to be a nurse. Ava tried to remember what the advice had been at that point: something about cold washcloths? Cold baths? Or had it been frozen peas? So much had happened since then, and on so little sleep. It was like trying to remember a different lifetime.

Pulling Sophie into her lap, Ava reached for the bedside phone, punching in the number so familiar to her now it was essentially muscle memory.

"Hello?"

"She's got a temperature."

Her best friend didn't need to ask who. "How high?"

"103.4."

"Shit." An audible exhale (was Livi smoking? Ava wondered). "Are you sure?"

"Yes."

"Where's your mom?"

"I don't know." Ava felt her throat tighten. "She was supposed to be back by seven thirty."

"Christ. Okay. Don't panic." Livi's voice shifted into a harder, quicker register; her *let's get this shit done* tone. "I don't know if Fran is even in town," she said. "But let me try her. Okay? If she's not, Daniel might know someone." Daniel was Livi's current boyfriend, a burly amateur boxer who was also an EMT. "Just sit tight. If I don't call back in ten, you call me. All right?"

Ava nodded, by now too anxious to even verbalize a response. Hanging up, she rested Sophie's head against her shoulder and rocked gently, feeling the baby's heart skittering against her skin as she tried to think through the heavy haze of heat and alcohol that seemed to have filled her head. What had happened? When she'd put her daughter down she'd seemed lethargic, yes. Maybe even a little clingy. But Ava had attributed both to Sophie's napless state, to the heat. If her skin had felt warm, she'd assumed it was from being held against Ava's own body in an oven-hot kitchen.

A sudden, warm dampness on her bare thigh: she'd forgotten to re-diaper. "Fuck," she said.

She wiped her leg off with a burp cloth and unfolded a fresh Pampers. A siren lowed into the distance. Ava stared at the phone, which didn't ring. And didn't ring. She started pacing: from the crib to the window. Then back. On her third round her bare foot landed on something hard and sticky; looking down, she saw the cooking spoon she'd given Sophie to chew on.

Foot half lifted, Ava squinted down at the sticky utensil. Then, leaving it where it lay, she raced back to the phone and dialed again.

"Eggs," she said, the minute Livi picked up.

"What?"

"There were goddamn eggs in this pudding I was making. Raw eggs. I gave Sophie the spoon to chew on."

A measured pause. "You think it's salmonella?"

"I don't know. I don't know what else causes this kind of a fever. God. I'm such an idiot . . ."

"Stop it, sweetie," said Livi sternly. "You know that's not helpful. Okay, listen. Daniel said you should take her to an emergency room."

"You mean call an ambulance?"

"No. Just go. The heat is causing a crazy backlog on the phone lines. You're better off with a cab. Or even just walking her over."

"To where?"

"Wherever's closest."

"I don't know wherever's closest."

"Are you serious?" Livi sighed, exasperated. "Av, you've lived there for two years!"

"So I'm fucking stupid, okay?" Ava snapped. "I'm a complete *Dummkopf.* I'm the reason we have to go in the first place."

Sophie stirred at the outburst. Reflexively stroking her hair, Ava noticed that it was wet before realizing that she'd been weeping into it. She hiccupped, took a shuddering breath. "Sorry. I think I'm—" She struggled to remember the English term. "Losing it. I'm losing it." Then: "Oh God, what if I lose *her*?" It came out a shuddering half wail.

"Just—listen," said Livi sternly. "Can you just listen to me for a minute?"

"Yes." Ava swallowed. "I'm listening."

"Go outside. Hail a cab. Tell them to take you to Cabrini. If you can't find a cab, walk. Fast. Just take Second uptown. Cabrini is on Nineteenth, between Second and Third. Did you ever buy that pepper spray stuff I told you about?"

"No."

Another pause—this one inaudibly annoyed. "Okay. It's not that late, so you should be fine. But it's dark now. So walk fast. Be aware of your surroundings. I'll meet you in the ER in, say, twenty minutes. Okay?"

"Yes."

"Repeat it back," Livi prompted.

"Cabrini. Nineteenth. Between Second and Third."

"Good. I'll see you there."

The heat had seemingly heightened taxi demand as well, since hailing one outside proved outright impossible. After the fourth had sped by in a checkered blur Ava started walking: past the prostitutes in their cropped halters and shortest of shorts, past the ragtag boys aiming basketballs at a broken air conditioner. A few looked in her direction, and the hooker in thigh-high boots asked Ava for a light that she didn't have. Her skin tingled with an unspecified vulnerability as she pushed the stroller along. She'd dismissed Livi's pepper spray suggestion as American overkill, but now she wished that she'd bought at least one can. As Ava quickened her pace, the pulsating beat she'd heard earlier—heavy and syncopated—was growing louder. In her exhaustion and the lingering remnants of her pink wine buzz she had the surreal impression that everything in the airless city, even her own quick-paced trot, was somehow set to its rhythm.

She'd just crossed East Houston when the lights above her flickered: not just the lamp she was passing, but all of them. For a few seconds the effect was almost festive; like fairy lights twinkling against the urban grit.

Then everything went black.

It happened not all at once but rather in a slow, almost graceful progression; a broadening swath of blankness that started somewhere above her head and swept its way up Second Avenue. *Poof, poof, poof*: as though each streetlight were being snuffed out by ghostly, synchronized lamplighters.

Ava stopped in her tracks. So, it seemed, did everything in the clamorous, filthy city. It all fell eerily silent, as though sound itself were being swallowed by the sudden blackness: two million television shows shrinking into tiny light points before vanishing. Five million radios falling into static-framed silence. A million humming air conditioners freezing midrumble. Oddly enough, nonelectric sounds stopped too: shrieking sirens and honking car horns, the shouts and greetings of passersby. The wary, rhythmic barkings of dogs. Even the pigeons stopped cooing, as if the sudden shift in atmosphere had caught them off-guard. Rooted where she was, Ava looked up into a sky filled with newly numerous stars.

For a moment she just stood there, transfixed by the sight: the revelation of such unfamiliar and unexpected beauty. Then someone somewhere near her—deep-voiced, male—let loose a three-note song: *"Hooooooo! Blackout!"*

As if on signal, the urban street sound blasted back on, though its tone felt somehow different from before: the sirens amplified and more urgent. The shouts shriller and more heartfelt, as though roused by a sudden call to battle. Ava heard the word again—*blackout*—and distract-edly searched her brain for the corresponding German, finally settling on *Stromausfall*. It was a term that—until tonight—she'd associated with aerial bombings: a verbal relic from the War No One Willingly Men-tioned. As she squinted into the sudden gloom, though, it seemed par-ticularly apt: but for the light of passing cars, she felt almost blinded by inky darkness.

She resumed briskly walking, fear of the dark ceding to a New York-er's instinct to keep moving on streets where hesitation implied suscep-tibility. She kept her gaze fixed ahead, and so it was only after twenty or more minutes and a furtive glimpse up at a street sign that she real-ized she'd veered completely off course: she was heading not uptown but westward. Groaning in frustration, she wheeled the stroller around and set back again the way she had come.

What felt like hours later she turned back onto Second, where she began to make out shifting outlines and shapes in the dark: a glint of headlight-limned skin here. A chalk-white tank there. The lit tips of cig-arettes, free-floating constellations in the gloom. At some point she no-ticed a group of shadowy figures drawing together several blocks ahead, like metal shavings clumping toward the end of a magnet. There were more shouts: not just *blackout* but exulted whoops and catcalls, and the rattling cough of steel gates being pulled shut. A chant started; slowing slightly, Ava strained to make out the words over the pounding of her pulse in her ears: *"Hit th' stores! Hit th' stores! Hit th' stores!"*

Then, from somewhere even closer, came the abrupt and unmistak-able retort: a gunshot. Then another.

Ava froze, as shocked as though she'd just been shot herself. Sophie burst into a fresh round of startled tears. Without a further thought for the hospital Ava swung the stroller around and set off back downtown at a jog: however sick Sophie was, it wasn't worth risking their lives over.

As she raced over the steaming pavement Ava kept her eyes fixed ahead and her limbs loose, like a wrestler in the ring, stunned by how quickly order had deteriorated around her. How long had they been walking? The street now felt as populated as it had at noon; she found herself darting left and right with the same tight-jawed focus she'd once turned on arcade games. Swerving to avoid two men dragging a full-sized sofa between them, she nearly hit another with a mattress balanced precariously on his head. A woman with a boxed Barbie Disco Playset and a pile of buxom dolls dropped one right into Sophie's lap, though a moment later the lone policeman who appeared to be giving chase (where on earth were the rest of them? Ava wondered) snatched the toy up again indignantly, as though Sophie were an accomplice to the heist.

"Be-be-be!" screeched Sophie.

"I know," Ava panted, pausing to allow a woman practically mummified in cheap clothing to pass, plastic hangers clacking, price tags fluttering like tiny victory flags. "We'll get you a new baby. I promise," she said, though part of her was wondering whether there would be any merchandise left in New York after this. It couldn't have been more than an hour since the blackout started, but the damage already seemed overwhelming: Doors defaced. Windows splintered. Walls splattered with food or paint or (could it be?) blood. The sidewalk was strewn with glass; pushing through one larger pile she felt a shard working itself into her sandal's insole, pushing into the soft flesh of the arch of her foot with each step. She limped on, past a man grimly attacking a padlock with a saw and two more prying steel shutters open with crowbars. Across the street the crowd had jimmied a hardware shop gate up with a hydraulic jack, propping it open with a city garbage can and proceeding to strip it clean, some of the men even loading the stolen items into a waiting U-Haul. A few stores down, someone had driven a tow truck up onto the sidewalk in front of an appliance shop and was attaching the hook to the gate. As Ava passed she heard the truck's engine rev and whine briefly, before the gate clamorously ripped away from its steel frame. A profane cheer went up. A man pushed past her, a KitchenAid blender held aloft like a sports trophy.

In the absence of working traffic lights the East 4th Street intersection was like the site of some vast, experimental urban art project. Cars honked and dodged in the darkness, loot-laden pedestrians maneuvering around them like gleeful mice in a maze. At first glance, it all appeared to be under the balletic direction of a barefoot man in dreadlocks and a striped tam, though neither drivers nor pedestrians were paying him any attention. After several false starts she got them across, though her heart remained in her mouth for the last few blocks home.

She awoke in grayish sunlight on the bathroom floor they'd collapsed on together following a prolonged battle to give Sophie baby aspirin. Sophie lay starfished on the mat, her blond curls damp and wild, her lips parted to reveal tiny pearls of budding teeth. She was so still that for one petrified moment Ava feared she'd stopped breathing. But then the baby flung one arm into the air and sighed, as though trying for a cloud she knew was beyond reach.

Carefully resting the back of her wrist against the damp pink forehead, Ava found to her amazement that it felt cool. She wondered whether the surreal events of the past twelve hours had simply been her own fever visions: a midsummer night's nightmare, sparked by spiking temperatures and too much sugary wine. But the bathroom nightlight still wasn't on, and the flip-clock on her bookcase remained frozen at 9:22.

For a moment Ava felt frozen as well: overwhelmed anew by the inky panic of the streets, by how quickly a known place could turn both unfamiliar and perilous. It was an awareness she'd had as a child and as a survivor of the Berlin bombings, but one she'd somehow lost since making New York City her home. She found herself wondering whether Ulrich had lost it too, in his brief window between moving to Israel and dying for it.

There followed a wash of yearning for him so sudden and dense that Ava's insides seemed to physically ache with it. Squeezing her arms across her stomach, she found herself thinking: *Why? Why did I let him go?* Why, after that last night in Berlin, hadn't she demanded that one of them change course? That he come to New York, or she go to Tel Aviv, or they go together someplace entirely their own?

But of course, she knew why. It was the same reason that, a decade before their parting, she'd put a stop to their teenage romance before it had really started. At the time she'd blamed the horrific history they'd uncovered together: *Look who my dad was.* But it was later, only after a string of disastrous affairs with fast, unfaithful men, that she understood the truth: for in fact Ulrich—brilliant, funny, unconditionally-supportive-from-the-moment-they'd-met Ulrich—had quite literally been too good for her. Too considerate; too gentle. Too altogether safe, at a time when what Ava craved was the breathless distraction of danger and pain.

Now, though, staring up at the paint-blistering ceiling, her sleeping, nonfeverish daughter by her side, she realized just how completely she had changed. Gone were the self-punishing yearnings of her teens and early twenties; the greedy urge to lose herself in a man's cruel whims. Instead, and for the first time in her life, she needed exactly what Ulrich had once tried to give her.

The revelation was so crushing—and the yearning so potent—that when the bedside phone started ringing her first thought was that it was Ulrich himself, showing up (as he always had) at precisely the moment she needed him. It wasn't until Sophie whimpered quietly that Ava forced herself back to the moment.

Standing as quietly as she could, she made her way to the bed, her back aching from the hard tiled floor.

"*Ja, hallo?*" she whispered.

From the other end came a staticky, compressed version of the chaos she'd escaped hours earlier on the streets: people shouting and arguing. Scores of phones ringing in an atonal chorus. A machine-gun *tat-tat-tat* that at first sounded like a war zone but she quickly realized was merely battling typewriters.

"Is this Ava Fischer?" Gruff and deep, the man's voice sounded as weary as she felt.

"Yes." Eyes glued to the sleeping Sophie, Ava slouched onto the still-perfectly-made bed.

"This is Officer Michaels down at the Seventh Precinct."

She sat upright. "The police?"

"Yes, ma'am," he said, with exaggerated patience. "I'm calling because I believe we have your mother here."

"My mother?" On the bathroom rug, Sophie stirred again.

"Is your mother Elsie Fischer?" the man asked. "German lady? Older?"

"Ilse," Ava said numbly. "Ilse von Fischer. Yes."

"We picked her up around five a.m. on the Bowery."

Ava gasped. "She's been arrested?"

"Not arrested. She was fighting with a couple looters when our team showed up. She didn't seem to know where to go, so we brought her along with the group we brought in."

"You say she was *fighting*?" Ava shut her eyes, trying to process what she was hearing. Her head felt as though it were stuffed with silt. "My mother was fighting in the Bowery?"

"She's *fine*," the officer said, as though she'd asked the question she should have. "A little shaken up. But not injured in any way that we can see. However, just to be sure, we don't want her leaving alone. We'll need you to come pick her up."

Ava glanced back at Sophie. Now awake, she had rolled onto her stomach and was on hands and knees, reaching for the open bottle of St. Joseph's that Ava had left on the tub. "Ah, *shit*."

The policeman cleared his throat. "Excuse me?"

"Sophie, sweetie. *No*." Scooping up the phone base, Ava raced toward the bathroom, stopping short as the cord reached its limit. "Please wait," she said breathlessly, before dropping the receiver. "Just wait a moment."

She reached her daughter just as Sophie reached her bottled quarry, scooping infant and aspirin up in one fell swoop. Failing to find the St. Joseph's top, she tossed the whole thing in the garbage before speeding back to the abandoned receiver.

"Sorry," she said breathlessly, clamping the device between shoulder and ear and reaching for a pencil. "Where exactly are you guys again?"

Outside, the morning light was ashy and wet-looking. Across the street from the precinct office a low-end boutique lay ravaged, its entire front window gone, its mannequins stripped and beheaded. Ava picked her way down the debris-strewn sidewalk, stepping carefully around more broken glass, burst bags of garbage, and two sleeping junkies. On Mott Street the Lincolns, Datsuns, and Buicks jostled and screeched, stopping short like irate bumper cars, honking at one another like lowing cattle. A fire hydrant spewed a foaming white jet of city water beneath which a homeless man, naked but for his briefs, appeared to be joyfully showering. Still in last night's sweat-stiff sundress, Ava momentarily yearned to join him—Snugli, baby, and all.

Inside the precinct office, the chaos seemed only marginally more controlled. Disheveled detainees sprawled on the wooden benches and spilled onto the tiled floor, mostly men, many shirtless, some wounded. An emaciated woman in a plunge-neck romper and red stilettos slumped before the exhausted-looking cop who was taking down her information with two fingers, his slow-pecking pace clearly no match for her rapid-fire Spanish. Scanning the room, Ava felt a shudder of recognition. The last time she'd been in a place like this had been a decade earlier—and unlike Ilse, she actually *had* been arrested. She pictured Ulrich's wry face when he came to sign her out and felt her throat tighten almost painfully.

Swallowing, Ava bounced Sophie against her chest and fed her small bits of bagel while surveying the room. She finally spotted Ilse on a bench by the far wall, seated between an enormous blue-black man in a pink rainbow tank and a teenage boy who seemed asleep with his mouth open.

"Mutti," Ava called, pushing her way through the crowd.

"Oma," crowed Sophie, twisting in her Snugli and spitting gluey dough onto the wooden floor.

Ilse was slouched where she sat, with her wire-rimmed glasses on, reading something in her lap. As she looked up Ava suppressed a gasp. Her mother looked terrible: disheveled, worn. As Ava approached she refolded her paper with shaking hands and tucked it hurriedly into her worn crocodile purse.

"Da bist du ja," she said tersely.

"Jesus," gasped Ava. "What happened?"

Her mother snapped her handbag shut. "Two hooligans tried to take my purse."

"But why were you even in the Bowery at five a.m.?"

Her mother shrugged. "I was taking a walk."

"A *walk*?"

"Oma!" Pushing off against Ava's chest, Sophie was trying to torque her body around to see her grandmother, who greeted the greeting with a tepid smile.

"And why did you try to fight off muggers?" asked Ava, still flabbergasted. "In the Bowery, of all places?"

"I told you. They were after my purse." Ilse scowled, looking fleetingly the way Sophie looked when Ava scolded her or denied her something she wanted.

"But you don't even have anything valuable in it! You left your ticket and passport at the flat!"

"Don't tell me what I have in it," her mother snapped, slinging the bag over her shoulder. "Can I finally leave? These horrid men wouldn't let me before." Without waiting for an answer she turned on her heel and started marching toward the door.

Two release forms and sixty-five minutes later they were back in Ava's apartment, where Ava had just managed to put a squalling, overtired Sophie down for an early nap. Carefully closing the bedroom door, she returned to the kitchen and set about making coffee in the stovetop Moka. Ilse sat at the kitchen table, staring blankly at the ruined feast that had been in her honor, a sight that made Ava furious all over again. The *Schweinebraten,* so brown and inviting just a few hours earlier, had taken on a sickly, grayish-pink color, though this did nothing to discourage the handful of fat houseflies gleefully skating over its larded surface. The second candle had burned out after bleeding an opaque streak of white wax that ended just before the tallow-toned streak of melted cheese and butter from her Camembert dish. Ava was half tempted to wrap it all up in the tablecloth and haul the whole thing to the trash.

Instead, while the Moka percolated and popped she curtly cleared the remnants of the wasted meal, throwing the food unceremoniously in the garbage, the plates and forks and knives and wineglasses in the sink. Throughout it all Ilse sat like a statue in her chair, her purse in her lap. The first thing she'd done when they reached the apartment was to retrieve her Lufthansa ticket and passport from the television console drawer. Now she had them in front of her and stared down at them without expression. As Ava set a cup of coffee in front of her she looked up and nodded distractedly, as though acknowledging a distant acquaintance.

Pouring a cup for herself, Ava sank into the chair across the table from her mother and tried to calm her churning thoughts. *Above all, don't get into a fight*, Livi had said.

"You really have to learn to let go of things," she said carefully. "Physically, I mean. One of these days you'll really get hurt."

"Hurt," Ilse repeated. Her face bore a look of bone-tired desolation, as though she'd traveled a thousand miles through a desert on foot. Then again (Ava reflected), traveling the Bowery during the early hours of a summer blackout probably hadn't been much easier.

"*Are* you hurt?" she asked, more gently.

"A few scrapes." Her mother seemed annoyed by the question. "From where I fell. Nothing serious."

"The police didn't seem so sure."

"The police here are idiots. Did you see what was happening out there? That would never have happened in Berlin."

"It would happen anywhere, given the right circumstances."

"Not in Germany."

Ava didn't have the strength to challenge her. "The bigger question is where the hell you were all night."

"Out," said Ilse stonily. "I told you. I couldn't sleep."

"I mean before that. You were supposed to be here at seven thirty. For dinner. I cooked all day."

"I had something to do." Her mother hugged the bag to her chest, as if she still feared having it ripped away. "I lost track of time," she added vaguely.

"For an entire *night*? How?"

"It doesn't matter." Ilse frowned as Ava lit her cigarette. "Didn't you quit?"

"I still smoke when I'm anxious," Ava said dryly.

To her surprise, her mother held her hand out for the pack, extracting a cigarette and lighting it. Her movements struck Ava as strangely mechanical. It was as though Ilse were operating herself remotely, the way people navigated radio-controlled cars in Central Park.

"Sophie was sick last night," Ava said, more abruptly than she'd planned to. "Really sick."

"*Krank?*" Ilse seemed momentarily roused again from her fog. "Why? What happened?"

"She had a 39-degree fever. You weren't here to help and I tried to get her to the hospital but then all hell broke loose and . . ."

"But she's all right now." Ilse's eyes were cool and gray-blue in the morning light.

"Yes," Ava said, unexpectedly stung by her mother's sudden shortness. For all her prior doting on her granddaughter, Ilse sounded less concerned than impatient.

"*Gut.*"

Resting her cigarette on the ashtray, Ilse unsnapped her purse and slipped her passport, ticket, and traveler's checks into it. Ava caught the glimpse of a silver compact, the same white folded paper she'd seen at the precinct. She tried again. "Can you at least tell me what part of the city you were in? And how you got there?"

Her mother sighed. "Why does it matter?"

"Because you're my *mother*. Because I had no idea if you were safe."

Ilse studied the cigarette in her hand. "I think I should not have come," she said quietly.

Stricken again, Ava blinked. "Why would you say that?"

"I'm just better off back in Germany. It is where I belong."

The words triggered a familiar surge of anxiety: *She's going to leave.* "Nonsense," said Ava stiffly. "You belong with us. You belong with your family."

"You have no idea," Ilse said tersely, "where I belong."

Ava took a deep breath. "You're right," she said. "I have no idea about you at all." She exhaled a stream of smoke, struggling to regain her composure. *Just don't let it go there*, Livi had advised her. *If you see a fight coming, change directions.*

But it was already too late: Ava couldn't have changed directions if she'd tried.

"All I understand is that it's always been about *you*," she said, her voice heating. "*Your* convenience. *Your* rules. *Your* private plans and . . . and secret stories that you never think to let me in on."

Ilse gave her a hard look. "What on earth are you talking about?"

"I'm talking about the fact that even here in New York, and even after all this time, you still can't be honest with me!"

The words seemed to finally puncture Ilse's weary remove: "Nonsense," she said indignantly. "I've practically been here from morning to night since arriving! I've taken the baby out and put her to sleep. I've rubbed my hands raw cleaning out your dirty firetrap of an apartment."

The abrupt shift into attack mode caught Ava's breath in her throat. "That's not what I'm talking about!" she said. "I'm talking about *honesty.* You weren't just wandering around last night—any more than you were wandering around for a whole damn year after the war ended." And oh, the sheer, electric relief of simply letting the words *fly*—of aiming them right at Ilse's rigid face. How many times had she played out this confrontation in her head? It felt so exhilarating that for an instant she was almost thankful. "You think a couple of air conditioners and a quick bathtub scrub makes up for it all?" she added. Her voice was rising now; for once she let it. She didn't care.

"What do you mean, 'all'?"

"All the secrets! All the *lies!*"

Did Ava imagine it, or had Ilse flinched at the word *Lügen*? If she had, she recovered quickly. "At least *I* had a real job," she shot back. "At least I raised you in a proper home. Not some tenement in an urban war zone."

"But you know what else *I* did here?" Ava's pulse was beating in her throat; her voice shook as though disrupted by its rhythm. "I made a real, honest-to-God family. It may just be the two of us, but at least there are no boundaries between us. Not of the sort you always kept up between me and you."

She held her breath, waiting for Ilse to deny this. But her mother merely tightened her lips. When it became clear that she had nothing to add, Ava allowed herself another slow exhale. There it was again: the icy certainty that if she pressed even a little, her mother would respond not by opening up but rather by shutting herself off completely—and very likely forever.

"Mutti," Ava said, softening her tone again. "*Bitte*. I just need to know the truth. You always said that someday you'd answer my questions. For God's sake. I'm almost thirty-seven. Don't you think it's finally time?"

Ilse's eyes were fixed on her, as steely and unrelenting as the Atlantic in late afternoon. Ava watched as she plucked the Parliament from her lips and wordlessly stubbed it out in the ashtray.

"I was going to tell you," she said. "I was going to tell you everything. It was actually why I came."

It was so precisely what Ava had longed to hear for so long that for a moment she felt as though her heart stopped. *Don't fall for it*, she told it.

"*Und?*" she asked, quietly.

"I can't." Ilse shook her head. "It's—it's too late now."

Despite Ava's own self-warning it still felt like a blow to the solar plexus. For a moment she couldn't meet her mother's eyes. When she did, she realized to her horror that her own were dangerously close to tears.

"Is—is this some sort of perverse *game* for you? Some sort of silly story you are just making up as you go along?"

Ilse shook her head. "It's not a game. And it's not a story."

"How can you say that, when my entire life you've refused to tell me anything meaningful?"

"What do you mean, 'meaningful'?"

"I mean like where I *came* from! I mean like where you were during the war, and all those months after it ended before you finally came for me!" Ava was crying now, openly. She no longer cared.

"Everything I did, I did so that you'd have a *good life*." Ilse spoke rapidly, her voice low and level. "An education. Clothes. Food."

"But not your *trust*! Can't you see that I never had that?" Ava dashed at her damp eyes with her wrist. "And without that, it was as good as never having you at all. I need that to change, Mutti. I need to *know*."

"Know what?"

Ava clenched her teeth again in frustration. "*Everything!* I need you to sit here with me—right here, right now—and answer every single question I ask you with full honesty."

For a long moment Ilse said nothing. She simply stared at the table, her face white and her eyes closed. When at last she opened them again there was a dullness to them that Ava had never seen before, as though some light deep behind them had flickered out.

"*Das kann ich nicht,*" she said, quietly.

I can't.

It came back to her then, the old, haunting image: a bone-bright day. Her mother walking away. She swallowed, fully aware of the weight of what she was about to say. Wishing desperately for a way not to say it. But it had been in her for too long, holding her back like a rusted anchor in the tempestuous current of her current existence.

"Then," she said softly, "I can't have you in my life."

Ilse remained still—so still, in fact, that for a moment Ava wasn't certain if she'd been heard. Then she nodded, albeit so subtly that it might as easily have been a shifting shadow.

"If that is what you need," she said.

Ava squeezed her eyes shut. Suddenly, she was feeling it all over: the juddering sift and tumble of the world collapsing on her. The blacking out of all light, all air. All life. For a moment she even thought she heard the whining buzz of the bombers, taking aim at the cornerstones of her life.

But then she heard something else: a sleepy, singsong tune floating gossamer-light from the bedroom.

"*Oma,*" Sophie was singing. "*Oma-oma-oma-oma.*"

When she opened her eyes Ilse was staring at her, her gaze quiet, bereaved. She lifted her pale brows in question.

"All right," Ava said numbly. "Go ahead."

It wasn't until after Ilse had pushed heavily to her feet that Ava realized why it had been so hard to shape the words: they had felt strangely like *good-bye.*

4.

Ilse

1935

*I*t is five thirty-five, and Ilse can't find the new lanyard that should be the crowning touch to her uniform.

"Are you sure you didn't put it in with the washing?" her mother asks, carefully combing through her golden finger-wave with two fingers. She's wearing a black silk dress that Ilse hasn't seen before, and she has to admit it's very striking: the sweetheart neckline and dropped shoulders make her mother's pale skin glow like moonstone next to a darkened lake. The little diamond drop earrings are also new, an anniversary gift from Ilse's father last month.

"Did you ask Katinka?" her mother adds. Katinka is the new housekeeper.

"I didn't. But I'm sure. It was on my bureau in my room. I always leave it there," Ilse gripes. "So I won't *lose* it."

"Well, the way you keep your room it's no wonder you can't find anything in it." Her mother crooks an eyebrow at her in the mirror; Ilse's chronic sloppiness is a point of ongoing contention. "Anyway, don't you have more than one?"

"My other one isn't the right color now that I've been made a Group Leader."

"Well, I really don't know what to tell you." Zella von Fischer spritzes her décolleté with Vol de Nuit. "You can either wear the old one or go without one altogether."

"But I can't go without it!" Ilse cries. "Especially not tonight! Everyone is going to be in full uniform!"

"Renate won't."

"Renate isn't going. It's a Hitlerjugend outing and her parents still won't let her join." In fact, Renate has at long last capitulated on the BDM front and now plans to join despite her parents' opposition, though in the end it wasn't Ilse's urgings but those of Rudi Gerhardt that got her to change her mind. Ilse can't help but feel slighted that after years of dedicated lobbying on her part, it took a boy who (as far as Ilse's concerned) barely knows Renate at all to change her mind on the subject. But she takes solace in the fact that once Renate does join, at least she and Ilse will be able to spend more time together. As of late, nearly all of Renate's free time seems to be shaped around Rudi's availability: taking walks, seeing movies, studying together in cafés and Herr Steinberg's library. And while Ilse is ostensibly invited on these activities, the few times she's joined have been distinctly uncomfortable—like trying to fit three people onto a two-person love seat. It doesn't help that Renate treats everything out of Rudi's mouth like the most fascinating story ever told. Even though it's usually another silly *Mein Kampf* quotation.

Or that every time Rudi takes her friend's soft pale hand in his own he might as well be hammering a small nail into Ilse's spleen.

"Well, anyway. It's just a *film*," her mother is saying. "It's not as though the Führer is going to be looking back at you from the screen."

"It's *not* just a film," Ilse says. "And everyone *else* will be seeing me!"

"I rather suspect they won't be quite as interested in your appearance as you seem to presume they will be," her mother retorts.

It is such a typical put-down, with such typical, casual cruelty that Ilse actually has to stifle a scream.

"You don't understand," she says instead, as coldly as she can manage. "You don't understand anything at all."

Fuming, she spins around toward the door. But as her mother begins powdering her nose, Ilse turns back again. "Don't you think you're wearing too much makeup? You know the Führer disapproves of face painting." She looks pointedly at her mother's feet, clad in black T-strap pumps. "*And* high heels."

And without waiting for a response, she stomps morosely back to her room.

With barely half an hour to make it to the Ufa-Palast am Zoo, she rummages first through her sock drawer, then her underwear drawer, still seething in silence. Not only does her mother seem to know nothing about her life, but she quite frankly doesn't seem to care. The fact that Ilse managed to become a *Mädelgruppenführerin* after only a year in the BDM barely elicited a reaction, even though in her performance review, the head of Ilse's leadership training unit described her as *one of the hardest-working and resourceful girls I have had the pleasure of meeting.* But all Ilse's mother said when presented with the news was: "That's wonderful, dear. But they don't actually *pay* you at that level, do they?"

She'd been similarly unenthused when Ilse brought home her very first piece of published writing in the BDM monthly, *Das Deutsche Mädel. The German Girl.* A short poem titled "Why We Work," it was about the role of German youth in carrying their country back to greatness. The day it came out in the February edition was among the happiest of Ilse's life: something her best friend, at least, easily understood.

"You *did* it!" Renate had shrieked. "My best friend's a published *author*!" Humming a snatch of "You're the Cream in My Coffee," she'd tried to pick Ilse up and twirl her around the way John Boles does Shirley Temple in *The Littlest Rebel.* Of course she failed, since Ilse is the significantly heavier of the two and Renate is such a weakling. But her exuberant pride and the steady stream of impressed compliments Ilse received as everyone got their issue of the magazine made Ilse realize that she truly has found it: not just the thing she wants to do with her life, but the thing she truly believes she was *meant* for.

Because yes, she wants to *write*. Not just for herself, or Renate, or her instructors at school, but for the nation. For the movement. For the *cause*. She wants to write knowing that what she's writing will be read far and wide; that her voice and her own thoughts and ideas will shape voices, thoughts, and ideas across the Fatherland, perhaps even some-day the world. Seeing her name in print that first time had felt like seeing it writ in lightning across the sky: electrifying, staggering. Even more so when she realized what it meant: that with BDM membership approach-ing two million, those neatly typeset words might well pass before four million eyes, or even more.

Four million eyes. All pondering her words:

The door that leads to the future is found in our young hearts
The fruit that sustains the nation ripens in our sinless souls
Our mission is holy, our will pure and true
Our destiny: eternal victory, endless glory!

All of which only made her mother's nonplussed response—"It's re-ally quite short, isn't it!"—sting all the more.

Slamming shut her underwear drawer, Ilse rifles through her jew-elry box a second time: the old yellow lanyard is there, but not the new red-and-white one. It occurs to her that her mother might have simply taken the stupid thing out of spite. After all, she and Ilse's father have only just joined the Party, even though Ilse urged them to do it over a year ago. Sure enough, almost the moment they did their lives took an immediate turn for the better. Ilse's father, for instance, was given the bank promotion he'd been denied for two years straight. "You were right, Mousebear," he'd crowed to Ilse that night, pouring her her very first half glass of real *Sekt*. "It's something I should have done from the start!" Ilse knew how *that* had irked her mother: not just that Vati was letting her drink wine like a grown-up, but laying credit for the family's fortune at Ilse's (sensibly shod) feet.

Removing Renate's friendship ring (accessories are frowned upon in the BDM), she drops it in the box and shuts the lid, then glances again at her bedside clock. Lanyard or no, she'll have to leave in ten minutes or else she'll be late to meet her troop at the theater. The idea of showing up in her yellow lanyard is disproportionately infuriating. Not wearing one at all actually seems worse in some ways. Not just because this is the first BDM event where she's actually responsible for overseeing thirteen younger girls, but because they are going there to see *Triumph of the Will*, which from everything Ilse has heard is almost like partaking in last year's legendary rally in real life. Showing up in anything less than her full BDM attire seems not just lacking but actually immoral.

"It's *amazing*," her friend Marta had rhapsodized last week, after seeing the film with her parents. "It's hard to explain. But it captures *exactly* what we are doing. What the movement is all about." Without an ounce of self-consciousness, she admitted that she'd spent the last half hour of the movie in tears. "Though I don't imagine *you* will cry, Steel Girl," she'd added. *Stahlmädchen* is the nickname the other *Mädchen* gave Ilse last summer on a group hike in the German Alps: after turning an ankle, she'd marched on for eight kilometers, not even relinquishing the troop flag she'd been assigned to carry. She laughs gamely at the moniker, but like that stupid story about the U-Bahn burglar Renate claims she "fought off," Ilse is never quite sure it is meant as a compliment.

Now she gazes gloomily at her reflection: the black beret pulled sportily over one ear. The white blouse she'd had Katinka iron, looking plain and barren without the colorful cord that runs from collar to breast pocket. Sighing, she pulls on her jacket and buttons it all the way up; she will simply have to keep it on throughout the two-hour documentary. Hopefully it won't be too hot in the theater.

She's just about to head out the door when it opens abruptly to reveal her mother, holding the missing lanyard out between two red-tipped fingers.

"Katinka *did* have it," she says in triumph. "You left it in your pocket yesterday."

Ilse all but snatches the accessory back, her annoyance that her mother was right briefly outweighing her relief that the cord has finally been located. "Can you please at least *knock* before just barging in?" she says feebly.

"You're welcome, *Liebling*," her mother says. And with a tight smile, she turns away.

An hour later Ilse sits with eleven of her charges, the other two having been kept home by the latest bout of influenza. After significant scolding, cajoling, and threatening (and four last-minute washroom trips), Ilse has finally gotten everyone in their velvet-covered chairs, a task made all the harder by the edgy excitement that fills the room like a palpable force. Even though the movie hasn't yet started, it already feels like a momentous occasion. The theater has been accessorized with *Haken-kreuz* banners and flags. The speakers—which usually pipe out cheerily bland *Volksmusik*—tonight emit brass-heavy Party tunes like "Kampf-lied der Nationalsozialisten" and "Sieg Heil Viktoria." Ilse casts a quick glance around the room for Rudi and is quietly relieved not to find him.

Then the lights dim, and the curtains sweep open, and a respectful hush rolls over the rows like a soft heavy wave. As the familiar chords of the Horst Wessel song sound, the first title cards roll: *"On the 5th of September, 1934, 20 years after the outbreak of the World War, 16 years after the beginning of Germany's suffering, 19 months after the beginning of the German rebirth, Adolf Hitler flew again to Nuremberg to review his faithful followers."*

And then suddenly, amazingly, they are in the clouds, soaring like angels above a field of shining white. As it becomes clear that they are on the Führer's plane with him, the wonder is both immediate and palpable—most of them have never been on a plane. And as the clouds part to reveal old Nuremburg's fairy-tale-perfect skyline, its gingerbread gables swathed in Imperial and Nazi flags, it's as if every volume switch but the film's has been turned off completely.

The plane lands to a sea of marching men in brown shirts, all perfectly united in rhythm and pace. Ilse knows all of this happened months ago, but her heart still pounds as the plane door opens and its passengers begin their descent: first Hitler himself, in his neat uniform and jackboots, his smile quiet and self-deprecating, almost shy. He is followed by a trench-coated Goebbels and then other members of the administration, mostly dressed in business suits.

But on the tarmac, as in the theater, the crowd clearly only has eyes for their Führer. The camera pans across the outstretched arms and beaming faces of old and young alike, and their love seems to pass through the screen like light passes through glass, filling the breathless theater with that same sense of worship. Ilse all but feels it in the air, an extra current of excitement and adoration, heightened by a startling sense of proximity. For while she's seen the German leader's countenance a thousand times, she has rarely seen it like this: so close, so casual, so entirely *alive* that it seems possible he might turn his head to address her personally.

Day turns to night, then back to day. They are now in a place so familiar that a murmur of recognition sweeps the rows of uniformed youths in the Palast: a Hitlerjugend campsite filled with circular tents, from which a thousand boys sleepily emerge and begin preparing for the day's pageantry by bathing, eating, and doing calisthenics: a thousand Rudi Gerhardts joyously offering themselves up to Führer and Palast viewers alike. *It's so huge*, Ilse finds herself thinking, and is unexpectedly awed by this realization. For how many times has she confided this in Renate: her desire to *matter*, to *be part of something bigger*? And yet even in her most hopeful moments, it never occurred to her that that something could ever be quite *this* big, this mammoth and panoramic in scale. It's like spending one's entire life knowing only a single constellation, then suddenly being shown an infinite universe full of stars.

On the screen, Hitler is now addressing legions of young men bearing shovels. But again, it feels as though he's really speaking to the room: "The whole nation will be educated by you," he tells them. "And at this moment, it is not merely we here in Nuremberg. All of Germany sees you for the first time."

All of Germany, Ilse thinks, with the same shiver she'd felt upon realizing that millions might soon be reading her poem. But it's more than simply the thrill of it she's feeling. She is also, she suddenly realizes, so profoundly *grateful*. Not just that this man—this marvelous, miraculous man!—is saving Germany from enemies both beyond and within its borders, but that he's offering *her*, Ilse, a role in this all-important battle. And as the Hitlerjugend line up before their namesake in scores of straight-edged blocks of two hundred, and as the surrounding stadiumgoers—thousands of men, women, and children, packed like sardines but clearly not minding it one whit—stand on tiptoe to cheer on the marchers and marvel, their chant ("One People! One Führer! One Reich! Germany!") seems to be picked up by her own pounding pulse.

Someone gasps aloud behind her, and twisting in her seat Ilse sees that District Leader Meindel is unabashedly weeping.

Mädelschaftsführerin Meindel is one of Ilse's favorite BDM leaders. Slight, dark-haired, and pretty, and still only in her midtwenties, she comes from a working-class background: her father, a fruit vendor, lost literally everything after the war. She's told Ilse stories that make Ilse's own childhood seem unspeakably luxurious: about being turned onto the street after the banks took her family's flat. About having to move from house to house for over a year. About leaving primary school even though she loved reading and art and going to work in a factory, since her family needed the money.

Since Hitler took over, however, Mädelschaftsführerin Meindel not only has been able to resume her studies but has a steady income from doing what she loves most: working with girls like Ilse. Even better, her father has not only climbed out of debt but been able to open up his own little grocery shop. Last autumn he even bought a car. "You can't understand what the Führer means to us," she said to Ilse over coffee once, "unless you understand what it's like to live without hope. To wake up hungry. To constantly be running away from creditors." She'd shaken her head. "To have all that gone! It's like being brought back from the dead."

Ilse turns back to the screen. Now the sun is setting in Nuremberg; torches illume a thousand black-and-red flags carried in concert in the evening's rally. Hovering over it all is an enormous gleaming eagle, wings outstretched. And in the center, on the podium, the great man stands alone. On his face Ilse sees something she's never noticed before: a kind of sorrow, mingled with another emotion that at first she can't quite put words to, until she recognizes that it is love. Hitler's face, she suddenly realizes, is the face of a prophet. And even as she understands this she finds herself leaning forward, as though to bring herself as physically close to him as she can.

"A year ago," he begins, "we met for the first time upon this field of the political leaders of the National Socialist Party. They were brought here by nothing other than the call of their hearts. They were brought here by nothing other than their loyalty. It was the need of our people which moved us . . . and which brought us together. We wrestled and struggled together." Around her, she senses the older members of the audience nodding; hears faint grunts of assent and agreement. *One people*, thinks Ilse. *One Führer. One Reich.* It's like an incantation; a magic spell that makes them all as invincible as any righteous fairy-tale prince she has dreamt up for Renate in her stories. (A faint pang: she so wishes Renate were here to see this. *But soon*, she thinks. *I'll see it again with her soon.*)

Around the theater some people are starting to stand now: wave upon wave of them rising from their cushioned seats to join the thousands standing before them on the screen.

"This is our vow tonight," Hitler intones, his voice echoing in every corner of the vast hall. "Every hour, every day, think only of Germany. The people, the Reich, the German nation, and the German people!"

And then: *"Sieg Heil!"*

And from all around him and all around her the cry comes thundering back, each incantation louder and more potent than the last:

"Sieg Heil!"

"Sieg Heil!"

"SIEG HEIL!"

Ilse has also leapt to her feet, along with every other person in the room, so instinctively that she didn't realize she was doing it. As she flings her hand toward the screen her voice joins the endless, reverberating chant that seems to somehow be filling the entire world; the words at once losing their meaning with repetition—*SIEG-HEIL-SIEG-HEIL-SIEG-HEIL*—and yet gaining something much deeper than mere words could ever embody. As the chorus reaches its crescendo she is almost physically lifted by its power: as though it, and not her own strength, is what is truly holding her up. It feels dizzying, but also exhilarating. As though she's learning to escape earth's gravity; to launch herself like a comet toward the sky, and fly.

5

1935

"*C*an you speed up?" says Ilse. "You're moving like my grandmother."

They have just emerged from the Wittenbergerplatz U-Bahn station and are standing on the street by its steps. Rather than speeding up, however, Renate stops altogether. "I'm sorry," she says, and leans against one of the railings. "I didn't sleep well last night. I kept worrying about the letter."

"I keep telling you. They probably won't even ask for it."

"But what if they do? And what if they can tell?"

Ilse heaves an exasperated sigh. "All right. Let's see it, then."

Renate pulls the envelope from her satchel, then pulls the thrice-folded sheet of paper from the envelope. She hands it over, swallowing her anxiety as Ilse runs a well-chewed fingertip down each carefully typed line:

Dear Fräulein von Schmidt,

Please allow my daughter Renate to register as a Hitlerjugend Jung-mädel and provide her with the appropriate physical exam: she has our full approval on both counts. I apologize that neither my wife nor I could accompany her today, but we've had a death in the family and must leave town immediately. Thank you for your consideration.

Heil Hitler!
Otto Bauer

"Completely fine," pronounces Ilse. "The signature is spot-on." Folding it back up, she winks. "Next you'll be pointing guns at bank tellers. You and Raina."

"Don't *say* that!" Renate smacks her on the shoulder. "I already feel like a criminal."

Ilse laughs as her friend snatches the page back, carefully refolding it and stowing it in her skirt pocket. "Like I said," she adds. "You probably won't even need it. Ursula Koch said they didn't even ask for hers. It's just better to be safe."

She is in a good mood. In fact, she's in the best mood Renate's seen her in for weeks—probably because she's just been offered a position as a junior reporter for the BDM monthly. Though her main job will be to write about BDM track events and charity drives, she is hoping to be promoted to more ambitious assignments—covering the lifestyles of German nationals living in the Sudetenland or Silesia, for instance. Or the Berlin Olympics next year. Or interviewing *Triumph des Willens* director and filmmaker Leni Riefenstahl—or (who knows?) even Propaganda Minister Goebbels himself. Renate sees her as a kind of uniformed Bette Davis in *Front Page Woman*, fighting to prove that girls can report the news too.

Ilse's face is bright, her hair tidy for once: two sleek Gretchen braids wrap her head, like a textured golden crown. The late-afternoon sunlight gives her pink skin a golden sheen and turns the loose white-blond tendrils of her hair silver. *She is so brilliant*, Renate thinks. *And so pretty. And I'm so lucky to be with her. I'm so lucky that she has chosen me.*

"What is it?" Ilse is looking at her oddly.

"Nothing." Renate ducks her head. "I'm stupid today."

"You look nervous."

"I am." Renate yawns. "Being tired always makes me anxious."

"Well, try to calm down. They're not recruiting nervous wrecks."

"You'll still wait for me during the exam, though, right?"

"I've told you three times now—yes!" Ilse resumes walking, humming "Deutschland Erwache!" under her breath and pulling Renate along like a mother towing a sluggish child. Renate finds herself almost stumbling to keep up. For an instant she imagines falling and simply staying there where she lands. And maybe going to sleep.

For as usual, Ilse is right: Renate is a wreck. Her hands are clammy, her mouth dry, her stomach clenched in hungry resentment. She'd known it would be this way almost from the moment she switched her light off last night; had known the next eight hours would be filled with limb-tossing and sheet-thrashing. Her teeth and jaws ached from unconsciously grinding them, and her legs felt taut and jumpy, as though ready to run a race.

Even more disrupting were her thoughts, though she'd tried to think of only good things—*Demon of the Himalayas*, which she and Rudi are going to see on Sunday. The special meal Maria's promised her for her birthday next week. Rudi's sea-glass eyes when he sees her in the navy skirt, the crisp white shirt. For in the end, of course, she is really doing this for *him*: her statue-perfect, beautiful boy.

He'd come for her the day after the library incident. Renate had been waiting for Ilse in the *Gymnasium* courtyard, so buried in her novel that she didn't even notice his approach. It was only when the page she'd been reading was suddenly obstructed by the Book Lady's now-familiar depravity that she registered he was there, right behind her shoulder, smiling smugly.

"So you apparently like books too," he said, lifting a fine blond brow as she snapped the book—with its incriminating new content—quickly shut.

"I do," she'd managed, feeling like a deer in the limned spell of a hunter's lamp.

"I hope that one's more decent than what I just put inside it."

"Oh, no." Starting, she turned breathlessly to face him. "I mean, of course. It's—" Lamely, she turned the cover to show him. "It's about a Chinese family that goes from being very poor to being rich. She grew up in China, you know. The author, I mean."

"You should be careful," he said sagely, "of American authors. A lot of them are Jews. But I do applaud that you're interested in world events." He smirked. "Among other things."

Renate felt her cheeks heat like small suns. "The card wasn't mine," she said quickly.

"Oh? My mistake, then." He held out his hand.

"I mean," she corrected herself quickly, "it was from my *house*, obviously. Well, not obviously. I mean, I did bring it in. But that was a mistake. Well, a kind of dare. And it really belongs to my brother." She sounded, she realized, fully insane. She forced herself to take a deep breath. "Either way," she went on, carefully, "you completely saved my life. I don't know how to thank you."

"I have an idea." He smiled a sleepy Cheshire Cat kind of smile, and for one dreadful moment she thought he was about to suggest something Book Lady–level filthy. But he simply said: "Let me walk you home from school. You can tell me more about your Chinese American lady writer, and I'll tell you about my favorite German writer." He winked. "That at least will be a start."

And he did, that afternoon and then nearly every afternoon thereafter when he didn't have Hitlerjugend affairs. He carried her satchel and held the door for her, and even though he wasn't particularly interested in the books Renate loved, he listened indulgently as she'd rattle on about them, just as she did when he'd quote from *Mein Kampf* and other writings of the Chancellor, for which he clearly felt an equal level of passion. By the second month he held her hand as they walked, and the month after that he put his arm around her in the Babylon, even as they both kept their eyes carefully trained on *Tarzan and His Mate*. After several more months of secret courtship (for Renate knew better than to introduce him to her parents; they'd forbid the romance in a heartbeat) they'd ceased to watch the movie at all. Instead, they spent the time twined together over the wooden armrest that separated their seats, their lips and tongues and limbs and fingers in various heated combinations, their breaths damp and quick in that darkened, flickering space. The way he looked at her in such moments—with vulnerability and pain, almost with a kind of reverence—made her think: *This is it— this is what real love feels like.*

But last night, when she had tried to distract herself from her nerves by summoning those deliciously disorienting feelings, her brain had other ideas. Remaining rebelliously fixed on the next day's application, it presented one calamitous scenario upon another: not just the *Ober- gau Führerin* seeing right through Renate's application, but the letter slipping from her satchel like the Book Lady did in the library that day, landing face up at her mother's or father's feet. Or somehow ending up in her trigonometry homework bin, leading to expulsion. Possibly even im- prisonment. Or what if rumors of the Book Lady incident—even though it happened nearly two years ago now—have somehow made their way to the *Obergauführerin*? Rudi had scoffed at this idea, citing Renate's "over- active imagination" (which he also called "adorable"). Overactive or not, Renate can still picture it all too easily: the woman in charge of her very future looking down at her with scorn and disgust. *Ah. So* you're *the one.*

Then there's Renate's terror of the physical examination itself. Both Rudi and Ilse have assured her that it's nothing arduous; that the Party doctors just want to make certain she is of sound German stock. But Re- nate is still worried they'll see how frail and weak she is and easily intuit that at school, she's always picked last for games of football or Capture the Flag.

Ilse, on the other hand, is always among the first. Strong and stocky, she can climb a rope and perform a cartwheel and then pinwheel around a metal bar in rapid sequence. When she flexes her biceps, its muscles rise like milky hills beneath her skin. When Renate flexes her biceps, nothing happens. There is just her arm, thin and floppy, as useless as an overcooked piece of *spaetzle*.

If her muscles are soft, though, her resolve is firm: she *will* go through with this. No matter what. Everyone but her parents says it's the right thing to do. The Chancellor himself would approve. After all, the very pledge of the Hitlerjugend (which Rudi had her memorize and recite to him until she got it completely perfect) states this fact: *Leader and country before family. I swear to devote all my energies and my strength to the savior of our country, Adolf Hitler. I am willing and ready to give up my life for him, so help me God.*

Help me, God, Renate pleads silently now, nearly colliding into Ilse, who has come to a sudden stop.

"This is it?" Renate asks. Ilse nods.

Before them is a stern gray *Volksschule* whose thick walls and deep-set windows might have once housed Prussian warlords. Its modern-day purpose, however, is clearly marked: billowing between the roof and the first floor is the now-familiar scarlet banner, centered by a spidery black *Hakenkreuz*. As they pass beneath it Renate finds herself glancing up at the arching doorway, half expecting steel spikes to trundle down in their wake. But the only thing moving is the red-white-and-black fabric, shivering in a breeze she cannot feel.

Inside, the lobby is just as dark and ancient-looking. As her eyes adjust to the dimness she makes out two more banners on the walls, on either side of an enormous portrait of Adolf Hitler himself. The Chancellor holds a riding crop and glares balefully over her head, as though he'd been expecting someone far more important.

Directly below the portrait is a curving center staircase, flanked on either side by a heavy oaken desk. The man sitting on the left side looks up and smiles briefly before going back to his paperwork. The woman on the right, however, stands up smartly and gives the Führer's salute. The girls respond in unison—*Heil Hitler!*—and as always Renate thinks of Franz's interpretation of the gesture (that it is only so stiff and upright because the men who invented it were compensating for less-erect parts of their bodies).

"Welcome, girls." The woman's mouth is painted the exact same blood-red shade as the flags behind her. Renate finds herself at first ad-

miring it, then wondering at it: everyone knows that the BDM discour-
ages cosmetics. Perhaps the rule gets waived for patriotically hued lips.

From the neck down, at least, the *Mädelschaftsführerin* is in strict
compliance with Bundestracht uniform regulations. Her white short-
sleeved blouse is embellished with the black-and-white district insig-
nia; her black kerchief neatly secured by a leather lanyard. Her navy
skirt is knee-length and modest, her shoes sensible lace-up pumps. Each
item of clothing is meticulously creased and ironed and polished, spot-
less enough to have been purchased that very morning. "You're here to
register?"

"Yes," says Renate.

"She is," Ilse clarifies. "I'm here to get an identification card for *Das
Deutsche Mädel*."

"That would be in room 210 upstairs." The woman indicates the
stairwell with her chin, then turns to face Renate. "Your name?"

"Renate Bauer. I'm fifteen," Renate offers, though no one has asked
her age yet.

The woman frowns and jots something in her notebook. "You have
your identity papers?"

"Of course." Renate's fingers tremble slightly as she fishes into her
bag again. She knows she has them. She always has them, because it's
the law to always have them. Lately, though, she's been strangely terrified of inadvertently breaking the law. She has had dreams where she
finds herself in a white-walled room that she knows is a cell. And last
Saturday, when her mother took her to Wertheim to buy new gloves,
she spent the entire hour convinced the sales lady thought she'd stolen
something.

"I wouldn't worry about it," her mother said, when Renate confided
her concern. "It's a classic response to the dilemma of adolescence.
You're being robbed of your childhood. Your innocence is being threatened. It's only natural that your thoughts would turn to theft and guilt."

To her relief, Renate spies the green corner of her *Ausweis* poking
out from beneath her history textbook. "Thank you," says the woman as
Renate hands it to her. "You have an appointment, correct? Good. We'll

start with the physical examination." The *Führerin* indicates the stair-well with her chin. "Up the stairs, first room on the right-hand side. Dr. Braun's office. He has someone else in with him right now, but you may wait on the bench outside until she's done."

"Thank you," says Renate, and forces what she hopes is a confident smile (*they're not recruiting nervous wrecks!*) before following Ilse up the stairs. On the top landing she pauses, patting her hair and pinching her cheeks to make them pink.

"You're not going dancing with Rudi," Ilse tells her, rolling her eyes.

"I just want to look healthy." Glancing at her reflection in another glass-covered image of their dashing leader inspecting a Bund Deutscher Mädel unit, Renate suppresses a sigh. She doesn't look healthy. She looks peaked and tired. Not at all like the wholesome, smiling girls in the pho-tograph (or like Ilse, who might have sprung directly from it). Uniformly blond, white-toothed, and smiling, the BDM maidens salute their Chan-cellor from several meters away, lithe arms outstretched like the pale fronds of an anemone. The Führer smiles back at them but keeps his own arms clasped behind his back. The effect is an odd mix of approach-ability and remove.

To her right, Ilse has settled onto the bench and is pulling out her homework. Renate settles in next to her, but she's too nervous to study. She takes in the literary offerings on the table by her elbow: a newly minted copy of *Mein Kampf* on a stand, behind a neatly fanned selection of *Wille und Macht*, *Das Deutsche Mädel*, and *Die Mädelschaft*, the BDM newsletter. There are also two editions of the HJ yearbook, *Jungen-eure Welt!*

Eschewing the Chancellor's tract (she's heard almost all of it from Rudi anyway), Renate leafs through last year's yearbook. It seems to be composed largely of maps of Germany and its borders, odes to the *Sturmtruppen* martyr Horst Wessel, and assorted images of other sincere-faced, stiff-armed youth, though toward the back she discov-ers a busy graph comparing Germany's current birth rate to the (much higher) rates of Poland and Russia. Beneath it appears yet another smiling blond girl, this one holding a cherubic-looking baby boy. *"Mädel!"* reads the caption. *"It is your Sacred Duty to propagate, and be the Future Mothers of the Fatherland!"*

Propagate, thinks Renate, blinking. She thinks of her and Rudi's outing last week to the Volkspark Friedrichshain. They'd been lying together, postpicnic, off one of the less-traveled pathways, half obscured by flower banks and well-manicured shrubs. She'd found herself beneath Rudi on the blanket, his mouth moving on her neck in a way that sent almost unbearably lovely shivers through her; his hips pressing against hers and between them both, the *thing* she can't name aloud feeling hard and warm and urgent between them. And while the idea of it had long frightened her (for what to do if he wanted to bare it for her; or—even less thinkably—for her to *touch* it?), the reality felt entirely, dreamily different. As though her skin—so taut and tingling beneath his featherlight touch—somehow expected and even wanted this odd, firm pressure; wanted to meet and surround it and become part of it. And so even as she was pushing his chest away with her palms, her hips— despite Renate's best intentions—had wanted to rise to meet his of their own accord. Not trusting herself, she had finally rolled away, flushed and giggling, and lied about her mother wanting her home early.

At the Babylon last week there had been the same bodily mutiny: her torso squirming and writhing as Rudi licked and nibbled at her earlobe, his fingers creeping beneath her skirt's hemline and over her bloomers before settling directly over the very spot where she most felt that strange new ache to be touched. It had all seemed to happen with breathless speed. And yet in retrospect, what had frightened her wasn't even that they'd gotten that far so quickly. It was that it had been so hard to *keep* herself from going further. In fact, if the midfilm newsreel hadn't come on showing the Führer celebrating his forty-sixth birthday, Renate honestly has no idea what might have happened.

But it did come on, and of course Rudi released her like a hot plate and all but leapt to attention in his seat.

Thinking back on it now, Renate realizes that she actually almost can understand it, how those nine hundred BDM girls Ilse told her about came back from last year's Nuremberg Rally pregnant. Nine *hundred* girls, who simply did with their bodies what her own body seems to be begging her to do.

And those were just the ones who got in trouble from it. The ones who actually did end up *propagating*.

"What?" asks Ilse, looking up from her history book.

"Nothing," says Renate, flushing slightly (had she said it aloud?). "Just—this notice. It's telling us that we have to have babies. I don't know if they mean when we're married or not."

"Does it matter?"

"What?"

"Well, a baby is a baby." Ilse shrugs. "If the point of having them is to boost the population, it doesn't really matter what their parents do or don't do, does it? Just so long as the silly things get born."

"I feel like I'm talking to Ida Fuchs." Renate laughs. And then stops, struck by a sudden, stunning possibility. "Hold on," she says. "You haven't actually . . ."

Ilse stares back at her, at first looking confused. Then she laughs. "Oh, good God. Of *course* not."

Renate lets her breath out in relief. After the Book Lady incident they'd sworn to share any and all details of their love lives with each other. And to date Renate faithfully has, whispering and giggling and blushing. Ilse, however, has had nothing to report (and for that matter, seems more annoyed than impressed by Renate's breathless recountings).

Tossing the yearbook back onto the table, Renate flips quickly through a small book of blood purity poetry (*Keep your blood pure / it is not yours alone*) before abandoning it for the April issue of *Das Deutsche Mädel*, the magazine that published Ilse's first poem, and for which her friend will now be writing regularly. "Your Duty to Be Healthy!" reads the title article, which turns out to list the steps every *Deutsches Mädel* should take to ensure that her body and mind are primed for patriotic motherhood. *Get ten hours of sleep a night. Exercise your body daily. Be domestically capable. Avoid stuffy cinemas and overcrowded smoky bars.*

Frowning, Renate rereads the list. She'd expected to have to catch up in things like running and gymnastics. But sleeping? *Ten entire hours?* For better or worse she is constitutionally a night owl, regularly reading until three a.m. and deeming every moment of exhaustion over it well worth it if the book was a good one. Domestic prowess is equally dubious. She can bake a little—but is only allowed to do so under the careful guidance of their housekeeper, since the one time she and Ilse attempted a Linzer torte they somehow set the oven rack on fire. ("You're marvels," Franz told them, with genuine-sounding admiration. "I didn't even know that was possible.") But even this skill seems of dubious value given the last "warning" on the list: *Be mindful of what you put in your body: too many sweets will make you lazy and plump!*

She thinks of Ilse, joyously stuffing her mouth with Herr Schloss's poppyseed cake. She thinks of their long-lost, quiet moments after school, now so much rarer since Ilse has the BDM and Renate has Rudi (when he doesn't have Hitlerjugend). Once she's accepted into the ranks of the BDM she and Ilse will spend more time together. But based on what Ilse's told her, that time will center on things like flag-toting and hiking . . . sighing, she slips her blue composition notebook out of her satchel and begins carefully copying down the magazine's mandates. She might as well begin getting used to them.

After what seems an hour, the examination room door opens and a squat, spotty-faced girl with brown hair steps out, straightening her skirt.

"How was it?" Renate asks her eagerly.

The girl shrugs. "Fine." She doesn't look at all like the BDM ideal—the strong, long-limbed, sylphlike Aryan. But it also doesn't look like that matters—from her sanguine expression, it's clear that she, at least, has passed the physical exam.

"Did he check how strong you were?" asks Renate. "Ask how fast you can run?"

"Yes," interjects Ilse. "And he made her climb to the very top of a big rope that hangs from the ceiling—just like the one you couldn't climb in Athletics."

The brown-haired girl looks puzzled. "No, he didn't. Why would a doctor's office have a climbing rope?"

Ilse bursts into laughter. "Your *face!*" she says, giving Renate's narrow shoulder a push. "You really believed it."

"No, I didn't," says Renate, blushing.

"There was nothing like that." The brown-haired girl is still looking confused. "He checked my height and weight, listened to my heart. Had me cough."

"That was it?"

The girl nods.

"See? Like I told you," says Ilse. "Child's play."

Renate lets her breath out, relieved. "So I should just go in?"

"I'd knock first," says the girl, sitting down on the bench by Ilse and pulling her satchel into her lap. "But he's expecting you."

Renate turns to Ilse. "You'll wait?"

Her friend lifts an eyebrow. "For the millionth time: yes!"

I love you, Renate thinks, but she doesn't say it. Instead, swallowing hard, she retucks her blouse and runs her hands over her braids before stepping toward the door.

Child's play, she tells herself. *Nothing more than a straightforward checkup.*

She raps her knuckles against the glass and then drops her hand to the brass doorknob.

"Come in," calls a friendly male voice.

But as she pushes the door open another voice—this one female—sounds from the other end of the hall, punctuated by the sharp clip of heels on hardwood.

"Fräulein—wait a moment."

She and Ilse turn around together to see the red-lipped *Führerin* walking briskly toward them, a manila file in her hands. "I mean Fräulein Bauer."

Stopping short, the *Führerin* draws herself up formally. She looks down at Renate over her pinched nose. Renate looks back up, offering a small smile (*not a nervous wreck!*). The red lips don't return it.

Behind them, she hears the door to the exam room open further; she glances over her shoulder to see an older man in a white coat. "Is there a problem?"

"Not a big one," says Red Lips. "But you won't need to see this girl today, Doktor Braun."

"No?"

"No. As it turns out, she's not eligible for BDM membership."

The prognosis is so completely what Renate most feared hearing today that her protest is almost reflexive: "But he hasn't even examined me yet!"

"I'm afraid an examination would be pointless," the *Führerin* says crisply. She nods at the physician; the exam room door quietly closes. The *Führerin* licks a finger, flicks open her folder.

"I don't understand," Renate falters.

"I can see that. I'm also not sure you fully understood our requirements when you completed this." The woman taps a page with an unpainted fingernail.

"Yes, I did."

"I mean our *racial* requirements."

Renate glances at Ilse. Her friend's face reflects the same bafflement she is feeling.

The woman is now running her finger down the page. "You see, you neglected to include your full family history."

"Yes." Renate exhales in relief; if that's the problem, it's easily resolved. "My parents have misplaced their ancestry tables. But as I wrote in the margin, I was told that you'd have access to the city's census records."

The *Führerin* nods. "As we do. We had had them sent over before your arrival today. But I didn't get a chance to pull them up until now." Leafing through the folder, she removes another piece of paper—an older one, slightly yellowed at the edges, with the Berlin City official stamp on the top. "Surely you are aware that you're not German."

Renate blinks. "I'm sorry?"

"Sie sind keine Deutsche," the woman repeats, slowly.

For a moment the entire hallway seems to flicker slightly, like a flame in the pathway of a small breeze.

Renate shakes her head. "Of course I am. My mother's family goes back five generations in Berlin."

"Yes. But we require *both* parents of our appellants to be of sound German stock."

"I-I'm afraid I don't understand."

The woman clears her throat. "I see," she says crisply, "that this will be news to you. I am sorry to have to be the one delivering it. But our records indicate that your father is a Jew."

Ein Jude. The words land like short blows to Renate's lower abdomen. Behind her, Ilse and the brown-haired girl gasp.

"That's—that's impossible," Renate stammers.

"I'm afraid it's not. Your father is Otto Andreas Bauer, correct?"

She nods.

"He was born of two fully Jewish parents. That makes you—in the best-case scenario—a *Mischling*. And hence ineligible for any aspect of our organization."

She holds something out; Renate recognizes the dull green cover of her *Ausweis*. Dazed, she takes it. "It's impossible," she repeats. "No one in my family is Jewish."

"She's right, Fräulein." Ilse has made her way over. "I can vouch for her."

As Renate throws her a grateful look, an image flashes past her mind's eye: the two of them baking stollen with Maria this past December. The girls making a joke out of sneaking pieces of the raw, sweet dough into their mouths whenever the housekeeper wasn't looking. And later, lying prone and groaning on Renate's bed, arguing over whose stomach hurt the most. She sees them perusing the *Christkindlmarkt* arm in arm a few days later, advising one another on gifts for their family members, and then parting ways just long enough to buy for one another. Ilse gave Renate a cloth-bound copy of Hoffmann's *Die Elixiere des Teufels* from a book dealer who swore it was a real second edition. Renate gave Ilse a jade-embellished fountain pen with a carry chain and a fancy holder.

"There was an error in the records," she repeats now, as firmly as she can manage.

The woman smiles tightly. "Frankly, I believe this is an error on your parents' part. They should have informed you about your heritage."

"Heritage?" Renate repeats numbly. Something in the air—a new density, as though the oxygen has somehow jellied like aspic—makes the *Führerin*'s meaning lag slightly behind her words.

"I'm sorry to say that I've seen it before, too," the woman is continuing. "I honestly don't know what these *Juden* are thinking, sending girls like you here. It's quite inconsiderate. To all involved."

That word again: *Juden*. Renate fights the urge to flinch. "I'll—I'll just talk to them. Tonight. After we sort it out I can come back tomorrow."

The woman gives her a long, cool look. Her round face reflects disapproval, distaste, and just the faintest touch of—could it be pity? "At any rate," she says to the brown-haired girl, "*your* papers are all in order. We should go finish your registration and talk about getting you your uniform. Come with me. And you, Fräulein von Fischer—I can show you to room 210."

"Wait!" Renate feels her throat constrict in panic. "Can't I—can't I just register too? As long as I'm here?"

"It would save time," Ilse offers, though her tone turns the statement into a question.

The *Führerin* swivels slowly to look at Renate again. "Fräulein Bauer," she says, articulating each word clearly. "I fear I *still* haven't made myself clear. It is against regulations for any non-German to wear the uniform of the Bund Deutscher Mädel. In fact, it goes against nearly everything we stand for. If you can, as you say, supply proof that you meet our requirements, then we can discuss taking further steps toward membership. Until then, however, this discussion must be finished. It is late, and we have other matters to attend to. *Kommen Sie*, Fräulein."

Turning on her heel, she begins walking briskly back down the corridor, the brown-haired girl scurrying behind her.

Renate stares after them, her gut hollowed by shock, her mind a buzzing blank. "Ilsi?"

It comes out barely a whisper, and when at first there's no answer she assumes Ilse hasn't heard. She turns back to see that Ilse also is staring after the *Führerin*'s receding shape, with an expression that Renate—who can usually read her best friend like a beloved book—this once finds completely unreadable.

"I must go get my press card," Ilse says at last. "You should go home—it will probably take some time. But I can come back with you tomorrow."

"You're sure?"

Ilse nods. "We can fix this." Her voice is certain, though Renate can't help but notice that the other girl doesn't quite meet her eyes. As she turns away, the thought of being left behind becomes inexplicably devastating—as though she were being cast into a stone gray ocean. *Don't leave me!* she wants to cry out. *Please stay!* But the words won't or can't come, and Ilse is already several steps away.

"Call the Albrechts tonight," Ilse calls over her shoulder. Her family doesn't yet own a telephone, so they share the neighbors'.

And then she is pacing quickly down the hallway after the *Führerin* and the brown-haired girl who looks more Jewish than Renate but is somehow fully German nevertheless. She pauses at a door, checks the number, knocks. The door opens. And then she is gone.

Slowly, Renate turns back toward the staircase. Her lungs feel strangely tight. Her hand hurts. Looking down, she sees that she is clenching her identity card hard—hard enough that its sharp edges dig into her skin. Forcing her fingers to loosen, she slides the card into her satchel.

As she starts her descent she imagines the Chancellor's picture watching her; feels the set of small, dark eyes studying her from behind, checking her stature, her alignment. It's an absurd thought, she knows this. Nevertheless, she lifts her shoulders and straightens her back as she makes her way down the stairs.

When she reaches the first floor she stops at the landing, unsure of where she is actually going. Home, of course, makes the most sense. But she can't really ask her parents about the District Census records—obviously, that is out of the question. She could ask her grandmother, who seems to know every detail about every ancestor on both sides of Renate's family. But knowing her *Oma*, she will doubtlessly report the query right back to her parents.

That leaves Renate's own brother—Franz. He had to register at the university this fall, so he will know where to find the right paperwork. And while he ridicules the BDM—he says the letters actually stand for *Bubi, drück mich* ("Squeeze me, laddie") or *Bund Deutscher Milchkühe* ("League of German Milk Cows")—at least he won't judge her for having gone behind their parents' back. Not when he himself sneaks out to meet his friends at the *Bierhaus*. Not with the Book Lady and those other postcards beneath his bed.

Outside, a church bell sounds out the hour in silvered tones: *One. Two. Three . . .* By *Five* she has decided. She will go home and—directly, before doing anything else—she will go straight to Franz, tell him what has happened, and ask him what to do. And by the evening's end she'll be able to call Ilse at the Albrechts', and they'll laugh over the misunderstanding.

"Fräulein?"

She turns to see the man seated to the stairwell's left, looking up from his desk. "Is there something more we can help you with?" His tone is clipped and cold. She realizes with a hot flush that he must have heard the entire exchange.

"No," she says. "I just—I just need to go locate my family records. The correct ones."

"The correct ones."

She nods. "The ones the city had for me are incorrect."

"Hmm," he says. His expression says *preposterous*. She wants to tell him that the *Oberrottenführer* of their district's Hitlerjugend is her very own secret sweetheart. And that *he* says that she is just the kind of German girl the BDM needs.

Instead, she does the only other thing she can think of: she salutes.

"Heil Hitler!"

"We close in thirty-five minutes," he says.

He doesn't even bother to stand up.

❧

The journey back feels surreal, the lights of the U-Bahn too brightly yellow against the dank darkness of its tunnels. As the train approaches the station a group of boys platform-jump it, leaping from between the cars with Indian-style whoops, letting the engine's momentum hurl their bodies onto the platform and past the stationmaster's tiny glassed-in office. As they land—*one, two, three*—just at the top of the stairwell, one of them whistles at her. "That was for you, little beauty!" he calls. If Ilse had been there they'd have shrieked and giggled together. Now, though, it's as though his voice reaches her from a distance. The way a breeze might carry cries from far-off gulls.

As she picks her way toward a seat, her schoolbag feeling as though it's filled with cannon fodder rather than textbooks: her *spaetzle* arms ache. The U-Bahn itself feels different; the lighting less light. The fixtures and seats somehow ominous and sharper around the edges. The next seat over, a middle-aged woman and a younger one in her twenties pause in their discussion to look up at her before resuming chatting. And though they both smile politely, there is something toothy and raptorial in their faces that makes Renate's stomach tighten in apprehension.

"I still don't think you should shop there," the younger woman is saying.

"But, you know, it's so much cheaper!"

"It's cheaper only because the things are more cheaply made."

"No, really," says the matron. "The goods there are just as well made as at German shops. They last as long. They are just so much cheaper. It's a much better deal."

The younger woman grimaces. "I'm sure there's some other way they're going to make you pay," she says. "That's what they do, you know. Those *Juden*."

Renate stares at them, confounded. Do they know? Something Ilse said recently floats through her thoughts: *What if all the world really is a stage, and everyone but you is acting, and you don't know it?*

At the time Renate had laughed. Now she shivers a little and hugs her satchel to her stomach. She focuses on the *clack-clack-clack* of the rails below, losing herself in their predictable, harsh rhythm.

At Friedrichstraße she gets off and descends to street level, distractedly planning the next hour. According to the station clock it is now six fifteen: Franz should be home, presuming he's keeping to his normal Tuesday schedule. As she makes her way toward Unter den Linden, passing blind old Fritz and his pencils without a glance, Renate tries not to think about what will happen if Franz *isn't* there. If, for some reason, he doesn't get home until late, until after she goes to sleep. In the worst case she will simply stay home tomorrow—say she's sick. At least it will get her out of school, and out of having to tell Rudi about the mix-up. Though—*oh, no*—what if Ilse ends up telling him anyway? That would be even more disastrous than Renate telling him herself.

She'll have to call Ilse tonight either way.

She pushes the front door open as quietly as she can. Her parents are in the parlor, having one of their hush-toned "discussions." Hanging her coat on the wall, Renate carefully unlaces her boots and takes the stairs in stocking feet, hoping that Sigmund is shut up in Franz's room so he won't give her away with his whimpering welcome. At the top she pauses again, tilting her head. No sign of the Schnauzer.

Below, her parents continue their tense murmuring. Renate makes out only a few words—*exams* and *committee*; then what sounds like *attendance*. Why, she wonders irritably, do they even bother to whisper? Must *everything* seem like such a weighty, secretive matter all of a sudden? Why do adults always think they're so very important?

Soundlessly, she deposits her satchel in her own room before continuing on tiptoe toward her brother's. She finds herself hoping Franz has one of his jokes for her—she needs one. At the moment she'd probably even laugh at something dirty . . . the thought is interrupted by a muffled whining and the soft scratch of canine nails against oak.

No, she thinks. *Stay.*

"All right, buddy," she hears her brother say. "Go say hello."

Almost before she's registered the words Sigmund is tearing toward her like a furry bullet, barking joyously, as though he hasn't seen her for years. Smiling despite herself, Renate drops to her knees and hugs the wriggling pup, turning her face away as he lunges at her cheek with his floppy tongue.

Downstairs, the tones of hushed conversation stop.

"Reni?" her mother calls. "Are you home?"

"Yes," she calls back reluctantly, holding the squirming Schnauzer at arm's length.

"Come have some dinner!"

"I'm not hungry. And I've a lot of studying to do."

"You have to eat something."

"Can I eat it in my room, then? I want to go to bed early."

A pause. Renate hears her father murmur something; hears her mother sigh. "Fine. We'll send Maria up with a plate. But please come down before bedtime to say good night."

"Fine," Renate says, though she has no intention of complying. As Ilse frequently notes, Renate's the worst liar on the planet. One look and they'll know something is up.

Standing, she pushes Sigmund back onto four paws, then wipes his kisses from her forehead with her palm.

"Good day?"

She looks up to see Franz leaning against the wall, his arms crossed and his sleepy eyes wry.

"Good enough."

"You don't look it," he says. "You look like you've been eating lemons."

Worst liar on the planet. Once more she breaks into a brief, glum smile. "It's been a very strange afternoon."

"A good kind of strange?"

Shaking her head she stands, brushing the short dark hairs from her skirt. "Actually, can I speak with you for a moment?"

"Aren't we speaking right now?"

He says it with one of his indulgent *you're such a child* smiles, which normally would infuriate her. Today, however, she simply says: "It won't take long," and prays to Nobody in Particular that this is true.

After he's shut the door she sits tentatively on his bed, with Sigi settling back into his usual spot at the foot. Renate finds herself relaxing a little bit, for the first time in what feels like hours. Franz's room has always had that effect on her. In part it's the smell: tobacco-tinged like her mother's, but also aromatic in a way that has nothing to do with perfume or cologne. It's a kind of boyish element, a faint whiff of musk to it. There is also a sourness, but it's an almost pleasantly sweet sourness— like condensed milk left too long out of the icebox. It's a smell that, for as long as she can remember, has made Renate feel safe. She watches in silence as he shuffles to the oaken secretary he works at, leaning his cane against the desk before falling into the cracked leather office chair he inherited from their mother's clinic. Hoisting his bad leg up onto the desk he locks eyes with her, and Renate has a momentary image of the two of them, twelve years earlier.

It was a cold winter morning, and he was six and she was three, and she'd woken up early and gone to bounce on his bed as she often did since their parents had forbidden them both to wake them before eight. Franz had groaned and complained. But eventually he'd made room, putting his arm around Renate's shoulders and pulling her close. Reading to her from the books he loved—Schwab's *Heroic Legends*, the kings and monsters of Hauff. An old version of *Alices Abenteuer im Wunderland* that had once belonged to their mother. Even then he'd had that sweet scent, though not yet infiltrated by the oily, adult pungence of perspiration, brilliantine, and tobacco.

"So," he says.

"So." There doesn't seem to be any graceful way to launch the subject, so she just plunges in: "Are we Jewish?"

"Ah." He leans back slightly, tents his fingers before his nose. Behind him, Karl Marx stares down from his postered position above Franz's desk, his hair wild and his expression inscrutable.

"Ah?" She'd expected the question to shock him—or, at very minimum, to make him laugh. That it doesn't makes Renate's stomach knot with dread. "Ah?" she repeats. "What is that supposed to mean?"

He holds up a finger: *Wait*.

Opening his top drawer, he takes out his cigarette tin. Renate's chest feels suddenly tight—as though her breastbone is expanding. *I should leave*, she thinks. *I should leave now. I should go . . .*

But she finds she can barely breathe, much less move. Immobilized, she watches Franz place a Mona between his lips, holding it there slackly as he lights it the way Humphrey Bogart does in *Big City Blues*. The match's flame casts her brother's long dark lashes in relief against his cheeks. Ilse once said—only half in jest—that he has the loveliest eyes of any woman she's ever known.

"How did it come up?" he asks at last.

She takes a shaky breath. "I applied to the BDM today." And as he rolls his eyes: "It was my decision to make."

"Unfortunately, it isn't. The Hitlerjugend have strict standards about the sort of blood they want pumping in their young folks' veins."

Her heart plummets within her chest. "You can't mean that what they told me is true."

"That depends. What did they tell you?"

"They said that—that Vati is Jewish." Renate's voice is shaking, but she forges on. "That his parents were both *Juden*. And that that makes me a—" She pauses, trying to recall the term.

"A *Mischling*," he says quietly. "At best. But in their eyes, we are probably no better than *Juden*. It's like poison, you see. One drop spoils the entire cup of water." He taps his cigarette over his own half-filled water glass.

Renate stares at him, then at the black specks as they swirl and whirl toward the bottom of the drinking vessel. And in that moment it seems the rest of the world has frozen: the walls, his books, the light fixture. Even Franz seems to take on a faint but impenetrable shine, as though he, too, might shatter if thrown or dropped. She pictures him, pictures everything tinkling to the ground in glistening shards. She feels as though she might vomit.

"No," she manages. "No, that can't be right. Even Ilse said it was a mistake."

"I'm afraid it's not."

Nonono. "But . . . but how can that be? We have photographs from my baptism!"

He shrugs. "There are photographs from Vati's baptism. They mean nothing."

"They mean he's *Christian*!"

Beside her Sigi starts, then turns to gaze at her with liquid-brown concern. Renate realizes that she was nearly shouting. Franz presses the air down with his palm: *softly.*

"Not if his parents were Jewish," he says quietly. "Which they were, originally. They converted to Christianity together just before they married. A lot of Jews were converting around that time. It was apparently quite the fashion." He lets out a low, long stream of smoke. "Before that they'd both grown up in practicing Jewish homes."

Practice, Renate thinks numbly. *What do Jews practice?* Piano? Violin? She pictures the somber-looking, dark-dressed people who live near Hackescher Markt and Mulackstraße: the women in their false-looking wigs and heavy, unbecoming clothing. The men with their corkscrew curls and furry hats. It's like trying to connect her cultured, Christian father to aliens.

"How long—how long have you known?"

"Vati told me last winter."

Renate gasps. "Last *winter*?!"

He holds up his hands again, once more pacifying. "He had to. Not only did I need the information to register at Friedrich Wilhelm, but it's common knowledge there now that he's a Jew." He takes a final drag of his cigarette, then uses it to light a second before dropping the spent stub after its ash. "He managed to survive the first few rounds of firings because of his wartime decorations. The word now, though, is that with the new law about civil positions he'll be out of a job by December." Grimacing, he hefts his bad leg up with both hands to shift it. When it stays still for too long—which it often does, since he forgets to move it—it's susceptible to pins and needles.

Renate presses both temples with the heels of her hands. She imagines cracking her own skull like a walnut, if only to stop the sickening spinning in her head. But her mind keeps whirling and swirling, pausing sporadically and only briefly on things she's seen every day without really registering them: the troops of Brownshirts who swagger their way down the streets. *Der Stürmer*'s announcement boards, with their lewd cartoons and vehement headlines: *The Jews Are Our Misfortune! Women and Girls, the Jews Are Your Doom! When You Recognize a Jew, You Recognize the Devil!*

"It makes no sense," she whispers, or at least she thinks she whispers it. The blood roar in her ears is deafening.

"They wanted to tell you when it became more . . . relevant. I think they knew they'd have to break it to you soon." Seeing her face, he leans forward. "Look. At least for the moment, it doesn't really change anything for you."

"Are you insane?" She gapes at him. "It changes everything. My God. *Everything.*" Nausea forces a path up her throat; she presses her handkerchief against her lips. Other moments are rushing to mind now, ones she'd barely noticed because she'd assumed they didn't apply to her. The new government quotas on the number of Jews in German schools. The bizarre and (she'd thought) silly prohibition on using the names *David* or *Samuel* to spell out words on the telephone (*Dora* and *Siegfried* are to replace them). Rudi expounding on a scientific study he'd read into what he described as "that unique Jewish smell": "It's a bit sulfurous," he'd told her. "Like rotten eggs. Though these days, they're more adept at covering it up—it's why Jew women like that fancy French perfume."

Franz noting at the dinner table last week how a sign had appeared on the Friedrich Wilhelm Student House, announcing that Jewish students and staff were no longer allowed to write or publish in German. *What are they supposed to write in, then?* Renate had asked.

Hebrew, he had said, and laughed as though it were the world's funniest joke.

"I thought about telling you myself last month," he's continuing now. "But it was going to come out anyway, sooner rather than later. Especially if all this talk about limiting the number of Jews in schools is true."

She frowns. "But if we're only half Jewish . . ."

"To be honest, I'm not sure how much that will matter." He smiles dryly. "Their logic can be somewhat hard to follow."

The room is suddenly too small, too stuffy—that familiar Franz-scent no longer comforting but suffocating, like being trapped in a closet filled with rotting candy. For a moment Renate almost thinks she does detect a hint of sulfur. The thought is enough to make her want to retch.

"I have to go," she says, and she is somehow already on her feet, the kerchief floating gently to the floor.

He lifts a brow. "Go where?"

"Out. Air." Not trusting herself to say more, she picks up her bag and slings its leather strap over her shoulder.

"Wait," he's saying. "Sit a moment. I know it's hard to . . ."

Renate just shakes her head, making her stumbling way to the door, ignoring the peripheral glimpse of him struggling to shift his leg, to get up; ignoring the heavy *thump* of Sigmund dropping down from the bed and making his tail-wiggling way after her. Slamming the door in his furry face she rushes down the stairs, past the murmuring parlor, to the white-painted front door that—could it really be just moments earlier?—she'd painstakingly and quietly entered. Jamming her feet into her boots, she flings the door open and hurls herself down the stoop, her untied bootlaces flapping, her heart pounding out a rhythm to which her mind supplies cruel lyrics: *JudenJudenJuden*. She trips on her laces and is leaning down to tie them when the front door flies open behind her.

"Reni?" says her father, looking sleepy and surprised. "Where on earth are you going?"

"Go *away!*" she shrieks, ignoring the startled gazes of an old woman and her companion, the giggles of two passing, pigtailed schoolgirls, both in crisp BDM uniforms. "Just leave me alone!"

And then, turning her back on him, she runs. She runs hard and fast, for the first time in her life feeling as fleet as a fully German *Deutsches Mädel* would feel, even though each step is still a pounding drumbeat of that word. That inconceivable hideous word:

Jude

Jude

Jude.

6.

Ava

1968

Ho! Ho! Ho-Chi-Minh! Ho! Ho! Ho-Chi-Minh!

The name thundered through the Berlin air, an angry incantation above a bobbing sea of protest posters and placards: here a beret-clad Che Guevara, dashing as a movie star. There a President Johnson embellished with a Hitlerian mustache and underscored by a scrawled *USA* in which the *S* was replaced by a swastika. Scattered throughout the marchers Ava also spied several images of the North Vietnamese Chairman himself, looking wise and somewhat bemused by the proceedings. So far, though, she hadn't seen a banner anything like the one she and her current lover, Fiete, carried stretched out between them.

Peering up at it, a Käthe Kollwitz–style take on the AP photo that had shocked the world in February, Ava felt a flush of weary pride not unlike what she felt during her art class exhibitions. Ava had spent the night working and reworking it, while Fiete—a rising Neo-Dadaist who looked like Paul Newman's pudgy brother—emptied a bottle of iced vodka and offered useless suggestions: *Aren't they shorter than that over there? Should his eyes look so big? Hey, is that even the right kind of gun?*

Ava hadn't had the answer to any of those questions. All she knew was that from the moment she'd seen it in *Der Spiegel* the image had sparked the same sickened fascination she usually felt over grainy images of Auschwitz prisoners and *Einsatzgruppen* massacres, though she knew the story behind the AP shot was more complex: Bay Lop, the Viet Cong captured at the moment of his shockingly casual execution, had himself summarily executed women and children just hours earlier. Still, the stark brutality of it continued to mesmerize her: the executioner's oddly relaxed stance. The doomed prisoner's grimace, a sullen mix of resignation and loathing even as his brains were being blown from his head. Ava had originally planned to integrate a Pollock-style spattering of bright blood into her banner reproduction. But when she'd applied the tone to the bedsheet, she'd quickly discovered why Kollwitz stuck with her famously monochrome pallet: the splashed color detracted from the picture's gravity, like lurid sound bubbles (*Pow! Wham! Crack!*) in an American comic book.

And so at three a.m. she'd started over, rousing Fiete from the mattress he'd passed out on in order to strip it of its remaining sheet. Somehow, between the two packs of Larks she'd smoked and the black sea of coffee she'd imbibed, the image was complete—if still slightly damp—by the time they were due to leave for Berlin's Technical University.

Pulling her end of the banner tighter now, Ava noted a crick forming in her neck even though they'd been marching for less than twenty minutes. Then she flinched as something soft and wet blew into her eye and popped there, a fleeting, burning kiss.

Ducking her head awkwardly to try to rub the spot with her shoulder, Ava traced the attack to her left, where two girls were waving bubble wands while bobbing along on the shoulders of their marching male friends. The one bobbing nearest—a pale blonde in a plaid jumper— mouthed an apology as Ava caught her gaze. Then she apparently lost her balance, swaying forward and back atop her human transport, shrieking giddily with laughter.

Despite the burn in her eye Ava found herself laughing too, less from the sight than from a sudden crest of glee. The opening moments of a protest were like this, she'd learned. It was not unlike buckling into a Trabant just before it took its first tilting spin: a vertiginous cocktail of exhilaration and terror made all the more intoxicating by Ilse's full-on disapproval of carnival rides. "I've lived through too much," her mother had once said, "to pay good money to risk life and limb." Though of course, when pressed on "too much" she would never elaborate.

Unsurprisingly, Ilse considered street protests an even more dangerous waste of time: "Hooliganism, pure and simple," she called it. And for all of Ava's genuine outrage over the state of things—former Nazis running the government; the U.S. war machine burning through Southeast Asia; Soviet jackboots grinding Prague's springtime hope to bloody dust—she sometimes wondered how much of a role her mother's disapproval played in driving her into the movement's riotous swell. Though in fact Ava's first sojourn into student dissent had been prompted not by Ilse but by a conceptualist "happening" she'd gone to see with Ulrich in Berlin. The show consisted of a heavyset artist sawing open a female mannequin, yanking out her cottony innards, replacing them with toy soldiers, all while screaming "TELL ME A FAIRY TALE!" And despite Ulrich's deadpan asides ("I'll bet *he's* fun in bed"), the performer's howls had connected somehow with Ava's own inner, widening well of despair over the life she found herself living: fitting her art and sporadic love life around a grueling waitressing schedule, living with Ilse to save up for graduate school in New York.

So when the *Fräulein Saigon* artist urged his audience to attend the next day's demonstration at the Deutsche Opera she'd found herself leaping at the chance, even as Ulrich dismissed it as "more self-congratulatory exhibitionism." And from the first jostling half step she'd found the experience exhilarating. Not just the camaraderie she felt within the crowd's collective fury, but the thrill of shouting—no, of *screaming*, until her cheeks ached and her throat was raw—at her mother's generation-wide wall of silence and complicity as the world erupted in napalm, flame, and corruption.

"Careful, baby! You're walking too fast!"

Snapping back to the protest at hand, Ava registered Fiete huffing and red-faced a few steps behind her, his banner pole dangling at a precarious angle. Slowing down slightly, Ava let him catch up while briefly fantasizing about doing just the opposite: swiping the plywood pole from his grasp and putting as much distance between herself and him as she could, given the crowd's density.

She'd met him two weeks earlier outside a Deutsche Bank near Ulrich's flat, sporting pinstripes and a sandwich-board-style sign: *Ask Me What I'm Thinking About.* Passersby who complied were offered an improvised pornographic fable on the spot, one that supposedly illustrated "how advanced capitalism fucks us all." "He's a fool and a fraud," Ulrich warned Ava at the time. But Ava was intrigued enough by Fiete's "bankporn" story in her honor (one involving ice cubes, Spanish fly, and handcuffs) to leave him her number, only to discover that for all his street-side bravado the man was pathologically insecure in the bedroom. It was a disconnect that Ulrich had found riotously funny: "Told you he was a fake," he'd hooted. "Trust you to bag a performance artist with performance anxiety."

"You weren't always so smooth in the sack yourself," she'd shot back, in an uncharacteristic reference to their own short-lived affair in their teens.

"I was seventeen," he retorted. "And the *least* of my problems was getting it up."

As Fiete pulled even, Ava threw another quick glance at Bay Lop's clenched face. It seemed to shiver in some unseen breeze, and Ava found herself shivering too, unexpectedly brushed by apprehension. Shaking the feeling off, she threw her head back and added her own smoke-sore shout to the crowd's: *"Ho! Ho! Ho-Chi-Minh!"* It felt both furious and playful; a primal nursery rhyme howled in breathless time with a thousand marching footsteps. But as they entered the plaza the mood suddenly shifted. The crowd's pace quickened into a jog. And as the chant swelled into a full-fledged roar—*Ho! Ho! Ho-Chi-Minh! Ho! Ho! Ho-Chi-Minh! HO! HO! HO-CHI-MINH!*—it was quickly underscored by the sound of sirens in the nearing distance and the rhythmic chop of a helicopter that had materialized above the campus buildings.

And then all of it—the chanting, the marching, the bracing, energizing outrage—was stopping, so suddenly that she nearly ran into the line in front of them.

Confused, Ava stepped back and peered around her banner pole.

"It's the bulls," Fiete shouted.

Following his gaze, she made out a dark block of *Polizei* at the demonstration's front lines. They were decked out in full riot gear.

"But why are they stopping us?" Shifting her grip again, she lifted onto the tiptoes of her white patent boots. As the chopper bobbed and whined above like an uneasy hornet, she watched as the two sides faced off: cops on one side, students on the other. "Don't we have permits?"

The attack came in lieu of an answer, though looking back Ava wouldn't be able to pinpoint the exact moment of its launch. All she'd recall was that one moment the *Polizei* were in their tight battalions, as stiff and stone-faced as so many tin soldiers. And then they were laying into the demonstration's front lines with a strangely mechanical-seeming fury that left Ava both stunned and sickened.

"What's happening?" she cried, to no one in particular, but no one around her seemed to have the answer. And already the neat, forceful rows were unraveling into a panicked scramble to safety. She looked back at Fiete again, uncertain whether to move forward or back before registering that it was too late to do either: the *Polizei* had already reached them. At the same moment she saw one of the bubble-blowers tumble from her friend's shoulders, inadvertently falling on top of a policeman who then proceeded to smash her head with his club. Ava gasped as the girl attempted to stagger back to her feet, the blood running in bright, spiked rivulets down the side of her face. As another *Polizist* pushed past her she extended an arm, mouthing something that might have been *help* or *stop* or *doctor*. Ava turned reflexively to try to offer aid, but the girl had already disappeared from view entirely, replaced by a writhing scrum of dissidence and enforcement.

A moment later the banner shaft jumped in her hands like a fishing pole with a strong bite. Looking over, she saw that her partner had dropped his end and was racing off toward the Tiergarten.

"Where are you going?" she shouted after him.

"I'm splitting," he shouted back, his blue eyes blank with panic. "You know I can't afford another arrest."

And without waiting for her response he sprinted into the crowd, Ava staring after him in mixed disbelief and disgust. *Bastard*, she thought. Why was Ulrich always right about these things?

A sudden sprinkle of cold water jolted her back to the moment. Turning, she saw the police had brought in tanks equipped with *Wasserwerfer*: black, boxy vehicles topped with gunlike hoses that were advancing on the crowd, forcing back water-battered bodies. A few meters behind her a white van had pulled up; the *Polizei* were already herding protesters inside.

Dropping to her knees, she scrabbled for the plywood handle Fiete had dropped, awkwardly lofting the painted sheet back up on her own: she'd worked too hard on the image to simply leave it in the street. A pole on each shoulder, she began gingerly moving toward the beckoning green of the Tiergarten: If she could make it to the park she could follow its outer rim south until she reached the Zoologischer Garten station.

She'd barely made it three steps, however, before a hand clamped down on her shoulder. "Where do you think you're going?"

Staggering, Ava turned to see a bull in his tall black hat and long black coat.

"To the park."

He snorted. "Why? Planning a picnic?" He looked to Ava to be in his forties; roughly Ilse's age, or perhaps older. His jaw had the blunt squareness of her mother's garden hoe.

"I just want to go home," said Ava truthfully.

Ava watched the man's gaze trace its way to the ruined painting that now sagged between them. As he studied the latter she found herself searching his face, an artist's greedy, reflexive need for even a faint indication that her work might have moved its viewer. But he just held out his gloved hands.

"Hand it over," he said.

"What?" Blinking, Ava took a step back. "I made this. It's mine."

"It belongs to the city now," he said. "Hand it over."

As he reached brusquely for one of the poles, Ava tried to sidestep. But her foot slipped on something slick and soapy that had spilled on the ground. As she fought for her balance the banner poles swung wildly, the left one striking the *Polizist* on the side of his helmeted head.

"Oh," she gasped, horrified. "I'm—"

Before she could apologize he was lunging straight at her, his truncheon whipped from its leather holster. Then somehow she was on the ground, her arms covering her head while blows rained down on her ribs and bare thighs. The pain was searing, breathtaking; it numbed with the force of electric shock. A burst exploded in her knee, and for one fleeting, red-veiled moment she thought she'd felt the bone snap in half. Then there were hard hands beneath her armpits, dragging her away from where the banner lay crumpled on the street, now stained with smears of her own blood.

"Stupid cow," the bull was shouting. "I warned you!" They'd reached the van now. Pushing her face-first against it, he patted her down before spinning her to face him again. His blunt face was beet red.

"What do you have to say now, you commie bitch," he said.

Ava registered that she was shaking: huge, harsh spasms. It wasn't until she tried to speak that she realized she wasn't crying but laughing: juddering, gasping peals that felt like another attack on her bruised ribs. But they elicited such a comically baffled look from the cop that she found herself laughing harder despite the pain.

"Tell me a fairy tale," she gasped.

❧

Four hours later she was curled up on Ulrich's couch, an ice pack on her knee and a mug of whiskey in her hand.

"How's it looking?" he asked.

"Empty," she said, extending the mug.

"I meant your knee, you lush."

Grimacing, she set the cup down and peeled the pack from the scraped, swollen flesh, eyeing it dispassionately before shrugging. "Still disgusting. But the swelling's gone down." She grinned grimly. "I should be back in my miniskirts in a week or two."

"I'm sure Bank Boy will be thrilled to hear it. Oh, wait—he's probably in France by now."

"Ass." Ava groaned. "Don't rub it in."

Smirking, Ulrich picked up the bottle of Jack Daniel's he'd set between them on the coffee table. He poured them both another fingerfull. Ava downed half of hers in a single gulp.

"Careful, sailor," he chided.

"What?"

"You're putting those away quickly."

"I was beaten up by fucking Nazis."

"They weren't Nazis," he said quietly.

Ava felt herself flush. "Sorry," she said. "It's just . . . it was hell." And it had been. The seats in the police van had been crowded and unpadded; every jostle and bump had hurt Ava's beaten body. Ten minutes into the ride, the woman crammed in next to her had leaned forward and vomited on Ava's boots. And that was before even reaching the Tiergarten's Precinct E, where her repeated requests for water, paracetamol, and a phone call had been ignored for hours. As awful as it had been, though, she knew she—of all people—had no business flinging around that particular term. Especially not with him.

"*Verzeihung,*" she said again, swirling her whiskey in its mug. He was right; she *was* drinking too much again. And making the same foolish romantic mistakes. And getting herself needlessly into trouble and injury. And speaking thoughtlessly to the man she cared most for in the world.

She'd start over in New York. She'd start *everything* over in New York.

To New York, Ava thought.

And tipping the mug back, she finished off the last few mash-sweet drops.

"That's the last time I'll be able to bail you out, by the way," Ulrich was saying. "Next time, you'll have to call Bank Boy."

"Fuck you," she retorted; but she was smiling. When the *Polizei* had finally allowed her her one five-minute phone call, her trembling fingers had practically dialed Ulrich's number of their own accord. After he signed the release papers, his first comment had been *Ask me what I'm thinking about*.

"You're actually lucky you got out when you did." He waved his mug at the Jurassic-era Zenith he'd inherited from his father back in Bremen. On Channel Three, the riots were still in high gear, policemen huddling behind a military tank as frenzied protesters hurled things at them: rocks, trash, and what looked like Molotov cocktails. Ava shuddered. *Who are these people?* she wondered. They didn't look at all like the ones she'd marched with by the university. The latter had been boisterous, yes. But not belligerent. This crowd, by contrast, seemed to want only to inflict as much damage as it could. In fact, the scene looked less like a demonstration than wartime devastation. Smoke billowed from burning and overturned cars; the wounded limped and dragged themselves toward shelter. She searched for the cop who'd beaten and arrested her earlier, but they all looked the same on the screen: stern, grainy ghosts.

"True." Reaching for the impromptu dinner he'd set out—a hunk of Emmenthaler, a loaf of bread, and some rock-hard smoked sausage— Ava sculpted off a piece of cheese before realizing that she had zero interest in eating. "At least this nonsense won't be happening in the U.S.," she added, setting it back on the plate.

"I wouldn't count on that. You'll be in Brooklyn."

"Brooklyn's not a war zone."

"The world's a war zone."

She lifted an eyebrow. "Some places more than others."

"What's that supposed to mean?" He patted his shirt pocket for his cigarettes, tossing his pack of Roth-Händles to her without her having to ask for them. *I love you*, she thought, the declaration sliding slyly into the jumbled slipstream of her consciousness before she had a chance to register and block it. Shaking her head, she reached for the cigarettes.

"Nothing," she said, tapping the pack against the tabletop. It had been three months since his abrupt announcement that he was leaving Germany for Tel Aviv, but it still felt as surreal today as it had then. "I just don't understand why you aren't coming with me instead," Ava added. "New York City is almost as Jewish as Palestine."

"It's Israel." He picked up her cheese bit, tossing it high into the air and catching it victoriously in his mouth. "And New York's not home."

"And Palestine is?"

"Israel," he corrected again, chewing methodically. "And yes. Or at least, it's as close to a homeland as I've got." He pushed his glasses up further on his nose. "Do you remember telling me—was it on the way back from that crazy trip to the Army Archives in Berlin—how New York suddenly just felt 'right' to you? Even though you'd never seen it?"

What she remembered of that bleakly silent ride back was the charred ache in her gut. The realization that nothing could be the same—not her sense of Ilse as a stern but essentially moral being. Not of Ava as a girl without a past and hence with no traceable link to the prior decade's horrors. And not, in the end, her newfound romance with Ulrich, though (typically) Ava had never had to put this into words. She simply pulled away until he understood that it was over. And then carefully, delicately, like a damaged ship at high sea, they'd navigated back to the safe shore of their former friendship.

"Not really," Ava said now, shaking herself out a smoke. "But anywhere away from Ilse felt right."

"I'm fairly sure you said that too." He picked up the sausage in his fist and bit off a chunk, not bothering with the knife. "The strange thing," he said, thoughtful again as he chewed, "is that I've always liked your mother. She's never been anything but civil to me."

Ava tightened her lips. "It's easy to appreciate civility if you're not entitled to more."

He quirked a brow. "Like what?"

"Like maternal devotion. Like *love*." She'd meant for it to come out lightly, but the sudden intensity of her longing broke her voice slightly on the word *love*. Mortified, she dropped her gaze to the cigarette.

"She loves you, Ava," he said, in precisely the warm, kind voice she did not want to hear at the moment.

She shrugged stiffly. "Do you have anything else to drink?"

"Just beer, I think." He climbed to his feet, making his way to the Westinghouse in the little galley kitchen and returning a moment later with two freshly decapped Pilsners. "Enjoy it," he said, sliding one her way. "You know American beer tastes like piss."

She grimaced. "Does Palestine even have beer?"

"*Israel*. And frankly I don't much care. If it's all that bad I'll stick with whiskey."

He tipped his own bottle toward hers. "Cheers."

"*L'chaim*," she countered glumly. It struck her anew that they'd soon be half a world apart; Ava and this brilliant, sardonic, insufferable being who had almost singlehandedly made her life bearable for two decades, who could make her laugh with the slightest shift of an eyebrow. It was true that they sometimes went for a week or more without talking these days. But it was the *idea* of his proximity that she depended upon: the knowledge that no matter what, she could always summon his wry, dry voice by picking up the phone's receiver. She had known this would change, of course; had known it the moment his emigration papers came through and her application to Pratt was accepted. But not until this moment had she fully felt the stark and gaping truth of it.

How did we let this happen, she thought miserably.

Cigarette between her lips, she leaned forward as he produced a lighter and wordlessly flipped its cap. As he lit her cigarette she studied his hand; the long strong fingers, the dark curling hairs. She felt a strange pang that she had never tried to draw them.

"Do you know," she said, exhaling and leaning back, "that she hasn't even congratulated me on getting into the program?"

He shook out a cigarette for himself. "I'm sure she's just upset that you're leaving her."

"Doubtful." Ava snorted, tasting the smoke's tartness in the back of her throat. "She'll throw a party. Even more so now that I've been arrested. She already thinks I'm a criminal."

"Why do you have to tell her about today?"

Ava shrugged. "I suppose I don't. But she'll find out somehow anyways. She always manages to find out about my fuckups."

"This wasn't a fuckup," he said, exhaling. "This was you standing up for what is right." He smiled. "At least until the *Nazi* knocked you down."

She gave him the finger. "Either way, it's another reason for her to hate me." On the television, a handful of protesters hurled themselves at a parked Volkswagen van and began rocking it from side to side.

"She doesn't hate you. She's in pain. She's losing her child."

"She never wanted her child," Ava said bitterly.

"How do you know?"

"I just do. Every time she looks at me I feel it. It's as if it takes all her strength not to run away from me, screaming. Not that I blame her, given what we know about my father." Ava toyed with her cigarette. "Do you know," she said, "that one of my clearest, earliest memories of her is of her leaving me. I was on a beach—Wannsee, I think. She'd been behind me. But then all of a sudden she was walking away. Just . . . going."

He cocked his head. "What age was this?"

"I can't remember. After the orphanage."

"But she picked you up *from* the orphanage, didn't she?"

"I know that. But I barely remember anything from that day. It doesn't make much sense." As Ava shut her eyes, for some reason she saw not the lakeside beach but Bay Lop's tooth-gnashing grimace. The simultaneous dawning of hatred and despair, even as life abruptly left his wire-thin frame. Where was he now? Ava wondered. Had they buried him? Burned his blood-spattered corpse? Her own body felt bloodless, as bleak and empty as starless space.

"Would you stay?" Ulrich asked.

"Was?" Startled, she looked up.

"What if she asked you not to go? To stay with her here in Germany?"

Ava contemplated this a moment: the novel thought of Ilse saying *I love you, Ava. Please don't leave.* Or even more improbably: *Let's talk.* In many ways, it was all she'd ever wanted from her mother. And yet at this moment the idea sparked not happiness but a swell of airless anxiety, the same sort that sometimes precursored her panic attacks.

"Not a chance," she said. "And you? Would anything make you stay now?"

He smiled. "Not all the blond tail on the planet."

"Pig." Ava flecked beer foam at him, though she was laughing again despite herself. In the years since their breakup it had become a running joke: his penchant for buxom milkmaid-types, as well as Ava's for dissolute artist types. There was truth in both depictions, though Ava had sometimes thought they evoked them to keep their own relationship safely in its platonic realm. After all, Ava—with her dark hair, slight figure, and mournful brown eyes—couldn't have looked less like a milkmaid. And Ulrich—sensible, sober Ulrich—had neither a creative nor a dissolute bone in his body.

"Anyway," she said. "There have to be blondes in Palestine."

"The bottle variety," he said disdainfully. "It won't be like here, in the Aryan paradise that is the Fatherland."

"I'd hope not much there is."

"Agreed," he agreed. "Ditto with New York."

"That's why I'm going," she said.

On Channel Three North the protesters finally toppled the VW van onto its side. As it lay there, a wounded whale, they crouched behind it as a shield, continuing to lob bottles and stones at the police squads.

"They'll make you fight," said Ava, watching one officer race past the screen, gloved hand clamped against the riot helmet on his head.

"Fighting was part of the draw for me." He toyed with his lighter. "At least there we *get* to be fighters. Not victims."

"You're not a victim here, are you?"

"Of course I am." He flicked his lighter, and she watched his flame materialize, then disappear again: *poof.* "The minute people hear *Jew* they see you differently. They wonder who you lost, how you survived—whether you lied or bribed or sold someone out to do it. They wonder why the hell you're still here, in a country that gassed your mother and would probably have gassed you as well, if things had ended differently." Sliding the lighter into his jacket pocket, he pushed his spectacles further up the bridge of his nose in that gesture that by now was so familiar, and so intensely dear all of a sudden, that Ava felt another pang.

"I wish I were coming with you," she said impulsively.

"As in making Aliyah? Is there something you haven't been telling me?"

She shrugged. "I just know how much I'll miss you."

She knew how foolish it sounded. Yet at that moment it was almost panic-inducing, the idea of an Ulrich-free world. She was suddenly uncertain if she could even survive it.

"I'll miss you," she repeated softly. Thinking, once more: *I love you.*

He held her gaze for a long moment. And though at this point she knew his gold-flecked eyes better than she knew her own, she saw something new and unexpected in them: a statement. A question. She caught her breath, instinctively summoning the nervous giggle, the offhand joke, the invisible gate she always slammed between them at these instances. For once, though, nothing came. She was aware only of his nearness; the scent of his English soap and aftershave. The faint spice on his breath left from the bite of sausage. That, and her pulse pounding in her throat.

It was he who looked away first, but only to stub out his cigarette and set his spectacles with careful deliberation on the table.

"What . . ." she managed.

But he was already pushing the table out of the way, and pulling his body over hers, and cupping her face in the warm, strong hands she'd never drawn. Ava found herself not pulling away but pushing forward, pushing back. Obeying an impulse long buried all these years, not just from him but from herself, she wrapped her arms around his neck;

twined her scraped, still-bleeding legs around his hips. As she started unbuttoning her blouse, though, it was he who paused.

"You're sure," he said, "that this is all right?"

For what felt like the first time in her life with him, she didn't have a flip answer. What she had were questions—hundreds, perhaps thousands of them, each one as cool and sharp as it was strangely weightless, swirling through her stunned mind like downy snowflakes: *why* and *why now* and *what is happening* and *what has changed*. But most of all: *what does this mean?*

But beneath the soft beat of their descent the answer lay already: that this wasn't romance restarting, but friendship ending.

That what they were saying was good-bye.

For a moment her ears rang faintly: the old panic threatening to overtake her. Pushing it aside, she clung to him even more tightly, squeezing her suddenly wet eyes shut, burying her damp face in his prickly neck.

"It is," she whispered. "It's everything."

7

Renate

1936

"*T*ake it. It's for you." Sophia Sitz holds the envelope out, her eyes as hard and sharp as broken shards of blue glass.

"What is it?" Renate asks warily.

Sofi shrugs. "I meant to give it to you last week. I forgot."

Which isn't an answer, but Renate extends her hand anyway, trying to look nonplussed even as her pulse skips a beat. Last week Sofi handed out invitations to her sixteenth birthday party. It's to be held in the ballroom of the fancy Hotel am Steinplatz, with a buffet table and a band and dancing. The whole class is buzzing about it. Renate had told herself she didn't care that she hadn't been included, but the thrill coursing through her now says otherwise.

Sliding the card into her skirt pocket, she darts a quick glance toward the front of the classroom, where Ilse sits scribbling furiously in a notebook.

"*Na*, aren't you going to open it?" Sofi is still waiting, her arms crossed over her chest.

Renate wavers, wondering whether she can extract the envelope's contents without her face giving away her relief and gratitude. She hears the singsong tenor of their geography teacher in the hallway, cheerily greeting some other staff member or instructor. *(Heil Hitler!)*

"I'll open it later," she says, relieved. "Class is starting."

As she sinks into her wooden chair she senses rather than sees Karolin Beidryzcki's hazel gaze. "What was it?"

Is it Renate's imagination, or is there a hint of jealousy in her voice? Feigning nonchalance, she pulls out her notebook. "I don't know."

"You were probably smart not to open it then." Karolin pulls out her own book and a pencil, then holds up the latter and frowns. *"Ach."*

"What?"

"Broken. Have you got an extra?"

Renate darts a quick glance at the metal sharpener screwed to the wall up front. A year earlier, Karolin might have risked a trip to it. These days, though, both she and Renate know better than to leave their seats unless summoned. The less attention they draw to themselves the better.

"I'll look." Renate rummages in her bag again. "And what do you mean, 'smart'? Do you know what it is?"

"I might. A few others got them last week." Her friend's freckled face is sober.

Poor girl, thinks Renate. Of course, she wouldn't have been invited. None of the full Jews were. "I'm sure it won't be much fun, anyways," she lies consolingly.

Karolin frowns. She looks as though she's about to say something more. But before she can answer, the room fills with *thunks* and screeches of chairs being hurriedly pushed back and girls springing from their seats. As Herr Hartmann strides through the doorway, pointer in hand, Renate reluctantly pulls herself to her own feet. Striding to the lectern, the teacher yanks down the retracting map they'd been studying yesterday: *Karte des Deutschen Volks—und Kulturbodens*, the title reads, over a darkly shaded area that includes large swathes of Czechoslovakia, Poland, and Hungary.

For a moment he studies it, rocking back on his heels. Then, swiveling around to face them all, he lifts his arm. *"Heil Hitler!"*

"Heil Hitler!" the class chimes, thirty-two girlish arms flung high. Renate and Karolin remain standing but don't salute. This is not from choice, but because "the German salute is for Germans only," as they and the school's other remaining non-Aryans were told at a terse meeting in the headmaster's office last term. By that point it had come as a relief; the daily inner battle between her longing to fit in and the last, defiant shreds of her self-respect had become almost as exhausting as pretending nothing had changed.

"And how is everyone today?" The teacher is beaming. "Scrubbed and fresh-faced and ready to work?"

Scattered titters. Barely into his twenties, Herr Hartmann just joined the teaching staff this year, replacing dour and darkly dressed Frau Cohen. Most girls welcomed the change: with his thick slicked-back hair and trimmed mustache he evokes Clark Gable wearing a red armband. A year earlier, Renate might have fancied him too. Now, though, his handsome face sparks little more than a sour spike of anxiety.

Picking up her pencil, she casts another glance up at Ilse, who is seated in her customary spot in the front row. As usual, she is scribbling away, probably finishing last night's assigned essay on the postwar redrawing of German borders. Between her BDM activities and her writing duties at *Das Deutsche Mädel*, Renate guesses that she's further behind than ever in her schoolwork. But in Herr Hartmann's class it doesn't seem to matter. A staunch Party man, he frequently assigns Ilse's newsletter items for Press Study. Last week's was about an upcoming visit by the British Boy Scouts to Berlin and the joint activities planned for them and the Hitlerjugend. *"Unsere kleine Journalistin,"* Herr Hartmann calls her. *Our little lady journalist.*

"On to business," he pronounces now. "I've got last week's essays to give back: *Expanding the Volksland: Our Need for New Space.*" Pulling a sheaf of papers from his briefcase, he lays the first one down on Ilse's desk with a flourish. "Fräulein von Fischer's paper gets the prize this week. Exemplary work. It will go in the usual spot." He jerks his chin at the side wall, upon which hangs a framed picture of the Führer, looking mournful. Beneath it, the week's showcase-able assignments are thumb-tacked in a neat row.

"The rest of you did acceptably well. With the usual exceptions."

Beside her, Karolin sighs. Indisputably their class's star student in past years, like Renate she now struggles just to pass. It's the same with all of the back-row students, including mousy-looking Amelia Kronberg and Rosa Sartro, rumored to be half Gypsy. It doesn't help that when-ever assignments have to do with *das Volk* and *Deutsche Politik* they—as non-*Deutsch* and non-*Volk*—are assigned different topics, almost al-ways on things not covered in class. (This one: *Water Systems in Ancient Mesopotamia*.)

"Is there even a point?" Karolin mutters beneath her breath now.

It's barely a whisper. Nevertheless, one row up Herr Hartmann pauses, his ear cocked like a hound hearing the hunt trumpet.

"Fräulein Beetle," he says, frowning and using the name he's given her (*Beidryzcki*, he says, is too much of a "foreign tongue teaser"). "What are you hissing and clacking about back there?"

"Nothing, sir," Karolin says quickly. "I was—just asking Renate for a pencil."

Renate half lifts her own pencil and nods. The teacher ignores her. "You came to class without a means of writing?"

"I—I have a pencil, sir," says Karolin. "But I just discovered the tip was broken."

"And no backup."

He is still smiling. But there's a tightness to his grin that Renate knows all too well. She feels her fingers clenching around her friend's alibi even as the axe falls: "Demerit for unpreparedness. You too, Fräu-lein Bauer."

Renate blinks. "Sir?"

"For your role in distracting the class."

"But I . . ."

"Shut your Yid trap," he snaps.

Renate's breath catches like a fishbone in her throat.

A stunned silence descends, followed by a single, nervous-sounding giggle from somewhere in the front. It sounds suspiciously like Sofi Sitz. Renate fixes her gaze on the pencil sharpener, biting her lower lip to keep it from trembling. A meter away Ilse sits in her chair, her shoulders stiffened, her figure motionless.

Turn around, Renate wills her, as Herr Hartmann resumes his distribution. But the blond girl doesn't move.

Upon reaching Renate's row Herr Hartmann announces its results for the general benefit of all: "Incoherent (*slap*) . . . Sloppy (*slap*) . . . Devoid of logic (*slap*)." But as he returns Renate's he merely lifts an eyebrow, slamming the paper facedown atop her notebook. Only when he's reached his lectern does she allow herself to quickly flip the page over and survey his commentary.

Despite the complete randomness of the topic, she'd spent extra time on this one, interviewing her father extensively and on his suggestion researching *Mesopotamia* and *Ancient Sewage* in the big Ancient Civilizations *Enzyklopädie* at the Charlottenburg public library. She'd included several carefully penciled diagrams and even typed it up on Vati's Adler, all in the hope she might break through the wall of *Substandard*s and *Disappointing*s her teachers have been piling against her. She certainly wasn't looking for the sort of praise she once took for granted; the *Beautifully worded*s and *Well done*s and *Quite Impressive Fräulein Bauer*s. She was aiming, at most, for *Good Enough*. But to no avail: overscrawled the neat black lettering, in Reich red, is Herr Hartmann's verdict: *Pathetic.*

Don't fret too much, he has added. *After all, as a foreigner you can't be expected to write in German with the fluency of a native.*

Renate fists her hands against her thighs: if only she could she'd scrunch the thing up and hurl it in his face. But of course, she knows better. The first and only time Karolin even contested a mark he'd given her he'd ripped the paper in half before the whole class and further degraded it from a *Poor* to a *Fail.*

Instead, Renate folds the assignment into the tightest wad she can manage before shoving it into her satchel's furthest reaches.

Closing her eyes, she breathes in slowly, out slowly. *Just get through today,* she thinks. She recites it over and over—*through today, through today*—until, eventually, her heart stops pounding in protest.

⤳

It's been her mantra ever since her *Mischling* unmasking. For a full week after that disastrous day she'd remained locked in her room, emerging only to return barely touched trays of food to the hallway, or to scurry to the washroom and back. She'd ignored Franz's quiet knocks and Sigmund's frenzied scratchings and her parents' pained pleas to *come downstairs,* to *let us help,* to *talk this over.* She ignored Ilse's four phone calls and two personal visits, not even answering when her mother knocked to let her know her friend was waiting in the downstairs hallway. She even ignored her beloved books, for when she tried to read one it was as though the letters and words had been somehow rearranged in some unintelligible format. The only thing she felt capable of doing was sitting and staring down at Ragdoll Alice from Wonderland: she of the boneless hug, the Mona Lisa–stitched smile, the unsurprised blue-button eyes.

Don't open the door was the doll's silent suggestion. *If you wait long enough you'll wake up like I did, and it will all have been nothing more than a dream.*

But after five largely sleepless nights and increasingly unwashed days it became clear that this wasn't likely to happen. And so on the sixth day—a Sunday—Renate pulled the chair from beneath her doorknob and crept down the hall into Franz's room—silently, and very early, the way she'd often done as a small girl. She had perched on his coverlet, hugging her knees until he somehow sensed her through his dreams, and—gradually, begrudgingly—emerged from them with groans and fluttering lashes to find her staring at him miserably.

"What do I do?" she whispered. "I can't go back. I won't survive the year."

"Don't think of the year," he said, his voice still gravelly with sleep, his black curls a tangled halo around his head. "Don't think about it that way. Just think about getting through today."

"I can't."

"You can."

"I *can't*, Franz."

"You can. Jews have gotten through worse."

"Stop saying that! I'm not a *Jew*!"

"All right, *Schwester*. I take it back." His tone was indulgent, as though she were three again and threatening to throw one of her tantrums. And just as he had when she was three, he pulled the covers back and moved over for her: *"Komm!"*

The bed was small now, of course, and they were both far too old. But after a moment's hesitation she slid in next to him anyway, settling on her back beside him with her arms folded behind her head, staring up at his white, sunlight-striped ceiling. They didn't embrace or even touch; for this (they both sensed) would have been *too* strange. But he did turn his head to look at her sympathetically.

"Another suggestion?" he asked.

And when she nodded: "Take a bath. *Du stinkst.*"

Renate glared at him: "Shut up." But she lifted her arm, taking a careful whiff of herself beneath it, blinking in mortification because he was right: she *did* stink.

And then they were both laughing; and after the laughter simply lying there, his brown eyes shut and hers open, the slowing sleepsong of his breath like a calming lullaby.

A day later, she bathed, dressed, and dragged herself back to the *Gymnasium*—or rather, to the strange, new place it had become in her absence.

∗

Recrossing her ankles under her desk, Renate feels the hard point of Sofi's envelope poking through the thin material of her skirt pocket. Pulling it out, she leans over to drop it into her satchel before stopping and studying it for a moment.

The sensible thing to do, of course, is to open the thing after school, away from Herr Hartmann's further wrath and Karolin's (inevitably) bruised feelings. But suddenly she doesn't care what makes sense and what doesn't. Not when nothing really makes sense to begin with.

Setting it in her lap, she runs her fingertip over the elaborate rendering of her name: *Fräulein Renate Bauer.* Just seeing it like that, written out so carefully and beautifully, feels like a much-needed affirmation: *I exist.* And not only that, she is going to a *party*—her first of the year. At least, her first not counting a dismal gathering last month at the Beidryzckis' home. Closing her eyes, Renate imagines it: a glowing ballroom, chandeliers casting glinting rainbows of life. Pink punch in crystal goblets. The sweet terror of being asked to dance by a boy. The joy of dancing. Really *dancing* again! True, they will probably only play dreary, boring German songs now that the government's denounced swing and jazz as *Judenmusik.* But it will be heavenly nonetheless to circle a dance floor in her best red shoes, in her best white dress. To feel a boy's arms around her waist.

The only downside is that Rudi will likely be there, doing his best to pretend Renate is invisible—just as he has since the news about her racial makeup came out.

The note had shown up in her notebook on Renate's second day back. Terse and neat, it had comprised two lines: *Due to incompatibilities of the blood, I regret that any future association between yourself and myself is out of the question. Please do not talk to me.*

Stunned, Renate had ventured upstairs to the boys' floor, wandering alone down a hallway full of whispers and half smirks and bemused gazes that didn't quite meet her own. She'd finally found him in the library, not at their usual study table but in a small corner table half hidden in the stacks. Note in hand, she'd walked toward him hesitantly, the girls and boys at the other tables monitoring her approach with the electric thrill of an execution-day crowd. When he looked up his face was so familiarly perfect, so perfectly familiar that she couldn't believe it wouldn't break into its usual bright smile.

But of course, it did not. "What is it?" he snapped. "What do you want?"

"I just—I got your letter."

"Then why are you here? I made everything quite clear." He looked angry—no, more than angry. Furious. He was, she saw in wonderment, actually shaking.

"I just thought . . ." She swallowed, aware that every eye in the room was trained on them. "I thought we could talk."

"Talk?" His voice rose sharply, cracking in a way that in the past they would have laughed at together. "About what? About how you tricked me into falling for you, with your Yid lies and spells?"

Renate gaped at him. "Rudi. You know I didn't know."

"Does it matter if a typhus carrier knows they have typhus, when they infect everyone in their path?"

The mercilessness of the attack left her breathless. "You can't really think . . ."

"It's not my 'thinking.' It's the Führer's word. *The discovery of the Jewish virus is one of the greatest revolutions that has taken place in the world. How many diseases have their origin in the Jewish virus!*" His ability to remember and quote passages from books after a single reading had become a sort of joke between them. Now the words felt like a weapon. Her heart pounding, she found herself unable to respond, to even move. She simply stood there, a willing, trembling target.

"Here's another one for you." He was blinking rapidly—not in anger, she suddenly saw, but on the verge of tears. Despite everything, her first instinct was to comfort him. *"The black-haired Jewish girl lies in wait for hours on end. Satanically glaring at and spying on the unsuspicious boy whom she plans to seduce . . ."*

And though Renate's hair is not black but brown, she found her own eyes welling up, her own heart shredding. And while all she wanted to do was hurl herself into his arms she'd instead hurled herself from the room, her satchel slapping against her thighs, whispered laughter spreading slickly in her wake.

The memory makes her throat tighten. *Don't think about it*, she orders herself. *Think about good things. Think about the party. Think about dancing.*

She flips the envelope over, casting a quick glance at Herr Hartmann. "As you all now know," he is noting, stabbing his pointer at the map, "our borders to the east should include this part of West Prussia, as well as Silesia starting *here*."

Holding her breath, Renate peels the envelope lip open and eases the oblong rectangle from it. Her first thought is that it's smaller than she'd expected. And more businesslike-looking: rather than the soft-curving letters of a typical invitation the words are printed in heavily blocked-out font.

Frowning, Renate holds the cardboard square higher, above the desk's shadow, and squints:

Einfache Fahrkarte nach Jerusalem.
Bitte kehre nicht zurück!
One-Way Ticket to Jerusalem.
Please don't bother returning!

The words circle a crude sketch of a somber-looking and faintly familiar face: bulbous nose, piggish eyes, stubble-covered double chin. It takes a moment to remember where she has seen it before. It's a typical *Juden* face, similar to those that in past months have festooned front pages and posters across the city.

Furiously, she turns the card over, hiding the hateful words and image from herself. It's only then that she realizes something is written on the back. Three words scrawled in blue:

Bon Voyage!
Rudi.

Quivering with shock, she shoves the thing into her skirt pocket again and forces her gaze back to the teacher. Out of the corner of her eye she glimpses Karolin watching her. But there's a vague sense that if she doesn't allow her gaze to touch anyone else's, then perhaps her shame and her hurt won't be registered by them. Or even by herself. So she fixes her eyes on Herr Hartmann's well-muscled back and manages to keep it there for several fleeting seconds. But then, somehow, she is looking directly at Sofia Sitz, twisted back in her front-row seat, her pink lips split in a triumphant grin.

Very slowly, the other girl lifts her hand. *Auf Wiedersehen*, she mouths.

Face flushing, Renate stiffly looks away, her gaze coming to rest on Ilse's back again. *Turn around*, she thinks again. *Look at me.* She wills it with as visceral a force as she can summon, a silent howl hurled across the rustling room. But Ilse's face remains turned toward the geographic display before her, the crosshatched shadows of German culture across the lands.

And somehow it's this—not the lingering sting of Herr Hartmann's grade or labels, not the hot humiliation of having walked straight into Sofi's trap, but her former best friend's back, white-clothed and ruler-straight—that pushes Renate past the edge. She is on her feet before she realizes it, moving swiftly toward the door, only faintly hearing Herr Hartmann's "Now where on earth are *you* off to, Fräulein Bauer?"

When she keeps walking he repeats the question, an octave higher. "Madame *Mischling*," he shouts. "Are you deaf? *Where are you going?*"

Renate pauses in the doorway, just long enough to turn back. The words lie there on her tongue, spiked with rage and fully formed: *Nach Jerusalem.* She opens her mouth to say them, gaze locked not with Herr Hartmann's but with Ilse's, as gray and blank as a cloudless sky before sunrise. But when she tries to speak her stomach clenches, her mouth and throat emitting nothing but a dry and silent rasp of air. She's like a car, out of fuel. She has just enough power to turn on her heel and continue walking.

⁂

The break with Ilse had been less abrupt than with Rudi, and yet ultimately, that had made it more tortuous. At first she'd let herself hope the lengthening silences between them were simply circumstantial: a phase. After all, they had both made new friendships: Ilse on her BDM camping trips and hikes and Renate within an informal *Judea* study group Franz had formed, half in irony but also half not. ("If we're to be citizens of this so-called Jewish Nation," he reasoned, "we should at least know a little about the place.")

The group included two members of his still-secret "Schiller" study group (one Jewish, one Catholic), the Beidryzcki twins, a boy from the Betar Zionist movement Franz had recently become intrigued by, and two other *Mischlinge* whose parents knew Renate's parents. Renate had agreed to join out of boredom at first: with the BDM now officially the only legal club at school, there was nothing else that she *could* join. Even then, she had braced herself to be as revolted by all things *jüdisch* as everyone around her seemed to be. To her surprise, though, in this instance too, her mother—who claims "engaging trauma often lessens its impact"—turned out to be right. The sessions not only helped her understand Judaism as a religion but leached away some of the toxic sting of being a *Halbjude*.

Part of it was because, when one studied it through history books and religious tracts (rather than through government publications and *Der Stürmer*) Judaism bore no resemblance at all to the parasitic, lecherous, and sinister cult she'd been taught to despise. For one thing, the stories they read from the mysterious-sounding Torah were largely ones she'd always considered Christian fables. Only their order really differed, and the way they were read: while Christians were simply told what the stories were supposed to mean, Jews were actually encouraged to argue about their interpretation, just as generations upon generations of rabbis before them had enthusiastically done in writing in the Midrash.

What was more, nothing in either the stories or the debates involved what she'd long been told was Judaism's version of the Holy Trinity: material wealth, ritual sacrifice, and world domination. Instead, they were about things like peace and mutual respect, learning to love both one's own people and the strangers among them.

But the biggest surprise for her had been the music.

Renate had first heard it on a warm night last September, wafting out of the enormous and stately Fasanenstraße Synagogue as she walked home. As it was mere blocks from her house, she had passed it by hundreds of times without giving it particular thought. This time, though, the sonorous organ tones that had washed into the darkening street had called out to her like the ancient, lonely cry of a siren. She listened to the end, and to the end of the next song. Then she found herself in a back pew, where she sat for the next half hour between a young woman with a sleeping baby and an older woman in a lacy black veil. The candles were lit, the rabbi reading from a list of the newly dead, his voice a soft-falling snow of gentle grief. And though she had no one physically to mourn, for the first time in months Renate had felt that it was not just permitted but somehow fitting to weep. And so she had.

"It was actually rather beautiful," she told Ilse the next day, as they perched together on the lip of the dried-up fountain in the upper school courtyard. "And to be honest, it didn't feel very different from church."

By that point, Ilse and Renate hardly saw one another outside school hours. But in school, at least, Ilse was still there when it counted. When Rudi broke things off, Ilse wrote a mock story for her newsletter titled "Hitlerjugend's Prettiest Boy Breaks with Sweetheart to Propose Marriage to Führer Himself." When the headmaster decreed that all non-Aryans had to move to the back of all the classrooms, she had agitated on Renate's behalf ("She's half Aryan! Shouldn't she at least get to sit somewhere in the middle?"). Upon losing that argument she continued to perch pointedly on Renate's desk until the bell rang. She still met Renate in the courtyard before and after school, even though it meant other girls started avoiding her too.

As gestures these all fell short of revolutionary. In fact, they weren't even particularly risky. But they helped make the days a little easier for Renate to get through, as did the flash of silver Renate still spied on Ilse's hand when she waved or gave the Führer's salute.

It wasn't until after Christmas that things completely changed between them.

Ilse had spent most of the winter holiday on an HJ/BDM-sponsored ski trip, and when she returned, it was without the promised telephone call announcing the fact and with (it was rumored) a new sweetheart. And while no one knew for sure who this mystery boy was, the name Renate heard mentioned drove a steel spike through her soul.

"Just ask her," suggested Karolin, when Renate confided in her. "She'll surely tell you, one way or the other."

But in that first week back at school Ilse was as maddeningly elusive as Rudi had been after Renate's fall from racial grace. She'd arrive in class after Renate but before the teachers, disappearing in the opposite order afterward. She was pointedly absent from all their old meeting spots—the courtyard fountain, the windowside table in the library. The old hitching post outside the school's main front entrance. When, in desperation, Renate finally cornered her on the route home one day, Ilse heard her out stiffly, looking intensely uncomfortable. Yes, she knew she'd said she'd telephone when they came back from Ischgl. And no, she hadn't, because she'd been *unusually busy.* No, she didn't know when she'd next come to Renate's house; it seemed likely she'd be *unusually busy* indefinitely. And no, Rudi Gerhardt was nothing more than a friend to her. But she didn't want to discuss it, she hadn't the time, there was a Winter Relief drive effort she had to write about for the newsletter.

As if to prove her point, she turned toward a passing Mädel and threw her arm up in the now-ubiquitous gesture: *"Heil Hitler!"*

It was a gesture Renate had seen a thousand times in past months. For some reason, though, this time it felt different: not merely reflexive but irrevocable. As though with that single upward swing of her right arm Ilse was severing their connection, once and for all.

It wasn't until she was in bed that night, staring up at the stars they'd cut together, that Renate realized what had really set it apart.

It was Ilse's hand: it had been bare. Renate's friendship ring had been nowhere in sight.

※

At home she kicks her boots off by the front door and is almost knocked over by Sigi's leaping, stub-wagging welcome. On another day she might have pushed him off in annoyance. Now, though, she buries her face in his wiry pelt, as grateful for his unshakable canine love as she is pained by all it can't replace. "You know what, Sig?" she whispers into his perked furry ear. "You may just be my new best girlfriend."

"Reni?" Her mother's voice floats from the kitchen.

"Guter Hund," she murmurs, releasing the Schnauzer.

"Welcome home." Her mother has long since dispensed with her former greeting, *How was school?* the answers have become too depressing for both of them. "Can you come here for a minute?" she calls instead. "I need an opinion."

"About dinner?"

"Yes."

Renate grimaces. They've had to let Maria go, as she's well below the legal age limit for an Aryan woman working in a Jewish household. Renate's mother tried to stress the situation's silver lining, the "opportunity" to "learn something about cooking" in addition to the monthly savings of fifteen *Reichsmark*, now doubly needed since Renate's father has been forced from his university position. But the fruits of this educational endeavor have been decidedly mixed. Whether by deliberate inclination or simply because she's too busy (with writing her own book, with taking on private clients in an effort to make up for Vati's lost income, with writing foreign clinics in search of work for herself and foreign universities in search of work for her husband) nearly every meal Lisbet Bauer produces has something noticeably—sometimes nauseatingly—wrong with it. The soufflé attempted last Saturday was so marble-hard that even Sigi had wanted nothing to do with it. The potatoes in the *Hasenpfeffer* were so overboiled and mealy that the salad tasted more like a potato soup, while the cabbage for the *Kohlroulade* was so undercooked that Franz joked he'd lost a tooth trying to chew it.

But worst of all was Sunday's *Sauerbraten*. Finding herself out of both vinegar and cooking wine, Renate's mother had improvised with vodka—specifically, horseradish spirits that had been in their liquor cabinet since her husband's service reunion two years earlier. It was like eating beef soaked in garlic and gasoline. Franz joked that he could blow up the police station he passed daily on Französische Straße by farting at it and striking a match—a comment that not only earned him no rebuke but actual laughter from both parents.

Hovering in the doorway now, Renate inhales with some caution. But the air smells deceptively appetizing.

"Komm rein, Liebling," says her mother, sounding slightly distracted. A cigarette clamped between her lips, she is stirring her pot with almost aggressive force, as though trying to beat the meal into submission. "What do you think?"

"About what?"

"What I'm making. How does it smell?"

Renate sniffs again. "It smells . . . good?"

"I followed the recipe this time. Proper ingredients. Proper amounts. Who knew it would make such a difference?"

"Who knew," echoes Renate, though she can't help wondering whether her mother's psychotherapeutic approach is similarly scattered. "How was work?"

"Getting worse." Her mother's lips tighten around her cigarette. "Now that Doktor Göring has forced out all the non-Aryans he's turned to the publications." The Psychotherapy Institute has recently been annexed by the Deutsches Institut für Psychologie, a government institute, and its new director is a cousin to Field Marshal Göring.

"Everything but Freud vanished over the weekend," her mother continues. "And even the Freud isn't available, since they're keeping it locked up in a cupboard for which only Göring has the key."

"Why keep it at all?"

Her mother shrugs. "It's a signed first edition. Perhaps they think it's worth something. Or perhaps even our esteemed government has to accept *Die Traumdeutung* as the foundation of the field—even if they don't want anyone to read it. *Na ja.*"

Setting her cigarette on a saucer, her mother extends her wooden spoon. Steam sloughs from it into the air; Renate takes a tentative taste. Meaty richness floods her mouth.

"Eintopf?" she asks. The stew is Ilse's favorite, one Renate has helped

her and her downstairs kitchen staff prepare a dozen times. But there is, of course, no reason to note this now.

"You win the prize," says her mother. The slight smile that appears almost looks strange on her thin face; it's been that long since Renate last saw one. For some reason, it evokes not a responsive smile of her own but a wave of grief strong enough that her body sways with it. She finds herself blinking back tears.

"Reni," says her mother, frowning. "What is it?"

"I just . . ." Renate licks the last salty trace of stew from her lips, trying to think of how to phrase it. "I know that I . . . don't have things as hard as other people. No one's arrested me. Or chased me out of a classroom. No one's told me to break up my family."

Her mother nods. Threatened with a beating by his former classmates, Franz and two of the other Jews in his class recently had to flee their lecture hall through a back window. Professor Bauer, meanwhile, has been brought in for "questioning" by the local Gestapo over rumors (false) of supposed Socialist connections. And Renate's mother has been visited twice by the same agents and urged to "seriously consider" divorcing Vati. "For the sake of my future career," she repeated in disbelief, over undercooked sausage and potatoes. "Next they'll want me to do what that awful woman in the papers did: claim my children aren't *Mischlinge* because their fathers were secret Aryan lovers from my past."

Renate is ashamed to remember how her thoughts buzzed at that. Not just the idea of her mother having a lover (and could she? She was certainly pretty enough, though to be honest Renate has no idea how she'd find the time) but the idea that by changing one small part of one's story, one could erase the damning blood in one's veins. She'd even allowed herself to imagine it: marching into the school office with the coveted Certificate of Blood Purity. Seeing Ilse by their fountain and having her pale face light up upon seeing Renate, instead of closing off as it always did now. And Rudi . . . Rudi. *Oh, Rudi.*

It took her several moments more to process that the fantasy only worked if she cut her kind, gentle Vati entirely out of her life.

"But . . ." her mother prompts.

"But . . ." Renate swallows, hard. What she really wants to ask is that her mother make it better; make it go away. That she magically dismiss the pathetic paper and the *Yid trap* and the one-way ticket to Jerusalem as she has always dismissed everything else. To take Renate into her lap, murmuring *shush-shush-shush*, stroking her hair and brow and cheek. What she really wants is to curl up into a ball and have her mother surround her, a fleshly shield against the world.

"Yes?" her mother repeats, her tone now slightly impatient.

"I miss her," Renate says quietly.

For a moment there's no sound beyond the bubbling of the pot's contents. Then she hears her mother sigh, feels her strong and wiry arms press lightly against her back.

"*Natürlich.* I miss her too."

Renate lays her head on her mother's thin shoulder, noticing that the seam of her sweater has split apart there. Noticing, too, how little flesh her mother actually has these days. Lisbet Bauer has always been bird-like, delicate. But now her face is drawn and peaked, the flesh stretched so sharply over her cheeks that Renate all but sees the underlying bone.

"I thought today that things might be changing back."

Her mother tucks a strand behind Renate's ear. "And why was that?"

"I . . . I left class. I walked out. And she came out to bring me back."

Her mother leans back to look at her. "You left class? Without permission?"

Renate nods, flushing a little. "They were being hateful. All of them. Even the teacher."

Lisbet Bauer shakes her head. "Reni. We've talked about this. You simply must learn to . . ."

"I know. *Get through the day.* But, Mama—that's the thing. Today I didn't think I could do it. I was pretty sure if I stayed there I'd do something awful. And so I left, and then Ilse came after me. And then . . ."

Her mother leans against the stove, crossing her arms. "And then?"

Renate squeezes her eyes shut, seeing it again: Sofi's ticket, which she'd pulled out again in the hallway. Its cheery message (*Please don't bother returning!*) cutting all the more cruelly because—as it slowly dawned on her now—there was actually nowhere she could go. She couldn't go back into the classroom she'd just stormed out of. She certainly couldn't waltz out the front door. She was as trapped as a Yid rat in a cage.

She'd just been contemplating trying to sneak unnoticed into the library when she heard—first, footsteps, approaching rapidly behind her.

And then the familiar voice: "Reni."

Renate looked over her shoulder, not daring to hope it was real. But it was; there she was. Ilse stood by a window, her blond hair lit by a shaft of afternoon sunlight.

In a single instant, months of built-up misery and solitude dropped away. A jumble of joyous greetings vied for vocalization: *I knew it* and *I've missed you* and *Why did you wait so long* and *I've so much, so much to tell you . . .* though only two materialized: "You came."

The old Ilse would have laughed dismissively and said, *Of course I came. I couldn't just let you leave, you idiot!*

This Ilse, however, merely shrugged.

"Herr Hartmann sent me. He said you're to stop this nonsense and come back."

She spoke looking not directly at Renate but behind her, vaguely, coolly. And just like that, the bolt of joy that had caused Renate's heart to jump became a leaden weight against her lungs. *Of course*, she thought. Of course Ilse was here not as Renate's best friend but as Herr Hartmann's most trusted and favored pupil. His *kleine Journalistin*.

"Are you coming?" Ilse prompted. "He says if you don't come back he'll have you dismissed."

"Why?"

Ilse rolled her eyes. "Why do you think? You left the room without permission."

"Not that. Why did you leave?" Renate licked her lips. "Me. Why did you leave me?"

The question seemed to catch Ilse off-guard. A look flashed across

her face: a look of anguish and something more (guilt? uncertainty?).
But then she tightened her lips and it was gone.

"This isn't the time to discuss that," she said.

"It is. It is *exactly* the time." Renate wanted to clench Ilse's shoulders, hard. To shake her until her enviably even teeth rattled. "If we don't, I won't go with you. And I'll—I'll scream. I'll scream and say you attacked me."

Renate had no idea where the threat came from, and even less of an idea if she'd have been able to put it into action. Happily, though, she didn't have to find out, because Ilse sighed and leaned against the wall. "I don't know if I can make you understand. Especially given your Jewish blood and everything."

Ilse had her eyes shut, so she missed Renate's flinch. Her pale face looked slightly pained, her lips pursed in thought. Finally she sighed.

"Did I ever tell you," she said, opening her eyes again, "about my ninth birthday?"

Renate shook her head.

"It was during the Inflation," Ilse continued. "My mother had promised me a cake. But we didn't have the money for ingredients. So she took an old cigar box of my father's, covered it with clean paper, and then spread shortening over it as though it were frosting. We sat with that on the table throughout whatever dinner was. Then, after she'd lit the *Geburtstagskranz*, and she and Vati had sung to me and had me blow out the candles, she scraped the shortening back into a jar and threw the box out."

Renate blinked. "Threw it out? Just like that?"

Ilse nodded. "She said it had just been there to make things look 'festive.' When I asked if there wasn't anything sweet at all—at least a biscuit or some fruit—she paddled me and sent me to my room. She said I was ungrateful; that I didn't understand how hard it was for them to even get bread on the table." She hesitated. "It was, I think, the worst day of my life."

"You never told me." Renate felt her throat tighten in sympathy. "Ilsi. I'm sorry."

"I'm not telling you because I need pity," Ilse said curtly. "I'm trying to make you understand. I don't ever want to experience anything like that moment again. I don't ever want my *children* to experience it."

"But why do you think I can't understand that?"

Ilse rolled her eyes the way she always did when Renate was being (as she'd put it) as *dense as cement.* "I don't think you understand what it's going to take to change things. The kinds of sacrifices that will have to be made. Anything that gets in the way of what we are trying to do has to go. It has to be eliminated. Even if . . . even if it's you."

"But how am I 'getting in the way'?" Renate asked, truly baffled. "I want a stronger Germany too. I know I can't join the BDM, but . . ."

"But that's just *it,* don't you see?" Ilse's cheeks were flushed, her voice hard in the way it hardened when she was trying to hide the fact that she was close to tears. "You can't join because you're not *part* of the new Germany. You can't be. I know that's not your fault, but it's the truth. We can't just pretend that it's not."

Renate stared at her, stunned. *Not part of the new Germany?* She knew other people believed this. But she'd never expected to hear it from Ilse. Not Ilse, who until last year showed every poem she ever wrote to Renate before anyone else. Not Ilse, with whom Renate had worked her way through Kant and Heine and Schiller and had just started Goethe when their friendship started to crumble. Not Ilse, who'd once predicted that Renate would be the first female German minister of culture.

It was as if someone had placed a tourniquet around her esophagus. Panic descended, not because she couldn't breathe but because she somehow sensed that this was her last chance to do it: to say something. To change things back, if she could only find the right, magical words. Try as she might, though, Renate couldn't even come up with one.

"Oh, and just so you know," Ilse was saying. "I told them not to give you one."

"One what?"

"One of the tickets. I told them to leave you alone." Message delivered, Ilse turns back toward the classroom.

"Wait," Renate said. "One more thing. Then I'll go."

Looking annoyed, Ilse waited.

"That—that signature."

"Which one?"

"The one on the back. From—it said *Rudi*." Renate licked her lips nervously. "Was it really from him?"

Ilse had gazed at her former best friend for a moment, and once more Renate—in the past so adept at interpreting her expressions— found herself unable to translate this one.

She did, however, recognize the tone of voice with which Ilse delivered this answer as well: "No."

It was the tone she usually used when she was lying.

"And that was it?" her mother asks now, absently straightening Renate's collar. "You went back into class together?"

Renate nods. "Herr Hartmann said he was going to report me to the headmaster. But then Ilse told him that she'd had to use the lavatory 'for women's problems,' and that that was why we took so long. So in the end he just made me stay after class and sand and wash all the desks." She doesn't tell her mother how the harsh soap and cold water caused her fingers to prune, or how the sandpaper blistered the pads of her fingers. Or the way Herr Hartmann made her stand straight without moving an inch while he pressed against her to "inspect" her work.

Instead, she says: "I know I shouldn't complain. But it's—it's so *hard*, Mama. And I'm lonely."

"I know." Sighing, her mother runs a tired hand through her hair. The emerald in her silver ring glints in the light. It's one of several heirloom pieces her mother's mother left her; this one a set comprising a finely wrought brooch, a set of earrings, the ring, and a stunning necklace. For as long as Renate can remember, these items have been kept in her mother's stocking drawer, in an enameled jewelry box inlaid with opalescent mother-of-pearl. Someday they'll be Renate's, though for now she has to settle for holding them only when her mother takes them out for a polishing. Or stealing glimpses of them when her mother isn't home at all.

"But for the moment," her mother is continuing, "there's nowhere else you can be. At least, not unless we leave Germany altogether."

"Are we seriously considering moving to another country?" Even saying it feels blasphemous, as though they were considering setting fire to their own home.

"*I'm* seriously considering everything." Lisbet Bauer sighs. "It's your father who is still resistant. He keeps saying all this will blow over, that it always has in the past. Though I think that's only part of the reason. He won't ever say so, but I think he's worried that he's not employable anywhere outside Germany."

"How can that be? He is—was—the most popular instructor in his department!"

"Yes. But he also doesn't speak another language. At least, not well enough to teach in it. And"—seeing Renate open her mouth to argue—"ancient Latin doesn't count."

"But he's brilliant. Surely he could learn . . ."

"Not quickly enough to qualify for a job in America. Or Shanghai. Or even Trinidad. And he'd need that in order to get a visa."

Biting her lip, Renate digests this. "Well, what do you think? Do you think it will blow over?"

Her mother purses her lips, tucking one of Renate's curls behind her ear. "I think," she says, "that it's better to be safe than sorry. But for now let's just get you to your *Abitur* without losing your sanity."

Turning back to her pot, she adds: "Go tell your father that dinner will be in half an hour."

8

Ava

1956

"*R*eady for trouble?"

Ulrich revved his engine roguishly, and despite her jangling nerves Ava couldn't help laughing. The car was his father's sedate '38 Opel Olympia. Its color was an unobtrusive mint green.

"You look ready to rob a nursing home."

"I thought you liked men with big motors."

"Only when they're balanced on two wheels, you idiot."

Ava slid into the passenger side and pulled the heavy door shut, leaning over to plant a kiss on his cheek that landed on his mouth as he turned toward her. She closed her eyes, registering the echo of Earl Grey tea and tobacco on his tongue, the stubbly scratch of his upper lip against hers before gently pulling away again. Kicking off her flats, she settled her skirt over her knees, drawing a small stack of bills from her jacket pocket. "Here."

He lifted a brow. "What's this?"

"For gas. Or bribes, if we need them."

If he took the bribes suggestion as a joke, he gave no sign. "Where'd you get it?"

"Ilse's purse. Where else?" She reached for the cigarettes on the dashboard.

He was thumbing through the bills. "Won't she notice? There's close to twenty marks here."

"I doubt it. I've been taking it bit by bit."

"Impressive. Just call us Bonnie and Clyde." He tucked the money into his jacket pocket, then absently tightened his collar. He'd dressed for the occasion, Ava noted, wearing her favorite blue striped tie that reminded her of stick candy tucked into one of his father's woolen V-necked jumpers. "Speaking of which . . . how'd our other criminal endeavor turn out?"

Rummaging in her purse, Ava tossed him the trifold license she'd spent most of the last night altering to make him appear old enough to drive unsupervised. "I was worried that my ink wasn't a match. But it looks more convincing now that it's dried." Shaking out a B&H, she pressed the dashboard lighter button with her bare foot. "What's up with the radio?"

"Should be working again. Just came back from the shop."

Still running the engine, Ulrich flipped the falsified document over to inspect its back. Ava fiddled with the radio's chrome knobs, skipping over alpenhorn-heavy folk music and a German quartet crooning over Hawaiian ukuleles. "For God's sake," she grumbled. "Why can't anyone play decent music in this town?"

Folding the fake license closed again, he gave a low whistle. "My girlfriend is a bloody genius."

"You think the border guards will buy it?" she asked, settling on an old-school swing number on the radio.

"If they don't they're either blind or stupid. My money's on the latter."

"God. I hope you're right." As Ulrich eased smoothly into morning traffic she rolled down the window and withdrew the dashboard lighter, pressing its heated tip to the end of her cigarette, studying him beneath her lashes. He'd been driving with his father for only a month now, but he was as naturally competent behind the wheel as he was everywhere else. In fact, with the possible exception of Ilse he was the most competent person Ava had ever known—and certainly the most trustworthy. At some point he'd also become surprisingly handsome, albeit in a gangly Jimmy Stewart kind of way. *I'm lucky*, she thought. *He's so much better for me than the others.*

It would have been a hard point to argue with herself. Before Ulrich, her two forays into romance had been with pompadoured, fast-talking boys whose sole purpose seemed to have been to get into her capris. One stopped calling when Ava declined; the other when she complied. Both abandonments—for that was how she'd felt, *abandoned*—had left her distraught and mortified for weeks.

Turning her head, she blew smoke at a gaggle of pubescent schoolgirls. It was barely seven in the morning, but the Bremen sidewalk was already bustling with ambling students, hurried dog walkers, and harried-looking commuters. Ava found herself searching warily for her mother's neat blond head, even though Ilse worked on the other side of town.

And yet, she thought, wouldn't it be just like Ilse to do that. To have discovered today's plan and found a way to ruin it, in the same way she ruined everything else in Ava's life. A few months earlier, for instance: Ava's *Gymnasium* drawing teacher told Ava her work was strong enough for a summer course at the University of the Arts, and offered to introduce her to the life study instructor there. It would have cost almost nothing financially, and interfered with nothing academically. Still, Ilse had put her foot down. "I don't want you staring at naked women in a room filled with boys," she'd said. "And you waste enough time on that drawing nonsense already." Similarly, last year when she'd gotten wind (probably by listening in on the downstairs phone line) that after six years of close friendship Ava and Ulrich had become something more, Ilse had immediately tried to put a stop to that development as well, appearing unannounced at the flat Ulrich shared with his widower father to inform a groggy Doktor Bergen that their children had crossed a "dangerous line," one that required firm parental intervention. She'd stated her intention to "monitor Ava and Ulrich closely" whenever they were at the von Fischer household. "I'd request you do the same whenever Ava is here," she'd added.

Happily, Ulrich's father—a night surgeon at Hospital St. JosephStift—had as little time for chaperoning as he did for anything else in his precious daylight hours. After relating the tale to Ulrich, he'd merely told him to "watch his step" with Ava—less because he agreed with Frau von Fischer than because he didn't want any further dealings with the woman. "Frankly," he'd confided, "she terrifies me."

On Radio Bremen the big band number gave way to a newscast about France withdrawing from the Suez.

"Why aren't we just driving to Paris again?" Ava asked, twisting the dial further. "I could enroll in the Beaux Arts. You could work at *Paris Match*."

"For starters, Magellan, it's in the entirely opposite direction." Ulrich checked his rearview mirror. "Also, I have exams tomorrow."

"So do I."

"Well, some of us actually want our graduation certificates. And it's bad enough that you have me skipping school in the first place."

"I have *you* skipping?" She switched the radio off in disgust. "This was your idea, remember?"

"My idea was that *you* go there."

"Which I couldn't do, unless you drove me. And you got your license a year early out of it."

"From a counterfeiter and a hussy. I love you, but you're a terrible influence. Here." Reaching under his seat, he retrieved a worn road atlas and tossed it into her lap. "See if you can steer us straight. Don't forget that north is up."

Ich liebe dich. She felt, as she had in past weeks, a strange sense of disorientation over the declaration, as though he'd unintentionally called her by the wrong name.

Shaking the feeling off, Ava flipped through the Michelin until she found the route to the capital. For a moment she just stared at the inkblot-shaped space: Berlin. Embattled city of her birth. Hazily recalled hometown of her happiest years. And, she now knew, the starting point of a story she'd been seeking practically every day since she'd been weepingly removed from that city by Berlin's wartime Child Welfare services. Not her own sad-sack tale of abandonment and reluctant reunification with a mother uninterested in mothering. Nor was it Ilse's story; her mother kept that narrative locked inside her nearly as tightly as she'd have liked to keep Ava locked into their little yellow row house. This was another story, belonging to another parent: the nameless, unmentioned third in Ava's incomplete family triad.

Only he wasn't nameless any longer.

Her finger still on the former capital, Ava silently recited to herself the three words that had felt like a magical incantation when she first read them:

Nikolaus Gunther Hellewege.

And then, experimentally: *Mein Vater.*

The day's extraordinary expedition had its roots in what had started as a quite ordinary afternoon three months earlier. Sitting (unchaperoned) together atop Ulrich's rumpled bed, Ava and Ulrich had been doing what they now did nearly every day after school: French kissing, smoking English cigarettes, and listening to American music. Ulrich had also been filling out an application for his automobile learner's permit, and Ava had his birth certificate in her lap, along with a photograph that had slipped out of the file he'd kept it in. Holding the latter to the light, she'd tilted her head appreciatively. "She looked like an angel."

Ulrich's mother had been a lithe redhead with dark green eyes, though in the black-and-white photo she looked like a brown-eyed brunette. Either way, she'd been ethereally lovely in that way only women who have been dancers can be. "Seraphina Sara Bergen," Ava read dreamily off the certificate. "Even her name sounds angelic."

"It was meant to sound Jewish," he'd said, flipping over the form. "Her original middle name was Ingrid."

"Why'd she change it?"

"It was the law." His eyes were still on the application form. "All Jews had to have a Jewish-sounding middle name."

Ava frowned, trying to recall whether this bizarre detail had been covered in any of their patchy history lessons. Information on both world wars—but particularly the second one—was usually dispersed cryptically and vaguely: a terse chapter on Hitler's seemingly self-propelled ascent to power. A chalkboard list titled "Enemies of the Reich" that included *Communists*, *Jews*, and *Jehovah's Witnesses*. Far more traumatizing was the day her class was led to the school's downstairs auditorium, where with neither introduction nor explanation they were shown Alain Resnais's brutally blunt concentration camp documentary, *Night and Fog*. After the last searing images—walking corpses, cloth made from human hair, shower-room walls scored by scrabbling fingernails—had faded, the stunned students were let out early to be bludgeoned by the wintry afternoon brightness. After vomiting in the school courtyard Ava had looked for Ulrich—only to discover that he and the school's one other student of Jewish descent had quietly been given the whole afternoon off.

"So Jews had to choose new names?" she asked.

"There was no choice," he said, copying down the Opel's year, color, and make. "Men got 'Israel.' Women got 'Sara.'"

"*Israel?*" Ava grimaced. "The women got the better end of that deal, didn't they."

At that he did look up, briefly. Then he looked down again.

"Not really," he said.

Immediately she recognized her mistake. She knew his mother's story: how her marriage to his Catholic father staved off the cattle cars and the camps until the very last months of the war, when the dreaded "Notice of Deportation" was delivered to the *Judenhaus* they'd been forced into. How Doktor Bergen had pleaded with her to go into hiding at the home of one of his patients, and how she'd initially seemed to agree—only to slip out of her hiding spot on the appointed morning of her summons with her designated single suitcase. *I can't bear the thought*, she had written, *that an attempt to save myself might result in repercussions for you or—worse—for our child. Better to go quietly and alone than risk the lives of those I love.*

She'd been gassed almost immediately upon reaching Auschwitz.

"Oh, Uli." Ava covered her mouth with both hands. "I didn't mean that. I just . . . I just wasn't thinking . . ."

"It's fine," he said quietly. Taking the certificate back from her, he'd folded it into the application papers and set them between them on the bed. Leaning his head back against the wall, his eyes opaque behind his thick lenses, he'd fixed his gaze on his *Die Gefahr von Superman* movie poster: George Reeves with his dimpled muscles stuffed into his silly sausage suit. Mortified, Ava pulled her knees up under her chin and rested her forehead against the scratchy twill of her skirt.

"I'm a monster," she'd murmured.

"You're not," he'd said, covering her knee with his hand. "You're the most beautiful girl I know."

She just shook her head, feeling as unworthy of the compliment as she was the offer of comfort. "At least you *have* her name," she said finally. "At least you know both your parents' names."

Even to her own ears her voice sounded defensive, almost petulant. But when Ulrich spoke again, he didn't sound angry. He sounded thoughtful, alert. The way he sounded when he was shaping a particularly interesting political argument, or offering suggestions on one of Ava's art projects.

"Actually," he said, "you might too."

"What are you talking about? I might what?"

"Have both your parents' names."

She blinked back at him, baffled. He knew she knew nothing about her father. That as a child she'd been told—first by her grandparents, and then by nuns in the orphanage to which she'd been sent when they died—only that he'd been "a brave German soldier." She hadn't even known for sure that he was dead, though a few years ago Ilse—in a fleeting moment of approachability on the topic—had implied that he might not be. In general, though, she'd only say that she would tell Ava more details "when the time was right." Which, of course, it never had been.

"Your father's name would be on your birth certificate," Ulrich said now, retrieving his own certificate and pointing to his own father's name. "If she knew who he was, there'd have been no reason not to put it down."

Ava bit the inside of her cheek. On the one hand, it seemed impossible. And yet it also made sense, if only in the way fantastical things— bulky, square-jawed men flying through the air without wings, or the idea that she might actually *have* a father—did. Thoughts racing, she tugged at a lock of hair that still felt startlingly short following an impulsive session with Ilse's sewing shears (she'd been trying for a Hepburn-style pixie but ended up with something more resembling a poorly executed military cut).

"Even if she has it," she said slowly, "there's no way she'd hand it over to me. Especially if his name is actually on it."

"But she could order another one for you."

"She'd never do that either."

"She wouldn't have to." Setting the application materials aside, he gave her a quick kiss (*See? Forgiven!*) before sliding off the bed and padding over to his desk. "All you need is her signature. And you can dash that off in your sleep." Excited, he yanked open one drawer, then another. "Actually, I think I have an extra request form somewhere in here."

Sure enough, eight weeks later the official-looking envelope Ilse had unknowingly sent in for arrived at the Martinistraße post box she'd unknowingly subscribed to. Opening it with shaking hands, Ava first saw the Reich's fading black eagle, hovering with ghostly authority over the Charité Hospital's official letterhead. Below the faded stamp was Ava's name, weight, and time of birth, and below that was Ilse's name and city of residence.

And directly below that was the name of Ava's father.

Nikolaus Hellewege, she thought again now, as the Opel sped along the Autobahnzubringer Hemelingen. *City of residence: Berlin*. She'd promised herself not to waste her time daydreaming about a man who in all likelihood was not only dead, but dead in service of a cause she now knew to be unspeakably evil. And yet, as usual, her imagination refused to sit quietly and behave itself: like the chatty girl in a classroom, it continued to spin stories and trot out scenarios in which her newfound parent played various heroic and villainous roles. Perhaps they'd been classmates, Ilse and Nikolaus! Or neighbors! Maybe they'd met in a bomb shelter, and made passionate love as the walls shook and trembled around them (and perhaps this was the real reason Ava had never fully escaped the nightmarish grip of the bombing she herself had survived)! Or perhaps he'd been a rakish rebel, like James Dean or the boys who'd dumped Ava before Ulrich, seducing Ilse with a few roars of his motorcycle engine. But couldn't he also have been an artist (Ava had to get her talent from somewhere, after all), or even a bookish outsider like Ulrich?

Of all the possible options, this last one somehow seemed the least likely—if only because Ava couldn't fathom her mother with someone as good and kind as Ulrich was. Then again (she reflected), it *would* explain Ilse's aversion to Ava and Ulrich being involved. Perhaps he reminded her too much of the man who'd left her pregnant and alone.

Rolling the window back up, Ava rested her cheek against the glass and watched the bark-bare trees flashing past. *Nikolaus Hellewege*, she thought again. What had her mother called him? *Klaus*, perhaps? Or simply *Gunn*—perhaps he'd preferred his middle name to his first? Could he have had any part in choosing *her* name? Had he even known she was going to exist? *Ava Lara Hellewege*. She whispered it under her breath, exploring it like an exotic sweet on her tongue. What would this other, two-parented Ava have been like? Perhaps, simply, a better Ava: an Ava as understood and beloved by her father as she was misunderstood and overlooked by her mother. An Ava who sketched and painted without shame or blame, dated freely, took university classes when she liked . . .

"Are you awake over there?"

"What?" Blinking, Ava turned toward her driver.

"You look like you're in another world." Glancing in the side mirror, Ulrich switched lanes in order to pass a tomato-red VW pickup truck. "Also, you're about to start a fire."

Glancing down, Ava saw that the cigarette in the hand she'd left resting on the atlas had burned itself down to the filter. "Damn it." Flipping open the ashtray below the lighter, she stubbed the smoldering filter fully out. "Sorry. I barely slept last night."

"The license?"

"Just nerves, I think."

"Like I said, don't worry about it. First off, it's almost perfect. Secondly, those GDR yahoos can barely read. Just make sure you don't give anyone any lip." Another quick, pointed look.

"Of course I won't give them any lip," Ava said indignantly.

"And maybe put a hat on." Reaching out, he ruffled her botched hair. "If anything raises questions, it'll be that haircut."

"I thought you said it wasn't that bad." Ava checked her reflection in the side-view mirror again, futilely pulling a few strands toward her ears on both sides, as though she could physically force them to grow faster. (Another reason to love him: he still somehow thought she was *pretty*.)

"What I said," he said, deadpan, "was that it could have been worse."

"Isn't that the same thing?" Rummaging in her purse, she found her lipstick and carefully applied it to her top and bottom lip, then blotted it against her handkerchief.

"Not at all." He checked the speedometer, then tapped the brake lightly. "You could have shaved yourself bald. Or stabbed yourself in the eye with the scissors. You could have . . ."

"All *right*!" Reaching over, she shoved him in the shoulder. "Does makeup help, at least?"

He darted a quick, assessing glance. "Decidedly. Is that new?"

"Max Factor." She pursed her lips, Monroe-style. "I got it at Kaufhof." She didn't mention that she hadn't paid for it but rather slipped it into her purse while the saleswoman was helping another woman pick out cold cream. Though in her own defense Ava hadn't really had a choice: she couldn't borrow lipstick from Ilse because Ilse never wore makeup. And she certainly wouldn't give Ava money to buy it. ("Only tramps paint their faces at your age," she had said; she used the same disparaging measure for high heels.)

"I was a little worried it was too bright," Ava said now.

"No, the color is good." He looked at her again carefully. "It distracts from the disaster up top."

"You're a jackass." But she felt her lips twisting into a smile despite herself. Recapping the tube, Ava tossed it back into her purse, then leaned forward to give the radio another try. This time she was in luck: after an advertisement for Hamburg's "most popular dance hall," Fats Domino broke through the static, the rich voice like a honeyed sunshaft through a cloud. Pleased with herself, Ava leaned her head back and closed her eyes, humming along with the lyrics she knew by heart even if she didn't fully understand them:

You made me cry when you said good-bye

She felt Ulrich's strong, long-fingered hand on her knee, and heard his voice joining in as well, his American accent impeccable as always, his melody perfectly in tune:

Ain't that a shame

They sang together until they lost the station and Ava switched the radio off again. She lit him a cigarette, then another one for herself as well, and they drove on a few kilometers in smoky companionable silence, his hands gripping the wheel and hers her cigarette and the lighter. Watching the latter's round eye turn from molten orange to deep red to ash gray, she briefly fantasized about pressing it against the pale soft flesh on the inside of her arm. For some reason the idea of it—the searing pain, the singed skin—seemed less frightening than clarifying. Even bracing.

"If I ask you something," she said suddenly, "will you be honest with me?"

"Am I ever anything but?"

Still, she hesitated. "If it turns out he was one of the bad ones—the truly bad ones . . ."

He shook his head. "Wouldn't change anything between us."

"Even if he was, say, the one who locked your mother in the chamber? You won't hate me?"

He didn't even blink. "Not a whit."

She hadn't expected another answer, but relief washed over her anyway, so unexpectedly comforting she swayed a little in her seat. "You're sure?"

"You have my word." He looked at her sidelong, his glasses glinting in the hazy morning light. "Though if you're really that worried about it, it's not too late to turn back. We might even make it back by the end of school."

I do love him, she thought. *I do.* For how could she not love a boy who not only stole a car for her, and used a forged document for her, and not only drove her fully across the country, but who halfway there offered to stop and drive all the way *back*? Ava shut her eyes again, pressing the tip of her pinky lightly against the lighter's disc. It now felt only pleasantly warm.

"The hell with that," she said, opening her eyes. "We've made it this far."

After three more hours of driving, with a brief roadside stop for gas and sandwiches, they reached Helmstedt-Marienborn and the double-sided entry point to the German Democratic Republic. The guard on the West side waved them through with barely a glance at their documents. On the GDR side, though—a dreary line of cement-gray checkpoint stations manned by men in mold-colored uniforms—it was another story. Their guard—who barely looked old enough to drive himself—blinked at Ulrich's doctored license for a moment or two before tossing it back at him. But he studied Ava's student card with such a dubious-looking frown that she felt her palms start to sweat.

"No school today?" His face was round and puffy-looking, his nose bulbous and pink. His eyes, however, were an almost startling shade of teal—the eyes of a much more handsome man.

"It's a family emergency," she explained. It wasn't really a lie. And yet her pulse continued thrumming at the base of her throat as though she were covering up a murder. She wiped her palms on her skirt.

"From Bremen, you say?"

"*Ja.*"

"Destination?"

"Berlin. Reinickendorf. Same as my friend's."

"Only friends, eh?" He leered openly at her breasts.

"Yes," said Ava, wondering why she said it even as she did. Crossing her arms across her chest, she scowled. "Yes," she repeated. "He's driving me to see my dad."

"Who doesn't live in Bremen, I take it."

"That's correct." Avoiding his eyes, she fixed her gaze instead on the flimsy-looking Trabi that had just pulled into the checkpoint station to their right. The man driving it had a long, glum face that resembled a camel's, though perhaps the glumness was because the woman next to him was shouting at him. Ava watched as the latter—with a final shot at the driver—stepped from the vehicle's passenger side and walked slowly around to the car's rear. She seemed visibly agitated, gesticulating with one hand and dabbing at her face with the other with a handkerchief. Ava couldn't tell if she was wiping tears or perspiration.

"Divorced?"

"What?" Ava snapped her gaze up again.

"Your parents," the guard said. His skin was so pale that it almost looked gray in the shade of the checkpoint's concrete overhang. "Are they divorced?"

"That's not really . . ." She'd planned to say *any of your business*, but before she got the words out she felt Ulrich's glance, as pointed as a physical dig in the ribs. "Not something I like talking about," she finished lamely.

The guard shrugged. "Seems to happen a lot with you *Wessis*. Bourgeois values, I suppose." Handing the card back, he pointed at the purse in her lap. "Mind if I have a look?"

"Seriously?" Ava looked at her watch. Their appointment in the city was in just under two hours; they were already cutting it close.

But Ulrich was already leaning over and reaching across her lap. "Of course we don't mind," he said firmly. Picking the bag up, he pushed it at their interrogator. "Take your time, comrade."

"*Danke.*" The guard lifted the bag with his black-leather-gloved hands, fumbling for a moment with the snap. Biting her lip in vexation, Ava returned her gaze to the Trabi. Its trunk was now open and the weepy-or-sweaty female was speaking animatedly while the guard rummaged through its contents. As Ava watched, he pulled out a box of some kind and held it up, a triumphant look on his face.

"So you're an artist?"

Glancing back at their own guard, Ava saw with dismay that he'd removed the little sketchbook she carried everywhere with her and had opened to a self-portrait she'd done of herself a few nights earlier. It was a full view of her nude torso, neck to navel, etched out minimally with a handful of charcoal lines. There was no way for the guard to connect the image to her personally (she'd left the head out because she hated her hair). But she found herself flushing anyway. "I try."

He held the book to the light, his head tilted as his gaze flickered back and forth between her face and the page. For a terrifying moment she wondered whether she'd unwittingly broken another law: trafficking in pornography, perhaps. But he simply shrugged.

"Nice tits," he said crisply, and tossed the sketchbook through the window.

Her face flushing, Ava flipped quickly through pages, checking for the carefully filled-out forms they'd need later and suppressing a sigh of relief when she found them. But the guard wasn't done yet: after digging a bit more he pulled out the fragrance spritzer Ava carried with her to cover the smell of cigarettes before she went home at night, since (of course) Ilse disapproved of smoking. At the moment, it contained the last of the Guerlain L'Heure Bleue that Ulrich had brought back for her from a recent trip to France.

"What's this?" the guard asked.

"Perfume."

He unscrewed the bulbed top of the little flask and held the vessel beneath his nose. "German?"

"French."

"*Ooh-la-la.*" He lifted his brows again. "Smells expensive."

"I don't know," she said shortly. "It was a gift."

The guard nodded pleasantly. Then, keeping his sky-blue gaze locked on hers, he poured the pale liquid onto the ground.

"What??" Ava sat up sharply in her seat. "What the hell . . ."

"It's fine," Ulrich muttered.

"Why did you do that?" she hissed, ignoring him.

"You clearly didn't read up on our rules." The guard smiled condescendingly. "You're not permitted to bring foreign luxury goods worth over twenty-five marks over the border."

"But it was a *gift*. How am I supposed to know how much it's worth?"

"Perhaps next time, simply ask."

Opening her mouth to argue, Ava threw a furious glance at Ulrich. Seeing his expression, she shut it again and simply glared. The guard laughed, clearly pleased with the reaction.

"Just be thankful I didn't arrest you for smuggling." Still smiling, he screwed the cap back on and tossed both the purse and the empty bottle back into her lap. Flipping his rubber stamp and inkpad from his pocket, he marked her card with a flourish.

"Have a nice visit with Papa," he said, handing it back through the window.

"What an *Arschloch*." As Ulrich pulled onto the dreary gray road Ava realized she was shaking.

"Could have been worse. That Eastern couple is still back there."

Ava looked over her shoulder and saw that he was right: the blue Trabi was now parked by the side of the road, while its occupants—the weepy woman and camel-faced man—huddled beside it.

"What's going on with them, do you think?"

He shrugged. "Either they were trying to smuggle something in, or the guard was in the mood for some extra cash. Or maybe both."

"And all that, for the honor of being *here*." Glancing out the window, Ava shook out another B&H. They were barely out of the FRG, and yet already the landscape seemed to belong to a completely different universe. The road itself—before the border black and smooth—looked bleached with age and populated mostly by more toylike Trabants. The fields flanking the highway flickered by in dried-out tones of brown and beige, broken by the occasional dirty-looking buildings. Even the air felt heavier, more stifling. She pulled her knees up to her chest, arranging her woolen circle skirt around them.

"And this is the good part," he said. "Once you get farther in, there are places where it looks like the war's still on." He looked at her again curiously. "Why'd you tell him we were just friends?"

She shrugged. "I don't know. I guess I thought that if I got myself into trouble it'd be better that way for you."

He nodded, his expression unreadable. For a moment neither of them spoke. "I can't believe you've never made the crossing before," he said at last.

"I know." The change of topic came as a relief. "Ilse sometimes goes to Berlin for work. But she's never taken me. She's always had the old witch next door spend the night."

"The one with the wart on her nose?"

Ava nodded, smiling slightly. "When I was little, I'd lie awake waiting for her to try to shove me into her cooking pot. Or turn me into a log and burn me. Like Mother Trudy."

"Interesting," he said in English, in his Sherlock Holmes voice. "Do you think our prim and proper Ilse was hiding a Berlin lover?"

Ava grimaced. "God, I hope not."

"Why not? She's a good-looking woman."

Ava looked at him flatly. "You're going to make me vomit. Seriously." She took another drag on her cigarette, then coughed. Her eyes stung from lack of sleep and surplus smoke. "Any man who touches her," she went on glumly, "probably gets frostbite. That's probably what we'll find out happened to my father. Poor Nikolaus. Frozen to death before he even saw his firstborn child."

"Lucky we don't have that problem." He flashed a sly smile in her direction. "If anything, touching you makes me too hot."

It was true: the first few times they'd consummated their new status he'd been so ardent that it was over before they'd technically started. Secretly, Ava found she hadn't minded; while not unpleasant, their lovemaking left her feeling strangely distanced, as though he were an embattled athlete and she a spectator, watching from the stands. She'd struggled to understand why this should be. After all, she hadn't felt this sort of remove with either of her prior boyfriends—both of whom had been immeasurably less devoted and considerate. Then again (she wondered), could that itself be the issue: that Ulrich's love was so certain, so densely unconditional that it actually pushed her *away*? The thought struck her as both absurd and unaccountably unsettling.

"Sorry," she said, and turned back to the window. As she started rolling it up, a building outside caught her attention: bone white and surrounded with rubble, it was little more than a bombed-out shell. It was like passing an enormous open grave.

The crossing into West Berlin took longer than out of West Germany, though only because of the backed-up traffic: once their turn came the harried guards barely glanced at either of them before waving them on their way. As they left the East behind, the scenery shifted with the same through-the-looking-glass instantaneousness: the roads once more freshly tarred, the cars shiny and large, the buildings taller and seemingly freshly minted. Even the pedestrians seemed cleaner and better fed, their clothes newer, their strides longer and more energetic. As Ulrich squeezed between a bright red bus and a Gevalia delivery truck sporting a coffeepot-style handle and spout, Ava took it all in with widened eyes and a pounding heart. To the left she spotted a palacelike movie theater with enormous posters advertising Charlton Heston in *The Ten Commandments.*

"Seem familiar?" he asked.

"We saw it together last week."

"I mean the city."

She shook her head. "But I haven't been here since I was five."

"You really don't remember anything at all?"

What she remembered were less memories than age-blurred flashes of image: the blue muslin coverlet on her old bed in her grandparents' house. The green kitchen table where she'd made her first drawing and spent hours every day, drawing more. The suffocating blackness of the collapsing cellar as the Allied bombs rained upon them; the chalky rubble she woke up to after they'd pulled her out.

The white sheets covering the battered bodies of Oma and Opa.

Her *Oma*'s slipper-shod foot, poking out.

She shook her head. "Nothing," she said. "Not a thing."

Twenty minutes later they were at their destination: an imposing red-brick structure on Eichborndamm Avenue in Reinickendorf. A blue-framed sign by the door somewhat pompously identified it as the Archives for the Notification of the Next of Kin of the Fallen Members of the Former German Wehrmacht. Reading it twice, Ava felt her chest contract. This was the organization the Census Department had suggested she contact to find out more about the man who was her father. "If he's a soldier," the woman had said, "they should have the basics, at least. It may take a few weeks for them to find the file, but as long as you can prove you're family they'll show it to you."

Family, she thought now. As a word, it had always felt foreign to her: it didn't fit her and Ilse's small, tense unit of two. Which was strange, since it seemed to fit Ulrich and his father, who were just as alone and (thanks to Doktor Bergen's schedule) together even less frequently.

She felt Ulrich's hand on her shoulder.

"Not to push the point," he said. "But it's still not too late to turn around and go home. I won't say a word about it."

She looked up at him; the amiable, ironic face. The close-cropped dark hair that he refused to grow out and wear slicked back like most boys did, because he said it looked absurd on anyone who wasn't American. *I love you,* Ava thought, but this time too it felt less like a declaration than a quiet reminder.

"No," she said. "If I don't do this, I'll hate myself for it." She straightened her coat. "I hate myself enough as it is."

Inside the building a burly attendant at the enormous *Auskunft* desk directed them up the stairs to the records room, a windowless space that smelled of dust and old paper and was lit by buzzing yellow fluorescent lights. Behind an even larger desk, a mannish woman with hair shorter than Ava's (but better cut) was typing furiously on an antique-looking Adler typewriter. Ava retrieved the two forms from her notebook. Smoothing them out, she slid them across the worn wooden surface.

"Tag," she said.

"Yes?" The woman looked up, waiting.

Ava cleared her throat. "I'm Ava von Fischer. We had an appointment for some research."

The woman scanned the forms, then glanced at her watch. "You are half an hour late."

"The crossing took longer than we'd expected."

"It always does," the woman informed them. "I'll have to see whether the results of your search are still available."

Ava suppressed a pulse of panic. "If not, we can wait."

"I'm afraid that's not an option. If they've been returned to the archives you'll need to file a new request, resend payment, and return another time."

Picking up the forms, the woman hurried back between the file-filled shelves as Ulrich gave Ava a sidelong glance. "Six-hour drive back," he murmured. "We can't wait very long."

"I'll take the bus back," she snapped, knowing full well that she wouldn't need to, that he'd stay with her for as long as she needed him to stay.

Fighting back a faint wave of claustrophobia, Ava returned her gaze to the records area. The boxes, she now saw, didn't only contain forms and files. Some were filled with objects: old, tarnished pocket watches. Brass buttons and pins. One contained a tangle of what at first looked like jewelry but which she quickly saw were old, rusted dog tags. She tried to guess how many soldiers they'd been stripped from, how many bodies they'd done their grim job of identifying. In her mind's eye, she saw a shuffling crowd of grimy-faced men in helmets, staring balefully back from the other side of their shared, blackened history. What were their final thoughts as they lay bleeding in the snow or mud? Had they died proud of their sacrifice? Or had they realized by then that it was all nothing more than a vicious trick; a foolish fable concocted by a madman whose only legacy would be the rest of the world's loathing and revulsion?

"Fräulein von Fischer?"

Looking up, Ava saw the mannish woman walking briskly back toward them, a thin file in her hand. "You're in luck," she said. "He still had the material out on his desk. Another ten minutes or so and it would have gone back to the stacks."

Ava felt her breath lodge in her throat. "You mean . . . you mean you found him?"

"Your father?" Setting the files down before them, the administrator nodded. "Which is itself remarkable, given that you didn't give a birth date for him."

"I didn't know one," Ava mumbled.

"And your mother?"

"She didn't either," Ava lied.

The woman studied her for a moment, her gaze lingering on the ridiculous haircut, the overcompensating red lips. "Nevertheless," she pronounced coldly. "Against the odds, he was able to narrow it down based on name and city of birth."

Reaching out, Ava touched the cardboard with the tip of her finger. Her mouth suddenly felt as though she'd swallowed ash. "It doesn't look like there's very much there." It came out sounding like a question.

"In general, all we have access to here at the notification service are the basics: drafting dates, dog tag numbers, training units, and war units. And of course, whether he was taken captive or injured. If you want more information, you might find it at the Bundesarchiv in Potsdam. They keep records on SA, SS, and Waffen-SS officers."

Ava looked up quickly. "Was he in one of those?"

"I don't know," said the woman curtly. "I haven't read the file."

She waved her free hand in the direction of one of the small wooden tables by the door. "You are welcome to take notes of this if you like. We also offer mimeograph services and a limited research facility downstairs."

And without another word, she reseated herself in her work chair and turned back to whatever it was that she'd been typing, the keys striking the canister with the force and impact of rapid gunshots.

Swallowing, Ava picked up the file. It was smooth and cool against her fingers. Across the top tab, someone had written in purple block letters the three words that had composed her constant inner mantra these past weeks: *Hellewege, Nikolaus Gunther.*

Clutching it to her chest with both hands, Ava made her way to one of the desks, Ulrich in tow. As they sat down together she felt his hand rest on her knee.

"Whatever it is," he told her quietly, "it will be fine. You know that, right?"

"I don't know anything," she said. "Nothing at all." Yet even as she said it, there came the slightly dizzying sense that some undefined stage of her life was ending. And with that came a strange grief, a kind of mourning for a self she somehow already knew would cease to exist, once she'd seen what lay between these two smooth, stiff covers.

Part of her wanted to stop then: to leave the file unopened and return it to the mannish, disapproving woman. To save that simple, naïve Ava before it was too late. Then she thought about all the years of silence that had led to this moment: silence on Ava's part, when asked about her father. Silence on Ilse's part when Ava asked the same. She thought about the empty ache of their two-person household: the sense that no matter how placid and content Ilse seemed within it, there was always that sense of something missing, something hidden. Something *wrong*. She heard it again: her mother's calm, cool voice: *We will discuss it when you are ready. When you're older.*

Nein, Ava thought. *No. We will discuss it tonight.*

She lifted the cover.

જ

It was after midnight, but lights blazed in every window of the little house: Ilse lying in wait.

As quietly as she could, Ava shut the car door and gave Ulrich a grim wave. Then she hooked her purse over her forearm and started making her way down the darkened street.

Behind her, she heard the Opel's window rolling creakily down.

"Ava," Ulrich called out softly.

Glancing back, she saw him leaning out, one elbow on the driver's-side door, the streetlight glinting off his glasses.

"I meant what I said in the car," he said. "He may have been your father. That doesn't make it your fault."

It was, in fact, essentially the only thing he'd said in the car, on the strained and interminable drive back to Bremen. Climbing back into the passenger seat, Ava had felt both numb and searingly hollow, as though the truth they'd uncovered were a bomb ripping through her, destroying everything she'd ever known of herself. "I don't want to talk about it," she'd replied curtly. "I don't want to talk at all." And so he'd sat stiffly at the wheel while Ava curled herself toward the window, alternately smoking and weeping in silence.

Now she nodded, not in agreement but to show that she'd heard him.

"I'll see you tomorrow," he added. Again she nodded, though for the first time in her life she found she didn't *want* to see him. Or rather, didn't want him to see *her* as she was now: shamed and shattered, indelibly tainted by the toxic secret they both suddenly shared.

When she reached the front doorstep she opened her purse for her usual tobacco-masking spritz, before remembering that her remaining stock of Guerlain L'Heure Bleue had long since evaporated along the East German border. Pushing past the empty bottle, she fumbled instead for her keys. The movement was all but noiseless (another habit formed by her frequent late-night escapes), but before she even had them in her hand the door was swinging almost violently open.

Flinching slightly, Ava blinked.

Ilse stood in the door frame, her silhouette briefly featureless and black against the bright spill of electric light. As Ava's eyes adjusted she saw her mother still had on her office clothes: the gray wool skirt and matching jacket she wore on days when she met with the magazine's chief editor. The sensible midheeled pumps. The only clue that she hadn't just walked in from work was the fact that her leather gloves were neatly folded on the front-hall bureau and her felt hat hung from the coatrack. As Ava set her own gloves and purse on the bureau, she felt Ilse's icy gaze raking her back. Her motions unhurried and careful, Ava began undoing her jacket.

"Well?"

Loosening the last button, Ava shrugged free from her sleeves and hung the coat on the rack before turning to face her mother. "Well, what?"

"Your headmaster called me today. At work. He wanted to make sure that everything was all right, since it's the third time in two months that I've excused you for doctor's appointments."

Ava allowed herself a small smile. "It's very nice that he cares."

Ilse's face seemed to go a shade paler. "How dare you," she hissed. "First you forge my signature. Then you come in at this hour—on a school night—reeking of cigarettes. After a day of God-only-knows-what. Have you no decency? None at all?"

Decency, Ava thought. But still, she didn't speak. Pressing her lips together tightly, she picked up her purse and made her way toward the kitchen.

"Were you with Ulrich again?" Ilse was hot on her heels, her outrage fanned by Ava's feigned ignorance of it. "You were, weren't you," Ilse continued. "I knew it. I told that man this would happen. How far have you gone with him, then? Dear God. Please tell me you haven't gotten yourself pregnant."

They had reached the kitchen now. Purse clutched beneath her arm, Ava took a mug from the cupboard, allowing herself a quick, longing glance at the little bottle of herbal digestif and the bigger one of sherry, the only alcohol Ilse kept in the house. Then she turned back to the sink, where she filled the mug with water and carried it to the kitchen table.

Placing the purse in front of her, she sank heavily into one of the kitchen chairs and folded her arms across her chest. Then, and only then, did she lift her eyes.

Ilse stood in the doorway, her gray eyes glassy in the stark kitchen light. Her arms were folded across her chest so tightly Ava could make out the rising muscles of her forearms beneath the fabric of her blouse.

"Well?" she prompted. "Are you?"

"Am I what?"

"Pregnant. Are you pregnant?"

Beneath the audible anger Ava sensed a new note: not just uncertainty, but actual fear. The realization made her shiver slightly, not from fear of her own, but from an unfamiliar and almost dizzying sense of power. Apart from one fleeting moment on the day Ilse fetched her from the orphanage, she couldn't recall a single time when her mother had seemed afraid of anything. It was almost enough to make her want to simply say it. To say: *Yes, I'm pregnant.* Just to coax that tiny seed of trepidation into a full-fledged bloom of horror.

Instead she took a sip of water. "No. All we did was drive."

Ilse's pale brows lifted slightly. "Drive where? Drive how?"

"In Doktor Bergen's car. To Berlin."

"Doktor Bergen drove you to Berlin?"

"Not Doktor Bergen. Ulrich. Ulrich drove us."

"*Ulrich?*" Ilse's face tightened further. "But he isn't old enough to drive unaccompanied. He doesn't have his *Führerschein.*"

"He does now." Ava shrugged, watching as comprehension dawned on her mother's chiseled face. It was closely shadowed by disbelief.

"And Doktor Bergen," she said tightly. "He knew of this expedition?"

Ava dropped her gaze to her mug. The water in it, slightly brown from the rust in the pipes, shivered slightly in response to some unseen vibration. It reminded her of the scene from *Godzilla, King of the Monsters!* when the giant lizard is closing in, still unseen.

"So let me repeat what you are saying." Each of her mother's words was barbed with fury now. "You forged my signature to skip school for the third time in the last two months. You let a boy you aren't supposed to be seeing unchaperoned, and who can't legally drive, drive you out of the country, with falsified documents, in a car he'd stolen from his father. And you drove to Berlin—*Berlin!*—and back. In one day." She gave a short laugh of disbelief. "My God, Ava. You've become a criminal! Right before my eyes!"

Ava jerked her head up. "*I'm* the criminal?" She felt it again now: the queasy stab of foreboding as she'd taken down the name of her father's division in the East. The raw shock when she looked it up in the little downstairs library. "If I am," she said bitterly, "it's your own fault, isn't it. You're the one who gave me a criminal for a father."

"*Was?*" Ilse blinked at her.

"My father," Ava repeated. "I know what he did. I found out about it today. That's why I went to Berlin."

For a moment her mother simply stared at her.

"Your father was a soldier," she said at last. "And you know nothing about him."

"I know more than enough now."

"What on earth are you talking about?"

Ava pulled her purse into her lap. Unsnapping the clasp, she withdrew the birth certificate and held it out.

Her mother took it warily, her pale eyes not moving from Ava's face until she had it in her hands. When she looked up, her jaw was tight. "Where did you get this?"

Ava allowed herself a small smile. "You ordered it for me."

"I . . ." Her mother took a sharp breath as this sank in as well. "My God," she said. "What has happened to you?"

"What happened to *me*?" Ava's voice was shaking now. She didn't care. "What happened is that you wouldn't tell me about my father. I decided to find out for myself."

Her mother was shaking her head slowly. "I told you I'd tell you when it was time. It isn't time yet. You're not ready. You're not . . ." She hesitated, bit her lip. "It was complicated."

"There's nothing complicated about murder."

"Murder?" Her mother's eyes widened, then narrowed. "What on earth are you talking about? It wasn't murder."

"What do you call it, then?"

Ilse hesitated. Ava recrossed her arms over her chest and waited. She could almost see her mother's mind working furiously through the pale windows of her silvery eyes, could see the mental calculus behind Ilse's next response. *What have I told her. How much does she know. How much can I get away with not saying.*

At last, sighing, she crossed the blue-checked linoleum floor and pulled the chair opposite Ava's out for herself. "You must understand," she said, slowly lowering herself into it, "that things were . . . different in those days. At the time, we—he—simply thought of it as journalism. We didn't think of it as propaganda."

"Is that what you thought he did?" Even to her own ears, Ava's laugh sounded shrill, slightly mad. *"Propaganda?"*

"It is what he did." Ilse looked affronted. "I know. We worked together. It's why . . ." Seeming to catch herself, she stopped and shook her head. "He was a journalist."

Ava started to laugh again, then stopped as it dawned on her that her mother was speaking in earnest.

"Do you really not know what he did in the East?" she asked quietly. "In Russia?"

"All I knew was that he was working for a general." Ilse didn't break her gaze; she didn't even blink. "I forget the name. Someone quite high up. I think Kai made his appointments, took letters. That sort of thing. When I asked for more details he told me it was all classified."

"It's not classified anymore." Heart pounding again, Ava reached into her purse and pulled out her sketchbook.

"What—" Ilse started.

"Notes," Ava interrupted. "From the army notification archives. That's where Ulrich and I went today. Would you like to hear them?"

Ilse looked dazed. "You went . . ."

But Ava was already flipping past her sketches to the shakily inscribed page where she'd jotted down phrases and dates. Not waiting for an answer, she started reading:

"Prior to his 1944 death at the hands of his Soviet captors, SS-Scharführer Hellewege was personal secretary and aide to SS-Obergruppenführer-General Max von Schenckendorff, commander of rear guard operations on the Eastern Front."

Ilse nodded faintly. "That was it. Von Schenkendorff."

Ava ignored her. *"Von Schenkendorff is perhaps best known for an infamous three-day field conference on partisan counteroperations in the*

Russian city of Mogilev, held in 1942. Conference participants were bused to the nearby settlement of Knyazhichi for hands-on antipartisan training. However, upon finding that the town did not harbor partisans, Hellewege screened the existent population and compiled a list of the town's fifty-one Jews."

At the word *Juden* Ava glanced up briefly. Her mother's face was ashen, her hands clenched before her on the table. She had gone very still.

"Of those," Ava continued, *"thirty-one—composed of men, women, and children—were summarily . . ."* She shut her eyes, overcome again by what she was about to read. It was the first time she'd said it aloud.

"Thirty-one—" she repeated, *"composed of men, women, and children—were summarily executed in the town square."*

As she finished, the words—furiously dashed off in what now seemed another lifetime—swam before her. She felt it return: that strangely weightless sensation of floating in murky, filthy water, pushed by a current over which she had no control: *He did this*, she thought. *The man from whose seed I came into being. The man whose blood is in my blood.* In her mind's eye she was once more watching Ulrich read the page, his jaw tightening. His brown eyes hesitating for just the briefest, the most heart-sickening of moments before lifting to meet hers again.

When she opened her eyes, her mother hadn't moved. Not a single muscle on her fine-boned face twitched. It was impossible to tell whether she was shocked or frightened or embarrassed. It was impossible to tell if she'd heard Ava at all.

Ava shut the sketchbook with a snap that sounded like a gunshot against the linoleum-limned silence.

"So that," she said, "was his *classified* work. Finding innocent men, women, and children for his special forces to murder." She laughed huskily. "A real hero, my father."

Ilse didn't answer at first. When she finally spoke she seemed to be addressing not Ava but her own strong hands. They were clutched together so tightly that the knuckles looked bluish.

"He told me he was just going to be taking dictation and writing more propaganda."

"And you expect me to believe that."

"It's the truth." When Ilse lifted her gaze, her eyes were unflinching. "I swear it. I had no idea at all."

"How is that possible?" Ava set the notebook down with a thud. "You went to see him."

"Never." Ilse shook her head. "He posted to Lodz first, that October. After you were born we wrote a few times. I never saw him again."

Ava stared at her. "October," she said. "He went in October?"

"October 1939." Ilse nodded. "Two weeks after the Polish victory. I remember it clearly."

"But I was born the next August," Ava said slowly. "You must have seen him at least once after he left."

Ilse's face was so white and still that she looked less like Ilse than a marble sculpture of herself. "I won't discuss this any longer," she said.

She stared back at her daughter with eyes the color of a river in winter. Ava stared back. And then it dawned on her, another sickening truth: that despite everything that had happened today—the endless drive, the horrific file, the harsh, dark shadow now cast between Ava and her best friend in the world—nothing with her mother had altered in the slightest.

The realization loosed within her a shock wave of sheer rage. She wanted to leap up, to scream out: *Tell me! Just tell me you knew about him. You knew it all. You knew he was slaughtering innocent people!* But it suddenly felt as though her throat, mouth, and lips were coated in the same plaster dust that had filled them when they'd dragged her from the wreckage of her grandparents' house. And just as it had hit her that day, it hit her again now: the fact that everything had changed in that world, but nothing in this one. That no notebook, no grainy image, no certificate forged or genuine, would be strong enough to pry open Ilse's locked chest of secrets. That when confronted with the proof of her lies and half truths, her mother would simply continue cleaving to the same, icy wall of silence she'd erected the first day of their joyless reunion.

Slumping forward, Ava covered her face with her hands, struggling to catch a full breath. She felt terrified and abandoned and shockingly alone. Yet when she heard Ilse stand up, a childish part of her leapt up too, in hope: *She's going to take my hand, and say she is sorry. She's going to tell me everything, at last.*

But when she looked up she saw that Ilse wasn't coming around the table to her. She wasn't even looking in Ava's direction. Instead, she was slowly making her way toward the kitchen door.

"Where . . . where are you going?"

Hand on doorknob, Ilse turned to face her. "It's late," she said. "I am going to bed, and I suggest you do the same. You are going to school tomorrow if I have to walk you myself. And you are staying there. Am I understood?"

Ava licked her lips. *No,* she thought. *No, not at all.*

But what she said, in a voice that felt thick and gravelly and strange to her, was "You are."

"Gut," said Ilse. "Turn out the light when you go to bed."

And with that, she was gone.

9

Renate

1937

*I*lse walks quickly, her eyes locked on the huffing train, valise swinging from her hand like a carpet-toned pendulum. It is raining. A half step behind her Renate half skips and half jogs, struggling as always to keep pace.

"What time does it leave?" she asks, breathless.

"Fourteen hours sharp," her friend replies. "But I want to make sure we get seats together."

"Wait—you mean I'm coming with you?" Renate's heart leaps: she'd thought she was here merely to see Ilse off on her journey. But she hasn't packed anything she would need for an eight-month posting to the Eastern border. In fact, she hadn't even applied for one. Only BDM members are eligible.

Ilse just rolls her eyes. "Of course you are, *Dummkopf*. You don't think I'd just *leave* you here, do you?"

"But I don't have my suitcase."

"So?" Ilse shrugs. "We'll share."

"And I don't have a ticket."

"I have one for you, silly." Grinning, Ilse holds it up in her right hand. The ticket is white with elaborate, embossed Gothic lettering that is as bright as the friendship ring on her best friend's finger. Seeing it fills Renate with a sudden sense of liquid lightness. *She didn't mean it*, she thinks jubilantly. *She didn't mean any of it.* She wants to throw her arms around the other girl: to cry and laugh in relief.

But Ilse has already resumed walking. "Hurry," she calls over her shoulder, as the train looses a long, sharp whistle. "They won't wait for us. Look—they've already started closing the door."

"Yes, I'm coming." Renate tries to run to catch up, but something is wrong with her shoes; the soles are slipping and scuffling against the wet asphalt as though seeking traction on ice. It's like Alice running with the Red Queen in Wonderland: no matter how fast her legs move she remains in the same place.

Meanwhile Ilse has already reached the train. "You have to *hurry*," she shouts over her shoulder. "Run! Do you hear me, Reni? *Run!*"

I do, Renate tries to shout. *Of course I do. Wait.* But when she parts her lips nothing emerges but a dry croak. Helpless, she flings her arms out as Ilse pounds on the carriage's closed door (*bang-bang-bang*), still shouting her name: "Reni. *Reni!*"

Bang.

"Reni? Are you up?"

Renate opens her eyes, her panicked heart pounding in the dream's dreadful wake. Her bedside light is still on, and the book she fell asleep reading sometime after two a.m. (*The Rains Came*, about floods and love in colonial India) lies half open next to her pillow. She pulls herself up in the bed slowly as the bedroom door bangs and rattles, her brother's annoyed voice sounding over the racket: "Hey, slug! Are you even awake?"

"I'm awake," she mumbles, reaching for her bedside water glass.

"Lisbet says you've a half hour to make your school trip."

The water tastes like dust. Renate drinks it anyway while simultaneously rolling her eyes. She finds Franz's new habit of addressing their parents by name both pretentious and profoundly annoying.

"I'm up," she lies, and throws the book at the floor to simulate the effect of her feet landing there. The door emits one final, aggrieved rattle before the sound gives way to her brother's heavy, uneven footsteps on their way back down the stairs. "She says she's up," she hears him call, his tone deliberately dubious.

Stretching painfully, Renate turns off the lamp and slowly slides from the rumpled bed. Making her way to the window, she stares out at the sleepy avenue, undisturbed but for a half-empty double-decker bus and a horse-drawn *Milchwagen* topped by clattering cans. Her heart rate has slowed, but there's a chill emptiness in her gut in the wake of the dream's cruel bait-and-switch: the dangled glimpse of that desperately longed-for reconciliation. The waking truth of its ever-clearer impossibility. *Textbook anxiety dream*, her mother would call it (and she would know, having written two textbooks on dreams). But why now? Renate hasn't dreamt of Ilse—who actually is off on a yearlong Land Service assignment—in well over a month. And it's certainly not as if Ilse has written her; not even a postcard, much less the long, newsy sort of letter she used to write when she went on holiday. Then again, as recently as this summer her former friend was still appearing in Renate's dreams nearly nightly. The possibility that that nocturnal haunting might be about to reassert itself is enough to spark a dull shudder.

Shaking it off, Renate resolves to turn her thoughts to pleasanter topics—and for once, there is actually something pleasant to contemplate. For at exactly eight thirty today, her class will depart for the Berlin-Charlottenburg station and ride the U-Bahn together to Museum Island. There they will wander the Nordic Antiquities collection at the Neues, making sketches and jotting down thoughts and notes. Renate has always loved museum trips: The marvel of craftsmanship that's endured for centuries. The way that age can be a ghostly presence in itself. This year, however, she has literally been counting down to the field trip. She's not entirely certain she could survive the regular routine for another day.

Things at Bismarck Gymnasium have been bad now for months.

But they got dramatically worse in late December, when Karolin Beidryzcki—the school's last remaining full Jew—was finally and summarily expelled. As with all the *Juden* expulsions it happened with ruthless speed: one minute her old friend was surveying a trigonometry midterm. The next, she was piling her desk's contents into a battered cardboard box, her eyes damp behind her perpetually broken glasses.

Looking back on it now, Renate knows that she shouldn't have been surprised. Karolin had been the last full Jew in their class, the others having departed either for Jewish schools or for other, more Jewish-friendly countries. Rumor had it that the only reason Karolin had kept her place for so long was that her father had paid the headmaster for the privilege. Though to be truthful, Renate couldn't understand why she'd even *wanted* to stay: from what she saw, the girl's life had become a gauntlet of daily torment. Not only had Karolin's teachers persisted in giving her poor and failing grades, but she'd been pushed, mocked, and even spit upon in the hallways; excluded from field trips, clubs, and films; and made to change into her gym uniform separately from the other girls. She'd told Renate that she could bear it all only because she knew that she'd soon be following her brother Martin to America—she was just waiting for her visa to be approved. But apparently Schuldirektor Heintz decided that she needed to wait elsewhere. Or else Herr Beidryzcki had finally run out of funds.

For her own part, Renate has managed school survival as a *Mischling* by keeping scrupulously to herself. She returns greetings when they are offered but initiates none of her own. All other verbal exchanges are kept short, and purely functional.

Most of all, though, she reads.

Reading, she's discovered, gives her an excuse to avoid eye contact, and avoiding eye contact goes a long way in avoiding the sorts of unpleasant encounters that last year sometimes left her in tears. Like Sophia Sitz's hateful one-way Palestine ticket. Or the time a few months later, when Trude Baumgarten waved her over in the library—only to ask her whether it was true her father killed "white" babies and drank their blood. Or the time a friend of Rudi's called Renate's mother a "Jew-loving whore"—right in front of Rudi himself, and Rudi not only said nothing but actually *laughed*. In such cases, Renate has learned, reading also gives her an excuse to not respond; she can simply pretend she hasn't heard them.

Over the last year, therefore, she's made a point of reaching her desk early enough to be reading (or pretending to) when other students arrive. She also reads in the school courtyard, in darkened corners of the library, and on the toilet when she goes to the WC. She even reads on the walk to and from school on some days, stepping slowly and very carefully.

She reads anything and everything, barring the books that have been banned. Lately she's even found herself doubling or even trebling up, as though one fictional storyline alone is no longer enough to distract herself from the troubling narrative of her own life. Before *The Rains Came* she reread every Pearl Buck book in the Charlottenburg library, followed by Baring's *Daphne Adeane* at the same time she was reading Shakespeare's *Henry the Eighth*. She read *The Wind in the Willows* for a third time and then read it again, between readings of Rilke and Heine and Tennyson. She read *Winnie the Pooh* twice as well, the first time to herself, the second aloud to her father, who clearly needed a laugh. In addition to *Through the Looking-Glass* she has read the new translation of *Alice's Adventures in Wonderland* and took Franz up on his challenge to memorize *The Hunting of the Snark*, Carroll's Jabberwocky-inspiring nonsense poem, in English. Initially she did this only to prove she could. But she came to find the poem strangely soothing in its absurdity, and now often recites it to herself when she feels bored or upset—which, despite all of her reading—is increasingly often.

For a brief period, she had dared to hope that in the wake of Karolin's ouster she might be able to let her guard down; that stripped of its final target, the vicious anti-*Juden* spotlight that had shone so hotly on her friend would dim a little, or perhaps a lot. Or maybe just shut off altogether. Instead, its loathsome focus simply shifted to the school's remaining *Halbjuden*, its new targets for mockery and scapegoating. Already this month, Renate's books have been knocked from her arms or off her desk four times. Notes that read *Dirty Jewess* and *Half-blood Abomination* have been slipped into her bookbag and coat pocket. The Racial Hygiene instructor makes her and the other *Mischlinge* wipe down their seats after his class, "to minimize the reach of Jewish contagion." Last Monday, he even called Renate up to the blackboard so he could measure her face with his caliper, cheerfully inviting the class to call out *Juden* or *Deutsch* as he went over her features. "The nose," he'd noted, "is arguably Aryan in its overall size, though the sharp angle suggests some Hebrew influence. On the other hand, look here! These lips are all Jew."

As her classmates snickered and scribbled, it had taken all Renate's willpower (and six verses of *Snark*) to remain something resembling impassive. But when the instructor asked for a show of hands on her "dominant" half and *Jude* won overwhelmingly, she barely managed to excuse herself and run to the lavatory before bursting into hot tears yet again.

But today will be different, she thinks, as she rummages for a clean pair of socks. For one thing, there are strict rules regarding field-trip deportment: no whispering, giggling, or other "disrespectful" behavior is permitted, which effectively strips her classmates of their main source of weaponry. Moreover, the only book she will have to carry is her little blue-covered sketchbook. After toting around two novels at a time in addition to all her regular textbooks, the prospect seems hugely liberating.

She even finds herself humming as she goes through her morning routine; splashing her face and armpits, braiding her newly brushed hair. And she actually has an appetite for breakfast, finishing off her poached egg and wiping up the leftover yolk with her toast. After kissing her father on his cheek, she hugs her mother by the sink and wishes her a pleasant day.

"Not likely," Lisbet Bauer retorts dryly. Still barred from her clinic for remaining married to her husband, she's been volunteering instead at the Jewish Hospital in Spandau, which has been inundated by mental breakdowns and suicide attempts.

But even this bleak response does little to dampen Renate's mood. As she steps out onto Unter den Linden, for once bookless beneath the lemon-white sun, the street strikes her as almost surreally detailed and lovely. And when the first butterfly of the season flutters its golden-winged way before her eyes, it erases the last bit of leaden sadness left over from her dream.

When she reaches her classroom, though, almost immediately she senses that something is off.

For one thing, even though she's here even earlier than usual (ten to eight, according to the delicate wristwatch that her grandmother gave her for her sixteenth birthday last year) the rest of the class is already there. Coats are off, bags are down, hands are clasped expectantly on their desks. It's a sight unsettling enough that for a moment she wonders whether she'd written down the departure time incorrectly.

Moreover, although it's not a BDM meeting day, every girl in the room is in uniform. To get to her desk, she has to navigate row upon row of blue serge skirts and crisp white shirts, to swim a bobbing sea of jauntily angled black berets.

As she sets her bag down, the class teacher, Herr Bachmann, unfolds his long-limbed form from behind his desk. "Ah, Fräulein Bauer," he says. "A word, if you don't mind."

He is speaking in a normal voice. But against the sudden silence that falls he might as well have shouted at her from across the room.

Sweat prickling her palms, Renate shrugs off her coat and makes her way toward the front of the room, spine-tinglingly aware of the twenty-two sets of eyes that are locked on each hesitant step.

When she reaches the blackboard, Herr Bachmann clears his throat uncomfortably and runs a spidery hand through his ginger hair. He has narrow brown eyes and a face that has always reminded Renate of an otter.

"Good news," he announces. "You are getting the day off!"

"Off?"

(Behind her a hissing whisper: *Jude!* Or is she imagining it?)

"Yes. Today."

"From what?"

(There it is again: *Juuuuuude!*)

Herr Bachmann chuckles, the sound mirthless and forced. "From everything. School. Schoolwork." He clears his throat again. "And of course, today's expedition to the Neues."

The mention of the museum lands like a leaden shot put in her gut. "But . . . why?"

Behind her someone half suppresses a snort so that it comes out sounding like a flattened sneeze. Like a stone dropped in a pond, it sets free a wider ripple of titters. Renate feels her ears turning red.

"I'm *allowed* to go," she says, pulling herself fully upright. "By the museum, I mean. It's only full Jews that aren't permitted there." She tries to say it as assertively and as calmly as she can, the way her mother responded when their local Geheime Staatspolizei agent came by last month to again "discuss" her marriage to Vati ("We married in 1916," Lisbet Bauer had informed him crisply. "The race laws don't apply in our case.").

But Herr Bachmann just shakes his head. "This isn't actually about the museum." He rubs his thin hands together. "I'm afraid that there has been a—a request."

"A request," Renate repeats mechanically.

"Yes." He nods. "To keep this particular outing exclusively German."

"Who . . ."

But he cuts her off quickly. "It is more than one, in fact. In fact . . ." He lowers his voice slightly, almost pleadingly. "It was almost unanimous. And given that we are, in fact, exploring Germany's Nordic roots, and that you are in fact neither German nor Nordic, the headmaster has decided to honor it."

For a moment she is back in the dream: running breathlessly, yet unable to move. A *Snark* verse floats like a baleful soap bubble through her mind:

> *"Be a man!" said the Bellman*
> *in wrath, as he heard*
> *The Butcher beginning to sob.*

"Should we meet with a Jubjub
that desperate bird
We shall need all our strength for the job!"

When she'd first learned the poem, the word *Jubjub* alone had been enough to set her giggling. Now, though, it feels faraway and fractured. She shuts her eyes, ordering herself not to cry. When she opens them again Herr Bachmann is gazing at her with what looks like real concern.

"Actually," he is saying, "this way you'll have more time to write your essay on how Marxism led to Germany's defeat in the Great War and shaped the Treaty of Versailles." He winks. "Silver linings."

In happier days he'd been one of her favorite teachers. He'd even lent her history books about ancient China and Egypt at one point, when she'd told him she wanted to write about foreign countries, like Pearl Buck. Last year, though, he wouldn't even sign her autograph book at year's end. "It might get us both in trouble," he'd said, sadly.

"Are you all right?" The teacher is still gazing at her with that uncomfortable not-quite smile. "You seem pale."

He is throwing her a lifeline. Renate scrabbles for it blindly. "Yes," she whispers. "I mean, no. I do feel ill, all of a sudden. I should probably go home."

Cheeks burning, she turns and begins what feels like the longest walk she has ever taken in her life; past Sophia Sitz and Trude Baumgarten and all the other uniformed girls who look on in undisguised triumph.

⚜

The trip home is almost as interminable. Without a book before her she feels defenseless, shiveringly vulnerable to the gazes of strangers who she is sure must be wondering why a schoolgirl is on the streets at half past nine. Too anxious to ride the tram back, she walks instead, quickly, keeping her gaze glued to the ground, ignoring the budding trees on

Unter den Linden and Potsdamer Platz and the bright display window at the Konditorei Schloss, with its official Star of David sign in the window oddly juxtaposed against the lamb-shaped *Osterkuchen* and Easter bread. She pauses before it, staring not at the sweets but at the familiar six-pointed symbol, remembering the long-ago day when she and Ilse had put the stars up on her bedroom ceiling. Or more accurately, Ilse had put them up for Renate, since they both knew Renate would almost certainly fall to her demise if she tried to stand on the chair they'd precariously balanced atop her homework desk in the center of the room.

Did you know, she remembers Ilse saying, cellotape in one hand and paper cutout in the other, *that a lot of the stars we see at night are actually dead already?*

How? Renate had asked. *If they're dead, how can we still be seeing them?*

Something about how long the light takes to get here. They die, but the light they send out takes such a long time to reach Earth that it only reaches us after the dying. Squinting at the ceiling, Ilse pressed one paper star above her head, then looked back at Renate (who was holding the constellation chart) for approval. Renate nodded.

So if they're dead, what we're seeing, Renate said, *is like a ghost? The ghost of a star?*

Ja. Ilse had nodded. *A beautiful, shining ghost star.*

Gazing at Herr Schloss's six-pointed star of shame, it strikes Renate now that he—that *all* of them—are not unlike those dead stars Ilse had spoken of. They go about their lives, reading and baking and hoping, sending out the impression of still being fully living, engaged human beings. The truth, though, is that they are simply sending out ghostly light into space, obscuring the fact of their own erasure.

The observation hits with a chilly bleakness that feels like the touch of death itself. Spinning away from the window, Renate races past the Fasanenstraße Synagogue, still fighting back tears, until she finally reaches her building and all but sprints up the front steps in relief.

Inside, she kicks her boots off and leaves her bookbag beside them, pausing only for a muttered inquiry:

"Hallo?"

As expected, there is no response: at ten o'clock in the morning the only Bauer at home is Sigi, who greets her with a sleepy tail wag from beneath the dining room table. She makes her way through the foyer, pausing at the bottom of the stairs to listen again, just to be sure.

Up until last week her father would have been home, at least, doing whatever it was that he did in his office all day. Now, though, he works at the Jüdische Gemeinde on Kantstraße helping aspiring emigrants navigate the baffling process of leaving the country: Filling in emigration and visa applications. Working out departure taxes and bank fees. Itemizing and assessing hundreds of pages' worth of household belongings down to the last spare trouser button. He calls the work "demoralizing," but Lisbet Bauer insists he do it. She has confided in Renate that without a structured schedule and daily interaction with others, she fears her husband will fall into full-blown depression.

Still battling tears as she half slides, half walks in her bobby socks, Renate makes her way into the sun-filled sitting room. There she rummages around in a cubby in the antique oak secretary until she finds the half pack of Monas that she filched from her mother's purse last week.

Dragging the desk chair to the wall, she sets the ashtray on the sill and cracks the window, deftly pulling one of the cigarettes out with her lips, a trick picked up by watching Marlene Dietrich in *Shanghai Express* two years ago, though the smoking itself is a new habit, taken up more from boredom than anything else. She initially found it vile but has since come to appreciate the nicotine's softening effect on her nerves. Not to mention the much-needed sense of glamour and sophistication it seems to add to her gloomy existence. Her parents, she knows, would certainly *not* appreciate these things—yet another double standard, since they let Franz smoke at sixteen. But since neither of them will be home for several hours at least, Renate doesn't bother herself with what they'd think.

Silver linings, she thinks, tipping her head back and exhaling a low and misty-white groan.

Staring up at the paneled ceiling, she tries to push past the despair, to fully absorb what just happened and what it means. Certainly it's a bad sign, if she's now seen as so loathsome that her classmates won't even let her come on a class outing with them. And yet why? What has changed? She's no more or less Jewish now than she had been when her ancestry first came out. Or is it possible that Franz was right; that the Jewish "blood" everyone seems obsessed with doesn't remain constant but rather spreads, like black ink in her veins, eventually tainting the entirety?

Experimentally, Renate holds a thumb over her wrist's pulse point, as though she might be able to detect the answer in her own muted bloodbeat. But of course, it feels the same as it always has felt, merrily pumping her cells on their endless anatomical loops.

Perhaps, she muses, the best thing after all would be to go to a fully Jewish school, like Karolin has. She's heard mixed things about them: that they are terribly overcrowded, but emotionally much freer and more open. That the instructors are overworked and exhausted and—as the law limits Jewish teachers to just five students—mostly Aryan, but not pointedly abusive as they are in German schools, where they must take pains to demonstrate their Reich loyalty. That the student body changes daily as various students leave the country, their spots filled by other students liberated from their former schools, by force or by choice. That there are no *Hakenkreuz* flags or daily pledges to serve the Führer, and no Hitler portraits glaring down in pale disgust. "It's so much easier to write now," Karolin reported when Renate ran into her on the street a few weeks ago. "I can't describe it. It's as though the pens there are lighter, somehow. Or magic."

Clearly, she still hadn't found anyone to fix her glasses (all but impossible since Jewish eye doctors have been stripped of licenses and Aryans declared off-limits to Jews). But despite that, despite *everything*, she had actually seemed almost *happy*. And this, in turn, had sparked an unexpected surge of jealousy on Renate's part.

Now Renate wonders: would it be worth it? Or is she better off clinging to her spot at Bismarck—no matter how awful—in the hopes of finishing her *Abitur* there and having a chance at university? At least, presuming universities still admit *Mischlinge* at that point? Sighing, she shuts her eyes. It's like trying to chart a course through life-threatening waves in a toxic ocean, with neither a compass nor a map.

Dispiritedly, she picks up the paper Franz left on the desktop, rifling through its cheap, gray-toned sheets. It's *Der Mischling Berliner*, the mixed-race biweekly he started bringing home last month from somewhere. Still smoking, Renate skims a story about half Jews enlisting in Hitler's army and an advice column on reading the Nuremberg Race Laws correctly before paging to the classifieds on the back page. Franz likes to read them aloud in a nasal, news-announcer voice: *Tall and kind 2nd Degree of 32 years seeks like young lady with marriage interests. Blond/blue-eyed preferable, not essential. Pleasantly plump 1st Degree lady—35 but young at heart!—seeks 1st Degree Gentleman age 30–50 for companionship and possible commitment.* But it's a struggle to keep her eyes on the page. Renate's head throbs, and she keeps seeing Herr Bachmann's careful face; keeps hearing his voice, low and tight with discomfort: *Almost unanimous. Neither German nor Nordic.* And behind it, that ever-flowing, malicious-whispering river: *Jude. Halbjude. Mischling. Jude . . .*

She tosses the paper onto the floor and balances her cigarette on the edge of the ashtray. She needs better reading material, she decides. In particular, the plight of Lady Edwina Esketh and her forbidden love for a Brahmin doctor in colonial Ranchipur. Hauling herself up, she sets up the stairs in her stockinged feet to fetch *The Rains Came* from beneath her unmade bed.

At the landing, though, she pauses. For the second time today something feels off. It takes a moment to realize that it's the door to her parents' bedroom. Her mother generally leaves doors open during the day ("closed doors lead to closed minds," she explains). Now, though, it is shut.

Perplexed, Renate reaches for the doorknob. Then she freezes, hearing voices inside. One of them is her mother's. The other, however, is unfamiliar: low and heavy. Unfamiliar.

And definitely male.

Barely allowing herself to breathe, she edges closer.

"I don't *have* anything else," her mother is saying. Her voice is taut and high; she sounds close to tears.

"Well, then, I'm afraid the case will close."

"But you can't do that. If you close it, my husband . . ."

"Your *husband*?" The man gives a short laugh. "May I remind you, Frau Bauer, that your husband is the reason you're in this situation. If you'd simply comply with our request, then this could all go away." A pause. "Even *I* would. I dare say you'd even miss me."

This last assertion, delivered mockingly, is followed by another pause, this one longer. Then her mother's voice again, barely audible: "I can't do that."

"Then we have nothing more to discuss today." The creak of bedsprings (Renate's stomach curls into itself, hard as rock). A heavy tread as he moves toward the door. Trembling, Renate takes a step backward at the same time her mother speaks again: "*Wait*. Wait. Perhaps . . ."

"Yes?" And a moment later:

"Not today. I'm not in the mood for a Jew's leftovers."

Renate registers the comment at the same moment her mother cries out furiously: "You *Schwein*!"

The sound of scuffling; of skin sharp against skin. Then the door-knob turns abruptly. Leaping back, Renate trips and nearly falls on top of Sigi, who has somehow materialized behind her without her knowing. They both yelp as the door flies open, revealing her mother's wiry, disheveled form.

"Reni?" Elisabeth Bauer's chest is heaving beneath her heavily pilled cardigan. Her neck and chest are flushed a damp pink. "What are you doing home? I thought you were going to the Neues today with your class."

Renate opens her mouth to answer, but nothing comes out. Her mouth is as dry as a cup of sand.

"Who is there?" she finally manages to say, but her mother just shakes her head.

"Take the dog downstairs," she orders tightly.

"But . . ."

"*Now*, Renate."

Renate stares at her. *A Jew's leftovers.*

For a moment she thinks she might vomit.

"Who is—" she asks again, but before she can finish her mother has slammed the door in her face. As she stands there, quivering, she hears the man laughing, hears her mother murmuring something in a low voice. Then the door opens and her mother appears again. *"Take him downstairs."*

Feeling strangely outside herself, Renate forces her limbs into action, yanking the stiff-legged dog back toward the stairwell. Picking him up when he refuses. Swallowing back the taste of bile on her tongue. As she descends slowly, pet in arms, the words still circle her mind, inexplicably mixing with the Snark: *There was one who was famed for the number of things / He forgot when he entered the ship (a Jew's leftovers) / His umbrella, his watch, all his jewels and rings (a Jew's leftovers) / And the clothes he had brought for the trip . . .*

After what seems an eon she reaches the foyer. Stumbling slightly, she carries Sigi through the dining room, shoving him through the swinging door into the kitchen, then leaning against the dining room table.

Upstairs, the door opens yet again. There comes the sound of the man's tread, slow and deliberate, on the stairwell. Still clutching her stomach, Renate tiptoes back to the dining room doorway, positioning herself just far enough behind the door frame to keep the stairwell in sight.

When he comes into view she gasps.

He is short, dark, and stocky, with skin that looks sallow and loose, and heavy eyebrows that almost meet in the middle. He is buttoning his trench coat and carrying a fedora beneath his arm, and the sight of this sends her pounding heart into her throat. For this, of course, is the informal uniform of the Gestapo, in its own way far more sinister than the Waffen-SS's blatant skull and bones.

As he reaches the bottom stair, the man turns his head in her direction, and Renate holds her breath. But he is only checking the time on the grandfather clock that stands against the dining room wall.

"How long, then?" her mother is asking, trailing after him in her bedroom slippers. Her eyes are swollen and red; there is a bright pink mark on her left cheek.

"Perhaps the next week or two," he says.

"Only that?" Her mother stops, her hand at her throat. "But the ring—the ring at least must be worth another month, no?"

Very slowly, the Gestapo agent turns around to face her. "Frau Bauer," he says coldly. "As I've now explained more than once, the value of your donation is not something I alone can determine. It will be assessed in the proper venues. Once I have that assessment I will be better able to calculate its worth toward your case."

Renate's mother gives a laugh that is so high and uncontained that it sends a shiver down Renate's spine.

"You speak as though this were something other than sheer extortion," she says, her voice brittle.

"Of course," he says, his tone suddenly both lower and more menacing, "I can return it to you. And recommend that the office close the inquiry today."

For a moment they just eye one another. And while neither makes a sound—neither (so far as Renate can tell) even *breathes*—the room fills with such taut and vibrating tension that she is struck by the wild urge to shriek, simply to break it.

At last, her mother gives a barely discernible nod. "Keep it."

"Smart lady." The agent flashes a nicotine-stained smile. "Even if you did marry a kike."

And to Renate's utter astonishment, he reaches a hand up and lays it against her mother's cheek, directly on the spot that is inflamed and angry.

It is not a gesture of affection. It is a statement of ownership. Even more shockingly, Lisbet Bauer, the outspoken, irrepressible Doktor Bauer, does nothing whatsoever to discourage it. She simply stands there, erect and frozen, her dark eyes snapping with fury as the Becker ticks ponderously into the silence.

"It's a pleasure, as always," the agent says at last.

He turns toward the door, setting the fedora on his head at a rakish angle. Lisbet Bauer stands where she is. She remains there as he unbolts the door with a deftness suggesting he's done it often, as he says *"auf Wiedersehen"* and touches the rim of his hat mockingly. As he jogs down the front steps, she still doesn't move, though he has, seemingly deliberately, left the door open. It isn't until the sound of his footsteps, and his cheerful whistling of "Ich hatt' einen Kameraden" has faded that she finally seems to waken again.

Taking the last few steps slowly, she moves to the door and shuts it. She turns the bolt with deliberation: *click.*

Then she turns to face the dining room.

"Renate," she says wearily. "You can come out."

Renate steps from her hiding place, a small voice in her head wondering, as always, *How does she know?*

But of course, this isn't the real question.

She parts her lips, then closes them. Her mouth is bone dry again.

"How much did you hear?" her mother is asking.

A Jew's leftovers.

She can only shake her head.

"Who *was* that?" she finally manages.

Her mother opens her mouth, then frowns. "Was someone smoking in here?"

"For God's sake! Answer the question!"

It comes out a shout. Outside a horse-drawn omnibus passes, a midday medley of horse hooves and brass bells. In the kitchen, Sigi whimpers slightly; then there's a furry *thump* as he settles onto his rug by the pantry.

Rubbing her eyes with her hand, her mother leans against the door.

"That," she says quietly, "was Agent Schultz. From the local Staatspolizei office."

"But why was he . . . why was he upstairs?" Renate can't bring herself to say the word *bedroom*; it feels obscene. Even thinking the word makes her want to retch again.

"We had a business appointment."

"Your hair is mussed. Your shoes are off."

"He was—he was early," says her mother, as though this actually explains anything. "He was supposed to come at eleven. I wasn't ready."

"Ready for *what*?"

"Reni," her mother says softly. She steps toward her, reaching out.

"No." Renate steps back quickly. "No. Don't *touch* me."

Her mother's expression doesn't change. But something about her seems to deflate; her thin shoulders weaken. Her chin lowers, just barely. For a moment she looks as though she might dissolve into tears. Instead, she steps past Renate to the stairwell and sinks onto the third stair in a movement that would have seemed more natural on a far older woman.

"All right," she says, seemingly to herself. She takes a deep breath. "You know that the Gestapo has been after me to divorce Vati, yes? The same way they're pressuring all intermarried couples."

Renate nods.

"Last month, Agent Schultz came by with some information he said might have a bearing on our case."

"What sort of bearing?"

"It seems that someone did some digging in my family's records in Silesia. Most of them are quite clear, of course—the Church records go back for nearly two centuries. But the office has apparently found a weak spot in my grandmother's parental lineage."

"Weak? As in, sick?" Renate knows next to nothing about her mother's grandparents, other than that her grandfather was a visiting professor of politics at a famous Polish university, who died relatively young of angina.

Her mother shakes her head. "Not physically weak. Genetically."

And when Renate still stares at her, uncomprehending: "They say that there is insufficient evidence that she was fully Aryan."

Renate gapes at her. "How is that possible?"

Her mother shrugs. "It happens. Particularly with Germans living abroad. People move houses, change countries. Records get damaged, lost. Even stolen."

"But . . ." Renate shuts her eyes, struggling to think clearly. "Even if your grandmother was Jewish, that would only make you one quarter. That hardly means anything at all."

"The problem isn't about what it means for me."

"What, then?"

"This is about you. And Franz."

Renate's legs feel suddenly weak; she sinks slowly to sit on the carpet.

"If you calculate it," her mother continues, "it comes to one extra eighth. An extra eighth of Jewish for each of you."

Renate shakes her head. "I still don't . . ."

Her mother sighs. "According to Herr Schultz, it means that you are now both five eighths Jewish. In other words, in their terms, fully Jewish."

Vollständig jüdisch. For a moment the words are merely sound, the way words repeated over and over become merely sound. Then, slowly, it starts to sink in. *Vollständig jüdisch.* The horrible pictures in *Der Stürmer.* The stories about killing babies, drinking their blood.

Jüdisch.

"If he's right," her mother goes on, "and there is really no way to challenge him, it changes virtually everything for you both. All the regulations you weren't subject to as *Mischlinge* they can apply to you as Jews. Franz would have to leave the university. You'd have to leave *Gymnasium.* But that's not even the part I'm worried about."

"It isn't?"

Her mother shakes her head. "I'm worried about what happens when things get worse."

"Worse?" Renate almost laughs. "How could they get any worse?"

Her mother uncrosses her legs, revealing a stocking ladder that runs directly over her left knee. "Mandatory factory work," she says. "Tighter

2 JENNIFER CODY EPSTEIN

curfews. Arrests for even more ridiculous excuses they use now. There are other rumors too." She rakes a hand through her hair. "I'm hearing horrible rumors."

Renate rubs her aching temples, trying to translate. She knows that Jews are being arrested now for infringements as minor as jaywalking. That a man was jailed for merely being in a department store elevator alone with an Aryan woman. People are sent off to work camps for such things—her friend Abi Feingold's father, for instance. He was sentenced to two months at the new Buchenwald facility after a traffic altercation with an *SS Staffelführer.* Shackled on his feet day and night during his imprisonment, he now can only sleep standing up in his own bedroom.

Numbly, she licks her lips. "Why was he upstairs?"

"He had," her mother says, carefully, "said that he could negotiate on our behalf. But he said it would require 'expenses.'" And seeing Renate's face: *"Money, Liebling.* He wanted money. That's all." She sighs, rubbing her cheek in the same place the agent's fingers had lingered. "The problem was that we don't have it. Our savings are all but gone through. He offered to take the dining silver, but as that belonged to your father's mother I would have had to tell Vati everything."

"Why haven't you told him? Surely he has the right. . . ."

"Nein," her mother says, so sharply Renate starts. "You have to promise me, Reni. You can*not* tell him. Not what you saw today, or what I'm telling you. Not any of it."

Renate feels the color draining from her face. It's one thing to keep something from both parents, as a unit. It feels strange—transgressive, even unclean—to keep this secret with one, against the other.

Especially after what she's just heard.

"Why not?" she asks, tonelessly.

"He'll tell me to give in to them—to divorce him," her mother says. "He'll see it as the only way. He might even try to divorce me himself. And once he did that . . ." She stops for a moment and swallows, seeming to lose her voice. "Once he did that they'd arrest him immediately. I'm sure of it. We might never see him again." She covers her face with her hands. "I couldn't stand that. I couldn't live."

"But . . ." Inevitably, Renate's own eyes fill, and squeezing them shut does nothing but push the tears over her lashes and down her cheeks. Keeping them closed, she wraps her arms around her belly and hugs herself, trying to counteract the hollow feeling that's still growing there: the bleakness that feels like a physical ache.

"Reni."

When she opens her eyes, her mother is gazing at her in a way that's almost physical in its intensity, as though she could somehow wring the answer from her with her reddening eyes.

"Promise me," she says.

Helplessly, Renate nods.

"So what did you pay them with?" she manages.

A Jew's leftovers.

"All I have . . . had." She takes a deep breath. "Oma Hildegard's pieces."

"The emeralds?" The four-piece set has been passed down from family matriarch to family matriarch on her mother's side for at least five generations. It had never occurred to Renate that this pattern wouldn't continue; that after her mother received them from her mother the jewels, in their lovely Oriental box, would one day reside in Renate's own stocking drawer and—on very special occasions—lie against her own pale skin.

Her mother nods. "The necklace bought us four months. The earrings two. The brooch just one." Breaking off, she dashes at her eyes with her sleeve. "Today he took the ring. But he said that it wasn't going to be enough."

Renate stares at the floor, at a dark, whorling knot that is about the same size as Sigi's pawprint, and as the brooch she will now never wear.

"I was hoping by this time that we'd have some sort of a plan in place," her mother says. "That Onkel Felix—that wretch—would have finally agreed to sponsor you and Franz from New York. Or that our Cuban or Harbin visas might have come through. But it's all just taking too long. The man at the Japanese consulate said it could be another *year* before we get permission to even go to Manchuria."

"So . . . so they get all the jewelry, and you . . ." Renate swallows, still unable to say the words. "And they still are going to make us full Jews in the end?"

"*Ja*, if the agent has his way. Unless I divorce Vati." Her mother nods slowly, as though just reaching the conclusion herself. "Yes. They will."

It's suddenly too much: Renate covers her face with her hands. "It doesn't make sense. It doesn't make any *sense*." By this point she's not even trying to hold them back; the tears simply stream down her cheeks. She tries to imagine their life without her father: no hat tossed upon homecoming, no tickling beard or sweet pipe smell when he hugs her. No rhythmic and reassuring *clack-clack-clack* from his office, when he's working on his books that no one will ever publish now.

"It doesn't make sense," she whispers. And then despite everything, she is crawling forward toward her mother; she is laying her head in her lap as though she were again three.

"Oh, *Mein Liebes*." Her mother makes a small, tight sound; she strokes Renate's hair, her wet cheek.

"Why did he touch you?" Renate whispers.

At first her mother doesn't answer. When she does, her voice is low and dull. "He touched me because he could."

"Only because of that?"

Her eyes are closed, but she can sense her mother hesitating, debating. "Sometimes," she starts, then shakes her head and falls silent.

A moment later she starts again. "Some men—very weak men—feel stronger and bigger when they can do that."

"Do what?"

"Touch us. When they know we don't want it. It's . . . it's a way for them to pretend to themselves that they are powerful. Important."

Renate turns her head slightly, looking up at her mother's face at the angle from which she saw it most often as an infant. In some ways she wishes she could simply go back to those days: to shrink and fatten and soften, lose her hair and her grown-up clothes, lose the aching need for nicotine and friendship and Rudi Gerhardt's perfect, long-lost lips.

"But they can't touch your mind," her mother continues, nodding now as though she's trying to convince herself. "They can only touch your mind if you let them. And they might change what they call us. But they can't break us apart. We will remain a family. We'll stay together. No matter what happens."

She strokes Renate's cheek again. "Yes?"

Renate hesitates. Then she nods. Inside, though, she is still hearing the man's voice: *A Jew's leftovers.* She is still seeing his fingers on her mother's face. He has, she realizes, more than simply touched her mind. He has cut into it, the way he might cut into an apple with a knife.

10

Ilse

1937

APRIL 10
NEUKRAMZIG, EAST PRUSSIA

Dear Renate:

I will never send this letter to you. In all likelihood, I won't keep it at all. I will finish it, and burn it, and scatter the ashes in the vegetable garden the other girls and I have planted behind our house. And yet as I go through my days in this strange German-but-not-German town, I find myself writing it anyway.

At first it was just in my head, so subtly and naturally that I didn't realize it was a letter at all. When I did, of course, I tried to stop. But this little mental pen—I picture it as the fancy jade one you once gave me for Christmas—just continued scribbling away, and the more I ignored it the more insistently it scribbled. Last night it actually kept me awake—and this after a morning spent sowing a ten-hectare potato field, with no help but a German farmer and a doddering workhorse named Bobik. I finally dragged myself up before dawn and down to the darkened kitchen to let the words out onto the page.

Which leaves me here, at half past three in the morning, composing a letter I can't seem to not write, to a person to whom I know I can no longer write.

Ilse chews on the tip of her pencil, rereading what she's written in the flickering light of the single candle she has lit. She sounds, she knows, utterly insane—she can all but hear her former best friend laughing in derision. And yet the truth is that there have been moments in these past weeks when she has never felt quite *so* sane; so certain of her purpose on earth. What she and her fellow *Arbeitsmaiden* are accomplishing in this tiny Polish border town astonishes her on a daily basis, while confirming everything she's ever believed about the revolutionary truth of their movement.

There are twelve of them in the labor camp, six per bunkroom, with Campleader Kass in her own little room at the end of the hall. The house was formerly a rectory; rickety and timeworn, it groans and hisses at night like an overworked old woman. A few of the Labor Maidens are convinced that it's haunted. Indeed, a few days after arriving—when it all still felt like a holiday—they'd held a secret séance at midnight, holding hands and chanting improvised runes to summon whatever restless spirits might be sharing their residence. In the end, though, none appeared, and the ritual only served to make their own five thirty a.m. summons to work and breakfast that much harder.

Five-thirty, she thinks now, checking the clock by the window. It reads 4:05—barely an hour before the rest awaken. Shifting a little in her chair, she resumes:

Our first order of the day is to make our bunks and clean our rooms so that they pass the Lagerführerin's *daily inspection. You would be amazed at how neat I've become; I can now make perfect hospital corners and tuck a sheet so tightly that a* Pfennig *will bounce off it. Since a significant part of our mission here is to impart German cleanliness and order to our German farming households, Lagerführerin Kass insists that we ourselves model those qualities at all times.*

After inspection we troop outside for flag raising, singing, and exercise (all of which I know you'd loathe, particularly at that hour). Then it's time for breakfast, by which point we are all ravenous since we've already been up for nearly two hours. We all line up in the kitchen and are given our plates by whichever of us Service Maidens are on cooking duty that day. After eating, we divide up according to our respective assignments and work until nine. Then it's on to our bicycles and off to our main mission: serving the Volksdeutsche of Neukramzig.

For me, this has mainly meant digging potatoes. I can hear you laughing at this image, but I am quite serious: Over the past week, I've spent twelve to fourteen hours per day in the potato field of a Volksdeutsche family named Michalski (that even their name sounds Polish gives you a sense of how confusing this world is). My duties consist of digging holes, dropping seed potatoes into them, and then covering them back up again. Row by row. It sounds easy, but I can honestly say it's the hardest work I've ever done. The soil is still cold and hard from the last snowfall, and the potatoes, though small, feel like leaden weights by midday. By sunset my back aches like that of an old woman, while my arms and legs feel like I've been at a daylong track meet. On top of that, my hands are so chapped and raw from working in the camp laundry this week that the mere act of gripping something—a potato, a spade, the old workhorse's leather reins—makes them bleed.

I had a hard time getting out of bed after the first two days. It wasn't just the physical soreness, either. It was the overwhelming dreariness of this kind of existence. Between the starkness of the field, the muddy slogging, and the ceaseless ache of my limbs, I almost couldn't face another day of it.

But I forced myself to rise. I will admit to fighting back tears during the first hour. But then I reminded myself of the millions of good people who, for centuries and generations, have devoted their entire lives to such work. And not just to feed themselves and their families, but to feed all the rest of us too! The thought made me—a privileged city girl who is only here for a few months—feel very small and ungrateful indeed. In fact, I resolved to change my attitude immediately by forcing myself to whistle instead of weep. After a while Herr Michalski joined in with me, even adding some harmonizing chords and trills.

And ~~Reni~~ Renate, something strange and amazing happened after that. It wasn't that the work became any less physically taxing, but I began to feel the most extraordinary sense of contentment. It came from a sudden, overwhelming sense of connection: not just to Herr Michalski, but to all those generations of Germans who had tilled this very land before us and—for all I know—might even be a part of it now. And for the first time, I felt as though I understood that oft-used term Blut und Boden. *It is more than a slogan. It is a sacred truth: as Germans, our blood is the soil we till. And the soil is in the blood in our veins.*

I can see you rolling your eyes here, in the way you always did when I talked like (as you and Franz called it) a "one-hundred-and-fifty-percent Nazi." And in truth I must have looked idiotic even to Herr Michalski, because just as I'd had this revelation he suddenly stopped whistling and gave me a rather odd look over his shoulder.

"What is so funny, then?" he demanded.

Realizing that there was no way to explain myself in a way that wouldn't send him scurrying for a Labor Maiden who wasn't barking mad, I improvised. "Oh," I said. "I was just thinking how grateful I am that our Führer gave us this opportunity to be here."

And believe it or not, his weathered face actually lit up.

"The man is a miracle from heaven," he said. "For all of us."

Shifting uncomfortably in her chair, Ilse tries for a moment to re-claim the jolt of sheer joy she'd felt in the field. But while the memory of the day itself comes easily enough—the pebbly soil beneath her fingers, the hay-sweet scent and soft nicker of the swaybacked workhorse, the craggy lines of the German farmer's face—the feeling itself seems to hover just beyond it; a luminous life raft of well-being bobbing and dancing away atop a swelling sea of revulsion and confusion.

Still (she reminds herself) she *had* felt it. *And that*, she reminds her-self sternly, *is why I am here. That's what makes everything else—even what happened today—worth it.*

Leaning back in her chair, she sets her pencil down and rubs her aching neck. Technically she isn't supposed to be downstairs until six— even on days when she's on breakfast duty. Tonight, though, after hours of tossing and turning beneath her rough-but-tightly-tucked sheet, she'd known that she had to get up, that if she spent another moment in the crowded room—with Josepha whimpering in her sleep and Susi snoring below her and Petra somnolently passing gas that smelled like beef sausage—Ilse would finally have let out such a howl of frustration that she'd have woken the entire floor.

So shrugging into a cardigan and woolen socks, she'd scooped her notepad from her wall cubby and noiselessly lowered herself to the cold wood floor, pausing just long enough to ensure that no one else was awake before carefully tiptoeing into the hallway and down the back stairway. Shifting again in her seat, she wonders whether she should have entertained her farm family's offer of putting her up with them, rather than remaining here with the camp.

The Michalskis are good people, after all. But like most villagers here they are quite simple—not to mention lamentably ignorant of their Nordic heritage. When Ilse first saw their modest farmhouse she'd actually thought the Service Board had matched her with a Polish family by mistake. The décor was cheap and tawdry, the tables groaning with false flowers. There were horrid little knickknacks everywhere—a google-eyed duo of ceramic frogs watched over by a gaudily colored shepherdess; a bisque "piano baby" with its dimpled rear end in full view. The parlor had even sported one of those eyeball clocks Ilse and Renate used to laugh about together, this one shaped like a little Negro genie whose white eyes rolled around to show you the time—*enough*, Ilse had written Renate in her head, *to give you nightmares!*

She'd found the house physically sanitary enough at least, as the Michalskis do well enough to keep a maid. Unfortunately, said maid— Marzia—also happens to be Polish, which means that her idea of cleaning doesn't even approach the rigorous German standard the Service Maidens have been charged to impress upon their respective *Volks-*

deutsche households. As she's since discovered, having Marzia around also makes it that much harder to maintain a German-speaking environment, as the housekeeper speaks next to no German and Frau Michalski and the children prefer Polish to begin with.

Still, Ilse has done her best given the circumstances; when she's not farming with Herr Michalski or helping his wife awaken her long-dormant *Hausfrau* instincts, she sings the children German songs or reads to them in their mother tongue, usually from the Grimms or *Struwwelpeter*. It's clear they don't understand everything. But they at least *seem* engaged, laughing at Ilse's impressions of thumb-sucking Conrad and fidgety Phil. They also leap at the chance to put on puppet shows together, especially if they involve Punch-and-Judy-style head-whacking. They're particularly enamored with one of their own invention called The Villagers Chase the Jew Out, based on the popular board game *Juden Raus!*

Unfortunately, though, not all the chasing in Ilse's life here is make-believe. The Dam-Großer Labor Service outpost is still fairly new, and some of the villagers—particularly the Poles—are clearly resentful of its presence. Just last week, two Service Maidens were unceremoniously knocked from their bicycles on their way back from their respective assignments in German households. Neither was seriously injured, but both were badly shaken up—one to the point that she was sent home to Munich to recuperate.

According to Lagerführerin Kass, such assaults stem from a belief on the part of some of the villagers that the Reich Service League is both "meddlesome" and "anti-Polish," though of course nothing could be farther from reality. (*Our hard work benefits everyone*, Ilse wrote Renate mentally, *Polish and German alike.*) What's more, to Ilse's mind these were not mere "boyish pranks," as Lagerführerin Kass seemed inclined to write them off. Rather, they struck her as deliberate, targeted assaults on the Reich itself, and she found it unfathomable that their perpetually harried-looking camp leader didn't seem more perturbed by them. "If we as the Reich's emissaries can be attacked like this, with impunity, what's to stop it from happening again?" Ilse had asked her. "And what sort of a message would that send? Not just to the villagers, but to Warsaw?" Everyone knew the Polish government—long angling for war with Germany—was actively seeking chinks in Germany's national defense system, particularly in these smaller border towns.

Despite its obvious logic, however, this line of reasoning got Ilse precisely nowhere with Lagerführerin Kass, who seemed more intent on protecting her camp's relations with the villagers than protecting the girls entrusted to her.

"Marita and Lies were ultimately unharmed," she told Ilse, "and the *Bürgermeister* assures me that the boys' families have been spoken to."

"The *mayor*?" Ilse sputtered. "Do you really think that someone with a name like Szczepański is going to come down hard on the Polish thugs who knocked our sisters to the ground?"

"Fräulein von Fischer," the *Lagerführerin* said, her jaw tightening slightly. "I understand your concerns. But I must request that you trust my judgment on this matter, and that it is being handled responsibly and properly."

Then, more gently (if inevitably): "You really must learn to let these things go."

And she had tried—Ilse truly had tried. In addition to her daily farm and farmhouse duties she threw herself into preparing for the bonfire her group was planning for the spring solstice, modeled on an ancient Norse ritual of Orasta. The other girls contented themselves with weaving ivy candleholders and wreaths, but Ilse composed a special verse for the event, and received permission from Lagerführerin Kass to not only read it aloud but to make copies to pass out to other attendants:

Hail to the offerings of coldest winter
Hail to the offspring of night
With hair of sunrise yellow and cheeks of peach hue
They dance in eternal Spring's light!

But as she'd walked back from the mimeographer's yesterday she became aware of a group of Polish boys walking far too closely behind her. She ignored them for as long as she could, but when one of them called out with a shrill, mocking *Sieg Heil* her indignation came slamming back.

Ducking into a nearby meat shop, Ilse pointed at the rude gang through the window and asked the butcher to write down the names of its members. When he claimed not to understand German she fetched the tailor next door, a bespectacled little man who initially offered his assistance with an indulgent smile, though it faded slightly upon hearing her request.

"They're gone now," he pointed out, indicating the empty street.

"He saw them," she insisted, pointing her chin at the worried-looking meat vendor. "He knows who they are."

After a whispered conference with the butcher, the tailor turned back to Ilse: "He'd like a promise that none of them will be hurt," he said, his smile now one of apology.

Why shouldn't they be hurt? Ilse wanted to snap back. *Why not, when Marita cried for the whole night after they set upon her, and Lies had to be sent home like a delinquent in disgrace?*

Instead, she pulled herself up to her full one-hundred-and-fifty-eight-centimeter height. "I want to make it quite clear," she said stiffly, "that I'm a representative of the Reich, and that the Reich doesn't negotiate when it comes to justice. If you fail to comply with my request, then I'll be forced to report you—both of you—to the *Hauptsturmführer*'s office."

Hauptsturmführer Wainer was the highest-ranking Party representative in the village. Ilse had never met him, but from the mixture of apprehension and deference that usually accompanied mention of his name she assumed he was someone to be reckoned with—an assumption further confirmed by the way the tailor's smile now evaporated completely.

"Report us for what?" he asked, blinking rapidly behind his spectacles.

"For—for aiding and abetting anti-Reich activities," Ilse improvised. "It's a very serious charge. People are sent to the camps for less in Berlin."

She actually had no idea if this was true, but it had its desired effect: still blinking furiously, the tailor launched into another rapid-fire, whispered consultation with the butcher, this one accompanied by equally terse shrugs and head shakes.

Finally, he turned back. "You have paper?" he asked.

She handed over the little notebook she carried with her. "Do you have a telephone?"

A half hour later she was pedaling down Dam-Großer's Hauptstraße, the damning notebook page carefully folded in her pocket and her heart beating somewhere near her throat. To her amazement, after being put through to the *Hauptsturmführer*'s office by the village operator and briefly explaining her mission, Ilse had been offered a meeting with the commander that very afternoon. "He had a four-thirty cancellation," the secretary explained. "I'd take it, if I were you. The next opening isn't for over a week. Do you have our address?"

The *Hauptsturmführer*'s office was in a large villa in the town's center, which up until recently had been Bürgermeister Szczepański's home. The first-floor parlor has been converted into a reception/secretarial area, in which a dark-haired young woman was typing so painstakingly it made Ilse wince just to watch it. Ilse couldn't help noticing that the girl also wore an exceptionally low-cut blouse, a rare sight in a town where many dressed with turn-of-the-century modesty. She appeared both aware of her exposed cleavage and blithely unconcerned by it: as she hunted, squinted, and pecked at her keyboard she'd periodically reach a hand around her back to yank the neckline back into place. Watching her, Ilse was reminded of the way Trude Baumgarten would hike up her skirt in school and pretend to be adjusting her stockings, when everyone knew she was showing the boys her legs. *And they're not even very nice legs*, Ilse remembered Renate hooting. *Don't they remind you of two skinny, hairy, white turnips?*

The memory triggered a snort of laughter, followed by an almost painful stab of loneliness and longing of the sort that Ilse thought she'd fully immunized herself against. *You have nothing in common*, she reminded herself, sternly. *She is a Jew. Your real friends are your colleagues in the movement.*

Which, while true enough, didn't address her mind's persistent habit of squirreling away thoughts and observations for later recitation to her former confidante. Nor did it change the fact that amid all of Ilse's BDM and *Landjahr* companions there's no one she can imagine whispering and laughing with for hours, sharing secret hopes and deepest fears and the occasional all-out pillow battle.

Sighing, she looked up at the office clock: it was already five fifteen. What was *taking* so long? If she didn't get in soon she'd risk missing dinner at the *Lager*—a fairly serious infraction, especially given the *Lagerführerin*'s dual obsession with food and punctuality.

Clearing her throat pointedly, Ilse looked back at the secretary, now angling her barely covered bosom over the typewriter keyboard while angling a pencil's eraser at the paper above it.

"It—it seems very busy today," Ilse said brightly.

"*Ach, ja.*" Without looking up, the girl rubbed at a spot, licked the eraser, and rubbed a bit more. "Since the year started the Reich's moved twenty new families from other areas near the border and settled them all right here in Dam-Großer. *Twenty!* You can't imagine the paperwork!"

"A lot?"

The secretary rolled her eyes. "Housing permits. Building permits. Farming permits. Not to mention registering the children with the appropriate schools. And Mother above, there are so many *children*! Four of the women have the gold Mothers' Cross, and eight of them the silver. The rest all have bronze or are working on getting it. Honestly, I don't know how some of them are still walking . . . oh *no*."

Dropping the pencil to the desk, the girl yanked the form from the typewriter's canister and held it to the light. "Ripped again," she pronounced in annoyance, tugging her shirt up once more from the back. "I don't know why they insist on using such cheap paper."

Tossing the disgraced sheet aside, she pulled a fresh one from a drawer and set about inserting it into the machine, her puckered brow and pursed lips making it clear that she had neither time nor patience for small talk.

Sighing again, Ilse settled back in her armchair, aware that her stomach was growling. Dinner was at six, a good quarter hour away by bike. Unless this was a very short meeting with the *Hauptsturmführer* she'd have to come up with a good excuse for her absence. Shutting her eyes, she tried to summon one, but what came instead was an image of all those gleaming maternal medals: *four gold, eight silver*, she'd said! It was like an exam question from Herr Kohler's math class last year: *If the Gold Cross is awarded to women who've had eight children or more, the Silver for six or seven, and the Bronze for four or five, what is the largest number of children the settler families might have between them?*

Shuddering, Ilse pushed the thought from her mind. The three Michalski offspring were more than enough for her.

Twenty minutes, two ruined forms, and a curt intercom exchange later, the secretary stretched and stood up. "He'll see you now," she told Ilse, shrouding the typewriter with a boxy black cover and herself in a sumptuous-looking fur-trimmed jacket. "Just knock before going in." Checking her face in a compact mirror, she added casually: "How old did you say you were?"

Ilse hadn't. "Seventeen," she said.

The secretary looked her over assessingly. Then she snapped her compact shut and nodded.

"You'll be fine," she said reassuringly.

It was a comment Ilse would look back on later and ponder, wondering how it was meant to have been taken. Was it merely an assurance to an obviously nervous young girl, one who'd been waiting for this meeting for over an hour? Or was she trying to reassure herself that it was sufficiently proper to leave that young girl alone, in that office?

Either way, the worker left. And gathering her courage and her satchel, Ilse stood and made her way to the heavy wooden door, upon which—after a deep breath—she knocked.

"*Herein,*" came the response, both authoritative and graveled.

Opening the door, she slipped in.

Inside, the *Hauptsturmführer* sat at an enormous desk, directly below a portrait of the Führer that was quite unlike any Ilse had ever seen. It showed Hitler in full Party attire, which in itself was not unusual. What was unusual was the fact that on top of his crisp uniform was an unexpectedly rumpled tan trench coat. Even stranger was the background, composed of the sort of luminous landscape sometimes found in Italian Renaissance paintings: rolling hills and shining rivers. A breathlessly blue sky filled with puffy white clouds. The Führer stood, hand on hip, beneath a pink flowering tree that seemed somehow at odds with his stern and solemn expression.

"I see you like my painting."

Ilse dropped her gaze, realizing that while she'd been taking in the odd portrait, Hauptsturmführer Wainer had been taking in his young visitor. Fighting back a wave of shyness, she studied him in return. A large man in his forties, he had the sort of face she associated with Party posters and Hollywood stars: bright blue eyes, square jaw divided by just the faintest hint of a cleft. A little like an older Rudi, in fact. *Reni would swoon*, she found herself thinking reflexively.

"Yes," she replied. "I've—I've never seen our Führer portrayed that way before."

The *Hauptsturmführer* nodded, as though this were the answer he both expected and wanted. "Very few have. I like it that way. Too many people simply stick up the standard photograph and then forget about it. I like to make things more . . . personal."

Lifting one large hand, he beckoned Ilse over. She obeyed hesitantly, noting that the ring on his middle finger might or might not have been a wedding band. As she drew nearer his features seemed to soften the way bread swells in humidity, weakening the initial impact of his handsomeness. She noticed, too, that one cheek bore the silvery mark of a *Schmisse*, one of those university dueling scars that her parents' generation considered high-status for some reason. There was a heavy layer of cigarette smoke in the room, and beneath it the distinct scent of some sort of Schnapps.

"I understand," he said, "that you are here with a complaint."

"Ja, Hauptsturmführer." Ilse cleared her throat. "I don't know whether you know it or not, but two of my fellow Service Maidens were recently attacked in town. In broad daylight, in the village." She cleared her throat again. "By—by Poles."

"Ah." He shook his head regretfully. "I hadn't heard of this incident. I have to say, though, I'm not surprised. Poles are practically animals— barely a notch above Jews, in terms of evolution." Leaning back in his chair, he folded his hands over his belly. "In fact, the farther across the border you go, the more interbred the two are, to the point where they become almost indistinguishable from one another. Did you know that, Fräulein von Fischer?"

Ilse did not. But she also had no interest in an impromptu eugenics lesson—she was late enough for dinner as it was. She decided to get to the point.

"I've been told," she said carefully, "that the mayor has spoken to these young men's parents. But a number of us—myself included—worry that without more serious repercussions, these—these incidents might be repeated."

The *Hauptsturmführer* tipped his chin up thoughtfully. "You have the names of the culprits?"

Ilse nodded. "Yes."

If it came out with conviction, it was because she'd thought this part through. It was true she had no proof that the boys who'd trailed her to the butcher's were the same ones who'd knocked Marita and Lies down. Nor did she know for sure that the names the butcher had written down were the actual names of the boys who'd bothered *her*. Logically speaking, though, it seemed far more likely than not that there was *some* overlap between the three categories. And even if these weren't the exact same Poles who'd knocked two girls off their bicycles, they were Poles nevertheless, and *someone* had to pay for the transgression. One way or another (she reasoned) the point had to be made—even if it meant that one or two of the boys might be wrongly disciplined in the process.

It was as she'd told Renate the day she'd fetched her back to Herr Hartmann's class: *Sacrifices have to be made. Anything that gets in the way of what we are trying to do has to go.*

"Yes," Ilse repeated now. "I have the names."

Reaching into her pocket, she retrieved the folded page upon which the butcher had carefully written down his list. Unfolding it, she placed it on the commander's desk. Lips pursed, he picked it up, perused its contents. Then he set it back down, leaned back again.

"I am impressed by your resolve, Fräulein," he said. "But can you tell me if either of your lovely Maidens were assaulted in a way that— how do I put this—*compromised* their purity?"

It was a straightforward enough question. But something in his demeanor made her stomach tighten uneasily. It might have been his bemused smile, which seemed to imply less concern for Marita and Lies than titillated interest in the details of their abuse.

"No," she said, feeling herself flush again. "No, they weren't. But given the current environment—and your own observations about the Polish nature—such things certainly can't be ruled out in the future. That is, not unless proper measures are taken. As I'm suggesting."

"No," he said, "they certainly cannot." He chuckled a little. "I'm curious. What measures do you believe would be 'proper'?"

Ilse blinked again, again taken aback: wasn't it *his* job to know these things?

"I'm not certain," she said slowly. "But whatever it is, it should be well publicized. In the paper, and on the bulletin board and such."

"How about a whipping?" He said it almost gently, tenting his fingers under his chin. "Would you like me to have them whipped?"

This left her even more flustered: "Perhaps," she stammered. "Or—or perhaps a day or two in detention. Or perhaps they could be assigned to work one of the German farms without pay."

"You've thought about this quite a bit, I can see."

"I have," she conceded. "Out of concern for both my fellow Maidens and the future of the Labor Service here as a whole. You see, I believe some of these—some of these hooligans are actively trying to discourage us from our purpose. I think some of them even want us to leave. And if they succeed, who knows what will happen to the poor *Volksdeutsche* in this town? They're practically outnumbered as it is!"

It came out in a rush; impassioned, almost accusatory. For a moment she worried she'd gone too far. But the *Hauptsturmführer* just nodded again, still smoking, his bright eyes still tightly trained on her face. He kept them there for what felt like an uncomfortably long time.

At last, stubbing out his cigarette, he stood. "How about this," he said. "I'll have my men round them up tomorrow. Then you can come back and decide for me what should be done with them."

"Ich?" The proposal caught her so fully off-guard that she actually took a half step back. "I—I believe it would be more advisable for you to make that decision, *Hauptsturmführer,*" she stammered.

"And why would you believe that?"

"Well, you obviously—you obviously have more experience in these things."

Almost sadly, he shook his head. "Ah, Fräulein von Fischer," he said. "The problem with *experience* is that it's very hard to get it without committing to action. But I'm more than happy to help you with that."

As he spoke, she saw that he was opening a drawer in the desk, from which he pulled out a bottle and two small glasses. He filled one, tossed it back, then filled both of them and picked them up. As he circled out from behind the desk with them, there came a pulsing sense of disorientation, as though the solid ground she'd thought she stood on revealed itself to be the floor of a moving train. As he drew even with her, she fought a foolish but intense urge to turn on her heel, to bolt breathlessly toward the door.

"It strikes me that you just might be headed for great places," he was saying. "And I believe that I can make that journey both shorter and more . . . comfortable for you. What do you say?"

He was slurring slightly, and she realized that he actually seemed somewhat drunk—a fact she found less worrying than infuriating at first. For here he was, this man sent to represent the Reich to the village! Here he was, taking meetings on the safety of his people, on the needs and concerns of Germany's vulnerable new settlers. And he was *tipsy*! It struck Ilse suddenly that he might not even remember their discussion later. In which case the entire endeavor—the hard-earned list of names from the butcher; the hour wasted with that idiot of a secretary; not to mention the fact that Ilse would need some sort of excuse to explain missing dinner (and by now she'll *certainly* have missed it)—all of it, apparently, was for nothing.

"Bitte," he was saying. "Let's toast."

"No thank you." She shook her head. He pretended to be shocked. "Why not?"

"I am here to work," she told him tightly. "Not to drink."

"Oh, come now," he said, chuckling again. "You're a city girl, aren't you? You must be. All you *Arbeitsmädchen* are. I'm sure you have all sorts of decadent habits."

He was standing very close now, and still holding the glass out so that it was practically beneath her nose. Because she could think of nothing else to do, Ilse finally took it from him.

"Good girl," he said. *"Prost."*

They clinked; he once again tossed his back. After a moment, holding her breath, Ilse did too.

"There," he said. "That wasn't so bad, now. Was it?"

In fact the liquor tasted like petrol and felt like fire against her throat: she immediately started to cough. Still chuckling, he took her glass back and set it on a coffee table by the couch against the side wall. For a moment he seemed to study it, and Ilse felt her pulse leap in a warning she didn't have time to fully decode. But he turned back again and started walking toward the door.

That was it, she told herself, with a silent sigh of relief. *All he wanted was a drink. And now, he'll tell me that I can go.*

But when he got to the door, the *Hauptsturmführer* neither held it open nor ushered Ilse out.

Instead, he closed it firmly and turned the bolt.

As he strode back toward her, Ilse found that she could neither move nor breathe. "*Hauptsturmführer*," she gasped, trying frantically to think of something to say to distract him, to bring the situation back to something even approaching normal.

But by that point he was upon her. And without another word, he took her into his arms.

What she'd remember most of what followed was not the meaty feel of his fingers against her neck, or the tobacco-and-Schnapps smell of his breath. What she'd recall was the icy *shock* of it: the abrupt recognition of the bizarre, colossal chasm between what she'd thought her purpose here was and what he'd probably seen it as from the start. The stinging realization that such things can happen with such speed, and with such irrevocable force.

That in the end, it really only takes a few moments.

In the *Lagerhaus* kitchen the cuckoo clock above the icebox chirps once, to mark the half hour past four. Blinking up at it, Ilse realizes she's been staring blankly at her letter for something approaching thirty minutes, and that she needs to get back upstairs before the rest of the house wakes. After missing dinner last night she barely avoided outhouse duty by arguing that she'd had to walk her bike all the way back from work. Which was only half untrue: Ilse *had* had to walk it, though not, as she'd claimed, because of a flat, but because while the bleeding hadn't lasted for very long it had still been too painful for her to perch upon the hard leather saddle. Dazedly, she wonders whether this will still be the case today, and if so, how she'll get herself to the Michalskis'.

For a moment that strange, moving-not-moving sensation from the

Hauptsturmführer's office returns. Squeezing her eyes shut, Ilse waits for it to pass before setting her pencil tip back on the page.

Do you remember when you were with Rudi, our pledge to share with one another all the "juicy" details of our future love affairs? I finally have started one, though I will admit that it is not at all the sort of affair I ever expected to be sharing. In fact, it is with a man much older than myself, though of impeccable Aryan lineage and an impressive Party standing. It came about this evening, quite suddenly. So suddenly, in fact, that I will admit that I was somewhat shaken by it all. But as I lay in bed tonight, failing to fall asleep and finding myself instead writing this impossible letter to you, it occurred to me that perhaps what happened with Hauptsturmführer Wainer was like that moment in Herr Michalski's field, when I pushed through the invisible gateway between tedium and pain and emerged with such overwhelming love for my country and its people. After all, he agreed to help me ensure the security of myself and my fellow Arbeitsmädchen *in town. And he told me that he saw potential in me, and that he was going to help me realize it. Surely these two outcomes alone are worth the ~~pain~~ initial ~~discomfort~~ surprise of the* Hauptsturmführer's *romantic attentions.*

Sacrifices have to be made to secure the future of our nation.

And in the end, isn't that what matters—Germany's future? Working together in order to make it great? Isn't that far and away more important than my naïvely girlish ideas of romance?

As I write this, I am realizing anew that it is for the same reason— Germany's needs, and my commitment to meeting those needs—that I had to sever our friendship in the way that I did. For whatever our shared history, and whatever promises and plans we made, the facts remain irrevocable: First, that you are a Jew. Second, that your family also has unapologetic ties to Socialism: Not only was your mother's father a former leader of the Socialist party, but your brother has attended Socialist meetings and even held them in your very home. In fact, as far as I know he is continuing to attend and hold them now.

So in the end, you are really an enemy of the nation on not just one, but on two counts. And that is precisely why I must not send this.

In fact, as I leaf through these pages now I can see that it really wasn't even you to whom I was writing in the first place. Rather, I was writing a kind of ghost; the ghost of a friendship that has long since died. The ghost of who I thought you were, and who I truly am now.

Because the truth is, I long ago wrote you out of my life.

Ilse

Setting down her pencil, Ilse pauses for a moment, reading and re-reading her last line.

Then, very carefully, she picks up the pages in one hand and her candle in the other. Carrying both over to the metal basin where she washed the dinner dishes last night (in penance for being late), she holds the candle to the corner edge of the missive until it catches. Then she drops the whole thing into the sink, watching dispassionately as it turns to ash before her eyes.

11

Ava

1949

"*S*he's a housewife," declared the boy two rows up from Ava's seat in the back of the classroom. "And my father is an accountant."

"*Gut,*" said Frau Klepf. "And do you know what an accountant does, Klaus?"

"He does sums with other people's money."

The teacher smiled, displaying yellowing teeth. "Something like that. You may sit. Next?"

A girl in the second-grade section leapt up, and Ava felt herself shrink in her seat. She'd been dreading the first day of *Grundschule* enough before walking in and discovering she'd have to "talk a little about her family" before the class. Now she found herself wishing she could simply sink below the earth so that when her turn came, the teacher would skip her.

"Abbi Schumer," the second-grader piped, her looped braids swinging slightly. "I have a baby sister whose name is Marte. She cries all the time. My father owns a candy shop on Hochofenstraße. Mother's a *Hausfrau* too, but she'd rather have a job."

"Is that so."

"*Ja.* She says she only doesn't because Vati is a caveman."

The classroom erupted with hushed giggles, and someone grunted gutturally—*Ooga-Booga!* Ava kept her eyes glued to her desk. Its wooden surface was worn and battered and—despite traces of frequent sandings— still tagged with symbols, phrases, and initials: mysterious messages for the future from pupils past. Tracing one with her forefinger (*L.G.N.* + *G.F.R.* = *W.L.f. I.*) she wondered whether, decoded, it might instruct her on what to say when her turn came. Experimentally, she gave it a try: *My mother is a magazine editor. My father . . .*

Nothing came: no self-forming thought finished the phrase in her head. No miraculous epiphany transmitted itself from the old wood into the whorled surface of her fingertip.

Before her to the left a girl in a crisp seersucker dress was standing. "Lotte Reinhardt," she was saying. "My mum is a dressmaker." (Of *course* she is, Ava thought, glancing glumly down at her own patched and worn frock.) "I have one brother. He's a bother. He's named Frederick, after my father."

Frau Klepf smiled. "You may find him less bothersome now that you won't be spending all your time together this year. And what does your father do?"

"He was a *Generalleutnant.*" Lotte paused. Then, lowering her voice: "He fell in Stalingrad."

The teacher nodded. But she didn't press for further details, or say *my condolences* as she had when first-rower Jeni Gruenbaum tearfully noted that her mother had recently died of stomach cancer. In fact, she hadn't pressed for details on any of the fathers who were reportedly felled by the War. *Fell*, Ava noted, being the word they'd all used. As though they'd all just toppled over like wooden soldiers.

They were on the row right in front of Ava's now; she felt her palms prickle with sweat. *Eins, zwei, drei:* six more desks to her turn.

Mein-Vater-mein-Vater-mein-Vater . . . Still nothing. She slumped a little deeper in her chair, intending to keep both her eyes and her head down until the very last possible moment. Barely a moment later, though, something high and tinny in the teacher's tone made her look up again.

"A camp?" Frau Klepf was repeating. "You say she died in a camp?"

The gangly boy she was addressing—Ava had missed his name—was standing in a way that suggested he'd rather be doing anything else: his sharp shoulders hunched forward, his chin tucked into his chest. His fists clenched at the ends of his bony arms.

"Yes," he said. "Auschwitz." He shuffled his feet. "That's a KZ," he added, still speaking to the floor.

"I'm aware." Frau Klepf sounded slightly breathless. "So your mother was an . . . was employed by this place?"

"Employed?" The boy blinked at her. "You mean like working there for money?"

Flushing slightly, the teacher nodded her head.

Placing a finger on the taped-up bridge of his glasses, the boy pushed them further up on his nose. "No," he said shortly.

Frau Klepf waited a moment. When he said nothing more she cleared her throat. "Well, Ulrich," she said. "I'm very sorry for your loss. You may sit."

As the boy slumped back into his chair Ava studied the neatly shaven back of his head. It looked both soft and prickly, like a porcupine's belly; if she were to draw it she'd do it with a series of short, dark lines and dots. She didn't know what *KZ* stood for, but she knew it was one of those terms that—like *the War, the Defeat, the Russians*—only surfaced in very serious adult conversations.

"Who is next?" Frau Klepf asked brightly, even though it was obvious since they were going in order.

As the next two students went (Lena, Max, only children, *Hausfrau*, judge, baker, banker), Ava wiped her palms against the skirt of the let-out-both-ways dress and willed her jackhammer heart to be quiet. *My father is . . .* What on earth could she say? She couldn't tell them the truth, that she didn't know who her father was, beyond that he'd been a soldier and had died. She could maybe just say he'd fallen, as a dozen other students had. But then she'd have to say *where* he'd fallen, and she didn't know, and she couldn't trust herself to repeat any of the strange-sounding names (*Stalingrad? Kursk? Voronezh?*) correctly—much less convincingly. Particularly given how nervous she was, and that nervousness made her say things she didn't really mean to say, like *Yes, thank you* when someone had just asked her name, or *You as well* when they'd asked how she was. It was almost as if she were missing some magic incantation or charm that made chatting so natural and easy for most people. She'd tried to tell her mother about this, but Ilse had dismissed it with an *"Ach, there's that colorful imagination of yours again."* As though Ava's imagination were a gaudy and unwelcome guest.

As the girl next to her rattled off that her father was a dentist and her mother a dental hygienist, another thought struck: if Ava convinced *herself* she was invisible, she actually would be by the time her turn came. *I am air*, she told herself, squeezing her eyes shut. *I am empty air in a chair. You can see right through me to the window.*

But as the dental duo's daughter sat back, Frau Klepf was already launching into her query: *"Und am Ende*, we have . . . ?"

Air, Ava thought.

But even as she thought it she could feel them: thirty-odd curious gazes brushing like hovering bees against her clearly-still-very-visible skin.

She opened her eyes.

"Ava," she murmured.

The teacher frowned. "Ava what? And please stand."

Reluctantly, she clambered to her feet. "Von Fischer."

"I'm certainly very pleased to meet you, Ava," said Frau Klepf, in the shiny voice grown-ups use when they really are saying *I'm a grown-up and you're certainly not*. "Can you tell us a little bit about your family?"

Family, Ava thought. As usual, she had trouble connecting the term to herself. She and her mother were related, of course, and yet as a unit they somehow felt less "familial" than simply pragmatic: as though they'd been assigned slots in the same living space.

"My mother is, ah, a writer and editor," Ava said, scuffing her right calf with the worn toe of her left shoe. "For *Favorit*. That's a women's magazine."

"Ah!" beamed the teacher. "I read *Favorit*! And do you know what she writes about?"

"Women's issues." It came out more like a question.

"And could you tell us what, exactly, 'women's issues' might be?"

And of course, Ava could have. She could have mentioned keeping house like a proper German housewife, and cooking wholesome meals on a tight budget. She could have told them about refurbishing one's husband's Wehrmacht jacket into a child's winter overcoat, or repurposing old *Hakenkreuz* flags into cheerful holiday coasters. Or letting one's daughter's dresses out in both directions in order to make them last another year. She could have spoken about Ilse's advice column, entitled *Liebe Tante* even though as far as Ava knew Ilse had no aunts and wasn't one herself.

Instead, she said: "If you really read *Favorit* you'd already know what they are."

The hush that fell on the room was so cotton-thick that she all but felt it on the top of her head.

"That," said Frau Klepf slowly, "is a very good example of how one ought *not* speak to one's teacher. On any other day, in fact, I'd be forced to consider whether punishment might be in order." She turned her gaze to the far classroom corner, and for the first time Ava noticed the branch there, casually propped in the crevice where the two gray walls met. Stripped and supple and thin as a whip. She had heard of children being switched by parents, though her own mother preferred the back of her paddle-shaped hairbrush, applied with expert aim and efficiency.

"Given, however," the teacher continued, "that it is our very first day, I am prepared to make some exceptions. Ava, would you like to try that answer again? Politely, and with the respect due to an elder?"

A bead of sweat started a slow, tickling journey down the center of Ava's spine. "She writes about housekeeping. And—and other things."

"Thank you. And the rest of your family? Brothers? Sisters?"

Ava shook her head slowly, thinking *bitte-nein-bitte-nein-bitte-nein*. But inevitably, Frau Klepf did. "And your father?"

"He . . ." Ava swallowed. "He . . ."

"I'm sorry, Ava. I didn't catch that."

"He fell," Ava mumbled, only slightly louder.

"He fell in battle?"

"He fell . . . he fell in a KZ."

"A KZ?" Frau Klepf seemed caught off-guard by the statement. "Do you know where?"

Ava shook her head numbly. "I don't know. I don't know anything about him at all. Except for that he fell."

She stared at the sand-colored wooden floor as shocked giggling and rustling arose softly around her. It dawned on her that she actually hated her mother—really *hated* her—for keeping the truth locked away like this. As though by not telling Ava anything she was somehow protecting her, when in fact it was the opposite of protection.

When she looked up again, Frau Klepf was studying her with a look much like the one Ilse had worn when Ava showed her a dead pigeon on the street. "Very well." She sighed. "You may sit."

Ava sank into her chair, her limbs rubbery with relief. But as the teacher turned toward the blackboard, she was also aware, deep in her belly, of just the slightest sense of letdown. It was the same feeling she got when her mother listened to her without seeming to hear her, or looked at her without seeming to see her. At those times Ava felt as invisible as the magically cloaked prince in the Dancing Princesses story. At those times, she felt like a ghost in her own life.

❧

In the afternoon they were given a half hour in the garden, which was less a garden than a big dirt square filled with cigarette butts and rubble. As the other children picked out rocks for goal markers and one another for teammates, Ava hung back, half hopeful, half intimidated.

She had no real sports skills beyond skipping rope, and had had little chance to build any up, since after one dismally failed conscription into a neighborhood snowball fight she never played with other children on her block. But the possibility of being included was tempting enough that she lingered as the others organized themselves—at least, until one of the boys called out: "Hey you! Bastard smartmouth! Was your missing dad a baller?"

"Didn't you hear her?" someone else hooted back. "She doesn't know *anything about him!*"

Face burning, Ava scuttled in the opposite direction. She wasn't sure where she was going until she all but tripped right onto it: a flat, large rock beneath a dead-looking oak tree.

Sinking down, she pulled from her pocket a pencil stub and her little sketchbook, then paged through to the picture she'd started the prior night. It showed a girl roughly her own age, roughly resembling herself (lean-limbed, sharp-chinned, straight dark hair in two braids). Except that while Ava was sitting cross-legged on a big flat piece of granite, the sketchpad girl was hurling herself into a well. Or, more specifically, poised on the rocky rim of the well, contemplating its moist and murky depths. It had taken hours to get the body position right, using as a model her only doll (chipped and bisque-headed, named for the nation stamped upon its back). The well was based on a soup bowl against which Ava had painstakingly propped "Japan" after stripping her down to her tiny knickers.

Now it was time for the face.

Ava chewed on her pencil tip, which tasted woody and salty and strangely comforting as always. What kind of expression would a girl wear if her own mother had ordered her to jump into a deep, dark well, and possibly drown?

Shutting her eyes, she tried to summon it: the moment, the feeling. The fear. A mineral tang of shale and cement; a green algae hint. For the barest of moments, the footballers' shrieks and calls faded, and along with them the morning's sticky anxiety, the hot shame of her exposure as a "smartmouth" and a bastard within less than three hours of the starting bell. Instead she was almost there: in the half world that might actually exist between dingy Bremen and glimmering Grimm. The air around her quivering the way water shivers and glistens before parting before her . . .

"Are you asleep?"

Startling, Ava popped her eyes open to see Ulrich Something-or-Other, the boy whose mother really had died in a KZ. Ulrich stood directly in front of her, a battered paperback beneath his arm and somber curiosity on his face.

"Of course not," she said, quickly covering her notebook. *Go away.*

Instead he drew closer, pushing his glasses up again in that same anxious, jerky fashion that Ava suddenly identified as intensely annoying. "What are you doing?"

"What does it look like I'm doing?"

"Drawing." He said it almost gently, as though introducing her to the concept. "The question is, *what* are you drawing?"

She glowered down at his feet. His boots were worn straight through at the toe: she could make out a striped sock. On closer examination, the sock also had a hole in it, revealing a single, dirt-mooned toenail.

"A girl," she said, begrudgingly.

"What sort of a girl?"

"A girl jumping into a well." *Like you should.*

"Why would she want to do that?"

She glared up again, preparing herself for ridicule. But behind the fraying wad of tape and the scratched spectacle lenses his eyes weren't mocking. They were mahogany-dark with greenish-gold flecks in them. They were curious.

"She dropped her spindle in it," she said cautiously. "Her mother makes her go back to get it. And when she does, she finds the world down there is much better than the one up here."

He rocked back and forth on his feet. "Well, that's splendid," he said thoughtfully. "*I'd* sure like to find a better world underground."

Ava scrutinized his face again, but it still appeared guileless. He was even nodding slowly to himself now, as though the idea of a wondrous land inside a well made such perfect sense he was wondering why he hadn't thought of it himself.

"So what kind of place is it, down there?" he asked, taking a seat next to her.

"A beautiful meadow with butterflies. Talking bread and apple trees. A lady who showers her with gold."

"All underwater?"

She hadn't thought about this. "No. I think the meadow and everything is under the water—the next level down. But not actually *inside* the water."

"That's good. So she wasn't soaking wet. That would make things pretty uncomfortable." Cocking his head, he added: "Show it to me?"

"No!"

"Why not?"

Why not was that while Ulrich Something-or-Other had seemed decent enough to this point, there was still plenty of time for him to find something to laugh at her for. And there was little Ava hated more than being laughed at. By anyone.

Glancing at him sidelong, however, she had to admit that he didn't *look* as though he was going to laugh. In fact, with his sad eyes and his long serious face, he looked like he rarely laughed at all.

She rearranged her knees into a crisscross position like his and set the sketchpad in between them. Ulrich studied it for a few moments, saying nothing. Then he looked up at her grimly.

"It's good." He sounded as though he were delivering a fatal prognosis.

Ava glanced at the picture. Since her grandparents' deaths, no one had complimented—seriously, thoughtfully complimented—any of her drawings. The nuns at the Children's Home of the Holy Mother had been too busy to offer more than an occasional "that's nice." So unfamiliar was this sort of praise that for a moment she wasn't sure how to answer, though she knew gratitude was in order.

But when she opened her mouth, what came out instead was a question: "What's a KZ?"

"Didn't you say your dad died in one?"

"Yes, but my mother won't tell me anything."

He nodded, as though personally familiar with this conundrum. "It's like a jail, only worse." Picking a stick up from the rock's surface, he studied it intently.

"Did people do bad things to be put inside them?"

"No," he said shortly. "That's part of why it's worse."

"How else is it worse?"

"My father won't tell me." He began stripping the twig of its silver skin. "He says he'll explain when I'm older."

"That's what my mother says to me," Ava exclaimed, abruptly giddy at this shared injustice. *"We'll discuss it when you're older. You're too young to understand."* Picking up a pebble, she threw it after his twig. "Like I'm a *baby*."

"They think being grown-ups gives them the right to talk that way," he said darkly. "But I've heard him cry sometimes. Like *he's* a baby."

"Really?" Ava had never seen Ilse cry. Not even once.

Ulrich nodded. "He thinks I don't hear it. But I do." Picking up another pebble, he tossed it so it landed between his twig and the little stone Ava had thrown. "So you really don't know who your father is?"

"No." For some reason it wasn't hard to say this to him.

"But you know he's dead?"

"I don't even know that."

He held her gaze a long moment, his gold-flecked eyes thoughtful. For a moment Ava had the strange sense that he was looking not into her pupils but *through*; right into the confusion and hurt and mortification that had made her blurt out the word *KZ. He knows,* she thought, with a cold empty certainty she felt in her stomach. *He knows that I was lying.*

If he did, however, her new friend opted not to say so. What he said, at last, was: "That's better."

"What is?"

"Not knowing whether he's alive."

"Better than what?"

"Than knowing he's dead."

She had heard this before. "What if he's alive, and a truly terrible person?"

Ulrich brightened. "Like a bank thief?"

"Or a murderer."

"Maybe he's an evil genius," said Ulrich, warming to the topic. "Like Lex Luthor."

Ava frowned at him. "Who's Lex Luthor?"

"He's Superman's archenemy, obviously."

"Superman? What's that?"

He gawked at her. "You don't know *Superman*? The American superhero?"

"I'm not American, am I?" Miffed, she tossed a pebble after his stick. "So how do you know about him?"

He shrugged. "An Ami soldier my dad treated gave me a stack of Action Comics before he went back home. They're in English, but I still understand most of it."

From the direction of the little schoolhouse came the silvered tinkling of Frau Klepf's triangle. Somewhat to her surprise, Ava realized she was disappointed to hear it. She wanted, she realized, to keep on talking to this odd but strangely familiar-feeling boy.

"He's the strongest man in the world," Ulrich continued, pulling himself to his feet as Ava repocketed her sketchbook. "Though he's not really a man, because he's from the planet Krypton. He can lift trains off the ground. And fly."

"That's impressive." Ava stood as well, brushing the dust and dirt from the backs of her bare legs. "Are his wings like bird wings or butterflies'?"

"He's not a *fairy*." Ulrich Bergen looked indignant. "He doesn't need wings."

"Then how does he fly?"

"He just does." They'd fallen into step together the same way they'd fallen into their conversation: with perfect ease and comfort. As though they walked this precise path together every single day. "The comic books explain it," he went on. "I'll bring a few in tomorrow if you promise not to touch them. They're pretty old. But they're still really good."

Tomorrow. The word and its unspoken promise were unexpectedly thrilling. What he was saying, she realized, was that they would talk again tomorrow. That it was a plan. What he was saying was that he liked being with her.

"I promise," she said, beaming.

Back in the classroom Frau Klepf stood before her desk, a wax paper bag in her hands and a stack of thin paper pamphlets before her. "In a few moments," she told them, "I will hand out the history textbooks that have been approved for our use for the time being. But before that, I've a very special surprise for you all. Abbi's father has given everyone a special first-day-of-school treat: a whole *Mozartkugel!*"

Abbi Schumer preened as the room filled with an impressed hum, and Ava wondered what it would be like to be her. Not only to have a father, but a father with the world's best job (*a candy shop!*) and the desire to secure his daughter's social well-being.

"Please note," said Frau Klepf, lifting her voice again to be heard over the excited whispers, "that I will normally not be permitting eating during classtime. But given Herr Schumer's extraordinary generosity, I am willing to make an exception just this once. Yes, Ernst?"

"Aren't textbooks still books? Those don't look like books." The pudgy boy in the front row pointed a pudgy finger.

"*Ja,*" said the teacher. "They are what we have instead of books for the time being. The occu—" She broke off, seemingly to correct herself. "The *government* is still working on new textbooks for everyone. In the interim they've given us these to start with."

"Why do we *need* new textbooks? What was wrong with the old ones?"

"I'm afraid that as I'm not in the government myself I can't answer that," Frau Klepf said, tightening her lips. "Now. Who still wants a sweet?"

A forest of childish arms shot up across the room; the teacher began making her way through them. Before she'd finished the first row Ava's mouth was watering, for Ilse relegated candy into the same category she did new toys and shoes and the pretty tin paint sets Ava constantly coveted: all *things we don't need* requiring *money we don't have*. So beyond the occasional festival candy apple and twice-yearly birthday cakes (about which Ilse was improbably insistent), the only sweetness Ava could regularly count on was the jam on her morning toast. As a result, she craved sweets now almost as much as she had in her orphanage days: an obsessive, gut-level yearning exceeded only by her craving to know the truth about her father. Now she could almost taste the buttery richness of the almond paste in sweet alliance with hazelnut cream, bonded together by their shiny cap of dark chocolate.

When she finally had the foil-wrapped treat in her palm she tried her best to savor it. Peeling the glimmering wrapping away slowly, she folded it with exquisite care and saved it to inhale wistfully later. She nibbled first one side of the bonbon, then the other, shutting her eyes after each taste so as to better savor every rich and glorious note. Around her the classroom fell into a contented lull broken only by the cheerful crinklings of wrappers unwrapping and occasional, breathy sighs of contentment.

Then a newly familiar voice broke the silence. "I thought you said we each get one."

Ava opened her eyes to see Ulrich from the courtyard frowning down at his desk, on top of which lay not one untouched *Mozartkugel*, but two. Standing over him was Frau Klepf.

"I did," the teacher said, smiling uncomfortably. Somewhat counterintuitively (at least to Ava), she looked like a child caught at the candy jar. "But as it turns out we had an extra piece. I thought that perhaps you might like to have it."

Ulrich stared up at her with open suspicion. "Why?"

"Why?" Frau Klepf smiled harder. "Why, don't you like candy?"

"*Klar.* But so does everyone else," he pointed out. "But no one else got two. Everyone else only got one."

"Well, Ulrich. You see . . ." Frau Klepf cleared her throat again. Her smile was starting to look like a grimace. "You see," she restarted, "sometimes when something is left over, rather than waste it, it is better to . . . to give it to someone deserving."

"But how do you know I'm deserving?" Pushing his glasses back up his nose, the gangly boy leaned back in his wooden chair. "It's only the first day of school. You don't know anything about me."

Her mouth still tingling with almond-paste transcendence, Ava found herself gawking at her new friend. It wasn't just that he'd landed this confectionery windfall, or that (incredibly!) *he didn't seem to want it.* It was that she'd never seen someone her age address a grown-up in quite that way: as though he were every bit as adult as she was. It was easily the most subversive thing she'd ever witnessed—and that included when someone at her old orphanage pinned a note to the backside of one of the plumper nuns reading *First Prize: Fattest Pig.*

"Well." The teacher coughed. "You mentioned that you've lost a parent."

"*Lots* of people did. Lotte, for instance. And Ava."

"I understand that." Was it Ava's imagination, or had the teacher's tone taken on a slightly pleading note? "The war was very hard on all our families. But in some cases . . ."

"I don't want it," he interrupted flatly.

A handful of gasps sounded audibly. Frau Klepf looked as though she'd been slapped.

"You don't . . . you don't want it?"

"No. Give it to someone else, please." Picking the bonbon up, Ulrich held it out at her stiffly.

Staring down at him, Frau Klepf's pinched face took on a rosy flush not unlike that on the candy's mini-Mozart portrait, while Ulrich simply stared right back. Ava bit her lip. She could practically feel the mounting tension displacing the close, quiet air in the room.

At last, the teacher sighed. "Bring it home for later," she said tartly, and turned away. "For everyone else: please have your wrapper ready when I come around with the bin."

"I won't want it later either." Ulrich glared at the teacher's receding back. But if she heard him, Frau Klepf didn't give any sign.

Ava waited until she was well past the first row of desks. Then, leaning over, she tugged on Ulrich's shirt. "If you don't want it," she whispered, "can I have it?"

He looked back at her with lifted eyebrows, and for a moment Ava worried that perhaps she appeared greedy, and that this would sever the thin thread of their new bond.

But Ulrich merely shrugged. "Sure," he said. And turning around, he picked up not one but both of the candies, depositing them directly on her desk.

"Really?"

"I don't really like marzipan," he said. He gazed solemnly at her from behind his scratched lenses. "Or Mozart," he added.

She wasn't sure if he meant it as a joke, but she found herself giggling anyway. It almost seemed too much: she'd not only acquired a friend who liked her drawing, and wanted to talk again tomorrow. But she had *two more whole candies* to herself. . . .

"Fräulein von Fischer!"

Starting, Ava lifted her gaze to see Frau Klepf glaring at her from the blackboard.

"Did you take those from Ulrich's desk?"

Ava licked her lips. "He—Ulrich said that I could have them."

Setting the bin she was holding down, the teacher strode back down the aisle. "I thought I'd made myself clear. Those were for Ulrich, and Ulrich alone."

"Yes, but . . ."

"But what?"

The teacher stood directly over her now, her fists propped on her slight hips. She smelled of old sweat and stale perfume and something deeper and slightly fishy.

"He doesn't *want* them," Ava said. "You heard him say it yourself."

"Are you implying that there's something amiss with my hearing?"

"It's true," Ulrich chimed in. "I really don't . . ."

"Not. Another. Word." Frau Klepf's face had gone from rosy with rage to as white as the chalk stubs she had just lined up neatly on her blackboard. "Give the candy back to Ulrich. And apologize."

Ava looked down at the two bonbons. It felt as though she had been told to give away the two sweetest pieces of her very soul. *Just do it,* she told herself. *Just say you're sorry.*

But her entire body, from her fingers to her lips, felt as fixed and frozen as Herr Andersen's Ice Maiden's.

"Well then!" hissed the teacher. "I'll do it myself!" Scooping the candy up, she flung it at Ulrich's desk so hard that one of the pieces bounced off again and skittered to the wall. Ava followed its trajectory. Then she looked at Ulrich, rendered speechless by the gesture's violence.

He stared back, his expression unreadable. Then, very slowly, he crossed his eyes behind his glasses.

As if on cue, they were suddenly laughing again together: Ulrich hooting and heaving and wheezing, Ava tittering and snorting and hiccuping, while the teacher and classroom looked on in utter amazement.

⁕

At five o'clock Ava sat at the kitchen table, her new magazine-style history textbook before her, along with more properly booklike math and English textbooks. On top of the older texts was her sketch of the Well Girl, upon which she was putting finishing touches. When she heard the sound of the key in the lock, however, she shut the sketchbook and opened her math textbook instead, staring unseeingly at rows of antlike multiplication tables as her mother's keys landed with a metallic clatter on the front hall dresser.

There followed a moment of weighted silence. Ava knew her mother was reading the note that Frau Klepf had dashed off *für deine Mutter,* which Ava in turn had considered ripping up, reading, or rewriting before finally, despairingly, setting it on the front hall bureau.

After a small eternity, her mother finally called. "Ava?"

"In here," Ava called back, fighting the urge to slide under the table.

She heard Ilse's hard-soled oxfords marching smartly down the hall. Then her mother was in the doorway, the note lifted in one hand. "Is this true?"

"I don't know what it says," said Ava, truthfully.

"Don't be smart. It says you stole candy from a—from another student. And then refused to apologize for it. And also that you were rude to the teacher in front of the classroom."

"He *gave* me the candy," Ava said. She realized her voice was trembling.

"Then why does she write here that you stole it?"

"I don't know." Ava stared at her shoes. "She told the whole class that. But I can prove I didn't." Reaching into her jumper pocket, she pulled out the last remaining *Mozartkugel.* "See? He gave them both back to me after school. I saved this one for you."

Lips pressed tightly, Ilse took the candy between two fingers. She studied it with a look that implied she suspected it might explode in her hand. "You swear to me you didn't steal it."

"Yes." Ava lifted her chin slightly. "He's my *friend.*" The word felt almost as sweet as the chocolate on her tongue.

"Your friend?" Ilse looked bemused. "How long have you known him?"

"We just met today." Ava felt her ears heat. "But we talked all throughout recess. He told me about Superman."

For a long moment Ilse said nothing. Her face seemed to set slightly, the way clay sets itself as it hardens. Finally, she sighed. "I'm afraid that the teacher is right. You will have to apologize to your new *friend* tomorrow."

"But that's not *fair!*" Ava felt her face heating again. "And it's not even important to Ulrich! He said . . ."

Her mother cut her off. "It's clearly important to the teacher. And you want to make sure you start the year off right."

"By *lying*? You always say lying is wrong!"

Ilse just shook her head. "We'll find a way to say it together. But I will check with Frau Klepf to make sure you've complied. And I want no more stories about you talking back in class. Do you hear me?"

"You don't believe me," Ava said hotly. "My own mother."

"This has nothing to do with me. To be fully honest—it has nothing to do with you, either."

"How can you say that?" Ava cried. "She called me a thief! And now you're making me lie about it!"

Ilse tightened her lips. "You're too young now to understand. I'll explain it when you are older."

"You *always* say that! You said that about why you work all the time! About why I can't get new clothes! About why you can't tell me about my father! I'm always going to be 'too young.' For anything!" *I hate you*, she almost added, but managed—barely—to hold it back. Still, Ilse's eyes narrowed slightly. As though she'd heard it anyway.

"You're not too young to learn one lesson," she said coldly. "Very often, life will not be fair, and there will be nothing you will be able to do about it. Your best hope is to simply keep your nose clean and your mouth shut."

"How clean is *your* nose?" Ava muttered.

If Ilse heard the challenge she opted to ignore it. "Speaking of keeping your mouth shut," she said. "Frau Klepf's note included one more fact. She wrote that you told the class that . . ." She hesitated. "That your father died in a camp."

"A camp?"

Her mother's jaw seemed to tighten. "A KZ," she said.

Ava dropped her gaze to the table. "I didn't know what else to say. Everyone else gave a job or the place their father died in. And I . . . I don't even know what my father's name was. All I know is that Oma and Opa told me he was a soldier somewhere. And that he was dead before I was born."

For a moment, the only response was a distant-but-growing low-ing: the grinding rise of a siren somewhere nearby. As it climbed in vol-ume—a plaintive, raspy howl of pending catastrophe—the panic struck again; the sudden certainty that the walls and ceiling were not solid plaster and wood but were about to collapse on top of them like so much crumbling chalk. As the familiar sense of suffocation set in, Ava gripped her pencil with both hands, so hard her knuckles whitened beneath the skin. For a moment it actually felt as though her lungs couldn't inflate; as though she might simply collapse herself right here, on the spot. Then the siren faded into the distance, and the terror moved on like the chilly shadow of a windblown cloud.

When Ava looked up she was expecting the familiar tight-lipped look of disapproval. Instead she saw that Ilse had her blond head in her hands. Her shoulders shook. Ava realized with shock that she was crying.

"Mutti?" Standing, she softly touched her mother's elbow.

For a moment, Ilse didn't move. Then, shaking off her daughter's hand she stood, wiping her eyes with her shirtcuffs. "Take your things upstairs, please," she said, her voice strained. "I need to get started on dinner."

"But . . ."

"*Ava.* Do I need to get the hairbrush?"

Ava felt her chin quiver. More upsetting than the familiar threat was the sense that a very rare window—one into her mother's secret, true self—had just been cracked, and then quickly slammed shut. But Ava knew better than to try to pry it back open.

Blinking back tears, she began gathering her books and papers be-fore making her way shakily to the door. Once there, though, she turned back again. "Mutti."

Her mother was piling things onto the counter: an onion, a jar of tomatoes, a bag of meat.

"Just one question?"

"*Nein.*" Ilse set the onion on a cutting board. "We'll discuss it when you are older."

"*Bitte.* Can you just tell me—how did he really fall?"

Slowly, her mother turned around. "Was he really killed in battle, you mean?" Her silvery eyes were now rimmed in red—a contrast that was somehow unsettling.

Ava nodded.

Ilse hesitated again. Very slightly, she shook her head, and Ava's heart gave a startled leap.

"Then he's *alive*?" she said, breathlessly.

Her mother shut her eyes. "I will not have this discussion now," she said, teeth gritted. "Go upstairs. This instant."

"But . . ."

A sharp retort echoed abruptly through the room, making Ava jump in surprise. For a confused moment she somehow thought that her mother had been shot, before realizing Ilse had simply slammed shut the knife drawer.

"*This instant!*" It came out almost a howl.

Ava turned on her heel and ran to the front stairwell, the salty warmth blurring her vision so that she miscalculated where the step was and almost tripped. Trying to steady herself, she reached her hand out for the banister, barely missing the framed picture that perched beneath it: her and Ilse, shortly after her mother magically appeared at the Home of the Holy Mother. In the picture Ilse's strong arms looped loosely around Ava's skinny waist; her blond plaits tangled with Ava's chestnut. Her smile was stiff; Ava's face solemn, faintly confused. Reaching out, Ava ran a finger along the sculpted edge of the sterling silver frame.

Then, with equal deliberation, she swiped the whole picture off the table, sending it skittering the length of the polished oak before crashing onto the floor, the glass pane shattering into a dozen glinting, jagged pieces.

12.

Renate

1938

*R*enate races down Kronberger Straße, deploring Daphne du Maurier and buttoning her too-small coat against the chill.

It is the second time in four days that she's completely missed her stop. On Friday, she'd caught the oversight almost immediately and got the driver to pull over, and so only had to run back a short way to school. Today, though, the number 8 made it halfway to Nikolassee before the conductor called out jovially over his shoulder. "Skipping class today, are we, Fräulein?" And even then, Renate was so immersed in Jack Favell's evil plan to blackmail Max de Winter that she had to be called again before she caught on.

Cursing beneath her breath, she glances down at her wrist before remembering that she pawned her watch last week so she'd have money for Christmas presents. But given the spectral silence of the St. John church bells (which chime on the quarter hour) she calculates that it is at the earliest 8:03, and at the latest 8:18. Neither of which would matter if her first class weren't English and her first teacher Herr Lawerenz.

A Great War veteran with a severe limp and a disposition so fero-
cious that he could shout down any Nazi instructor from Renate's old
school, Herr Lawerenz inspires raw terror in his overcrowded classrooms with a single bang of his walking stick. He has never been known
to smile, though opinion is divided as to whether this sobriety reflects
war trauma or the fact that he was simply born an *Arschloch*. He also
seems to have taken more of a dislike to Renate than to his other students, though she can't understand why. Her work in his class is strong;
she contributes articulately to class discussions and always raises her
hand before speaking. She even tries to make him smile, in part because
after her last school experience she's desperate to be liked by her teachers, but also for the simple challenge. Last Monday, for instance, when
informed by him that her tardiness meant she'd missed his introduction to the English pluperfect, she pointed out that she'd been reading
Gone with the Wind in the original English, and that it happened to be
in the past tense. "So you see," she'd said (in English), smiling in what
she thought was a winning way, "I really haven't missed anything at all."

The class laughed. Herr Lawerenz did not. Instead, he slammed his
cane on the parquet floor with such force that Renate half expected the
wooden slats to shatter.

"Be late again," he'd said ominously (and in German), "and you'll find
yourself facing suspension. And then we will see what you will miss."

He then sent her straight to the headmistress's office to contemplate
her "arrogance."

Happily, Doktor Goldschmidt, who is also the school's founder, has
both a sense of humor and a love of Margaret Mitchell. In fact, the *Doktor* admitted to just having finished *Gone with the Wind* herself, and she
and Renate had a nice chat about America's civil war and dark history
of slavery before walking back to Herr Lawerenz's class together, where
the *Doktor* urged Herr Lawerenz to accept Renate's sincerest apology.

Now flying through the wintry garden grounds behind the school
(the back entrance is less conspicuous and also tends to be unmoni-
tored), Renate knows that the consequences might be far worse this
time. If Herr Lawerenz does call for her suspension, what if even Doktor

Goldschmidt is unable to change his mind? And if Renate is suspended, what if she then doesn't have enough time to prepare for her university-qualifying *Abitur* exam? That, after all, was the whole point of coming here after leaving Bismarck last spring. Not only is the *Jüdische Schule: Doktor Leonore Goldschmidt* the only Jewish school in Berlin authorized to administer the exam, but it gives it in both English and German. At thirty-seven marks a month it is also expensive—she is only here because they gave her a scholarship. If she wastes this opportunity her parents will be furious.

She bursts through the double glass doors of the converted villa that, rumor has it, once housed Imperial family members and now houses some seven hundred banished Jewish students. Renate's mouth is dry and sour-tasting; her heart feels as though it has a violent case of the hiccups. Struggling to catch her breath, she jogs past the closed classroom doors in the school's East Wing, shrugging off her coat as she discards possible alibis: *My mother needed help at the Jewish Hospital last night and we got home late.* (No good: she'd need a note.) *The tram broke down.* (Too easy to disprove.) *I left my Kennkarte at home and had to go back for it.* That one is a little more plausible. The penalty for being caught without the mandatory identification card is stiff, even more so if it bears a glaring red *J* on its cover.

Reaching the classroom at last, Renate roots through her satchel for the document while listening for Herr Lawerenz's gravel-filled voice. To her surprise, though, she doesn't hear his voice at all. What she hears instead is the tense hum of fifty-odd students sounding very much unattended.

Which she discovers, as she opens the door, they are.

As always, the battered classroom is packed to bursting—not just with dozens of displaced Jewish youth, but with the jittery energy of a student body that has no idea what its near future might hold. Almost every family enrolled here is trying to emigrate or at least get its children out of the country, though between the mountainous paperwork, extortionate departure fees, and endless waitlists for visas and ocean passage, the odds of escaping Germany are slight and getting slimmer.

When it does happen, though, it happens quickly—students simply disappear, and are quickly replaced by others struggling against the same odds.

Today, though, Renate senses a darker element in the mood, which offsets her initial relief at not facing Herr Lawerenz. The atmosphere is not unlike that following the *Anschluss* last spring, when she came in to a hurricane of heated whispers about Viennese Jews scrubbing sidewalks with their own toothbrushes. Or after July's Evian Conference, when nation after nation expressed sympathy for German Jews but kept their borders resolutely closed. (*Jews for Sale, Der Stürmer* gloated the following day. *Who Wants Them? No One!*)

"What's happening?" she asks Bernhard Bhär, a pink-faced boy with red acne scars on his cheeks, whom the others have nicknamed Piglet. "Where is Herr Lawerenz?"

"Meeting," he says. "They're all in a meeting."

"About what?"

He looks at her as though she's asked him if the sky is blue. "You haven't heard?"

When she shakes her head he rolls his eyes, his face assuming a by-now familiar expression that roughly translates as: *Don't you ever pay attention to anything?*

"The pogroms," he says.

"What pogroms? Where?"

"Everywhere. Here, even. Good God, Bauer. Did you wear a blindfold to school? Didn't you see the Hitlerjugend out front?"

"I came in the back," she falters, wondering instinctively whether she might have missed Rudi.

"They've been setting synagogues on fire," he says.

"What?"

"I hear they're destroying Jewish shops and beating the owners," adds Kinge Lehmann, looking up from one of the five newspapers on his desk. Wire-thin and plagued by asthma, he reads the Nazi press obsessively.

"I've heard they've thrown people from windows," chimes in Piglet's best friend who is nicknamed Pooh, though his real name is Rolf Sumner.

"Which 'they'?" asks Renate. "The SS?"

"Along with the Gestapo and the Hitlerjugend. But pretty much everyone who's not a Jew themselves is falling in behind them." Kinge shakes his head in amazement. "You really missed it all? You didn't see any of this on your way here? The smoke? The crowds?"

"I . . ." Renate feels her face heat. The only thing she noticed was that the car seemed quieter and less crowded than usual. And, of course, that she'd entirely missed her stop. "But *why*?"

"The Dwarf's got the papers saying it's a 'spontaneous uprising' of the people to protest vom Rath's murder. But no one is buying it. They're saying the people in charge are *Sturmtruppen* wearing civilian clothes."

"Wolves, sheep, et cetera," Pooh adds darkly.

"And *spontaneous* my ass," says Kinge. "They have government lists of every Jewish business and residence in the city. And it's happening all over the country. I hear in Munich they've told all Jews to leave by sundown."

"What, like the sheriff in a Karl May novel?" Renate asks, but no one laughs.

She sinks into her seat, struggling to process. *Dwarf* means Propaganda Minister Goebbels (one of the many pleasures of her new school is that one can speak ill of the Party without worrying about repercussions). Ernst vom Rath is the German diplomat shot the other morning in Paris by a Polish Jew barely older than she is. Renate hadn't realized vom Rath had died, though. Chewing on one of her braids, she tries to remember more from the BBC broadcast the family had surreptitiously listened to. She wishes she hadn't been reading *Rebecca* under the table.

Kinge, meanwhile, is quoting from the *Völkischer Beobachter*: "*We shall no longer tolerate a situation where hundreds of thousands of Jews within our territory control entire streets of shops, throng places of public entertainment, and pocket the wealth of German leaseholders as 'foreign' landlords while their racial brothers incite war against Germany and shoot down German officials . . .*" Usually he reads Party news in a whining and sycophantic voice. Now, though, he reads it straight. And he sounds worried. "That's from last night," he says, looking up. "They planned it all. My uncle's wine shop in Munich was smashed to bits. Every bottle."

"Same with my father's friend in Leipzig," says Piglet. "He has a shoe store there." Looking apologetically at Renate, he adds: "They took shits in all of the shoes."

Revolted, Renate covers her ears and turns away, searching the rest of the classroom for some sign that the boys are lying, or at least exaggerating; some sign that her life isn't about to take another of the sickening jolts for the worse that have periodically marked the last three years. *Please*, she prays wordlessly, to No One in Particular. *Please don't let it happen again.*

As if in answer, the door flies opens and Herr Lawerenz limps in, his cane pounding the floor with even more vehemence than usual, his gray hair sticking up on his head in two places, like tufted horns on a crochety fawn.

"Achtung!" he bellows.

As feared as he is, it normally takes the teacher at least two tries to get the jittery classroom to quiet down. Now, though, the silence is so sudden and so complete that Renate hears a bird chirp chidingly from a distant tree. Even the instructor seems momentarily taken aback: his rheumy eyes widen behind his spectacles. But he quickly recovers.

"All right, then," he snaps. "Pack up your bags."

Baffled, the students exchange glances.

"For the day?" asks Piglet finally.

"No, for a holiday," the instructor growls. "Yes, for the day. You are all being sent home. Doktor Goldschmidt has determined that it's not safe for the school to remain in session."

As the buzz starts up again he slams his cane against the floor. "However."

He waits as the room falls silent once more. "You must go out the back entrance, not the front. Do *not* all go at once. Avoid large groups. Find a partner, and go two-by-two. *Two-by-two*. Out the back. Do you understand?"

"Why can't we go in groups?" asks Kinge.

"You'll make for too obvious a target."

"A *target*?" Renate repeats, incredulous.

The question is lost in the flurry of papers being hastily pushed back into satchels, of chairs being pushed back from the desks. Someone in the back shouts: "When is the Hesse essay due?"

"When school resumes."

"When will that be?" asks Renate, thinking again about her exam.

He just shrugs. "You'll be notified."

"How about the smaller children?" someone asks. "How are they getting home?"

"Some of their parents have already fetched them. If necessary, the *Doktor* is prepared to take the rest home with her driver. You just worry about yourselves."

For a moment he glares at them each in turn. A little uncertainly, Renate raises her hand.

"Yes, Fräulein Bauer," he says, looking pained.

Renate licks her lips, almost afraid to repeat the question. "What are we too easy a target for?"

Something in his expression shifts. And suddenly, he doesn't look so much furious and vengeful as tired, and brittle, and even strangely fragile.

"Just get home," he says. "Go straight home. No loitering. No stopping. No talking to strangers. No matter what. Am I understood?"

Renate nods. But her heart is pounding again. Not because she is terrified by her teacher but because it dawns on her that *he*—a veteran of the Kaiser's war, held captive by the Russians, twice decorated for bravery, is terrified. He is clearly terrified for them all.

They ride the tram car like frozen players in a game of statues: two standing in the front, two in the back. Two seated on each bench on either side. Though they'd left the school in pairs they'd all ended up at the same stop within minutes. When the first tram came along they'd hesitated for just a moment before clambering on together in silence. Now they don't speak with or even look at one another, or any of the other dozen-odd riders in the carriage. Renate can't help thinking that anyone seeing them could deduce the truth at a glance: that they are students, out of school, on a regular school day. In other words, that they are in all likelihood Jewish. She is almost tempted to point it out: how silly they all must look, sitting stiff and pale in frightened silence. But as the tram squeals and hums toward Charlottenburg no one will even so much as catch her gaze.

Instead they wait, eight young bodies sitting and standing motionless and ramrod straight. Sixteen eyes remain glued to the slow-passing street scenery as though it were a movie screen, and they were waiting for some monster—a trudging clay-trailing Golem, a maiden-clutching King Kong—to burst forth from the shadows.

For several stops they see nothing. But as they approach the Friedrichstraße the smell of smoke fills the air, and she hears a dull, rowdy roar punctuated by drunken singing and shattering glass. The trolley turns onto the main avenue, and Renate catches a glimpse of what at first looks like garbage strewn over the sidewalks and street. But as the tram pulls even she sees that it is not garbage at all but brand-new goods: clothing with tags still on it, some of it half ripped off headless mannequins. Cans of food, dented but unopened. Worst of all (for her): books, with pages and covers ripped.

And the glass. Everywhere, there is glass. Shards of porcelain, stained glass, crystal-cut pieces from a chandelier—it all sparkles sharply in the weak morning light.

The tram lurches onto the main avenue, where the view is partially obstructed by a double-decker bus at a dead stop in front of the action, its two-score-odd passengers watching the proceedings with the bemused expressions of opera attendees. As they pass the stalled vehicle Renate for the first time sees the full extent of the chaos. The hairs on the back of her neck prickle.

The stores are under siege by bands of men, egged on by a crowd of laughing, applauding pedestrians. Many of the rioters appear to be drunk, staggering as they shout and sing and smash. None of them are wearing the familiar brown shirts and red armbands, but most have the burly, beef-faced look of stormtroopers. And the songs they bellow about plunging knives and Jewish blood are as unmistakable as the SS's signature Horst Wessel anthem.

Barely breathing, she stares out at the roaming marauders, a mix of young and middle-aged men and boys. Some of the latter are in Hitlerjugend uniform; others in civilian clothes. They are working as a group; as the number 8 stops for a signal she sees one boy smash a wooden table that has been dragged from a nearby furniture store, pounding and hacking at one of the legs until he manages to pry it off completely. This he hands to another boy, who bellows in approval before he unsteadily clambers onto what appears to be a matching dining room chair. He then begins to whack at the neon sign over the shop door, methodically destroying its two-word promise of *Feine Möbel* letter by glassy, shattering letter.

As he demolishes the *l* the others burst into applause, which is quickly picked up by onlookers. The boy leaps off the chair, tripping and falling flat but never once losing his giddy grin. A *Polizist* offers an arm to help him back onto his feet, then pats him jovially on the back.

Renate finally breaks her silence. "I can't believe that all of this is because a Pole shot a German," she whispers to Stella Goldschlag.

Stella, her blond braids as perfect and parallel as golden tram rails down her back, shakes her head. "It's just an excuse."

A man in a tan trench coat who has been smoking and reading *Die Börsen-Zeitung* looks up from his position against the carriage wall.

"An excuse for what?"

"An excuse to destroy us," says Stella, her voice cracking.

"Get a grip," hisses Gartner Rabin, who is sitting across the car next to Rita Oelburg, a thin and studious girl with bruiselike shadows beneath her eyes. "We're not supposed to draw attention to ourselves."

Stella tightens her lips and stares down at her neat black boots. "I *hate* being a Jew," she murmurs.

Renate studies her sidelong. Stella is easily the prettiest female in the *Jüdische Privatschule*—or at least, the prettiest by German standards. With smooth pale skin and eyes as blue as the painted flowers on a Chinese teacup, she looks like a girl for whom nothing ever goes wrong. On a normal school day the boys try to outperform one another around her. In fact, Gartner, who has now returned to staring tightly out at the devastation, actually did a handstand on the railing of the school's second-floor balcony in September, purely for Stella's benefit. Losing his grip, he'd fallen right off and crashed into the hyacinth bushes below, ending up with an arm cast which, in fact, only came off last week. And yet somehow, it all seems like something that happened deep in the past already. An event in a book she's all but forgotten . . .

The tram, which had finally started to move forward, stops again with a metallic shriek and a shudder.

For a moment no one moves. From outside comes the crystalline crash of another window shattering.

"Oh, wonderful," mumbles a man in the rear corner of the car. "Right in the middle of it all."

As if to underscore the point, a passing group of rioters slap their carriage, hard enough that it rocks slightly on its rails. As the marauders bellow with laughter, the Goldschmidt students stare straight ahead, and Renate realizes with horror that they are trapped here, mere meters from the violence. It would take just moments for the mob to shift their focus.

"What should we do?" whispers Stella, as another nearby window breaks. "Should we get off?"

"But what if they see us?" asks Rita, her voice shrill with fear.

"Shut up," hisses Gartner, his teeth gritted. "Just shut up, all of you. Can't you?"

The girls fall silent. Outside, the air fills with catcalls and wolf whistles, and reflexively Renate turns to see the source of the laughter. It comes from a group pillaging a storefront she recognizes as a lingerie shop her mother has frequented. As she watches, one of the boys reaches into the display he's just broken into and begins tossing out handfuls of silky, fluttery clothing, which the others drape coyly over their jackets and sweaters before ripping them to shreds with their hands. A moment later the proprietor—a bearded, birdlike man who was once a dancer in the Paris Opera Ballet—appears at the front door, waving his thin arms. He is shouting something, but the looters don't appear to be listening. Instead they begin to laughingly push him back and forth among themselves, a human pinball in some nightmarish machine.

At another nearby corner the crowd hurls cakes and pastries and loaves of dark bread from a shop Renate recognizes with a jolt as the Schloss-Konditorei: the once-beloved cake shop she and Ilse so often frequented on their way home from school. The same shop into which Ilse crossed the first SS boycott, in a moment that now seems not just from another era but from some other, alien planet.

Herr Schloss is a good baker. I don't really care if he's Jewish.

Renate thinks of the *Mohnkuchen* she and Ilse would share daily, like a sacrament; the display window always whistle-clean, filled with brightly fragrant delicacies. The cheerful train set and snow-capped model village in the winter, the pastel lambs and painted eggs in the spring. Now the shop lies in wreckage: a doughy bedlam of baked goods and broken glass. The destruction is no worse than that of any of the other nearby shops, but the sight hits like a clenched fist to her gut.

Swallowing, she cranes her neck, trying to glimpse beyond the broken display to see if Herr Schloss or his wife is inside. But all she can see is the laughing crowd, tossing food and plates, trays and tongs, light fixtures and framed pictures into a growing pile on the street. As she watches, one of them pours petrol over the resulting heap and lights a match, and in an instant they are standing around a small, man-made mountain of flame.

"They're getting closer," mutters Rita.

Renate shivers, remembering her question to Herr Lawerenz: *What are we too easy a target for?* She again sees Herr Lawerenz's flushed, rough face: *Two-by-two.* Why hadn't they listened to him?

She is considering grabbing Stella's arm and simply pulling her from the car when the vehicle resumes its lurching trek forward. For a few minutes a relieved silence fills their car. But then they reach the

Tiergarten, and the Moorish-inflected arches of the Fasanenstraße Synagogue, and a collective gasp rises from the riders.

The synagogue's entrance swarms with barbarous activity. The huge oaken doors are hanging open; silver ornaments and ancient-looking scrolls fly through the air, the lambskin parchment flapping like lopsided wings. Chairs and bits of pew rain down from one of the upstairs balconies, where a red-faced man wears a prayer shawl on his head like a turban and is doing a kind of drunken jig. As was the case with the shattered shops, policemen stand on the periphery but make no effort to intervene. Towering above the entire surreal scene is an enormous pillar of smoke that seems to stretch straight up to the clouds, so thick and dark it looks unreal.

"It's on fire," says Gartner, forgetting his own directive. His voice is hushed, reverential, as though he is witnessing the burning bush.

The old woman sitting next to him shakes her head, her soft white bun vibrating with the movement. "Such a shame," she clucks. "Such a lovely old building."

"Was?" The interjection is so abrupt and so loud that both Renate and Stella jump in their seats. Turning, Renate sees the man who'd been reading the newspaper in the corner striding furiously toward them. As he draws near, Renate clutches Stella's arm in panic. But he passes them both, stepping up to the old woman and grabbing her frail arm.

"What did you say?" he shouts, yanking her to her feet, his mouth inches from her shocked face.

"Mein Gott!" she quavers. "What—what are you doing?"

He shakes her, so hard Renate hears the woman's teeth rattle. *"What. Did. You. Say."*

"I—I just . . ." The woman throws a petrified glance around the carriage. *Help her*, Renate thinks, to herself, no one, to anyone.

But no one, including herself, moves a muscle.

"You want to save the Jew house?" the man continues, shaking the woman again with each word. "You're a goddamn kike lover? Is that it?"

His captive shakes her head. Two tears travel the fleshly channels of her wrinkled cheeks. If the man sees them they mean nothing to him.

Still clutching her arm, he yanks on the emergency stop cord above the windows. "The building is a *Jew house*," he repeats, pointing, spittle flying from his lips. "It's where they gather to plan the demise of our country. Where they have their secret rituals of murder and sacrifice." As the trolley slows, he pushes the woman toward the door. "But if you love it so much, Oma, you can go take part. Go join the rabbi. They love German women. I'm sure he'd even love a wrinkly old ass like yours."

Yanking the door open, he shoves the woman out so that she falls sprawlingly on the curb, losing a shoe in the process. Stunned, Renate gapes as the man strides back on board, wiping his hands on his trousers.

"Anyone else have anything to say?" he demands, eyeing each of them in turn. "Any other kike lovers on board today?"

Beside her, Stella gives a small, terrified sob. Across the carriage Gartner stares at the floor, his face chalk-white. For a moment all Renate can think about is not vomiting before they get to her stop, which is next. But then she sees the woman's shiny black purse lying like a wounded reptile on the trolley floor. She remembers the woman's petrified face, almost childlike in its incomprehension.

And before she realizes fully what she's doing she has leapt up and grabbed the bag, and is throwing her weight against the door. She battles with it for a moment until it reopens with a sigh, spilling her onto the glass-littered street.

The fall knocks the wind from her. At first she simply lies there, purse clutched to her chest, eyes glued to the yellow, smoke-filling sky. She hears the noise of the riots and the strangled gasps of the woman weeping. Then the clamor fades slightly, as though someone has twisted the volume knob. A constellation of dull white light points dances before her eyes. As Renate sits up slowly, though, they dissipate, and the noise of the chaos returns.

Climbing to her feet, she brushes dirt and glass from her coat. Beside her, the woman has stopped sobbing and is straightening her coat and hair with trembling hands.

"Here," says Renate, realizing as she holds out the bag that she left her own school satchel on the tram floor.

The woman takes the purse, still staring glassily across the street. Renate holds out her hand. "Here. Let me help you up."

The woman allows herself to be pulled to her feet. Clutching Renate's arm, she fumbles for the missing shoe, then freezes as an unearthly sound—like a thousand geese, honking breathy death knells—fills the air. Turning, Renate sees the wreckage of the enormous organ that had led the congregation through song and mournful prayer each weekend. Its silver pipes are bent and smashed, its ivory keys shattered. Sheets of music slip and float through the hot air like a school of startled fish, dispersing.

"Madness," mutters the woman, working her stockinged toes and heel back into her shoe. Two fire trucks rumble and screech into view, looking like black ladder-backed beetles. As they stop in front of the synagogue the woman tips her head back, taking in the thickening smoke stream. Then she turns and looks back up at Renate.

"I'm not a fan of the Jews," she says dully. "Frankly, I don't care one way or the other. But this . . ."

She waves her hand helplessly, shakes her head. She is incapable of finishing the sentence.

Renate licks her lips. What she plans to say is: *It's all right. The fire department will take care of it now.*

But what she says is this: "I'm a Jew."

She has no idea where the words come from, has no comprehension of having even thought them, much less deciding to give them voice. In fact, she has never thought of herself in these terms. Not after being declared a "full Jew" by Agent Schultz; not after three years of name-calling and isolation. Not even after entering a fully Jewish school and occasionally slipping into evening services at this very synagogue—just (she always told herself) out of curiosity.

And yet here they are now: four indelible syllables, a terse incantation into the acrid air. *Ich bin Jüdin.* And here, too, is a strange new certainty inherent in the utterance, one born of these battered storefronts, these shattered windows, the flaming synagogue rooftop before her. As the firemen leap nimbly from their benches, their hoses unspooling and stiffening like waking snakes, Renate finds herself repeating it, defiantly holding the woman's gaze:

"*Ich bin Jüdin.*"

The woman blinks.

Very carefully, she removes her hand from Renate's arm.

"Get away from me," she says coldly.

And turning away, she limps off down the devastated street, cradling her purse before her like an infant.

Renate stares after her, her throat tightening and her eyes tearing in the smoke. A children's taunt she's heard lately runs inanely through her head: *Jew, Jew, spit on your head. Jew, Jew, better off dead.*

For a moment, she almost agrees. For a moment, she almost does want to die.

But very slowly, though it feels as though it takes all of her strength, she turns back to the burning building.

The firefighters have taken positions on either side of the structure and are hanging off their hoses like competing teams in tug-of-war. But as the jets start to spray, Renate realizes that they are aimed not at the flaming synagogue but at the buildings on either side of it.

She makes her way toward one of the *Polizisten,* who has been watching the scene with evident satisfaction. Hesitantly, she grasps his sleeve. "They're not spraying the fire," she says. "Why aren't they spraying the fire?"

He looks down at her, almost indulgently. "Because that's not their job, sweetheart. They're only paid to protect *German* buildings."

"But . . . but what if there are people trapped inside?"

He shrugs. "Let them figure it out. After all, the Yids brought this on themselves, didn't they? They're only getting what they deserve. All over the city, it sounds like."

Then his expression shifts, hardens. "Hey!" he shouts. "Stop that!" And he is running toward the inferno and a man who is plucking and scattering pages from a prayerbook the way he might pluck and scatter petals from a daisy. His target is not the book ripper, however, but a man with a camera who is taking pictures of the devastation.

Renate stares after him, her thoughts tangling, her breath heavy. *He means us*, she thinks numbly. *He means we are only getting what we deserve. . . .*

Then she thinks: *all over the city.*

A terrifying thought strikes her. *No*, she tells herself. *Surely not . . .*

Turning on her heel, she starts running as fast as she can.

When she reaches Bismarckstraße she's run over two kilometers and is panting so hard she starts coughing. Clutching her throat, she pushes her way through a small crowd of neighbors that has gathered across the street. They are people who used to smile and greet her and ask after her parents, but now quickly look away as she passes. When she reaches the far curb she sees what they were watching: another gang of boys and men, standing in a semicircle around another man who is wearing only a bloodstained undershirt and briefs. From somewhere in the background comes a woman's clear, outraged voice: "Let him go! Do not *touch* him!"

Oh, no, Renate thinks, starting across the street. *Nononono . . .*

But as she gets closer it becomes clear that it is. The woman shouting is her mother, who is attempting to pull the half-stripped man away from the crowd of leering, laughing youths.

The half-stripped man is her father.

And standing between the crowd and the couple is Ilse von Fischer.

13

Ilse

1938

*T*he man on the motorcycle wears civilian clothes: khaki slacks, white shirt, leather trench coat. But his hair is cut close on the sides and in the back, in the style favored by the SS. And his bike—a BMW, glinting with newness—is the type Ilse has seen SS officers riding.

"Heil Hitler," says Kai, Ilse's editor at *Das Deutsche Mädel*.

"Heil Hitler," says the biker, saluting back. "It took you long enough."

"Sorry," Kai says. "I had to confirm a few details on our list. You ready?"

"Never more so. Who's the skirt?" The biker pushes back his driving goggles, and Ilse realizes with some surprise that he's quite young, probably not much older than she herself is.

"A colleague," says Kai. "Berlin's answer to Torchy Blane. She's here to write about us making history." Grinning, he flings a thin arm across Ilse's shoulders. She forces herself to smile back, even as she subtly maneuvers away.

Whippet-thin and sallow-skinned, Kai Hellewege spends his work days circling his female staffers like an undernourished shark; general opinion is that the only reason he took the job was in order to have girls actually talk to him. And at least in Ilse's case it is working: she is here because he offered her her very first political piece. He declined to offer many details about it. But after two years of writing columns about racial hygiene and seasonal craft ideas Ilse leapt at the chance. It didn't hurt that Kai's personal connection to the Führer's extraordinary Propaganda Minister is said to be very close—some say Goebbels is practically his godfather.

"Good thinking," says the driver. Reaching into his jacket, he pulls a flask out. Deftly unscrewing the cap, he takes a swig and hands it to Kai, who in turn offers it to Ilse. After hesitating a moment, she tips it against her lips, discovering to her relief that it's rum and not Schnapps. After her experiences with Hauptsturmführer Wainer, even a whiff of the latter can trigger a sickening gag reflex.

She hands the flask back to the boyman biker, who restows it before turning to candidly look her up and down. "Want a lift?"

"How far are we going?"

Kai pulls out the map she'd seen him studying earlier when they'd stopped for a few drinks at a local *Bierhaus*. "First stop is Pestalozzistraße 14–15."

"What about the others?" asks the biker.

Others? Ilse thinks.

"They'll meet us there."

"Excellent." The driver pats the seat behind him. "Come along then, Torchy. You'll have to sit behind me, though. Sidecar's taken." He juts his chin at the latter, which Ilse sees is covered with a tarp.

"I think she wants to walk," says Kai possessively.

"Actually," says Ilse quickly, "I am rather tired. I'll meet you there."

Before he can argue further she perches herself behind the driver, smiling apologetically. Shrugging, Kai turns and starts off at a rapid clip down the darkened street.

Ilse's driver kicks the engine into gear. As he lowers his goggles he shouts over his shoulder: "I didn't catch your real name."

"It's Ida," shouts Ilse back, surprising herself. "Ida Fuchs." She hasn't thought of her old pseudonym for months, perhaps years, and for a moment she considers correcting the lie. But the rum is warm in her stomach, and the idea of assuming another persona is both titillating and unexpectedly reassuring. It's like she's donning a disguise.

"I'm Max," he says, revving the engine again. The leather seat vibrates against the insides of her thighs like a live animal, something forbidden.

Cautiously, she snakes her arms around his waist. Leaning against her, Max chuckles.

"You're going to have to hold tighter than that, Ida. It's going to be quite a ride."

Ten minutes later they stand with Kai and a dozen others in civilian clothes in front of an aged building that Ilse recognizes as one of Charlottenburg's smaller but gracious-looking synagogues.

"Ten *Reichsmark* to whoever hits it on the first try." Kai squints. "Twenty to anyone who hits the center of the kike star."

"You're on," says Max.

As he removes the tarp from his sidecar Ilse sees that beneath it lies a dense pile of rocks and bricks. Atop that are several sets of leather gloves, some welder's glasses, and a few crowbars. Removing a rock, Max winds up theatrically, like an American baseball player. They all watch with bated breath as he lobs his stone, sending it up and up, straight at the shining surface. It hits just to the star's left, shattering half the window.

With a whoop, two others in the small gang Kai's led here let fly their missiles. After reducing the big window to splintered wood and jagged glass teeth they take out the smaller, clear windows that flank the doorway, their shouts growing more exhilarated and confident with each throw. They lob a few stones at the door itself. When this has no effect beyond scraping off some paint, Max climbs the short stairwell and sets his shoulder against it.

"Here," he calls to Kai and the other motorcyclist. "Give us a hand."

The other two fall into position: *"Eins, zwei, drei . . ."* They hurl their combined weight into it with a heavy thud. Then another. And another, this one followed by a faint splintering sound.

"Almost there," shouts Kai.

Ilse's stomach has curled itself into a tight ball of anxiety, balanced out by a tingling anticipation. Her teeth are chattering even though it's not particularly cold. As the other three continue their assault she finds herself wishing she could have a few more swigs of Max's rum.

Meanwhile, the synagogue doors finally give way with an ancient-sounding, splintering complaint. Panting, Kai and the two drivers peer in, as though surprised by their own efforts. There's a round of applause from the newcomers; Max takes an elaborate bow. Then he ushers the others into the darkened interior. "Remember the instructions," Ilse hears him bellowing above the excited roar. "No stealing. We're only here to destroy."

He is greeted with catcalls and more mocking laughter. "Yes, Head-master," one of them shouts.

As the last of them files in Ilse hesitates a moment, certain that the *Polizei* must be on their way by now. But the street is quiet, save for a lone black van that has pulled up a slight distance from the parked BMWs. As Ilse watches, the driver cuts the engine and lights a smoke. He seems to be settling in for a wait.

She looks back to the shattered synagogue. From inside comes the sound of laughter and more shattering; the lights go on. Max sticks his head out. "Come on, Ida," he shouts, and gestures for her to hurry.

What she actually feels like doing is running away, and for a moment she even considers it. But then she thinks about the article Kai has promised to give her: the thrill of seeing her own words in a major Party publication.

Berlin's answer to Torchy Blane.

Throwing her shoulders back, she starts mounting the stairs.

Inside the building a dozen-odd men and boys lay waste to everything they get their hands on. Several are on the balcony, pulling books from bookshelves, ripping pages from them, sending them skating down like flat white leaves on an autumnal breeze. Two have just pushed over the lectern at the front and are laying into it with axes. Max and three others have ripped the curtain off a large cabinet and are pulling out enormous and ancient-looking scrolls.

"What are those?" she calls.

"Torah. The kike bible," he calls back, panting.

Ilse watches, both enthralled and aghast as he rips off the protective silver headpieces and sends the yellowing parchment rolling down the steps into the aisles. When one of the others unbuttons his pants and starts to urinate on the hand-inscribed texts, Ilse feels her bile rise—as much at the sight of the soft pink member as the way the careful lettering smears beneath the yellow stream. Yet it's like watching a horror film: she can't seem to look away. And as the boy splashes his last, Max, who'd disappeared briefly, reemerges wearing several skullcaps piled on his lank hair, his body wrapped like a mummy in prayer shawls.

"What do you think?" he calls to Ilse. "Is this my color?"

She shakes her head, both sickened and strangely exultant at finding herself here, in the heart of such astonishing transgression. Everywhere, ripped scroll paper is fluttering down like snow. The boy next to her is plunging his Hitler Youth dagger into the burgundy velvet of the pews, while Kai is stamping on a silver goblet of some sort until it lies squashed like a precious bug beneath his boots. She still can't quite believe the police won't appear at some point, though Kai had assured her that they will not.

"Are you getting all this, Ida?"

Turning back toward the lectern she sees Max, now hatless, about to take aim at an ornate wooden screen with his boot. At first she has no idea what he's talking about. Then, remembering the whole purpose of her inclusion in the event, she reaches into her satchel and pulls out a notebook and a pen. The movements feel almost embarrassingly inappropriate; like trying to read Shakespeare in the center of a tornado.

And yet this, she remembers, is what she has come here to do: to get the story.

Just get the story, she tells herself.

She sets her pen to her notebook, then hesitates, her mind a blank. Somewhere, someone has started singing what sounds like a gibbered approximation of Hebrew: *Dai-dai-dai. Dai-dai-dai. Dai.* Within moments the others have taken up the tune, singing in rhythm as they pound and smash and break: *Dai-dai-dai. Dai-dai-dai.* It's like the finale of the most frightening opera ever composed, as if Nosferatu had stepped from the screen into the screaming, deafening present. She has to remind herself that in this live version the attackers are the heroes, taking revenge on the true villains: *bloodsucking Jews.*

As she writes the phrase down, she becomes aware that a sudden hush has fallen onto the hall.

The rioters in the balcony area are all looking in one direction. Looking up, she follows their gaze.

A man is standing in a side door she hadn't noticed before. He is short and dark, wearing a long dark coat and a black hat, from beneath which corkscrew curls tremble on either side of his pale cheeks. He doesn't look like a vampire. He looks like a frightened, oddly dressed little man.

But even before the thought is completed there is a hoarse shriek from the balcony area: "KIKE!"

It's quickly followed by another: "Murderer!"

A rock comes flying from the pulpit area and hits the man on the forehead. As he staggers back, Kai and two others hurl themselves into the debris-filled aisles, fists and weapons raised.

"Go!" shout the others. "Assassin! Get him! Don't let the scum get away!"

Run, thinks Ilse reflexively; and as though he has heard her the man whips around. Still clutching his forehead, he staggers into the darkness, the three boys taking after him in hot pursuit. A moment later she hears thuds, screams. A garbled plea for mercy.

Then, nothing but the men shouting *KIKE! KIKE!*

They are laughing.

A few minutes later they reappear, arms around each other's shoulders as though they are coming back from a night's worth of hard drinking. There is blood spattered over Max's khaki pants. "One down," he shouts, to no one in particular.

"Two hundred thousand to go!" shouts someone back from the balcony, and the room roars its approval.

Looking down at her notebook, Ilse takes a deep breath. *Rabbi*, she writes, carefully. *Blood.*

After an hour and a half, there is literally nothing left in the chapel that hasn't been defiled or destroyed. Disappearing outside briefly, Kai and Max come back carrying four cans of petrol. These he and the others distribute liberally over the wreckage before retreating to the street. Standing in the splintered doorway, they flick lit matches into the darkness, watch them fall like tiny comets of doom. Within seconds the entire building is in flames. The mob stands before it as though it were a campfire, singing and swaying in triumph:

> *Germany, awake from your nightmare!*
> *Give foreign Jews no place in your Reich!*
> *We will fight for your resurgence!*
> *Aryan blood shall never perish!*

They finish with a communal piss into the flames, the urine hissing like a thousand hostile snakes. Then Max shouts out the next stop on his list—someplace on Unter den Linden—and the crowd sets off at a bellowing jog.

"What happened to the rabbi?" Ilse asks Max as she clambers back onto his BMW.

"Why?" Turning, he lifts an eyebrow behind his protective glasses. There is still blood on his left cheek.

"I just want to include it in my article," she says quickly.

He shrugs. "Write that he was taken into protective custody. Him and thousands of others."

"Thousands?"

He nods curtly. "Those are the orders. We're to arrest as many male Jews as we can fit into the vans." He points at the black truck she'd spotted earlier, the driver of which is now starting the engine.

"Where do the vans go?"

"Various holding sites. Then the camps. Dachau, Sachsenhausen. Oh, and a new KZ out in Ettersberg. Buchenwald, I think it's called." He revs the engine.

"How long will they be there?" she shouts over the rumble.

He shrugs. "Who cares?"

As the dawn breaks they make two more stops in rapid succession: a stationery store that explodes in flame with a single match. A delicatessen that they leave looking as though the floors and walls have been renovated in rotting meat. Both owners are beaten and dragged off like the rabbi, while policemen look on benignly. Meanwhile, firemen stand at attention in the early-morning light, soaking adjacent buildings and warning rioters to be careful not to get burned. They do nothing whatsoever to put out any of the blazes. Indeed a few actually feed them, tossing in bits of broken furniture and other debris.

As the sun streaks the gray sky with silver and pink the mob surges on to its next target, a small row of shops on Unter den Linden. The tea shop and sundries store bearing red-and-black *Christian-Aryan Enterprise* signs have been left alone. Gerstel's hat store, however, swarms with drunken rioters who have shattered the show window and painted *Jude* and a crude Star of David on the door. Hats and gloves lie flattened on the street, amid shards of glass and shiny mirror and puddles of what looks like drunken vomit. Scattered throughout are small yellow spheres that Ilse recognizes as lemon drops from the big crystal jar the jovial merchant used to keep on his sales counter. She also spots what she at first takes to be a pile of dirty, wet rags before realizing with a chill that the wet and dirt is actually blood, and the "rags" are a man lying face-down on the pavement. When one of the rioters turns the prone form over with his boot Ilse doesn't know which shocks her more: the sight of Herr Gerstel's lifeless face, the eyes open, blank and staring, or the casual way in which the man above him kicks the body before moving on.

She manages to tear her eyes away as Max pulls up next to three men who have dragged what appears to be a shop safe through the wreckage and are hammering at it ferociously with clubs and crowbars.

"No looting, right?" he calls out to them. "We're patriots. Not thieves."

"*Klar,*" says one, pausing and wiping his brow. "We're not after money. We're after records."

"What records?"

The man slaps his right fist into his left hand. "Customer records. To see who's been betraying their country by doing business with this scum."

Ilse looks back at the ruined shop, swallowing again. Though she and Renate probably tried on every hat in the store at one point, she has never bought anything from the Jewish merchant. She wonders uneasily what the punishment for his Aryan customers will be. At the delicatessen on Friedrichstraße, she'd seen the mob turn on one of its own with dizzying speed, a dozen or more of them pummeling an older man until he'd collapsed into a fetal-shaped ball. When Max asked a bystander what had happened, the man spit in disgust.

"He said that maybe they'd done enough damage for now," he said.

Cutting the engine, Max dismounts, as does Ilse. He begins walking the heavy machine across the street. "One more stop," he says, gesturing across the street with his chin. "This one's a special assignment."

"Special?" Following his gaze, she feels her mouth go dry.

"He's had offers from Aryan buyers but has been holding out for a better price. We're to give him a little incentive. Though by the time we're done with it I doubt the place will be worth more than a few *Pfennige.*"

Noticing something near the engine, he squats to get a closer look, then looks up, seeming annoyed. "You go ahead."

"I can wait."

"No, go on. I'll be there in a moment."

She makes her way toward the crowd, her heart pounding as she draws close. The target, as she'd feared, is the Konditorei Schloss, though it bears no resemblance to the fragrant haven of her younger years. The large glass display window has been shattered so thoroughly that the shards are tiny, piled high both inside the building and outside on the sidewalk like mounds of glittering snow. Baked goods lie in swollen, sodden piles on the ground, brown loaves mashed into gray pavement with lingering imprints of heavy boots, cakes oozing frosting and custard like sugary innards.

But most shocking of all is the sight of Herr Schloss himself.

It's been over three years since Ilse saw the baker, and he no longer looks as though he'd fill out the red robes and bishop's hat he used to sport at *Weihnachten* in years past. In fact, it's hard to imagine him even laughing at all. His formerly round, pink face is now pale and pinched-looking, and he has an angry welt on his left cheek. His apron has been marked with a lopsided Star of David, in what looks like the same yellow paint used to scrawl *Jude* across the shop's door.

As his bright blue eyes meet hers and widen in recognition, she feels a spike of panic: *No*, she thinks. *Nonono*.

But he is already calling her name. "Ilse!"

His voice is different too. No longer hearty and deep, it's the voice of a thinner, weaker man.

Pretending not to have heard, she searches wildly for Kai and spots him a few meters away, dousing a pile of towels and potholders with petrol and the fierce overfocus of the exceptionally inebriated.

The baker calls to her again. "Ilse!" he calls again. "Ilse von Fischer!"

Ilse shrinks into the crowd, still pretending not to have heard. Kai, however, clearly has: swinging around, he glares from Herr Schloss to Ilse and back again. Then, setting his can down with the same overstated care, he walks unsteadily over.

"Who are you talking to, Jew?" he says.

Though not especially loud, his voice cuts through the shouting and laughter. A queasy quiet descends as, as if on cue, two heavyset men step out from the group. Each one takes one of the baker's quaking arms.

Herr Schloss stares at him blankly.

"I asked you a question," says Kai more loudly. "Do you know this girl?" He points to Ilse.

When the baker doesn't answer, one of the men shakes him hard enough that he briefly loses his footing. Regaining it, he blinks.

"I do," he says quickly. "I do." Looking back to Ilse, he adds: "Tell them, Ilse. Tell them you know me. Tell them I'm a good man."

As the crowd turns its bleary gaze on her, Ilse is rooted to her spot.

"You know this Yid?" asks Kai, his voice now even quieter.

Ilse shakes her head. "No."

"Of course she does," says Herr Schloss, his voice rising in desperation. "She's been one of my best customers. Go on, Ilse!" he pleads. "You can tell them!"

For a moment, no one seems to breathe. Ilse keeps her gaze on the ground, on a raspberry turnover whose glistening innards splay on the street with obscene sticky sweetness. She feels rather than sees Kai approaching from the corner of her eye. He is walking slowly, as though taking a casual stroll. But when he puts his arm around her shoulders this time, there is nothing joking or affectionate about it. And when he presses his lips to her ear, there is nothing even faintly seductive in his voice.

"Is the Jew telling the truth?"

Pulse racing, she shakes her head again. "No," she repeats. "I—I don't know him."

"But of course you do!" exclaims the baker. He actually laughs, an obsequious smile spreading on his bruised face. "You even came during the boycott! Don't you remember?"

Kai's grip tightens. "Really," he says. His voice is tight and low. To Ilse, almost beneath his breath, he says: "Look at me."

Trembling slightly, Ilse meets his gaze. He is staring at her with a kind of gloating intensity. Pulling her close, he murmurs directly into her ear: "Did you break the boycott for a Jew?"

His breath smells toxic: beer and bile and molded cheese. Swallowing back a surge of nausea, she pulls away. "Of course not."

"Prove it." He lifts his hand, and it takes a moment for Ilse to realize that he is signaling Max, who is still holding his motorcycle up on the other side of the street. Nodding, the latter turns and begins rolling the bike toward them, the crowd parting to create a silent path. When Max reaches Kai, the editor reaches into the sidecar and selects a large red brick, which he hands to Ilse.

"Prove it," he says again.

Behind them, the mob begins to shift and mutter restlessly. *Boycott*, she hears. *Jew lover. Bitch.* The rough red block in her hand feels far heavier than it looks; her arm and shoulder ache with its weight.

"Well?" says Kai. He is sounding impatient now. "There's a good spot. Right there." He is pointing at the one glass expanse that hasn't yet been shattered: the door.

"Ilse, *bitte*," the baker stammers.

Ilse looks at him. His eyes are wide. His small pink mouth is pursed and trembling. "Please," he repeats. "You were always such a nice girl."

Nice girl, she thinks, numbly.

And suddenly, she is filled with a searing rage. At Kai, for putting her in this position as casually as he puts his hands on her body. At Max, for bringing her here, and for locking his dark eyes on her as though her next move will determine her fate.

But most of all, at Herr Schloss. For in the end this is all *his* fault. He was the one stupid enough to hold on to his business, rather than selling it and remaining safe. He was the one bringing up the boycott, getting her into trouble with her superiors, when all she'd ever tried to do was be kind to him, to help him.

Traitor, she thinks. *Coward. Liar.*

Greedy kike.

And then the brick is in flight, with all the velocity and accuracy of an arrow released from a bowstring. Ilse stares in amazement as it speeds through the air, heading not for the glass but the man: Herr Schloss himself. She watches, mouth agape, as the baker tries to duck and the men holding him hold him firm. The missile hits its target, striking the terrified Jew in the chest, just above the six-pointed star. And though she has never in her life done anything remotely this violent, never been aware of even harboring such an urge, the sight of his startled face and the sound of his pained cry spark a crystalline jolt of exhilaration that makes her want to do it again.

The crowd feels it too. It lunges forward, piling onto the tradesman, pounding and kicking, until he lies as motionless on the ground as the hat merchant. Shouting and cheering, the mob surges past him and into the shop through the window, toppling the cash register, tearing down oven racks and shelves, throwing the goods out onto the street. Sacks of flour land and split in clouds of dusty mist. Raw eggs crack, bleeding sunny yellow yolks onto the street. Two baking sheets come flying through the empty window, nearly hitting Ilse in the head. But by now she doesn't care; it's as though with that one action a spell has been cast: she's invincible. Invisible. Omnipotent. She could leap into one of the surrounding fires and emerge not just unscathed, but reborn.

Electrified, she takes the other brick from Max, marveling that it hardly feels heavy at all now.

"I thought your name was Ida," he shouts, as he picks up another for himself.

"It is," she shouts back. "The filthy Jew was lying."

 ❧

An hour later, Max curses the traffic for moving at a snail's pace as drivers and riders gawk at the ominous vista. Still, despite its coating of dust and rubble, the sidecar is significantly more comfortable than the back of the bike had been, and Ilse is almost tempted to close her eyes. It would be easy to simply fall asleep like that. But just as she's found a comfortable, slumped position Max is stopping again.

"*Hallo,*" he shouts. "Looks like the fun's still going on over here."

Lifting her head, Ilse sees with a start that they are idling on Renate's street. As she follows his gaze to the now-familiar sight of half-drunk men and boys jeering and shouting *Jude* and *Yid* and *Kike*, Max cuts the engine. And it's then that Ilse hears a woman's voice as well, high and shrill: *Let go of him! You animal! You swine!*

As Max swings his leg over the seat, she watches him groggily before clambering out of the sidecar and trailing after him toward the activity.

At first she can't make out what it's about. Then the group parts, and she sees the object of their derision: a tall, gray-haired man with a beard wearing only his underthings. One of the men has his dagger out; he appears to be lunging fencing-style, pricking his victim each time just enough to make him cringe. Two others hold a shrieking, struggling woman back from the cruel tableau. "Cowards!" the woman screams. "Swine!"

The voice makes the hairs on the nape of Ilse's neck stand up. A split second later her eyes make the same, devastating connection:

The man in the bloody shirt and drawers is Renate's father.

The woman is her mother.

This time, Ilse doesn't give herself time to think about what she's doing. She simply breaks into a run.

14

Renate and Ilse

1938

"*S*top. *Stop* it!"

Ilse hurls herself at the group, pushing past a surprised Max and the taunting semicircle that has formed around Renate's father and his torturer. For the second time in two hours she is surprising herself: just as her arm and fist made the decision to hurl the brick at Herr Schloss, her legs are carrying her toward the Bauers' familiar front door as her brain struggles to catch up.

"Let him go!" she shouts, knocking head-on into one of the men and in the process knocking him into the much younger boy beside him.

"What the hell," says the man.

The boy staggers and nearly falls, cursing before hauling himself back up and pointing an unsteady finger in Ilse's direction. "Who'sh that," he slurs.

Ilse ignores him, coming to a panting stop as she reaches the circle's center.

It's not just the blood, though that is shocking enough: Otto Bauer's white cotton shirt and shorts are soaked with it. A thick, paintlike streak drips down one arm; there is even blood smeared in his tangled hair.

But since Ilse last saw him, Renate's father has transformed into a man she no longer recognizes. His once-dark and rich hair is now thin and almost white. His lank form seems to have shrunk several sizes, not just in girth but in height. His face, which had exuded intelligence and perpetual bemusement, now looks heavily lined and confused, as well as startlingly vulnerable without his habitual horn-rimmed spectacles. At the sound of Ilse's voice he, like everyone else in the small group, has turned his blue eyes upon her. But they reflect no recognition; only a vague puzzlement. His wife stands a couple of meters away, struggling in the grip of two large, leering men. Coatless despite the cold, she is wearing only a thin blouse, one of the sleeves of which has been ripped from her shoulder. She, too, has changed: always bird-thin, she is now almost skeletal, her pale skin stretched so tautly over her exposed shoulder blade that it appears the bone might tear through at any moment. Slightly behind her is Franz, disheveled and pale and being held by another, much younger thug in Hitlerjugend attire. Behind him, the front door to the Bauers' home has been left open, displaying a front hall in complete disarray: the rug is rumpled and thoroughly muddied, the banister broken. The grandfather clock Ilse has always loved has been smashed and turned on its side. She wonders vaguely where Sigi is.

She tears her gaze away from the destruction, only to meet Franz's one good eye. The look in it is unreadable. But the gaze itself still lands like a punch to her gut.

Taking a deep breath, Ilse squares off with his father's attacker. He is easily twice her weight, with the burly frame of a day laborer and biceps that she likely couldn't fit both hands around. As he registers her presence his eyes—wide-set and beer-bleary—seem to have trouble focusing correctly. She wonders how long he's been drinking.

"You don't want to do this," she tells him.

"Who the hell are you?" He holds the dagger high and slightly behind him, as though preparing to attack her next. Its tip is crimson with the professor's drying blood. Ilse forces herself to look away from it as she tries to catch her breath.

"I asked you a question, bitch," he repeats, spraying spit as he speaks. "What's your name?"

"Ida," she says, trying to keep her voice from shaking. "Ida Fuchs. You need to leave this family alone."

He throws his head back and laughs contemptuously, the sound like that of a bull lowing. The jeer is quickly picked up by his cohorts. "Ooooh," one of them mocks. "Are you going to fight her next, Manfred?"

"She looks like she'd like a fight," says another insinuatingly. "I'll fight her if you don't."

"I'm the regional district leader of the Bund Deutscher Mädel." Ilse tries to state it as authoritatively as she can, though her blood is roaring so loudly in her ears that she can barely hear herself speaking. She forces herself to maintain his gaze as she reaches into her satchel and pulls out her *Untergauführerin* badge. She flashes its distinctive yellow crest at him, hoping her hand isn't visibly shaking and praying that in his alcohol-fueled haze he won't grasp more than the capital letters *U* and *F*.

He shrugs. *"Na und?"*

"This man isn't Jewish. No one in the family is. You're about to make a very big mistake."

As she slides the badge back she sees Elisabeth Bauer staring at her, her brown gaze hard and angry but also blazing with comprehension. "It's true," she says, in the *I mean business* voice that Ilse still remembers so well. "What she's saying is true. My husband isn't Jewish. Neither am I."

"I know *you're* not, you kike-fucking bitch," says the one they'd called Manfred.

The men holding her shake her violently in emphasis, so that her head seems to snap on the thin white stalk of her neck.

Ilse fights back a flinch. "You are only getting yourselves into a lot of very bad trouble. This man has powerful connections to the Party."

"Then why was his name given to us by Party headquarters?" asks

Manfred. Pulling a crumpled ball of paper from his pocket, he smooths it awkwardly against his thigh and squints at it, holding it up to the light. *"Otto Bauer,"* he reads, with exaggerated care. *"Number 265. Wife is Gentile."* He looks at Renate's mother, spits contemptuously.

"Some of those lists have the wrong names and addresses on them. It happened several times last night."

The lies hang there like desperate darts thrown into the chill fall air, Ilse holding her breath, praying that they'll land.

"The Party doesn't make mistakes," says Manfred, staunchly.

"I'm sure it wasn't a Party leader. They have secretaries, you know," she retorts, in a tone she hopes is both confident and contemptuous.

"Ida? What in God's name are you talking about?"

Turning, she sees Max staring at her, his dark eyes wide.

"These people aren't Jews."

"Not that. What are you saying about the lists?"

Swallowing, she tries to keep her expression matter-of-fact. "You didn't hear? Kai told me at the Windhund earlier. He had to call in with his list before we went out because we were told some of the addresses on it were off." She pauses before improvising: "It's why we were so late."

His dark eyes dart from her to the brutish Manfred to Manfred's blood-spattered victim. "He didn't tell me that."

"Well, it's true. And these oafs are going to find themselves in a cell if they don't listen."

Turning back to Manfred, she pulls herself up to her full height. "What is your full name and rank, anyway?" *Always ask questions with authority.* It's one of the interview tactics she learned last month at the National Leadership School in Potsdam, where she and other rising BDM regional leaders were sent as part of their training. Of course, the interviews they'd been prepared for were with adolescent girls, as part of the screening process for new BDM recruits. But the strategy seems to work just as well on drunken *Sturmtruppen.*

"Schumacher," Manfred says, frowning confusedly. "SS-Mann Manfred Schumacher."

A quick beat of relief: he's the lowest rank possible without technically still being only a candidate. "Put your dagger away, Manfred," she says. "This man served the Kaiser. He has two Iron Crosses."

"A kike who served is still a kike," says Manfred, though his tone is now more petulant than threatening.

"He's not any more of a kike than you or I are."

He hesitates, and Ilse can all but see him struggling to weigh the wisdom of contesting her.

"It's true! Please. Listen to her. It's true."

The voice—frightened, female, and familiar enough that even now Ilse's pulse leaps in recognition—breaks in from just behind them. Turning, she sees Renate pushing toward them, white-faced and breathing heavily. She is wearing the familiar green woolen coat she had at fourteen, her pale wrists extending nakedly from the cuffs.

Like the rest of her family she is much thinner than when Ilse last talked to her. But in that instant she strikes Ilse as beautiful in an almost otherworldly way: her cheeks flushed pink, her dark eyes wide with fear. The wave of joy at seeing her is so powerful that it is almost disorienting; Ilse actually has to shut her eyes for a moment to suppress it.

"It's true." Renate's voice sounds thin and childish to her own ears. She has to fight to keep the shock out of it: shock at the sight of her besieged family and home. Shock at that one moment when she thought Ilse was leading the attack. The almost equally shocking moment when she realized that in fact, Ilse was stepping in to try to protect them.

And yet she finds herself falling into line beside Ilse and the young man who stands beside her as though nothing at all has changed between them. "We're Germans," she says again. "None of us are Jews."

Which is true, she reminds herself. She has never been as good a liar as Ilse. But she knows instinctively that at this moment, it is her father's life that very likely depends on what she says next and how she says it. She stares up at the drunken stormtrooper, hoping desperately that she looks as authoritative as Ilse. "My father was baptized at the First Lutheran Church on Friedrichstraße."

She casts a quick glance at her mother, who has taken advantage of the interruption to yank herself away from the two men who were holding her. Lips set in a tight line, Lisbet Bauer makes a beeline for her husband and pulls him from his tormentor. Her father's face is the color of chalk. They must have taken him from his bed straight to the street, as he is wearing nothing but the drawers and white cotton vest in which he sleeps at night. Renate's throat tightens as she takes in the spattered blood. But while numerous, the spots at least don't appear to be growing. She desperately hopes that this means that his wounds are superficial, unlike those of some of the men she's seen on her way home.

"You're the daughter?"

The boy speaking is the one who seems to be here with Ilse, given how close to her he is standing. He strikes her as almost unnervingly young, his face and torso still padded with childish fat, his dark eyes long-lashed like Franz's.

She nods. "Yes."

The boy looks at Ilse. "You know her too, Ida?"

Ida? Renate glances at Franz. He gives a faint nod.

"Absolutely," says Ilse. "I'm telling you. I've known all of them for years."

"I don't think she knows her ankle from her *Arschloch,*" says the boy who is still holding Franz's arms.

Another round of chuckles, but the sound is uneasy now. And the boy in the leather coat doesn't even smile.

"It's easy enough to clear up," he says, and turns to Renate. "Go get his *Kennkarte.*"

Renate's heart lurches. But before she can respond her mother is answering: "He's had to apply for a new one. He dropped the old one in the water at Wannsee when we went boating there last month."

She rattles off the mistruth with the same calm, commanding tone she uses to dispatch orderlies at the Jewish Hospital. Renate holds her breath as the boy turns to her father.

"This is true?"

Otto Bauer looks dazedly from his questioner to his wife. "Is what true?" he asks, slowly.

Oh God, Renate thinks. *Not now. Please.* Over the past months, as his work has dried up, his post and pension remain revoked, and even his beloved typewriter and bicycle have been confiscated (Jews are no longer allowed either), her father has been increasingly prone to periods of unresponsiveness. Her mother says it's a symptom of his melancholia, that it will get better once life returns to normal. Renate knows better than to ask when that will be.

To Ilse, he looks as bewildered as a young child, the way her grand-father looked last year as he began to forget even the face and name of his own wife. "That your *Kennkarte* was lost in a lake," she repeats loudly, encouragingly.

He looks at her and his eyes narrow, as though he's trying to place a once-familiar face. *Please don't say my name*, she prays.

He licks his lips, clears his throat. "Yes," he says, in a weak, shaky voice. "In the lake."

Ilse exhales silently in relief.

Max still looks uncertain. Stepping closer, he leans in and whispers to her. "You're sure about this, aren't you? You could end up in a camp if you're wrong."

Ilse's mouth goes dry. She hadn't thought about that part, any more than she'd thought about what she was doing when she ran into the group. But she makes herself nod. "I'm absolutely positive." Her pulse racing, she turns back to Manfred. "Why don't you go find some real Jews to arrest. I hear there are plenty of them on this block."

The stormtrooper scowls, his thick fingers twitching on the blade's handle. For a moment Ilse fears he's going to challenge her again. But he doesn't, instead shoving his knife back into its holster and tucking it into his belt.

"All right," he tells the group gruffly. "Let's go."

"*Scheisse.*" The boy holding Franz releases him, though not before giving him a small shove. Deprived of his cane, Renate's brother staggers and falls before slowly climbing to his feet. As the thugs drift away, Renate's mother gives a small sob; she flings her arms around her husband. "Are you all right? My God. Let me see."

"It's nothing," Renate's father mumbles.

"It's not nothing. Come inside. If you need stitches we'll need to call Doktor Strauss." Pulling his arm over her shoulders and smearing her own blouse with blood in the process, Renate's mother leads her husband slowly back into the house, though not before giving Ilse another look that feels so loaded she might as well have shot it out of a rifle.

A moment later she and her husband are slowly taking the steps together as Ilse stares at the ground.

"Well," says Max. "That was interesting."

She looks up again, startled: she'd almost forgotten he was still here. "It makes no sense to spend our energies on the wrong people," she says, as diffidently as she can manage. "It just takes away from the mission."

He shrugs. "Do you still need a ride home?"

The thought of a ride is intensely tempting; her legs are still trembling so much from exhaustion and relief that merely walking to the U-Bahn from here seems daunting. Still, she shakes her head. "I should stay here and make sure they don't lodge a complaint. That would cause more unnecessary paperwork for everyone." Though what she's really thinking is that if he drives her to her house, he'll know her address, and once he has that, it's a quick step to finding out her real name. Of course, if he asks Kai about her at any point the ruse will be up just as quickly. For now, though, Ilse is too drained to think that possibility through.

"All right," he says. He hovers awkwardly for a moment. "Is it all right if I call you tomorrow?"

"Call me?" She blinks up at him.

He clears his throat, flushing slightly. "Just in case you need more information. For your story."

"Oh," she says. "Right." A bizarre urge to laugh sweeps her; she has to struggle to keep her face straight. "I'll call you," she manages. "We don't have a phone at the moment."

"I'll give you my number."

She nods, silently retrieving her notebook and pen and handing them over to him, waiting as he scrawls the digits. As he hands the book back he gives her the stiffly formal salute. *"Heil Hitler."*

"Heil Hitler," she responds.

As he walks briskly back to his bike she watches him go, uncomfortably aware of Franz's and Renate's eyes on her. *There is nothing between us,* she wants to tell them. But of course, that isn't true. Not at all. The smashing and the burning, the bloodying and the brick-throwing: it's all bigger than anything she's experienced in her life, including the unpleasant hours spent in Hauptsturmführer Wainer's flabby arms in Dam-Großer. And it will always be there between them, she realizes numbly. No matter what happens from here. Or what he thinks her name is.

For an instant she wishes she'd accepted the offer of a ride; it would be so much easier to simply roar off in a cloud of smoke. But she makes herself turn back toward her former friends.

"That was extraordinary."

Standing next to Renate, Franz leans on his cane as he stares at her. There is a strange look on his face, as though he's trying to read her face in the distance, or in rain.

Ilse looks away. "It was nothing," she says, stiffly.

"Don't be ridiculous. You just saved my father's life. And very possibly put yourself in real danger."

She shrugs, though at *danger* her heart skitters within her rib cage. She drops her gaze to her notebook. "They'll be back, you know."

"I know." He holds her gaze for a moment as the BMW's engine starts up at the curb with a cough. "Thank you," he says, simply.

Turning, he begins to limp toward the door.

Renate remains where she is. For a moment they just look at one another.

"Ida Fuchs," she says, finally. "I didn't think I'd hear from her again."

"Me neither." Despite herself, Ilse smiles. "Turns out she's not all bad in the end."

Renate smiles back—a weak curve of her full lips that makes Ilse's throat constrict again.

"I feel like I need to thank you," Renate continues. "But I can't . . . I can't think of the right words."

"Don't thank me. Just leave," Ilse says tightly. "All of you. There's no place for you here now."

"We're trying." Renate's voice catches slightly. "We've been on the waitlist for American visas for over two years. We've applied to five other countries as well. No one will take us."

The hurt and helplessness on her face hit Ilse in the chest the way her brick had hit the baker they'd visited as friends. Ilse fiddles with the bag's buckle, trying to keep her composure. "It was just this once," she says, in a low voice. "I can't do it again." She hesitates miserably, before adding: "I have to go."

Renate swallows. "Me too," she says. But she remains rooted to the spot, and Ilse feels her chocolate eyes locked on her back as she turns in the direction of the U-Bahn.

Keep walking, she tells herself.

But after a few steps she stops and looks back. "I wrote you a letter," she says.

Renate blinks. "When?"

"When I was in the East."

"I didn't get it," says Renate slowly.

"I didn't send it," says Ilse.

"Why not?" The look on Renate's face—confusion mixed with hope—actually almost hurts to see. *Because we can't be friends*, Ilse thinks. *Because I miss you too much. Because you are what's wrong with everything.*

"Leave," she repeats.

And turning on her heel, she walks away.

15

1946

"*Y*ou know she's dead," said Maja. Her black eyes danced as she stood on tiptoe, holding the crumpled paper just out of Ava's reach. "She was probably raped and killed by the Ivans. You know that, right?"

"Give it back," said Ava, and leapt again, in futility. She didn't know what *rape* meant, except that it was awful and hurt a lot, and that it had happened to some of the other girls at the orphanage. One of them, Katje, had only been five. After arriving at the Children's Home of the Holy Mother Katje hadn't made a sound for a whole week. But the first time she saw the orphanage's Ami supervisors—Kapitän Ron and Leutnant Tommy—she screamed and screamed until she outright fainted.

"Well, do you?" Maja said now. "Answer me."

"She wasn't," said Ava. Thinking: *I will not cry.*

"She was," said Maja, and reaching out she gave Ava's shoulder a shove. Behind her, Hanne Rossing and Anja Blum watched, their eyes shining.

"She was," Maja repeated. "Probably by a hundred of them at once. Big, stinky, dirty Russians. They probably split her apart so she looked like a slab of meat. And then they left her naked and bleeding in the snow, to die."

She shoved Ava again, hard enough this time to make her stagger. As Ava caught her balance her tongue caught in her teeth. The sick-sweet taste of blood triggered nausea and a hot rush of tears. She squeezed her eyes shut, but the droplets spilled out anyway, converging in stinging, salty tracks down her cheeks.

"Awww," said Maja, delighted. "Is Babypisse bawling?" *Babypisse* was the nickname she'd given Ava the first day she'd arrived here, when she'd discovered Ava still sometimes wet the bed.

Behind her, Hanne and Anja screeched with laughter.

"Look at this thing," Maja added. Ava opened her eyes to see Maja mockingly waving her drawing, back and forth. It was supposed to have been of a *Banane*, an item Ava had never seen in real life but had seen pictures of in books and magazines.

"It looks like a cock," Maja declared. "A big yellow Ivan cock. *Auf Wiedersehen*, Ivan."

And with a flourish, she tore the picture in half.

❧

"She's just jealous," Ava's friend Greta said later, as she brushed and parted Ava's hair for Presentation.

"But why is she jealous?" Ava sniffled, then wiped her nose on her sleeve.

"Stand still," Greta chastised, and yanked the brush down for emphasis. "She's jealous because you have a mother and she doesn't." Dividing the left side into three parts, Greta started to braid, pausing to check her work from both sides in the mirror. They were in the washroom, where the older girl—Ava's one self-proclaimed ally at Holy Mother—had just helped Ava splash her face with cold water.

"But no one knows where my mother is," said Ava. *A slab of meat.*

Naked and bleeding. She tried to black the words out of her mind the way she blacked out mistakes in her drawings.

"But not knowing is still so much better than knowing for sure that she's dead."

As she tied off the first braid and started on the other, a brief somberness clouded Greta's Delft shepherdess features. Ava knew she was thinking about her own parents. After Greta's father was called to the war, her mother had taken Greta and her younger brother to the East to escape the Berlin bombings. But then the war ended, and the Russians came, and all the Germans had to run away. Greta's mother led them on the long, hard trip back to Düsseldorf, sometimes in crowded, smelly trains that stopped for hours and had no toilets or seats. Sometimes simply walking. It was while they were walking, Greta said, that the Russians had raped her mother and made her so sick that she finally died. Meanwhile, her father had been shot at the Russian front.

"You still have hope," she said now, finishing the second braid with a gentle tug. "She doesn't."

"Someone might still adopt her."

"No one will."

"How do you know?"

"The same way I know your mother's alive. I just do."

Turning Ava to face her, the older girl surveyed the younger for a moment. Pulling out a tattered handkerchief from her skirt pocket, she licked a corner and rubbed a spot above Ava's mouth, and Ava kept herself statue still. She knew it made more sense to try to look as unkempt as possible for Presentation, since she certainly didn't want to be picked for adoption. But having Greta fuss over her—having *anyone* fuss over her—made Ava's insides glow in a way that was nearly as nice as actually having a full stomach.

"There," her friend said at last, tucking the handkerchief away. "You look beautiful."

"No, I don't." Ava looked at herself quickly in the mirror, taking in her pale, pinched face, her sunken eyes, her arms and legs that looked like white toothpicks. "But you do. You always do."

Greta laughed. "Now *that's* a lie. Let's go."

It wasn't a lie. But as Ava trailed after the older girl to the barracks she wished with all her heart that it was. The only reason she could think of that Greta was even still here was that she refused to be separated from her brother, who lived in the boys' barracks on the other side of the chapel. And as of yet, no one had wanted to adopt two orphans instead of one.

But for someone as lovely as Greta, it was only a matter of time.

Back in the bunkroom, Ava felt Sister Agnes's wooden ruler prod against her sternum. "Stand up straight, child," the nun chided. "Don't slouch!"

Ava pulled her shoulders back, trying to ignore the way Hanne was scowling at her from across the aisle, and the way that Maja, standing next to her, was sticking her tongue out. But both were quickly obscured by the woman who had just come to a stop directly in front of Ava's bed.

The woman looked Ava up and down, holding her chin in thought. "Hubert," she called.

"Ja, Bärchen." The stooped man chatting by the door with Kapitän Ron and Leutnant Tommy looked up.

"Doesn't she remind you of Ina?"

Separating himself from the bored-looking Americans, the man made his way toward them. He walked haltingly, with a cane and a limp that made his body jerk back and then forward with each step, as though he were doing a funny kind of dance. Ava dropped her gaze to the floor, studying first the woman's worn brown work shoes, then the nun's low-heeled oxfords, and finally the man's heavily scuffed brown-and-white wingtips as they drew up beside them.

"In what way?" he asked.

"Around the nose," said the woman. "And the eyes too."

"Hard to tell when she's got them stuck on the ground." The man gave a quiet laugh.

Go away, Ava thought.

"What's your name, *süsse Maus*?" the man asked.

She felt Sister Agnes's ruler again, this time under her chin. "Look up, child. Tell them your name."

Ava lifted her head. The couple standing before her were younger than her grandparents had been but probably older than her mother, though it was hard to know for sure. The woman had kind hazel eyes and black hair streaked with white, and she was gazing at Ava with a kind of dreamy wistfulness. The man was almost bald and had a huge silver-pink scar that ran from his left ear to the corner of his mouth. It pulled his top lip a little, making it look as though he was always smiling just the tiniest bit.

"Well?" said Sister Agnes. "What's your name?"

Ava swallowed. "Ava." She said it in the smallest voice she could manage while still technically not whispering.

"And how old are you, Ava?" the woman asked.

"I'm six," she muttered.

"Six! My, what a big girl," said the man, though Ava knew full well that she was small for her age. "And what do you like to do?"

"Do?"

"With your free time. What games do you like to play?"

Ava looked uncertainly from him to Sister Agnes. She really didn't know any games. Her *Opi* had started to instruct her in chess, but the bombing happened before he'd taught her how all the pieces moved.

"Ava," said Sister Agnes, "is our little resident artist."

"Isn't that lovely!" exclaimed the woman. "Our Ina loved to draw too. She especially liked drawing flowers and kittens. We still have some of them up on our walls." Kneeling next to Ava, she looked directly into her eyes. "What do you like to draw?"

Ava bit her lip.

"Go on," said Sister Agnes, laughing in a way that sounded amused but which Ava knew actually signaled annoyance. "Don't be shy, for goodness' sake. Tell Frau Dunkel all about your pictures."

Ava licked her lips with her still-smarting tongue. "I draw food," she said, still in her lowest voice. "Cakes and chickens and banana splits, especially."

"That sounds delicious," the woman said warmly. "I don't know about banana splits. But Humbert and I live on a big farm outside Norf, and we have chickens and baby chicks and a cow."

"A cow?" Despite herself Ava looked up again. Greta had lived on a farm during their time in the East, and still waxed rhapsodic about the food: real milk and eggs and fresh bread and fruit and honey. Sometimes there was even meat. At night, she'd tell Ava stories about the meals she'd had, the way Ava's grandmother had told her bedtime stories in the life that, looking back, now felt like a fairy tale itself.

Frau Dunkel winked. "She is a very skinny cow at the moment. Still, she gives us a little milk. And someday soon we might even manage to pull together a cake or two, if we have something nice to celebrate."

Her voice was gentle and low, and beyond her obvious interest in cake Ava found herself wondering whether Frau Dunkel ever sang lullabies. Her *Oma* had sung sometimes, at night: "Sleep Child Sleep" and "The Moon Is Risen." . . .

An image drifted past, her grandmother's white hair and little diamond drop earrings. Her quavering voice, a room papered with Ava's pictures of princesses and castles. A wave of homesickness and longing washed over her so powerfully that for a moment she was unable to speak.

"Our Ina," Frau Dunkel was continuing, "was a little older than you when she was taken from us last December." From the corner of her eye, Ava saw the husband's hand settle on his wife's shoulder.

"For a long time we were very sad," the woman went on. "But then we realized that there are so many wonderful children who have no parents now. And . . ."

"I also draw pictures of my mama," Ava blurted.

Frau Dunkel blinked. "Your mama?"

"Yes," said Ava. "And I'm not an orphan, because she isn't dead. She's going to come back for me soon."

Frau Dunkel raised her brows, looking up at Sister Agnes, and Ava

saw the nun's chin set in annoyance. "Ava's mother was in the Wartheland at the end of the war," she said, as though in apology.

Frau Dunkel gave a nod. "Oh dear. I see."

"But she's coming back," Ava insisted.

"Now, Ava. We've discussed this." Sister Agnes's voice was a tad too
bright. "Given how much time has passed, it seems safe to assume . . ."

"She's not dead!" It came out a shout, so shrilly and abruptly that
the entire barracks fell silent at the sound.

"She's not dead," Ava repeated, her voice only slightly lowered. "And
she wasn't raped and left like a slab of meat in the snow."

Behind her, she heard Sister Agnes gasp, while Frau Dunkel, still
kneeling, flinched. As the nun's hand clamped on her shoulder Ava's
heartbeat thrummed in her eardrums, so loudly that it almost drowned
out the *clunk-clunk-clunk* of Kapitän Ron's big black boots marching toward them down the aisle.

"What is happening here, ladies?" he asked, in his slow, cowboy-
sounding German. "Why the shouting, squirt?" *Squirt* was what he called
Ava and the other, younger orphans. He said it meant *little* in English.

"It's my fault." Frau Dunkel climbed awkwardly to her feet, smoothing her floral skirt with two hands. "I upset her, I think."

"Oh no." Sister Agnes's voice was as light and as calm as always,
but her fingers conveyed another message, gripping Ava's shoulder with
steely strength. "Not at all. Ava knows better than to speak like that. In
fact, I think Frau and Herr Dunkel deserve an apology." She shook Ava
lightly. "Don't you agree, Ava?"

Ava stared at the floor, mute. She hated apologies, especially when
she'd done nothing wrong. Her stomach felt like a clenched fist.

"Well?" said Kapitän Ron. He sounded cross now, and when Ava
hazarded a glimpse at him his hazel eyes were narrowed. "Say you're
sorry, squirt. These good people are just trying to help you."

"*Entschuldigung,*" Ava muttered.

Sister Agnes shook her slightly. "Louder, please. And look up."

Swallowing, Ava tilted her head back and looked up at Frau Dunkel's thin face. The expression on it now fell somewhere between horror

and pity, as though she'd just discovered that Ava had horns, or a hidden third leg. From behind her, Ava heard Maja snicker.

"I'm sorry," she whispered.

A half hour later she sat quietly, her hands folded in her lap and her eyes fixed on the Mother Mary statue perched just above Mother Superior's white-winged head. Apart from the requisite Evening Devotion, Ava didn't generally pray outside of Mass. It was clear to her by this point that if God existed, he was either deaf to or uninterested in her requests: that her grandparents and their house would return miraculously. That her mother would return from whatever mysterious, silent place she was now. That Maja would, like the cruel stepsisters in *Aschenputtel*, have her black eyes pecked out of her face by vengeful pigeons.

Now, though, something in the Virgin's gently vacant gaze gave rise to one last heartfelt, desperate request: *Please*, Ava asked her silently. *Please let her be alive. Please let her come back soon and take me home.*

"Well, Ava." The *Mutter Oberin*'s words were tight and terse. "I understand that you spoke very rudely to our visitors."

Ava squeezed her hands together hard enough that her knuckles grew nearly as white as the statue's smooth, pale cheek. "I was only telling the truth."

"And what is that?"

Ava looked up rebelliously. "My mama isn't dead."

"But you said more than that, didn't you." The nun leaned back in her chair, eyeing Ava over her glasses. Her face was as creased as a walnut shell: rumor had it she was at least a hundred years old. She'd been known to beat children with a heavy volume of *Starck's Prayer Book*, kept specifically for that purpose.

Ava bit her cheek and said nothing.

"I understand," the *Mutter* went on, her voice lowering in tone in a way that made it more unnerving than if she'd shouted, "that you said your mother had not been . . . not been violated."

"Violated?"

The Mother Superior cleared her throat. "It means—the word you used to the Dunkels. The thing you said hadn't happened to her."

"Raped?"

Frowning slightly, the nun nodded.

"That's because she wasn't."

"It doesn't matter if she was or was not. We do not speak in that way here. Ever."

Ava scuffed the toe of one shoe against the floor, feeling the sole pull back slightly where the seams had worn away. On rainy days her feet soaked right through. Until the next Red Cross clothing shipment arrived, however, there was nothing that could be done.

"What on earth made you think it was all right to say such things?" the Mother Superior went on. "Where did you even get those awful ideas?"

Ava shook her head mutely. She knew better than to rat out Maja; in her half year spent roaming Berlin's rubbled streets the latter had seemingly perfected every surreptitious torture trick in the book. The last girl who'd tattled on her had been so fiercely pinched in retaliation that her arms resembled those of a black-and-blue leopard.

"Ava." Mother Superior let out a short sigh. "Look at me. I must make one thing very clear to you."

Ava stared at her bare, grubby knees, knowing full well what was coming. Knowing, too, that it was wrong. *Wrong-wrong-wrong.*

"Your mother," the Mother Superior continued, "has not been heard from since before the end of the war. Indeed, she wasn't even present at your grandparents' funeral. We have waited over a year for her, or another relative, to contact us. Your photograph is in every Red Cross office in the sector. I understand that it's painful, but you must accept that your mother isn't going to come back."

"She is." Ava kicked the wooden rung on her chair. "Even Greta says she is."

"Greta is a *child*," the Mother Superior said sharply. "There are certain things in life that only adults can understand. But there is more involved here." Leaning forward, she looked Ava in the eyes. "You know that there are many, many girls and boys in Germany who don't have family or a roof over their heads. The mission given to us by God is to take them in and find them homes. But we can only do that if and when we have space. And even then we can barely care for them, especially since the Allies won't give food or clothing to Germans. Not even German children." She paused. "Do you understand what I am saying?"

Ava shook her head. The gesture felt strangely passive, as though she were a puppet and someone was making her move with strings.

"Every child that comes to our doors has a right to our care and protection. But we can only give it for a little while—just until we find a safe, good place for them." She sighed. "We've now had two fine opportunities to find such places for you. But both times, you have rejected them outright." Planting her hands on her desk, the Mother Superior heaved herself creakily to her feet. As she made her way around the desk Ava shrank against the chair's hard oak back, though the dreaded prayer book was nowhere to be seen. But the Mother Superior merely perched herself in the other chair and placed her hands on Ava's bare thighs.

"If you don't leave," she said, "it means we can't help another child. And do you really want that? To deprive another little girl of food, of clothes, of a home?" She leaned closer, so that Ava could smell the combination of mint tooth powder and the cod oil she took daily for her arthritis: a sick-sweet blend of pristine and putrid. "Do you really want to do the same thing to another child that the Americans and the Russians and the British did to you?"

Ava felt powerless to look away. What she wanted to say was *Yes. Yes, I do—just until my mother comes.* But somehow, all she could do was shake her head.

Mother Superior nodded. Releasing Ava's legs, she sat back. "I didn't think so. So tonight, you will apologize to Sister Agnes and Kapitän Ron for your behavior. And for Evening Devotion you will pray both for forgiveness, and that you might be lucky enough that a kind couple like the Dunkels will make you their daughter."

Daughter. Every cell in Ava's body wanted to shout out: *No! No, I won't!* But as the nun held her gaze she once more found herself unable to do anything but nod.

"Gut." Rising to her feet, the *Mutter Oberin* gestured for Ava to stand as well. "Now go back to your bunk, please, and spend the next two hours before supper thinking about what we have discussed."

Pushing herself to her feet, Ava smoothed her threadworn dress over her thighs and followed the nun to the door. As she was opening it, however, a soft knock sounded and Sister Agnes stuck her head in.

"Do you have a moment for some discharge paperwork?" she asked.

"Of course!" The Mother Superior's voice seemed almost relieved. "Who is the lucky child?"

Beaming, the younger nun pushed the door fully open while beckoning behind her with her free hand.

"Danke," said a familiar voice.

Ava looked up to see Frau and Herr Dunkel poised in the hallway. Between them, holding both their hands, stood Maja.

As the two girls stared at one another, for once Maja's gaze held none of its usual loathing and scorn. Joy and wonder had suffused her pinched features with a softness that Ava had never seen there before.

"Oh my dear! Congratulations!" Sweeping past Ava, the Mother Superior enfolded the older girl in her arms, a smile spreading across her withered cheeks. As she turned to the Dunkels, Ava looked up to see Sister Agnes looking down with a strange expression, one brimming with both pity and self-satisfaction. *You see*, it seemed to say. *I told you so.*

❧

"Is it a castle?"

"No." Tongue tip tucked between her lips, Ava carefully scraped off the top layer of her structure. Theresia pulled her thin cardigan more tightly against the April chill and jutted out her lower lip. A recent arrival to the orphanage, she was five but looked three, and even younger when she smiled since half her teeth were missing. Like other recent additions at the orphanage she'd lost her parents to the *Schwarzer Hunger* brought on by a winter colder and longer than even Mutter Oberin claimed to have ever seen. ("He is punishing us for our sins," she'd explained at one Sunday night sermon, though when asked what those sins were she'd just shaken her head.)

For some reason, Theresia had fixed on Ava as her new best friend, a designation Ava found irksome rather than flattering. She had no interest in making friends these days—and certainly not tiny, toothless ones who wouldn't stop asking her questions and had terrible breath to boot. Still, Theresia trailed her around the orphanage, nestling beside her at mealtime and perching uninvited on Ava's bunk. This morning, the younger girl had actually offered Ava half her breakfast ration of dry bread and margarine after Ava complained she was still hungry. It was an offer that took all of Ava's might to refuse, which only served to make the whole thing more annoying.

"Why isn't it a castle?" the smaller girl was asking now. "It *looks* like a castle."

"Because it's a house."

"What kind of a house?"

"Just a house."

"Can I help build it?"

"No. And stop bothering me."

Scowling, Ava shifted so that her back faced her interrogator and blocked her project from Theresia's meddlesome sight. The latter let loose a short, hurt sigh before resuming her own project, a hole she'd been struggling for the past half hour to claw into the still half-frozen sand. Ava huddled over her building again, focusing this time on the arching hole of the doorway. As she'd told Theresia, it was not a castle but a house, one as close in style and appearance to what her *Oma* and *Opi*'s had been as Ava could manage. Since the weather had finally warmed enough for them to play outside coatless (though few of them had coats in the first place), this had become her new obsession: molded versions of food items that she wanted to eat, and of buildings in which she'd like to live. She had crafted sand-cakes and sand-cottages, sand-pretzels and sand-palaces. She built them with a focus so intent that it sometimes made her dizzy, so single-minded that she often missed the bell that signaled the end of playtime. When she did hear it, she'd stand up and stomp her creations back into their original grit, an act that felt both transgressive and deeply satisfying.

She turned her attention to the roof, using the spade's tip to etch in the illusion of overlapping tiles. She was just trying to decide where the chimney should go when she heard someone calling her from somewhere behind her: "Ava! Ava!"

Looking over her shoulder, Ava spotted Greta flying toward her from the direction of the chapel, her cheeks pink, her face bright with delight. Frowning, Ava turned back to her structure.

Since Maja's adoption a half year earlier, their relationship had changed. Ava hadn't exactly stopped talking to the older girl. But she had stopped seeking her out; had stopped climbing into her bunk at night for whispered tales of mythic foods and famous paintings. It helped, of course, that since Maja was gone Ava no longer needed Greta's protection from her. But Ava herself had changed too. She knew better, now, than to let herself dream of things that would never come to be—and better than to believe people like Greta, who encouraged her to dream of them.

"Ava!" Greta called again.

"Ava?" Theresia echoed, poking Ava's shoulder with a sandy finger.

"Leave me alone." Turning back to her house, Ava began carefully carving out a chimney, not looking up until Greta hurled herself into the sand pit between Ava and the younger girl, her left knee knocking into a carefully lathed wall in the process.

"Look what you've done!" snapped Ava, angrily pushing Greta's thin leg away.

"She doesn't want to be bothered," Theresia explained glumly.

"Oh, yes, she does. Ava! Don't be a goose." Greta poked Ava in the ribs lightly. "And don't worry about the house. I've something much more important to tell you." Her eyes shone like rounded raindrops on a leaf.

"What?" asked Ava, cautiously.

"Deine Mutter," Greta said breathlessly.

Ava yanked her arm away. *"Sie ist tot."*

"She's not dead." Greta laughed, the same light and patient laugh she always laughed, no matter how rudely or curtly Ava behaved. "She's here."

Ava's mouth suddenly felt as dry as though she'd taken a bite out of her own building. *"What?"*

"She's *here,*" Greta repeated. "In the office with Mutter Oberin."

It was as though the air had been sucked from Ava's lungs, from the sandpit, from the whole coldly bright day. "My mother?" she repeated, the words thick and foreign-feeling on her tongue.

"Yes!" Greta clambered to her feet, yanking Ava up with her, not bothering to wipe the sand from her bare legs. "Come on! Don't you want to see her?" Leaping from the sand pit with the lightness of a blonde, bony rabbit, Greta started racing back toward the chapel. Ava remained behind for a moment, simply staring after her. Her tongue felt frozen inside her sand-dry mouth, her feet rooted to the sand pit's shifting floor.

Brushing her hands together, Theresia clambered to her feet. "Aren't you going to follow her?" she lisped, through her few remaining teeth. "Don't you want to see your mama?"

Mama, Ava thought.

And then she, too, was running—skipping, stumbling, racing—as if for her very life.

Ten minutes later, she was sitting in the same oaken chair, in the same dark office in which six months earlier she'd been told by Mutter Oberin her mother was dead. And miraculously, sitting directly across from her in the other big oaken chair, was Ava's mother, looking very much alive.

Ilse had pale white skin and perfect posture. She had eyes the color of storm clouds and braids the color of cornsilk that wrapped around her head like Greta's, only thicker and cleaner-looking. She wore clothes that had no holes or patches, and that fell smoothly over her frame in a way that suggested there was actually flesh and fat underneath. She felt familiar in the way that Ingrid Bergman was familiar: a face Ava couldn't quite place but knew that somehow she knew. And even if her mother's first reaction upon seeing Ava had not been the whirling embrace of Ava's dreams—even if, instead, she had almost seemed to flinch, and instead of saying *ich liebe dich* she'd said nothing at all—she was still the most beautiful woman Ava had ever seen.

Now she was studying Ava with a kind of troubled intensity that left Ava unsure where to direct her own gaze. "She's grown up so," she said, sounding almost frightened for some reason. "She looks . . ."

"Yes?" Peering over the tops of her glasses, Mutter Oberin waited to hear how Ava looked.

But Ilse just shook her head, seemingly unable to finish the sentence. Running a hand over one of her braids, she asked instead: "Are they all so thin?"

"This winter took a particularly hard toll on us," said Mutter Oberin, a little stiffly. "We've managed to scrape by somehow, and now that the weather is nicer we'll be able to supplement with our own vegetables and things like nettles and dandelions, when they come up." She nodded, looking the younger woman over. "The Americans seem to have treated you well enough."

Ilse flushed, which made her even prettier. "I suppose so."

An uncomfortable pause followed. Then Mutter Oberin cleared her throat. "Ava," she said. "I know it's likely a big shock. But isn't it wonderful? Don't you have anything to say to your mother?"

Ava blinked, her gaze still fixed on the vision, half afraid that if she spoke it would vanish.

"*Hallo,*" she said finally, almost whispering.

"*Ja*, hello." The woman stared back. Her jaw—square and strong and almost like a man's—tightened slightly.

"That's it?" said the head nun, laughing in her dry, coughlike way. "Ava. Show her your drawing." And to Ava's mother: "She worked on it for weeks."

Ava looked down at the image, which she had in fact worked on for weeks, back in the days before she'd decided Ilse was dead. Titled *Meine*

Familie, it showed herself and Ilse and a dog she hoped they might one day maybe have. Ava and the dog were both dark-haired and smiling; Ilse was golden-haired and smiling, and above them all was a smiling golden sun. It was Greta who'd remembered the image and fetched it out from under Ava's bunk.

Now, hopeful and shy, Ava held it out and watched as Ilse took it in her stocky, strong fingers. For a long moment her mother stared down at the slightly wrinkled picture, her face utterly stripped of emotion. Then she nodded and gave Ava the picture back.

"It's very nice," she said. "I like the cat."

"It's a dog," Ava corrected, but her mother had already turned back to the *Mutter Oberin*. "I assume that there will be some paperwork?"

"Of course." The Mother Superior nodded, appearing slightly flustered. "I'll need a few things from you as well. Your Exoneration Certificate, to begin with. And a work permit if you have one."

"The one with the yellow hair is you," Ava said, holding the image up again for Ilse to see.

But her mother was digging in a battered-looking purse. "I'm sorry," she said, seeming not to have heard. "Do you have a pen? Of all the days to not have one with me . . ."

Their voices softened and merged as Ava stared back down at her drawing, the wide sickle smiles, the bull's-eye eyes and stick fingers. It was horrible, she realized all of a sudden; like something Theresia would draw. Or a baby.

She should never have shown it to anyone.

Very quietly, she began to rip it in half.

16

Renate

1939

Item number: 16
Quantity: 2
Item description: hand towels
Year purchased: 1933

Renate pauses, pencil pressed to her lips. Will two be enough for the five-day journey to New York? Should she risk taking more and strike something else from her list? Or will there be enough space and dry air on the ship to accommodate an emergency hand washing if need be (*Item number: 9. Quantity: 1. Description: Box of Persil laundry soap. Year Purchased: 1939.*)?

Sighing, she sticks with two and moves on to the next line. *17*, she writes. The next item on her notebook list is monthly menstrual protection. But as her eyes drift to today's date—*Friday, November 10th, 1939*—she finds herself hesitating, pen tip hovering.

"Perhaps," she says, "if I just say they're pewter instead of silver?"

"What?" Her mother looks up from the health summary she is copying out for their records across the kitchen table.

"My candlesticks. What if I say they're pewter. How are they really to know?"

"Are you seriously still thinking about that?"

Lisbet Bauer stares at her daughter in disbelief. Renate stares right back, a faint flush creeping its way up her neck. "It's not as if you and Vati are going to use them," she adds.

The "them" in question is a pair of Shabbat candlesticks Renate acquired back in February, on her way home from the weekly hairdressing course she and Karolin Beidryzcki are taking at the Jüdisches Gemeindehaus. (Neither girl particularly wants to go into hairdressing, but prospective emigrants are encouraged to acquire a trade, and hairdressing seemed the most glamorous option—at least initially.) Hurrying down a darkening Oranienburger Straße, she'd passed a prim-looking old woman sitting next to a handful of items she was apparently trying to sell. It's an increasingly common sight these days: Jews who, having secured transport and visas out of Germany, find themselves unexpectedly having to unload items they discover they can't take with them, often at the last minute.

Renate usually walks past these spontaneous street sales quickly. Not just because she herself has no resources to make a purchase, but because the quiet undertones of self-conscious desperation only underscore her own growing despondency. On this day, however, she had paused, unexpectedly captivated by one of the woman's wares.

Thanks to a handful of "Judea study sessions" with Franz and a few surreptitious synagogue visits on her own, she had a vague understanding of what Shabbat candles were for, though she'd never considered performing the old-new ritual herself. And yet standing there that chilly day, her fingertips stained red with henna and her back aching from an hour bent over a rusty wash basin, the candlesticks had seemed unaccountably comforting. Tarnished, still spotted with waxen drippings from decades of Shabbats past, they struck her as symbols of flickering hope in the waxing darkness of her life. Picking one up, Renate had found herself stroking it as though it were some Aladdin-like talisman.

"*Jakubowski und Jarra,*" the seller said.

"What?" On closer inspection, the woman's age seemed more elusive than Renate had first assumed; her fine-boned face so deeply creased by fatigue and worry that she might have been anywhere between forty and seventy.

"The maker," she said. "Jakubowski and Jarra of Warsaw. Very famous." Renate could tell from the fluid way she pronounced the names (the *J*'s softened into *Y*'s and the *B*'s into *V*'s, the same way they did for Karolin's mother) that her native language was Polish.

"My mother's," the woman added curtly. "A wedding gift."

"They're very pretty," Renate said. It came out almost an apology, though as she turned the silvery objects over in her hands she understood that she fully meant the compliment. Adorned at base and stem with unfurling leaves and whimsical flourishes, the Polish pieces were nothing in style like the sleek Parisian Art Deco pair her own mother had recently and reluctantly sold. These were unapologetically ornate, like something a Jewish Louis the Fifteenth might have set upon his rococo table. Even the nozzles looked like regal flowers in full bloom, awaiting their holy waxen stamens.

"I thought they'd let us bring them," the woman was continuing. "You see, they're only plated in silver, not solid. At first our emigration officer said yes. Then yesterday, he said no. I think they make the rules up by the hour." She sighed heavily. "I couldn't stand the thought of them ending up with some bandit official or pawnbroker. I wanted—" She hesitated, peering into Renate's face.

"I want to keep them with Jews," she said.

For a moment Renate just stared at her, sitting there in the singed shadow of the Neue Synagogue that was itself still shuttered in the wake of what the papers were now calling *Kristallnacht* (such a patent misnomer, Renate still thinks, as though that ghastly event had been nothing more than a festival of dainty glass baubles). *How does she know?* The question shaped itself in her head, not with defensiveness or resentment but a vague sense of relief, even wonder. She thought back to another old woman; the one she'd helped after being thrown from a tram. The one to whom she'd said: *Ich bin Jüdin.*

"How much?" she asked. And then, breathlessly, without waiting for an answer: "I can give you ten *Reichsmark.*" Technically, the money was for materials for her hairdressing class; she was supposed to have handed it to her instructor last week. But even as she recognized this, Renate's grip on the silvery sticks was tightening, her mind working furiously to come up with a way to borrow Karolin's kit, or even steal the instructor's rusty spare set of scissors.

"Ten?" The woman laughed dryly. "At that rate I might as well throw them in the gutter."

She reached for the candlesticks, shaking her head, and Renate's throat tightened with something almost like panic. "Wait," she said.

Plunging her right hand into the pocket of her ever-more-ragged green coat, she pulled out the crisp banknote. Then she reached back into her pocket, fingers fumbling against the worn wool until she found the slim, hard circle she'd been seeking.

She'd carried Ilse's friendship ring like this for the past four years, rationalizing the practice with various little stories she told herself about it: that when she had time she would push it into Ilse's mail slot, or bring it to a jeweler to sell, or donate it to the Jewish Winter Relief Fund. For four years, however, she'd done none of these. The ring had remained snugly nestled in the right pocket of her only coat, retrieved only occasionally for a moment or so before being plunged back into its place of nubby rest.

"Here," she said now.

The woman picked the ring up with two fingers, studying it through slightly narrowed eyes. Then she looked up.

"Silver?"

Renate nodded, though in fact she had no idea; she'd have declared it platinum if it had meant the candlesticks could be hers.

The woman hesitated once more, her eyes still searching Renate's face. Then she shrugged. "*Ach,* well," she said. "Day's almost over." Wrapping the bill around the ring, she'd tucked both in her own pocket and held the candlesticks back out to Renate. "Better these end up with someone who will use them for their intended purpose. That's worth something in and of itself."

And since then, Renate has done just that. Despite not understanding the Hebrew prayers Karolin hastily taught her, or why she covers her eyes after setting the waxen wicks aflame, or why she mustn't blow out the candles before they burn to the base; despite, too, the fact that Franz dismisses the practice as "Judaic voodoo" and her mother shakes her head in unspecified disapproval, Renate lights the two candles every Friday in her room, murmurs blessings and sing-says *A-mein.* Afterward, she leaves them to burn down on her windowsill, weekly beacons to a transformation she feels in her bones but still doesn't fully understand.

"Renate," her mother repeats now. "Are you seriously still proposing not just smuggling a precious metal—which, incidentally, you were supposed to have turned over to the Reich's Treasury Division in March—out of the country—but actually lying, *in writing,* about it?"

"Of course not," Renate snaps, although of course this is exactly what she is proposing. "I just . . . don't want them to go to waste."

"Your whole emigration could go to waste if you try to take them with you," her mother retorts tartly. "You could very well find yourself arrested."

"That's fine." Renate finishes off the next row (*17, Sanitary napkins, 12*) with an irritated flourish. "I don't want to go in the first place."

"Enough." Her mother rakes a pale hand through her now mostly gray hair. Her voice is tired and sharp. "I don't want to hear any more about not wanting to go. Not after all the work I've done."

Renate opens her mouth. Then she shuts it again, since this, too, is not really a point she can argue.

Over the past year Elisabeth Bauer has registered with the Jewish emigration aid agencies in Germany and the Jewish immigration aid agency in New York. She has filled out endless questionnaires for the governments of both nations. She has haunted five different government offices in her quest to get the new, J-stamped passports now required of Jews, batted from one unresponsive, rude bureaucrat to the next in what seemed to be the Reich's idea of an inside joke. She has paid for exorbitant departure fees and overpriced ocean liner tickets, obtained sponsorship affidavits from a former colleague in Chicago and her brother-in-law in New York, found a way around the German prohibitions against wiring funds abroad to deposit the currency required of prospective immigrants by the U.S. government in two separate New York bank accounts. She has queued up for, harassed, and cajoled staff members at the American consulate general until the Bauers' numbers came up on the visa waitlist, three years after they'd been applied for but two years sooner than they otherwise might have. After hearing that even mildly "unfit" immigration applicants faced visa rejection, she enlisted the family doctor to concoct a sprained-ankle diagnosis for Franz's leg, and paid a discreet "sweetener" to the consulate doctor to ensure that her son passed the American examination.

She has procured affidavits of good conduct from the Charlottenburg police office, and from four other "responsible and disinterested" parties in America and Germany. She's collected school certificates to confirm Renate's passing of her *Abitur* last year and Franz's completion of three years of university. She's obtained proof of passage to the Western Hemisphere, included certified copies of Bauer family tax records and two copies each of the two children's birth certificates. Most recently, she brought home the petition Renate is currently working on for the office of Berlin's chief financial president, itemizing every object Renate plans to take with her when she boards their ocean liner in two weeks. It must be submitted to, checked by, and approved by a Reich official against the actual items in her trunks and carry-on luggage, after which she'll face *another* tax on the estimated value of those items and the pitifully small cash amount Jews are permitted when they leave.

All in all, it's been a heroic performance on a two-front bureaucratic battlefield that these days defeats almost everyone. Rita Oelburg's family, for instance, was approved for U.S. visas and secured boat passage, but had no money left for the exorbitant Reich "escape tax." Kinge Lehmann's father, a former banker, could cover the escape tax and visas but couldn't secure passage before the visas expired. Bernhard Bähr was rejected because he'd had acne radiation treatments and the U.S. consulate physician labeled him a cancer risk. And the affidavit supplied by Karolin Beidryzcki's New York sponsors—pledging all their assets as bond in the event Karolin was unable to support herself—was deemed inadequate by U.S. authorities, forcing her to start the whole application process again.

"It's as though they're trying to find reasons not to let us in," she'd complained, as she and Renate mixed peroxide, honey, and baking soda into a paste that their instructor guaranteed would lighten even the most "Jewish" of dark-haired heads. Renate hadn't had the heart to tell her that according to Franz, at least, this was precisely what "they" were trying to do. And when she and Franz had finally secured transportation, visas, and exit documents, she'd almost wanted to hide that fact as well. For despite everyone's congratulatory envy, despite the soul-crushing and steadily growing list of life restrictions in Berlin, when she thought about their departure date—November 25, 1939—all she felt was a chill sense of emptiness.

"I don't want to leave," she repeats (*18*, she prints fiercely; *Sanitary pad belt, 1*). And bites her lip to keep it from trembling. "I don't want to leave you."

"You'll have Franz. And your *Tante* and *Onkel*."

"It's not that. It's about not knowing what's going to happen to you and Vati. You always said we would all stay together."

"I said that before knowing how impossible it would be," her mother says. "And nothing will happen to us. What more could happen to us?"

It's such a drastic departure from her mother's prior, dire warnings that Renate snaps her gaze up in disbelief. "Do you really want me to answer that?"

"It was rhetorical," her mother says curtly. Pulling her cigarettes from her pocket, she starts to shake one out before frowning and returning it to the pack. Since tobacco rationing was implemented she's restricted herself to two a day, a sacrifice that has made her on-edge and snappish enough that Franz has taken to calling her *Frau Havisham.* Needless to say, the days of Renate pinching the odd smoke from her mother's purse are long gone.

"You know they're banning Jews from Aryan buildings next?" Renate continues. "They're going to crowd us—meaning you—into specific houses. *Judenhäuser.* They're making Aryan spouses go too. They're already doing it in other cities, supposedly. And in Poland they're making Jews wear a yellow star."

"They couldn't do it here." Her mother waves dismissively. "It'd be a logistical nightmare. On both fronts."

"In case you haven't noticed, they are rather good at logistics," Renate retorts. "Unlike you two."

Her mother frowns. "What is *that* supposed to mean?"

"Just that for all your degrees, for all your books, for all your 'understanding' of history and human psychology, you weren't prepared for any of this."

Her mother tightens her lips. "Not many of us were, Renate."

"But if you had been, even a little more, we might be able to stay together." Renate blinks, hard, before adding: "And maybe we'd even still have Sigi."

Her mother flinches. A month earlier she'd announced abruptly that she was having the dog put down. Her reasons were multifold: veterinary care for the aging Schnauzer was expensive and increasingly hard to find, and their reduced rations made it hard to even feed themselves. "It's also better we do it kindly," she'd added, "rather than risk someone else doing it cruelly." It was an oblique reference to Jewish neighbors who over the summer had found their cat stone-cold on their doorstep, a bloody *J* carved into its matted pelt.

Renate and Franz protested vehemently; she with tears, he with brittle fury. Each argument was gently but firmly countered: Yes, Sigi was only nine, but he was already limping with arthritis and struggling to digest the cheaper, coarser food they were forced to feed him these days. Yes, she'd thought about giving him away—but to whom? All the Jews they knew were leaving the country, and those who weren't were facing the same harsh decisions they were facing. No one from their shrinking circle of Aryan friends had expressed any willingness to take an ailing, elderly dog from a Jewish home. And when Renate, desperate, offered to eat less herself, her mother turned on her with her old imperiousness. "You're suffering enough because of the animals in charge now," she'd snapped. "I won't let you starve to death over one as well."

In the end Lisbet Bauer had her way, as she almost always had her way: Sigi had a last meal of cheese and blood sausage laced with poison, and the family doctor gave him an injection so that he slept through his own death. They buried him outside by the rose garden that was now a vegetable garden, where Franz and Renate gave him a short (Lutheran) funeral service.

But in the days since, Renate has felt her pet's absence keenly: in the barkless silence following a ringing phone or a rapping knock on the door. In the empty hallway when she comes home from class or tutoring students in English at the Jüdischer Kulturbund, or at her former school until it was shut down by the government in September. She still shifts her feet at night seeking the warm furry weight that had graced the bottom of her bed since she was ten; still reaches out whenever she wakes up, at night or in the morning, for a quick pat and rough-tongued kiss. And she still finds herself battling jagged and grief-stricken sobs when her toes and fingers find only empty, silent air.

She knows she's being unfair now. But arguing with her mother seems to have become one of the few ways she can lessen the leaden ache of loss and worry.

"You know that's not true," her mother is saying. She pulls her Lords out again, her hand trembling slightly. "You know New York was a long shot. The only reason we were able to afford it for you is that Oma died and we—I—was able to sell her flat. And even then it barely covers everything."

"I still don't understand why we can't find a place cheap enough for us to all go."

"Are you saying you'd prefer Aleppo?" Her mother lights her cigarette, inhaling deeply and slowly before finally letting the precious smoke out in a slow stream. "Or Cochabamba? Because those are the sorts of places that might possibly take us at this point—and that's *if* we could manage to get visas, paperwork, and passage for all of us. Which is becoming increasingly unlikely."

"Shanghai doesn't require visas," Renate points out. "And it's supposed to be very glamorous."

"Not the neighborhoods we could afford," says her mother tartly. "And passage there for the four of us would be nearly three times as expensive as the cost of sending you both to New York on your own." She stabs the ski-slope ashtray with the ashen tip of her Lord, and Renate sees that her hand is shaking slightly. "Besides," she adds. "I honestly don't think that your father would survive that kind of a transition. Not given his current state."

"You don't know that," says Renate, though now it's her turn to look away. Over the past year Otto Bauer's condition has gone from poor to worse. He has all but stopped eating, has to be cajoled into bathing and shaving, and refuses to even go into his former home office, instead spending hours in bed or in an armchair in his bedroom. Renate's mother still speaks of his "condition" as something temporary, remediable. But Renate has noticed that she keeps a keen eye on him when he's out of bed and has quietly removed the ties, sashes, and belts from his drawers.

Now she leans back in her chair, looking tiny, defeated. "What do you want me to do, Reni?" she asks wearily. "If you are truly telling me you want to stay here, in this suffocating nightmare, then I—" She shakes her head. As she inhales, her already hollow cheeks hollow further, making her look almost skull-like.

"It breaks my heart, too," she says finally, exhaling as she speaks. "It's not as if I *want* to send my children across the world. My God. But I know if I don't, if we let this opportunity pass us by . . ."

She breaks off as a sharp rap sounds at the front door.

Mother and daughter stare at each other, eyes wide. Friendly drop-bys these days are rare, especially since it's now illegal for Aryans to enter Jewish households. When heralded by the kind of forceful knocking they are now hearing, visits are almost invariably dangerous: they've twice preceded random searches by the Gestapo. On their last visit the agents took Renate's father's Prussian officer's sword from its decorative post above the dining room cabinet, then fined him forty Reichsmarks for illegally harboring a weapon. "You're lucky," the officer who issued the ticket told them. "Jews are sent away for less these days." He hadn't needed to elaborate on what *away* meant.

Renate rises tensely. "I'll get it."

She hurries to the door, still bracing for Sigi's bouncing, barking show of territorial supremacy before remembering he isn't on her heels. Hand on knob, she shuts her eyes and forces a deep breath before opening both her eyes and the door with a silent prayer.

There, on the doorstep, is Ilse.

She looks the same as when Renate last saw her, if perhaps a little thinner, a little more tired. On her face is an anxious smile. In her hands is a bouquet of purple-and-blue delphiniums.

"*Hallo,*" she says.

Renate stares at her, her mouth half open.

Ilse gives an uncomfortable-sounding laugh. "You look surprised."

Renate licks her lips. Her face feels odd—stiff and tight, as though her mouth has recovered from the shock before the rest of her features.

"I am," she manages.

"I suppose that's fair," says Ilse, shrugging. "Can I—may I come in?"

Renate hesitates. Five years ago she would have simply laughed off the question. She would have grabbed Ilse's wrist—*What are you waiting for, you idiot*—and dragged her over the threshold. Four years ago she would have felt a glittering wash of relief that her most heartfelt prayer had been answered. Now, though, she can barely process the fact of Ilse's expectant face less than a meter from her own.

Since that brutal morning last November, she has neither seen nor heard from the other girl. She briefly contemplated dropping by Ilse's house, or at least sending a note of thanks for her inexplicable but vital act of kindness. It was Franz who'd talked her out of it.

"She put herself in enough danger, lying like that in front of people who could easily figure out the truth, if they wanted," he said. "Don't add to the risk. And *definitely* don't put anything in writing. If she wants to see us she'll find a way on her own terms."

After which he'd smiled in the half-admiring, half-incredulous way he'd been smiling whenever Ilse's miraculous reappearance came up in conversation. "That girl," he said, shaking his head in disbelief. "Who would ever have thought."

Renate slowly steps back from the door, allowing her former friend to pass.

"Reni?" her mother calls from the dining room. "Who is it?"

"It's Ilse," calls Renate. And then adds, inanely: "Ilse von Fischer."

The silence that follows is more telling than anything Elisabeth Bauer might have put to words. Then there's the sound of the dining room chair screeching against the hardwood floor, a few short, clipped steps before her mother herself appears in the dining room doorway. Her expression mirrors Renate's: it is one of the few times Renate has ever seen her at a loss for something to say.

"Hello, Doktor Bauer," says Ilse, filling the vacuum. "I brought these for you." She extends the bouquet. "I remembered that you liked them because of the poem."

"Poem?" The doctor accepts the flowers as she might a ticking bomb.

"By the man who wrote *Pooh*," Ilse explains.

"A. A. Milne," supplies Renate, reflexively. "'The Dormouse and the Doctor.'" Sent by the same *Onkel* with whom she and Franz will soon live, the book had lived on her bookcase for years, initially undisturbed because it was in English and was supposed to be only for babies. One day, though, Ilse happened to take it down, and the girls discovered the rhythmic, nonsensical little verses with delight. They'd especially loved the Dormouse, since one girl could chant the narrative while the other supplied the colors in a shout:

There once was a Dormouse who lived in a bed
Of delphiniums ("BLUE!") and geraniums ("RED!")
And all the day long he'd a wonderful view
Of geraniums ("RED!") and delphiniums ("BLUUUUUUUUE!!").

They'd learned of Renate's mother's fondness for the dusky blossoms after asking her what they were called in German ("Delphiniums," she'd told them).

"Where on earth did you find these?" Lisbet Bauer asks now.

"My mother's become friends with a Kurfürstendamm florist."

As Ilse unslings her satchel from her shoulder, Renate watches her mother waver between delight and distrust. Though relieved and grateful for her husband's reprieve last year, she'd counseled caution as far as Ilse was concerned. "One of the few certainties of human psychology," she'd told Renate, "is that while people sometimes defy expectation, they rarely change."

Her nose pressed into the bouquet, Elisabeth Bauer closes her eyes now, inhales. She suddenly looks close to tears, and as the light sweetness of the blossoms fills the air Renate almost wants to cry again herself. There haven't been real flowers in the house for months. She can't help wondering how much they'd cost.

"I hardly know what to say," her mother says at last, looking up with a chagrined smile.

"You don't need to say anything," Ilse says. "I'm the one who should say something. I should say . . ." For a moment she seems to be fighting for composure. "I should say that I'm sorry. I'm sorry for disappearing."

"So why have you rematerialized?" asks Renate's mother.

Ilse colors, clearly thrown by the question's bluntness. "I have done a lot of thinking since . . . especially since last year," she says, after a moment. "I've come to realize just how wrong I was."

"About what?"

Ilse drops her gaze to the floor, touching the toe of her shoe to a dark knot in one of the floorboards. Renate wonders if she notices the absence of the Oriental carpet, which was sold last month along with all other household items deemed nonessential.

"Everything, really," Ilse says. "The Party. The Führer. The . . ." She glances at Renate. "The Jews. I hate what's happening to them. I can't stand it."

She looks from mother to daughter again, her cheeks pink, her gray-blue eyes wide. Elisabeth Bauer stares back, her gaze level but wary. Renate can all but see the flickering equation being tested in her mind: *Abandoned Reni. Rescued Otto. Old friend. Young Nazi.*

"I'm going to go put these in some water," she says at last, her expression impenetrable.

She turns and begins to make her way toward the kitchen.

The two girls stand awkwardly: Renate nervously wringing her hands, Ilse shifting from one booted foot to the other. At last she clears her throat.

"I'm sorry," she says again, a tremor in her voice. "I truly am. There were so many times before now when I wanted to come. Especially after . . . what happened."

"So why didn't you?" Renate meant her tone to be casual. But even she can hear the hurt in her voice.

"It never seemed the right time. No. That's not true." Ilse clears her throat. "The truth is, I was afraid."

Renate almost wants to laugh. "You were afraid of visiting us but not of lying to protect us?"

The other girl smiles ruefully. "I know. It makes no sense."

"But you came."

Ilse nods. "I heard you're finally leaving. I realized I might never get another chance."

Renate thinks of Ilse's command on *Kristallnacht*: *Leave.* She frowns. "Who told you?" She hadn't thought their social circles intersected anywhere any longer.

"I ran into Maria at the Concordia."

The names land like a double blow: the first the Bauers' beloved housekeeper, forced by the race laws to quit. The second Renate's favorite cinema and ice-cream counter before Jews were banned from the movies.

"And I brought you this," Ilse goes on. "I thought of you when I first read it."

She pulls a slim, dark volume from her satchel and extends it. Renate takes it and runs a forefinger over the gold-embossed title—*Meine Wunder.*

"Isn't she on the banned list now?" she asks, pointing to the name: Else Lasker-Schüler.

Ilse arches her brows. "So what?"

So are you trying to get us arrested?

It's the first response that comes into Renate's mind. She quickly discards it. Because despite herself, despite everything, a tender sprig of hope is vining its way through her anger, her shock.

"So is your mother friends with a book importer now as well?" she asks instead.

Ilse tips her head back and laughs. It is the first genuine-sounding sound she's uttered since Renate opened the door: loud and clear and almost startling in its heartiness. It is also so intuitively familiar—like hearing Sigi's distinctive, raspy bark after resigning herself to never hearing it again—that at least for the moment it breaks through some of Renate's icy reservation, and she finds herself laughing along. For a blissful moment it's as if they've traveled back in time together.

"I found it in Switzerland," Ilse says at last, after the giggles have ceded way to a new, slightly warmer level of discomfort. "I took a Mädelschaft group on a ski trip there. It's not hard to smuggle things in if you've got the right uniform and stamps on your passport."

"So you're still with the BDM?"

"For the time being." Ilse tugs on a braid. "It's easier to know what to fight against if you're working on the inside."

"Fight?"

Ilse parts her lips, then presses them together again, throwing a quick glance toward the kitchen. The chink and splash of dishwashing drifts toward them, underscored by the rare sound of Elisabeth Bauer humming under her breath: the melody to "Stardust."

"Can we go to your room?" Ilse asks quietly. "Not because I don't trust your mother. It's just . . ." She drops her gaze. "I'm still working through all this. I need you to help."

"My room's a mess," Renate says, shrugging to disguise the sudden leap her pulse takes at the words *I need you.*

"Fantastic." Stripping off her coat and boots every bit as naturally as she'd done when they both were still German, Ilse tosses the former onto the coatrack by the door and the latter next to Renate's battered black-and-white saddle shoes.

People don't change, Renate reminds herself, as she turns toward the staircase. But it's hard to ignore the rush of happiness she feels as, glancing downstairs, she sees the new-looking woolen swing coat covering her own threadbare trench.

Upstairs her father is asleep in his bedroom armchair, a dog-eared copy of *The Last Days of Pompeii* lying unopened in his lap. Tiptoeing in, Renate covers him with the Persian throw from the bed, then tiptoes out again with a finger to her lips. Ilse on her heels, she makes her way silently through the now-carpetless hallway.

"How is he?" Ilse asks, once they're inside Renate's room with the door shut.

"Not well." Renate props her pillow against the wall and leans back, while Ilse settles at the bed's opposite end—right above (she can't help noting) the Shabbat candle shoebox. Seeing her there feels surreal, like a visitation by a ghost. Renate suppresses an urge to reach her hand out, to make sure it doesn't go right through.

"He's taken everything very hard," she continues. "Especially since the Jewish Affairs Office turned down his appeal for pension resumption. Mama calls it 'acute depression.' She says he'll be better once all of this is over."

"I'm sure that's true." Ilse leans back against the wall as well, pulling Ragdoll Alice into her lap in a movement so natural and reflexive it's as though the past four Ilse-less years have been a dream. "Can he teach in New York?"

"He's not going to New York. Neither of them are. Did Maria say they were?"

"We didn't talk much," says Ilse quickly. "The film was about to start."

Renate can't resist asking, a little wistfully: "Which film?"

"*Bel Ami*. Have you seen it?"

"I can't see it."

"Oh." Ilse flushes slightly. "Is the ban really that strict? I mean, do they actually check your *Kennkarte* and everything?"

"It doesn't exactly seem worth finding out, does it?" says Renate, more sharply than she intends to. "Not when they'll arrest me for sitting on the wrong bench."

"I suppose not." Coloring slightly, Ilse fiddles with the doll's padded foot. "Well, anyway. The costumes were impressive. I thought the film itself was overrated. But you know me. I always like book versions more." Stroking Alice's woolly hair, she adds, consolingly: "I heard *Gone with the Wind* is coming out in color. And you'll be able to see *that* before anyone here."

"That's true," says Renate dubiously. She hadn't thought of this. Given everything, it seems small compensation.

"I'm sure there are lots of perks to moving to America. I wish *I* could." Ilse's smile turns wistful. "Maybe I'll come live with you in New York. Do you remember how we planned all those trips together?"

Renate nods, though the memory feels celluloid and oddly inauthentic, like a film montage filled with fake champagne bubbles.

"Why aren't your parents going along?" Ilse continues.

Going along. The phrase is so breezily divorced from the tortuous reality of emigration that Renate almost snorts, though she checks herself. It amazes her, how little non-Jews comprehend about what life has become like for her. When a former schoolmate she met on the street recently asked her whether the eight o'clock curfew was "restricting" her social life very much, Renate had been tempted to laugh in his face. The truth was that given how little Jews are allowed to do in the first place now, it barely makes a difference what time they aren't allowed to do it.

"It's too expensive, for one thing," she says. "And Vati will never pass the exams."

"The physical?"

"There's a written one now too. They're apparently looking for excuses to shut people out." In fact, the new exam was added just as Renate and Franz submitted their novella-length stacks of forms and papers to the U.S. consulate on Pariser Platz.

"That's ridiculous! Was it hard?"

"Absurdly. Do *you* know how tall the Bunker Hill Monument is, in feet?"

"So much for welcoming the huddled masses." Ilse shakes her head. "But you passed?"

"We both did." She doesn't mention that here again Elisabeth Bauer had come through, somehow obtaining a list of the written test's more esoteric questions that might otherwise have torpedoed her children's chances. Or that, waiting in her slip and panties for the consulate physical, Renate had suddenly found herself having trouble breathing, half-expecting as she did a red-lipped *Führerin* to appear and ban her from emigrating.

"Ugh." Ilse shakes her head sympathetically. "How is Franz, by the way? Is he here?"

Renate shakes her head.

"Schiller discussion group?" asks Ilse, making quotation-mark gestures with both forefingers. "Is that still going on these days?"

Renate opts not to answer. "He's at Alberti's with some friends," she says. "They've supposedly got some new discs in from New York."

"Jazz?"

"What else." Renate rolls her eyes. Officially, at least, the *fremdländische* "alien" music form is prohibited by the Ministry of Propaganda. For those in the know, however, the latest hits by Glenn Miller and Louis Armstrong can be clandestinely appreciated in the locked basement of the little music shop on Rankestraße. So it is there that her brother can often be found.

Ilse's face falls, and for a moment Renate worries whether she should have shared even this hardly incriminating information. Then again, she remembers, Ilse always did act a little oddly when it came to Franz.

"So tell me more about it," she says, changing the subject. "What made you change your mind? And what are you thinking about doing about it?"

"I suppose it's been building for a while." Ilse smoothes Alice's blue dress. "But last year was really when my thinking changed direction. I was supposed to cover the *Kristallnacht* story. But so much of what I saw sickened me. It was . . . it was just wrong. No matter what you think about Jewish influence in Germany, it didn't—doesn't—justify that." She frowns, picking a nonexistent speck from the doll's shoulder. "I couldn't get it out of my head. The image of your father. What those . . . *buffoons* were doing to him. What they'd already done. And then I had to write it up for *Der Angriff* as though it were this spontaneous and heroic revolution. Germany's storming of the Bastille!" She pauses, blinking rapidly. "I've always wanted to be a newswoman. But what we are writing isn't news. It's lies."

"Did you ever get in trouble for the other lies?" Renate hugs her knees to her chest. "The ones you told for us?"

"No." Ilse twirls the doll's hair around her index finger. "Believe it or not, those thugs were actually more stupid than they looked. *And* more drunk." She pauses, staring down at the worn paisley duvet cover, biting her lower lip. She really does look sick: drawn and pale, the purple shadows beneath her eyes deepening their oceanic grayness.

"So will you leave the Party?" Renate asks her.

"I'm thinking about it." Ilse leans back again. "I've actually applied to go to the Wartheland, to help with the *Volk* resettlement and with press and publicity in Lodz. But I'm thinking perhaps I'll apply to university as well."

Renate nods, dropping her gaze. University had always been a delicate subject between them. Until Jews were banned from higher schooling it had been considered a given that Renate would go. Ilse's mother, though, had discouraged it as impractical: in her mind university was wasted on girls, since their main destination was marriage. "Your parents are all right with university now?" she asks.

Ilse nods, tightening her jaw.

"And after?"

"I'm hoping this madness will be over." Sliding off the bed, she stands and stretches. Turning, she treats Renate to one of her old, rare, cheek-dimpling grins.

"I'm so glad I'm *back*," she says. The words seem to issue forth in a rush of breathy relief.

"Me too," says Renate, cautiously.

"May I use the toilet?"

"Of course."

After Ilse is gone, Renate picks up Ragdoll Alice from her facedown position on the bed.

What do you think? she asks her in silence.

The button eyes look back dispassionately.

It might be real, Renate tells her. *Think about it. It might.*

And for the first time since Ilse's forceful knock on the door, Renate actually almost believes this: that the change of heart for which she'd so desperately yearned might actually be possible, even imminent. And yet for some reason, her emotional response to this idea feels almost as muted as the rag doll's. There is no melting sense of relief. No flooding rush of joy. Merely a cool, almost clinical curiosity. It's as though her friend, like Lawrence Selden in *The House of Mirth*, has arrived with her flowery proposal too late.

And what would it mean now, anyway, she wonders, leaning back against the pillows again. How could they resume their friendship, when literally everything they once did together is either explicitly or implicitly forbidden? Their trips to the Concordia are prohibited. She is no longer welcome at the *Deutsche Oper Berlin* or the Odeon theater, so opera and drama are out too. So is the museum, the restaurants and cafés they used to visit. The Tiergarten is now out entirely, though last year they could have gone so long as Renate only sat on the Jewish benches. They can't listen to music or take bike rides together, since Jews no longer own phonographs, radios, or bicycles. And with the new ration restrictions, Renate isn't even allowed the sorts of sweets she and Ilse had once so loved eating together.

In short, any resurrected friendship would have to be limited to short, careful walks during daylight hours, or else sitting and talking here at home. And even then they'd *still* risk censure, since someone could report Ilse to the Gestapo for merely being seen in Renate's presence.

Down the hall, Renate hears the gurgling flush of the toilet, the rusty sink faucet squeaking in protest at being twisted. *I'm so glad I'm back*, she had said.

Restless, Renate picks up the little book of poems, flipping through the first few pages, reading a few passages aloud to herself. But she feels too confused, too tightly wound to be able to focus; after a few minutes she throws the book back on the bed, stands, stretches. Glancing at the bedside clock, she realizes that Ilse has been in the bathroom for a long time. What's keeping her?

Thinking perhaps she needs more newspaper (they've gone back to the old-fashioned, hand-cut squares of Renate's early childhood, *Toilettenpapier* being now an unnecessary expense) she makes her way down the hallway. But to her surprise the bathroom is empty. Hearing a rustling noise in the direction of Franz's room, she takes three stocking-footed steps to his doorway, where she sees Ilse standing over his desk, a look of concentration on her face.

"What are you doing?" Renate asks.

"Oh!" Clearly caught off-guard, Ilse starts. "I'm sorry. I suppose I should have asked. I'd just remembered Franz had a lot of Kafka. There's a quote I've been trying to recall for the past few days."

"Which book?"

"I can't remember. It's something about . . ." She cocks her head in thought, in that gesture Renate remembers so clearly. "It's about using one hand to wave off life's miseries and the other to write about them. But of course, put much more eloquently than that. Do you know it?"

Renate shakes her head. "I don't. I think he got rid of all his Kafka. Along with all the other books on the list." Though she actually knows that this isn't the case. Franz has a system of storing his forbidden books inside larger, permitted volumes, the pages of which he's hollowed out with his (also forbidden) jackknife.

"Right. I forgot about that." Sighing, Ilse makes her way to the hallway. "That's another thing I hate about the Party. Why should they be able to tell us what to read?" Something in her tone strikes Renate as a little too bright, just a shade too enthused. But then her mother is calling from the dining room.

"Reni? We're eating in half an hour. Can you wake your father?"

"Klar," Renate calls, faintly relieved for the excuse to end the conversation. Turning to Ilse, she says: "I'd invite you to stay. But you know my mother's cooking."

Ilse laughs. "I do. The boiled *Leberkäse* episode still haunts me." Faced with liver cheese that had been left out overnight, Renate's mother had had the bright idea of heating it in a pan of water, "just to soften it up." After leaving it on the stove for too long (she always forgets to set her timer) she'd ended up with a tasteless pink sludge that she salvaged by serving as "stew."

"I'd forgotten that one." Renate grimaces as they start down the stairs. "It's only gotten worse since rationing started. Though luckily, she works late a lot at the Jewish Hospital, so I have an excuse to take over."

Reaching the bottom of the stairs her friend pulls on her coat and shoes and ties her scarf. She turns to face Renate with another smile. "Can I come back?"

"Of course," says Renate, trying to toss off the response as casually as the question. "I'm out for a class on Tuesday and Thursday afternoons. But otherwise"—she shrugs—"I'm generally here."

"What class?"

"Hairdressing. At the Jewish Community Center. They want us all to learn an 'internationally viable' trade."

"So the next time I need a permanent I come to you?"

"I didn't say I was *good* at it."

They laugh together again, and once more, for just a moment it is almost like the old days. Then Ilse frowns. "Now I know what I was missing. Where's Sig?"

Renate swallows, hard. "He—he died."

The wound is still too raw for her to go into more detail; she tightens her lips and shakes her head.

"Oh, Reni," says Ilse softly. "I'm so sorry." She hesitates for a moment, her face stricken.

Then, wordlessly, she enfolds Renate in a hug.

Caught off-guard again, Renate lifts her arms and squeezes back, until the warm, familiar scent of her friend threatens to undo her composure for good.

Laughing self-consciously, she pulls back. Ilse laughs as well, though her eyes are suspiciously damp again.

"I'm sorry, too, for just showing up like this," she says, dashing at them with the back of her hand.

"It's all right," says Renate. "It broke up the afternoon."

"So I'll come back soon. Before you leave?"

Renate nods. "I'll look forward to it."

It comes out automatically: more politeness than assertion. But as she leans against the door frame she decides she does mean it. That despite the pain and the betrayal, despite the months of solitude, there is a part of her that is cautiously, sheepishly thrilled as she watches Ilse stride briskly away down Bismarckstraße, the early-evening light glinting silver in her gold hair. A verse from one of the poems she read upstairs comes back to her:

> *We are framed by stars*
> *And take flight from the world*
> *I believe we are angels.*

17

Ilse

1939

*S*he sits windowside at Die Arabische Tasse with her notebook before her, though in reality she's engaged in surveillance. The coffee shop—a former favorite of hers and Renate's—is positioned on Bismarckstraße and Leibnizstraße, within convenient viewing distance of the Bauers' arched doorway. Nursing her *Milchkaffee*, Ilse divides her attention between the familiar black door and her latest article: *Jews and Ritual Sacrifice: A History.*

Thanks to an introduction from Kai before his posting to the East, she's been taking on more Propaganda Ministry writing for various pamphlets and newsletters. There have also been two more *Der Stürmer* pieces written under her male pseudonym of Isador Frank: "Jew Alert! Ten Ways to Spot a Sex Predator," and "The Secret, Bloody Truth about Passover." Kai calls these "investigative pieces," though all Ilse really does is interview sources he assigns her, using questions he writes for her, then more or less transcribes their answers to be published. "It isn't bad journalism," her editor had said last week when she questioned him about this system. "It's just an alternative way of presenting the facts."

"But some of these 'facts' are laughable!" Ilse had been typing up quotes from a Talmudic 'expert,' a jaundiced-looking man with a monocle that kept dropping into his lap, who had punctuated his claims with hand movements so bizarre that Ilse at first suspected some sort of palsy. It was only later that she realized that he was trying to imitate the distinctive hand gestures of some *Ostjuden*, Eastern European Jews.

"Does anyone believe that matzo is made with blood from Gentile infants?" she asked now. "If that were true, wouldn't it at least be red? Or pink?"

The editor just waved dismissively. "If you write it often enough it becomes its own version of the truth."

"But surely there's enough real evidence of the Jewish problem that we don't have to fall back on such nonsense?"

"Of course there is," he'd retorted. "But which makes for the better story: Jews murdering babies or Jews cheating the banking system? And in the end, don't they amount to the same thing?"

She'd had to think about that one. But under certain circumstances, Ilse decided now, they very likely could.

Chewing on her pen tip, she reworks her second paragraph, periodically glancing back at the Bauers' flat. *In a secret companion volume to the Jewish Talmud can be found the command to "slaughter foreigners . . .* (No sign of Renate, though if her class is at three then she should be leaving now) *who are the same as beasts." Jews are ordered to do this in a "lawfully valid manner." According to Talmudic experts, this "manner"* (She had said Thursdays, hadn't she? Or had Ilse misremembered?) *is the very same manner in which Jewish butchers so cruelly slaughter and bleed animals, which is why throughout the ages the bloodless corpses of Christians, especially Christian children* (Ilse checks her watch again: it is now two twenty, and the U-Bahn trip takes well over forty minutes), *have been discovered in areas where Jews live, usually on or approaching the Jewish holidays of Passover and Purim . . .*

At precisely two forty, as Ilse starts her concluding paragraph (*While it hasn't been reported by the Jew-controlled press, cases of Jewish ritual murder have been authenticated as recently as 1932 . . .*) her vigilance is finally rewarded. Renate emerges from her apartment in her familiar green coat, looking typically flustered and rushed. As she races off toward the Charlottenburg station Ilse imagines her bursting into class, breathless and pink-cheeked, spouting the same apologies that used to drive Ilse herself mad: *The underground was slow. Franz stole my shoes. I couldn't find my hairbrush/change purse/jacket/Kennkarte.*

For a moment Ilse almost smiles. Then she remembers why it is that she's been waiting here in the first place, and the smile slides from her face like shifting light.

৵

She has come back to the Bauers' because her last mission to the household was judged unsuccessful by the only judge who matters in this situation: SS Obergruppenführer von Helldorff, Berlin's notoriously sadistic chief of police. "This was a very generous opportunity that we'd given you," he'd reminded Ilse after her last summons to his office. "A chance to redeem yourself after what I, at least, consider the rather serious transgression of interfering with the people's justice."

The reference had made Ilse's hands prickle with sweat.

Eight months after "Berlin's Night of Righteous Retribution" by I. M. Fischer had gone to press, two Gestapo agents had burst into the BDM editorial office and dragged Ilse outside and into a black sedan. They took her to national Gestapo headquarters, a darkly Gothic-looking building that wears its manicured front garden the way a dragon might wear a tiara. She'd been unsure on the drive what they wanted of her— after all, over half a year had passed since her Kristallnacht encounter with the Bauers. But it quickly became clear as they grilled her: Why had she given a false name to the stormtrooper last November? What was her history with the Bauer family, and Otto Bauer in particular? What were her views on the Jewish question? On Party loyalty? On "the underground Bolshevist movement"?

She'd denied everything, of course. Retrieving the excuses she'd prepared months earlier in anticipation of just this event (even as she dared hope that she wouldn't actually have to use them) she'd said the SS thugs had misheard her name, which was no surprise as they were utterly drunk. She said that while she'd been friendly with the Bauers at one point in her life, she'd had no idea that they were actually Jews. She'd said she truly had believed that the stormtroopers had made an error, and that her goal had been to protect them from the possible repercussions.

Still, for more than four hours the agents wheedled, cajoled, shouted. At points they'd even screamed directly into her face, a tactic that frightened Ilse enough that she'd almost urinated right there on the spot, especially since they'd also denied her use of the washroom. Even more frightening, however, was the sickening expectation that sooner or later the attack would turn physical. After all, she wasn't naïve. She knew that suspects brought to this particular basement quite often only left it on stretchers—or in coffins.

Instead of beating her, however, the agents had driven her to von Helldorff's office, where she was again denied the use of the washroom. Her bare thighs tightly crossed and her stomach knotted in terror, she'd stood trembling as the *Obergruppenführer*—whose round blue eyes and pointy ears might have reminded her of Dopey the Dwarf, had they not been topped by the death's-head-emblazoned cap on his head—laid out her options. Option A was securing evidence of Franz Bauer's suspected involvement in illegal activities, in which case not only would the black mark on her record be expunged, but von Helldorff would support her application for a choice position in the newly opened propaganda offices in Lodz—and after the war, perhaps even a university scholarship.

Option B was a return trip to Prinz-Albrecht-Straße 8. This time, he implied, it would be one-way.

It was a choice that, in other words, was not a choice at all. Still: "I'll think about it," she'd told him breathlessly, hoping to at least buy herself time.

"Don't think too long," he'd said coldly. "I'll be away for the summer's remainder. When I return I'll expect some intelligence."

True to his word, he'd called her back in October, his eyes glinting when Ilse confessed she still hadn't carried out her mission. "It's been very busy since the invasion," she'd said desperately. "There is so much to write about, and we've been quite short-staffed on the editorial desk."

"I will give you one more month," he'd said, ominously. "If you still come up empty you'll have far more to worry about than your schoolgirl newsletter."

Now, slowly walking the few short blocks to the Bauers' front door, Ilse reviews her plan. She isn't certain when Renate's class ends, but she doubts she'll be home until sometime after six. Her mother should be home at roughly the same time or later (*she works late a lot at the Jewish Hospital,* Renate had said). And Professor Bauer, hopefully, will remain in his room, where according to Renate he now spends all his time.

Which leaves just one unknown: Franz himself. Renate had said nothing about his schedule. And since Ilse hadn't thought to ask, she has no idea whether he is even home. During her three-hour vigil she'd been hoping to catch him en route in or out, or for a deliveryman or a letter carrier who might summon him to the door. She'd even toyed with the idea of sending something herself, as it rather strikes her as something Madeleine Carroll might have done in *I Was a Spy.* In the end, though, she had to recognize that she was really just procrastinating. And when she reaches the front door she still finds herself hesitating before finally lifting the tarnished brass knocker. After the three *rat-tat-tat*'s she presses her ear against the painted wood.

At first there is no response. But just as she is breathing a sigh of sheepish relief she hears a door upstairs slam. The sound is followed by the forgotten-yet-familiar rhythm of Franz's uneven footsteps, syncopated by the drag of his weak leg, punctuated by the thud of his cane.

With a deep breath, she forces herself to remain rooted, reminding herself of every reason she has found for coming here in the first place: the dank basement of the Sicherheitsdienst headquarters. The fragrant farmlands of the New Germany. The once-forbidden and hallowed halls of higher learning . . .

Franz reaches the entrance. There is another brief silence before the inside bolt is thrown back.

And then: there he is. Taller than she'd remembered, or than she'd noticed last November; he must have grown several centimeters. But there's the same mass of dark curls, though now shaggier and longer. The same brown eyes, warm and liquid and even larger-looking because his face is so much more drawn and thin. But they are still framed by those ridiculously long lashes. *The most lovely eyes of any woman I know.*

"*Ja?*" he says.

"*Hallo.*" It comes out between a giggle and a croak. Feeling her cheeks heat, she fakes a cough, forces a laugh. "Sorry," she says. "Fighting a cold."

"I'm sorry to hear that." His expression is wary but not surprised. "Ren's not here. She's off at the Community Center, learning how to finger-wave and backward roll."

This time the laugh is real. "You make it sound as though she's practicing gymnastics."

The quip slips out almost before she's aware of having come up with it. She worries briefly that she's already ruined it all; that now he'll know that she's really here for him.

But Franz just smiles the same smile she'd forgotten she'd always loved: sleepy. Sweet. Just a little bit impish.

"I'd give her ten seconds before she fell on her face," he says.

"If that." She manages another laugh. "What time is she back?"

"Six-ish, I think. Unless she burns the place down with her curling tongs before then." He shrugs. "I'll tell her you stopped by."

"Actually," she says quickly, "I'm glad you're here. I had a question for you."

He pauses, his hand still on the door.

"Renate and I were talking about a Kafka quote," she goes on. She hopes desperately that she sounds as natural and nonchalant as she did while practicing it in her head. Lying effectively, she has learned, requires sticking mostly to the truth: finding just enough honest bits to land on amid the flow of her fabrication that, by hopping from one to the next, she can credibly navigate her way through the deception.

"I was trying to remember which book it came from," she goes on now. "I even popped into your room, because I thought I remembered that you had it. But she said you'd gotten rid of your Kafka."

"She told you I'd dumped them?"

"Because of the ban."

"And you don't believe it?"

She shrugs, though the question sets off an alarm. What answer does he want? *Of course I do? I know you're a loyal citizen?* Though of course, that would be a lie in and of itself—not just the loyalty part but the citizenship too. They both know that he's no longer, legally, a German. He is simply a "subject of the State."

Franz is still waiting, his expression indecipherable. Ilse hesitates, then takes the leap.

"Of course I don't," she says, and offers a guileless smile.

As his dark eyes narrow there's a plunging sensation in her stomach. *I've ruined it*, she thinks again. But then he breaks into a laugh, those deeply husky peals of hilarity that always feel like their own rewards for unlocking. The relief is so sharp that her limbs weaken with it.

Stepping back, he opens the door fully. "I'll admit I've missed you, von Fischer," he says.

"Me as well," she says, and steps in.

His room hasn't changed much since the days when Ilse was a regular household member here. The carpet is gone, as are most of the carpets in the house (sold, Ilse assumes). So is the Karl Marx poster he'd had above his desk for years. In its place (and Ilse can't help but smile when she sees it) is a red-toned French movie poster for *Une Nuit à l'Opéra*, with cartoon pictures of Groucho, Harpo, and Chico.

"Have you switched political parties?" she asks, indicating it with her chin.

He smiles. "You might say I've raised my standards."

Giggling, she lowers herself into his creaky desk chair. As he surveys his crowded bookshelf, she surreptitiously studies the rest of the space: the worn leather armchair. The rumpled bed with the paisley bedspread. The ashtray perched precariously on the leaning tower of books that seems a permanent extension of his bedside table. There is no sign of anything even vaguely illicit.

"So when are you really leaving?"

"Two days, ten hours. Actually—" A quick glance at his bedside clock. "Nine and a half hours now."

The immediacy makes her gut plummet. Had Renate mentioned it would be this soon?

"I take it you're excited," she manages.

"Relieved, mainly. They made us jump through more hoops than you can imagine. On both sides." He is running his hands across the eighteen-volume set of the *Brockhaus Konversations-Lexikon* that has resided on his top shelf for as long as Ilse remembers. "What was the quote?"

"Something about warding off life's despair with one hand, but writing about it with the other."

"Doesn't sound like one of his novels." Pulling several volumes of the *Brockhaus* down, he limps to where she is sitting and sets the encyclopedias down with a thud.

"Would it really be in that?" When Franz likes an author, she knows, he becomes obsessive about collecting their works. Given how much he loves Kafka it seems odd to her that he'd seek the quote in a secondhand source.

"You never know what's in good old *Brockhaus*." Eyes twinkling, he pushes one toward her. "Take a look."

Ilse hesitates. She remembers this expression. It's the one he wears when he's pulling off a prank: pie-sheeting Renate's bed on a sleepover night. Replacing sugar with salt for afternoon tea. When Renate got her first two brassieres Franz hung one from the second-floor flagpole as she and Ilse approached the house after school. Ilse vividly remembers Renate's face upon spotting it: the way it went almost as white as the lace-trimmed cotton on public display.

"Go on," he says mildly. "It won't bite."

Holding her breath, she lifts the battered cover of the volume closest to her—and gasps. The tome's pages have been almost completely carved out, creating a large, hollow box. Nestled inside like bookish Matryoshka dolls are three slim volumes: *The Metamorphosis, The Trial*, and *Amerika*. Delighted, she lifts them out.

"Is the whole series hiding contraband?" she asks, looking back at the bookshelf.

"Just every other volume," he says. "That way if some dunderhead of an officer is sharp enough to take one down, the odds are that he'll open up a real book. Though I've enlisted a few other genres in the resistance." Turning back to the bookshelf, he points to a 1927 world atlas, the combined *Iliad* and *Odyssey*, and Volumes I and II of Musil's ponderous *The Man without Qualities*.

"You took a knife to Homer?" Ilse asks, covering her mouth in mock horror.

"We've got four editions. It's not as if Otto is going to miss one," he retorts dryly. Picking up the *Brockhaus Glied* through *Henare* edition, he drops onto his bed with it. "Especially not these days."

"Is he here?"

"In a sense. Locked in his room and his head."

His expression doesn't change, but there's a bleakness in his voice that makes Ilse want to reach for his hand.

"Renate told me about his condition," she says instead. "I'm so sorry."

"Don't apologize. You're the first one yet who's really tried to help us."

Ilse finds she can't look at him. "Surely there've been others."

"At first." He's pulling another volume from the hollowed-out encyclopedia. Setting the gutted shell beside him he begins flipping through its pages. "At first everyone was *horrified*. No one believed it was *happening*. No one believed it would *last*." He recites it in a mocking drone, running a fingertip down a margin. "But that's the strange thing about hell. The longer you're stuck in it, the less those who've been spared seem to notice." He flips a page. "Do you remember my university friend Diederich Schuchard? Tall fellow, blond? Long skinny nose? He used to come here to copy my Weimar Law notes every week."

"Was he the one with that insufferably affected Viennese accent?"

"Ha." A quick, approving look. "You've still got a memory like a trap."

She blushes again, absurdly pleased by the compliment.

He continues, finger still planted on the page. "About two years ago he, like almost everyone, had stopped coming round. Which is fine. No, really. It's dangerous to be seen with Jews, and I understand that. You just happen to be braver than most."

She picks at a cuticle, feeling loathsome.

"Anyway," he resumes. "I bumped into him outside a music shop. My mind is on something else, because it's always on something else nowadays. But I stop, just reflexively. Just for a quick *fancy-meeting-here* kind of exchange. 'Why, hello, Schuchard,' I said. 'It's been ages.' "

He looks up at her. "Do you know what he did?"

She waits, holding her breath.

"He spit on me," Franz says. "Landed right on my shoulder."

He lifts his finger to indicate the spot on his worn-looking navy jumper. "And it wasn't a very delicate sort of spit, if you get my meaning. I think he was coming down with a head cold."

The way he recounts it—a bitter-tart blend of humor and resignation, as though the main point is not *woe is me* but *see this foolish, marvelous world we inhabit together*—nevertheless makes Ilse's throat tighten.

"Odd," she says, trying to keep her voice steady. "He never struck me as an ideologue. I actually considered him more of a Marxist. Like you."

He just shrugs again. "He was. At first. And when Hitler landed as Chancellor he was as disgusted as any of us." He drops his gaze back to the book, turning a page. "But now that the current's swung the other way he just wants to ride it along. Who gives a damn if people like us drown."

"I do," she says, with an indignation that surprises her.

"I know." There is no trace of laughter in his voice now.

For a moment neither speaks. She feels his gaze like a ray of late-afternoon sun, its golden warmth just barely lessened by the melancholy promise of sunset.

He doesn't deserve this, she thinks, with a stab of remorse so over-whelming she grips the sides of the chair. *I should make up an excuse. I should leave now.*

And in her mind, and in that moment, Ilse does precisely this: gets out of the creaky chair. Races out the door and home to her room. In her mind she types up a report saying she found no evidence what-soever that Franz Bauer or anyone else at the house was involved in anti-Reich activities. And when questioned about this by Obergrup-penführer Helldorff, she looks him straight back in his fish-pale eyes and confirms it.

Because, after all, it is still the truth.

But then her mind shifts to the basement of Prinz-Albrecht-Straße 8, the two agents circling her chair like preying panthers.

Looking back, Ilse will later try to pinpoint the moment she decided to remain in Franz's chair, in Franz's room, and she will come up empty. But this, nevertheless, is exactly what she does: she stays just where she is. She holds the course.

Sacrifices have to be made.

"Ah," Franz is saying. Looking up again from his volume, he offers a wan grin. "Found it, I think."

Clearing his throat theatrically, he reads: *"Anyone who cannot come to terms with his life while he is alive needs one hand to ward off a little of his despair over his fate—he has little success in this—but with his other hand he can note down what he sees among the ruins, for he sees different (and more) things than do the others; after all, dead as he is in his own life-time, he is the real survivor."*

He looks up, his eyebrows arched in dismay. "Holy hell, von Fischer."

She laughs, a little self-consciously. "I don't remember it being quite that bleak."

"It is bleak, though, isn't it? Even for bleak old Franz."

"It is," she agrees. "I'd forgotten that part about the ruins. Where was it from, in the end?"

He holds up a slim blue volume. "One of his diaries. A rare private edition that I was lucky enough to stumble upon in an old bookstore."

The way he sets the slim volume back down on the bed is wary, as though it contained some potentially unstable chemical compound.

"Can I see?"

"Of course." He indicates the foot of the bed with his chin and hands the booklet to her as she settles in there, still shaking his head. "I'm amazed that that's what has stayed with you. There's plenty of Kafka stuff that I can pull up from my head, but nothing that obscure."

"I know." She laughs again. "You once recited the last two pages of *Metamorphosis* for us from memory. Do you remember? We were playing Truth or Consequences."

"*Ja.*" Now it's his turn to smile self-consciously. "I'd forgotten that."

"I used to love playing that game with the two of you." Ilse leans back against the wall, twirling a strand of hair around the top of her finger as she reminisces. "Do you remember the time we convinced your parents to join in?"

He cringes. "I've tried to block that out."

"Well, *you* were the one who asked them that awful question. What was it . . ."

"I asked my mother to share her most Freudian dream. I never thought she'd actually answer."

"None of us did!" The scene comes back in a rush, as sweetly potent as a shot of honey liqueur: the five of them in the parlor. Franz and his parents drinking wine, Cole Porter on the phonograph, a roaring fire in the fireplace. Was it the same night that Doktor Bauer had tried to teach them the jerky steps to the Black Bottom, and Renate tripped and landed flat on her back? Ilse can't remember. She just remembers the laughter, the flickering, sighing fireplace. And Franz's dark eyes, dancing as they are dancing now.

"What did she say again?" she asks. "Something about trains and tunnels, right?"

"Worse." He rubs his temple. "A 'very big' train that got stuck in a 'very tight and damp' tunnel. And she was riding it, afraid that it would explode." He shakes his head again, covering his eyes with a thin hand in feigned humiliation. "I think she was three sheets to the wind."

"And she kept going, and going," Ilse chimes in. "And your father kept saying, '*Lisbet. Lisbet? That's enough.*'"

"And when she finally stopped talking," he adds, "there was that shocked silence. And then Renate asked . . ."

Ilse recites it with him: *"But Mutti, what does it mean?"* She giggles. "We teased her with that for months, do you remember? Every time she said something clueless. *But Mutti!*"

They dissolve into helpless laughter together, Ilse clasping her arms over her belly as the scene plays over again in her head. The mirth feels like a feather blanket; light and airy and warming, and for the first time in months she feels nearly safe, almost happy. As she wipes her eyes with her sleeve she has to remind herself that this is an illusion; that it is precisely because she is neither happy *nor* safe that she has landed in here, in this room, on this bed. And that unless she accomplishes what she came for, neither fact will change.

"She might as well have been narrating my own conception," Franz is saying, rubbing his face with his hand, as though laughing has unexpectedly fatigued his features. "It was mortifying. I remember worrying that you'd never come back."

"Really?" She glances up, unexpectedly touched and thrilled that her presence was a cause for concern. "Why would you think that?"

"You always seemed so much more . . . proper than we were. I felt like we were constantly shocking you."

"But I liked it," she says, truthfully. "I loved being shocked. It made my life so much more interesting." She hesitates, then adds, carefully: "I loved how brave you were, too. That you kept going to your secret Socialist meetings even after they became illegal."

"Brave or stupid," he says dryly. "I'm still trying to decide."

"Are you still going, then?" She pretends to examine a split hair. When he doesn't answer right away she looks up and sees that he is studying her again, his expression unreadable.

"I'm sorry," she says quickly. "You don't have to tell me."

He runs a hand through his hair. "Reni said you're leaving the BDM."

She feigns a yawn. "It's so time-consuming. And there's more and more about it I don't believe in. I'd prefer to put my efforts into other things." (*True* and *true. Hop, hop.*)

"I don't suppose it matters, then." He shrugs. "Yes, I still go. Not that it accomplishes much. It's always been mostly about talk."

"Any revolutionary romance, at least?"

"At the meetings?" He snorts. "They're all bluestockings. Bookish harpies, every last one."

"What's wrong with bluestockings? Your sister is one. So am I."

"No, you aren't."

The quickness of the denial catches her off-guard a second time. "How do you know?"

He shrugs. "Various clues throughout the years, I suppose."

"Such as?"

"For one thing, bluestockings don't like swing."

"I'm sure some do."

"No." He shakes his head somberly. "They like classical music only. Bach. Schubert."

"Mozart?"

"Only the less dangerous works. And the candies, of course."

She finds herself giggling again. Crossing her legs, she realizes how little opportunity there is in her life for laughter and banter. With Kai—to whose attentions she finally wearily succumbed once he made it clear her job security depended on it—Ilse rarely even cracks a smile. And when she does, it is never over something clever on his part. Usually it's the opposite: that he behaves with such insufferable self-importance that Ilse has to stifle her derision.

"Also," he's continuing, "bluestockings don't devour romance novels the way you and Reni did. They prefer dry, academic works that they can then use to bully any poor male unfortunate enough to start a conversation with them."

"That sounds like experience speaking."

"It is." He rolls his eyes. "At the last meeting I was cornered by the lovely Karina Hafner and treated to a thirty-minute disquisition on Gramsci's views on economic determinism."

Karina Hafner, Ilse thinks, stowing the name away. "Is she pretty, at least?"

"Karina? Picture a face like a potato on top of a neck like a pencil." He grimaces. "Add a voice like a squeaking clarinet."

She can't help laughing again. "You're cruel."

"I have taste." He rolls his eyes, folds his arms behind his head. His physique has changed somewhat, she realizes; not only is he taller but his shoulders are broader, his arms more solid-looking, despite the obvious toll taken by his reduced Jewish rations.

"So no Duke Ellington. No Vicki Baum. What else?"

"Well." Reaching behind his stack of books, he retrieves a pack of Monas. "No smoking or drinking, obviously." Shaking out a cigarette, he offers her the pack, and after a moment's hesitation she takes it, aware of his eyes still trained on her face.

"And no postcards," he adds.

"Postcards?" Ilse frowns, rolling the slim white stick between her thumb and fingertip.

"Yes. A bluestocking would never have her friend steal a lewd postcard and be brazen enough to bring it to school." He puts the pack back on the bedstand, his dark eyes still trained on hers. "Though I suppose if they had to, they'd have chosen the same one you two did."

The Book Lady. For a heartbeat she simply stares at him, Mona motionless in her hand. He flicks the lighter on and off, smiling his small, bemused smile.

Ilse forces a laugh. "How did you know?"

"How did I know it had been taken? Or how did I know where it went?"

"Both, I guess."

Lighting his cigarette, he inhales, then exhales a stream of smoke. "You don't think I'd let my little sister go through *Gymnasium* without having one or two people there to look out for her, do you?"

"But why did you never say anything?"

He shrugs. "You put it back, didn't you? Or rather, that insufferable little stormtrooper my sister was seeing finally gave it back."

Ilse blinked: so he knew about Rudi too. "Yes," she says. "But surely . . ."

"Surely what?"

"Surely you thought it was . . . wrong. For us to have been looking at them."

He is smiling again, just a little this time, the movement casting the faint stubble on his upper lip into darker relief. Ilse finds herself wondering what it would feel like: those full lips, that sparse stubble. Hauptsturmführer Wainer's lips had felt wet and slack and slightly scratchy when he'd kissed her with them. Kai's were thin and chapped and smooth, and he hardly ever has to shave. Thankfully, she hasn't had to feel them since he left for the Soviet territories to work for some general Goebbels has set him up with. He's written a few times, but she hasn't written back yet. He'll be back on leave soon enough.

"Or at least, no more wrong than it was for me to," Franz is saying. "I suppose a part of me even liked the idea of it."

With the second statement his voice drops just a little, in a way that makes it feel both more intimate and confessional. As he holds the lighter out toward her his expression is both lazy and speculative; a boy tossing a bread crumb into a sleepy pond to see whether a fish will break surface for it. She's aware of the air somehow tightening between them, of her pulse beating butterfly-like, in her throat.

Very slowly she leans forward, until her face is a sigh's distance from his, her cigarette millimeters from the flickering flame.

"The idea of what?" she asks.

He doesn't blink. "Of you," he says. "Of you. Looking at that."

It's barely a whisper, but Ilse feels the words on every inch of her skin. She feels them in the same way she feels his gaze somehow flowing inside her, warm and wide, daring and questioning. With other men at such moments all she has wanted is to escape, mentally if not physically; to contract her sense and her essence deeply into herself as a sea anemone retracts its vulnerable tendrils.

To her amazement, though, what she wants now is precisely the opposite. She doesn't want to pull back. She wants to push past her own skin and his; to empty herself into him until there is nothing left to extend. It is what she has always wanted; a craving she only now understands has not lessened but ballooned in the years since she abandoned this house. Set loose by their banter, by the bubbling memories and drunken laughter, by the parted proximity of his soft full lips, it roars by every caution and every fail-safe mechanism she'd set up for herself, sweeping them away and out of sight even as it sweeps Ilse herself onto his lap.

And then her lips are on his, and her hands are in his hair, and the unlit cigarette is on the floor and forgotten.

❧

Two hours later she is walking toward the U-Bahn, braids hastily re-pinned, skin tingling, thoughts in turmoil. The banned Kafka, slight as it is, feels like a ten-kilo weight in her satchel. But even heavier is the scrap of paper sandwiched within it, hastily ripped from Franz's mole-skin notebook.

Lying there with him, intermittently kissing and conversing, she'd found herself dreamily skip-hopping across her stream of untruths: *I'm curious about your meetings.* (True.) *I think I'd maybe like to see one of them. Just to see if it's something I might like to join.* (Both true and untrue.)

He'd stared up at the ceiling, smoking the cigarette that she'd dropped, and it had taken him less than a minute to nod. *All right. I'll write down the information for you before you go.*

It had seemed impossible that it might be just that easy. But as she'd rebuttoned, tucked, and adjusted, he had scribbled the address, time, and cross-street, tucked it into the Kafka volume, and handed it to her with one last, slow kiss.

There may be hope for you yet, von Fischer, he said, as she made her way into the hallway.

It was so easy that it almost broke her heart.

Now, walking quickly, she struggles to reconcile it all: the giddy exultation of his whispered confessions: *You're so beautiful, I've always wanted you.* The tight-coiled power of the other confessions—the *yes, I still go*; the *I'll write down the information for you.* The salty, sated joy of lying there with him, his palm cupped over her navel and his glorious hair veiling her face and neck. The stark terror of realizing, as she took him into her arms, that she was taking his life—both their lives—into her hands.

What would Kai say if he knew she'd slept with Franz Bauer? What if she were, right now, to telephone his unit, right this very minute, and say: *I just made love to a Jew!* Would he be more upset about the faithlessness or the *Rassenschande*? Would he scream at her the way she'd heard him scream the night they'd burned down the synagogue; tell her how soiled and impure she had made herself? The thought is strangely satisfying; the way it might feel to slap him in the face after he says one of the stupid things he is so often prone to saying: *Why would you even want to go to university? Men don't like women who think too much.* Or: *My money's on you being a Gold Cross mother after we marry. You've a terrific build for breeding.* As though she were a prize cow.

Maybe I will go to New York, Ilse thinks now. Maybe during Kai's upcoming leave from Lodz she'll simply tell him it's over. That she's leaving. The thought is shocking yet intoxicating, like a shot of ice-cold vodka.

As she makes her way down the darkened stairwell of the Friedrichstraße U-Bahn station it's as though her insides are shattering into sharp and embattled factions: what she feels versus what she knows. What she wants versus what she is. What she said versus what she really, truly meant. At one point the dissonance is so overwhelming that Ilse almost turns back up the subway stairs and down the street and to his room, to burrow back into the cocoon of his adoration, to feel his warm firm skin against hers. It's only the knowledge that Renate and her mother will be back soon that pushes her through the ticket gate and into the waiting carriage.

I can make this work, she tells herself, pushing through the rush-hour crowd and taking hold of a strap by the far door. After all, von Helldorff hadn't specified an exact deadline for her report. He may not even know Franz is leaving the country, let alone in two days' time. So if Ilse simply times the delivery of her report properly, she can give the police chief what he wants while buying Franz just enough time to get out. In fact, maybe she can even hold off until after the meeting next week. She could say she was double-checking her intelligence. By throwing in a couple of days between the meeting and delivery she can ensure that the Gestapo doesn't have a chance to act. And that way, she can give them other names—not just potato-faced Karina Hafner, but all the others who show up Wednesday.

All the others, except for Franz. Who will be gone.

I can do it, she thinks again. But her pulse is pounding even harder, and Ilse forces slow and deliberate breaths to calm it while she stares at a bright advertisement poster directly before her.

The ad depicts a young couple in a shiny new KdF "Strength Through Joy" Wagon. Golden and chiseled, the man drives with a white-toothed grin. The woman—also beaming—is standing on the passenger side, her trim torso bursting through the fully opened sunroof. Her tanned arm is flung jubilantly into the air, against an impossibly blue sky. Behind them, white-capped mountains gleam next to rolling green fields, as though offering the best of all seasons in one landscape.

I can't believe you are leaving so soon, she'd said.

Will you come visit? Franz murmured. *Will you let me show you New York?*

Careful. If I come I might stay.

I'd be fine with that, he'd said. *Really.* He smelled like smoke and coffee and something else that was slightly musky; the way his eyes looked as though they'd taste, if she could lick them. His skin tasted like something else, though; salt and something faintly acidic, mixed with the faintest trace of amber honey.

Staring at the poster now, she feels another warm wave of elation, quickly trailed by anxiety that seems to sour her stomach. *I can do this,* she repeats to herself, as the train stops at Berlin-Mahlsdorf and she jostles her way off. *I can do this. I can do this.* As she hurries down Frankfurter Allee it forms a chant: a silent mantra of desperate optimism. It's like the "news" she writes, she tells herself: if she repeats it often enough it is bound to become true. And so she thinks it, and thinks it again. *I can do this.*

By the time she reaches her block she is murmuring it aloud, so caught up in the words—*Ich schaffe das Ich schaffe das*—she doesn't notice the black sedan parked across the street from her doorway. Nor does she notice, at first, the strange silence as she unlocks the front door, or the fact that her mother looks pale and frightened when she greets her.

"There are two men here to see you," she says tightly.

18.

Ava

1989

*H*eart thudding in her ears, Ava twists the bedroom doorknob. Her intention at first is to just crack the door a little, but the button lock has barely popped before the door flies open with enough force that she has to leap back to avoid getting hit.

Her daughter stands in the threshold, arms crossed over her chest, her smooth face pink with annoyance. "My *God*," she huffs, pushing past Ava into the bedroom. "What took you so long?"

Ava licks her lips again. "I'm sorry. I was a little distracted."

"Distracted? Or deaf? I have to be back at the park in five minutes!"

"Which park?" asks Ava reflexively. "Not Tompkins, I hope?" Over her vocal objections, Sophie and her friends have taken to congregating in Tompkins Square Park, currently home to half the city's homeless population.

"We're just hanging around outside it." Striding into the master bathroom, Sophie stares down at Ava's overflowing laundry bin for a moment before picking it up with a sigh. "I thought you said you were doing laundry today."

"Before dinner," says Ava, distractedly wondering if she can clear the box and letters from the bed before her daughter turns back around. But before the thought is even complete Sophie has the bin in her arms and is making her way back into the bedroom with it.

"So Erica's sweatshirt's still dirty then," she is saying.

"It's just a sweatshirt," Ava reminds her mildly.

"Yes, but it's not mine, and I promised her I'd take good care of it."

Reaching the bed, her daughter drops the basket at its foot and begins rifling through its rumpled contents. Ava watches warily, until it strikes her that Sophie's less likely to notice the letters if Ava herself isn't staring at them obsessively. Turning back to her drafting table, she takes a swig of cold coffee while feigning interest in her abandoned *Mutter Trudi* illustration. In reality, though, she is seeing not the wiry-haired old witch but Ilse's blue eyes, narrowed against the sun. *Dummes Mädchen. What on earth is the matter with you now?*

Everything, Ava thinks wearily. She still feels utterly disoriented—as though the past hour's revelations have severed her connection to her life the way an axe might cut through a ship's anchor, setting it adrift.

It's not just the sheer selfishness of Ilse's actions that has left her stunned: the empty justifications, the self-imposed blindness, the continual, cynical prioritization of personal gain over principle. Nor is it even that Ilse made these confessions not to Ava, her own daughter, but to a woman she hadn't seen for four decades; a woman she'd betrayed in the most callous of ways. It's also the *voice* of these pages; the fact that the person they reveal is a complete stranger to her own daughter. Affectionate and confessional, nostalgic and reflective, anguished and surprisingly, sharply humorous, she is someone who has been almost completely absent for Ava's entire life.

"What was in the box, by the way? What are all these?"

Glancing up again, Ava sees with dismay that Sophie's attention has indeed shifted from the laundry to the open carton and scattered letters.

"Nothing," she says quickly. *Shit.* "Well, not nothing. But nothing you need to worry about."

She takes a step back toward the bed. But already it's too late:

Sophie has scooped a handful of the envelopes up off the coverlet. *"Re-nate Bauer,"* she reads. "Who's that?"

"I have no idea." Ava fights to keep her voice even. What she wants to do is to leap across the room, to snatch the pages from her daughter's grasp as she'd once snatched dangerous items from her chubby toddler fists (topless bottles of baby aspirin; dusty ant traps; on one heart-stopping occasion an X-acto knife, capped but potentially lethal). But it's as though gravity has trebled its grip on her body.

"163 Eldridge," Sophie is reading. "That's, like, a couple blocks away, right?" She is turning the top envelope over in her hands now. When she registers the return address her eyes narrow.

"They're from Oma," she says, a new intensity in her voice.

The word *Oma* seems to break Ava's paralysis: she begins making her way back across the room. "Yes."

"If they're for Renate Bauer, why are they here?"

"I don't know." Reaching the bed, Ava holds out her hand. "Can I have those, please?"

Ignoring the gesture, her daughter continues shuffling through the papery stack. Then she stops again, and Ava sees to her horror that she is studying Bernard Frankel's note. "Who's . . ."

"I said *give* them." Leaning across the bed, Ava rips the paper and envelopes from Sophie's hands.

Her daughter jerks back as though she's been slapped. "What the *hell*, Mom?" Stunned, Sophie stares at her mother with her grandmoth-er's ice-blue eyes. "What is *wrong* with you today?"

"I'm sorry." Breathing heavily, Ava begins gathering the envelopes back up again. An ocean seems to be roaring in her ears. "I just—you weren't listening. But I'm sorry."

Her daughter is still staring at her now, her lips in a tight, pale line, her eyes narrowed the way they are when she works out math problems.

"LLP," she says. What does that mean?"

Ava takes a deep breath. "It's how lawyers sign things."

"Why is Oma's lawyer writing you?" Sophie asks slowly.

Standing up fully, Ava faces her daughter, the letters pressed against her chest. She can't think of a single thing to say.

Sophie's blue gaze hardens. "Read me the note," she says.

"What?"

"Read me the lawyer's note."

"It's in German," says Ava, stalling.

"So translate it."

"There's really no need . . ."

"Read it," Sophie repeats, in a low, even voice that—just like her late grandmother's—carries ten times the power of any shout.

Ava hesitates. Then, trapped, she sinks back onto the bed. Clearing her throat, she begins reading, aware that her voice is trembling. *"Dear Ms. von Fischer: As your mother's lawyer and designated executor of her estate, I regret to inform you that your mother—Ilse Maria von Fischer—passed away on the twelfth of April, after a long battle with uterine cancer . . .*

"In April?" Sophie interrupts, incredulous. "Oma died *last month*?"

"Yes."

"But . . ." Her daughter has both hands pressed to her forehead. "But you told me she died in a car crash. When I was a baby."

"I know I did."

Outside on the window ledge a mourning dove chooses the moment to release its throaty warble. Ava desperately wishes she and the bird could trade places; that she could sing her bereavement and take flight.

"So . . . I've had a grandmother?" Sophie asks, at last. "For my whole life, until just now?"

The tremble in her young voice is so audible, so devastated that for a moment Ava wants nothing more than to pull the girl into her lap; something she'd done so often, so *naturally* in years past. (When was the last time? When had Sophie stopped allowing it?)

"There were reasons," she says desperately. "I can explain. I just . . ."

But her daughter cuts her off. "I don't have time now." Her tone is stony, her face closed like a book. "I have to go. I have to go meet Erica."

"This is more important than your friends," says Ava.

"Oh, really?" Her daughter laughs a short laugh that sounds more like a sob. "At least my friends don't *lie* to me."

"Sophie!" Ava races after her. "I wasn't lying. Not really. I was only trying to protect you."

"Protecting me by lying to me?" Sophie's hand is already on the doorknob. "You've got a funny idea of protection. Then again, I don't know why I'm surprised by that."

Ava stops, stung. "What is *that* supposed to mean?"

"Nothing. I don't want to talk about it." And stepping into the hallway, Sophie slams the door in her wake, leaving Ava frozen in place.

As the front door's deadbolts are thrown back in rapid succession (*klunk klunk klunk*) Ava remains where she is, frozen in dismay. *She's right*, she realizes, as the front door thunders shut again. *Oh my God. She's right.*

Stunned, Ava stumbles back to the cluttered bed. The guilt feels as though it's coursing through her very veins. *She's right. She's completely right.* For all her excoriation of Ilse for lying about Ava's parentage, and for all of Ava's pledges to be an entirely different kind of parent, in the end she has repeated the exact same sins of her mother. She has lied. She has kept Sophie from her own story.

Sinking to her knees on the coverlet, Ava peers over the dust-coated air conditioner, down onto the sleepy Saturday street. Spotting Sophie's slim form turning onto Second Avenue—not strolling, this time, but nearly running, vest flapping with each violent step—she briefly contemplates throwing up the sash to shout after her, even though this would send the entire air conditioner crashing into the street. She refrains only because she realizes that calling after Sophie will only hasten—and perhaps prolong—her flight.

And anyway, what can she say?

Biting her lip, she stares down at the letters. Then she sweeps them back together and stuffs them into her battered *New Yorker* tote, along with her wallet. Wriggling into a denim skirt, she slings the tote over her shoulder and makes her way to the bureau mirror. The woman who stares back is a stranger: haggard and ancient. The circles beneath her eyes are shadowy troughs, the sun spots by her graying hairline a spreading crap-colored rash. *My God. How did I get so old? How did I let any of this happen?*

Looking-glass Ava returns her gaze coldly but says nothing. Suddenly Ava is so exhausted that she wants nothing more than to crawl back under the covers. Instead, she forces herself to meet her own gaze, unflinchingly, directly. *You did this*, she tells herself. *Now fix it.*

Outside she blinks into the late-afternoon light, for a moment flashing back to a terrifying night twelve years earlier: the city wrapped in eerie blackness and stifling heat, Sophie wan and warm against Ava's lips. Now, in part fueled by the extraordinary things she has just read, Ava feels the same visceral fear; that terrified epiphany of just how tenuous it all is; how everything that anchors her might vanish in the blink of a feverish eye.

What if I lose her, she remembers wailing to Livi.

Looking both ways down the sidewalk, she takes a deep breath, clearing her thoughts. Where had Sophie said she was meeting Erica?

Of course. Tompkins Square Park. *We're just hanging around outside it.*

Ava sets out at a near gallop, taking Allen to East Houston and taking a right, then another left onto Avenue B. As she pushes past the weekend sidewalk strollers—skinheads and punks, college kids and cross-dressers, a young man in tight pink spandex shorts—she scans them for Sophie's pin-straight platinum hair, to no avail. She scans for it again when she reaches the park, breathing through her mouth to escape the stench (urine, sweat, pot, beer, spoiled milk, and a hundred other notes too rankly entangled to single out).

In one corner a man drinks from a can of Miller while cooking hot dogs on a black Weber. Tall and tan, he might be a suburban husband presiding over a Sunday afternoon barbecue but for the track marks on his skinny arms and legs. Nearby a woman wearing just a bra and a pair of cutoffs lies on a moldy sofa, an old *Village Voice* over her face, her bare feet bruised, skeletal-looking, the toes painted a jarring shade of electric orange.

Behind them, the tents that are the subject of so much vitriol and conflict look improbably innocuous in the afternoon sunlight, their "walls" fluttering in the summerlike breeze like misshapen sails on some surrealist ship of the damned. They remind Ava of the bedsheet forts she and Sophie once built together in the living room, and as she peers inside those open enough to do so, she sees her daughter at age three: twinkle-eyed and giggling, smelling of baby shampoo and baby sweat, her plump arms up in supplication: *Hug! Hug! Hold me! Uppah!* Was there ever a time when Ava refused? Said: *No, Mama's too tired right now*? The possibility strikes her like a body blow now. *Stupid*, she thinks again: the idea that she'd have ever seen the chance to hold her daughter as anything short of precious and rare. Stupid that she'd ever assumed that Sophie's love would simply always be there: immediate. Instinctive. Imperative. *Stupid stupid stupid.*

After circling the square once more with no Sophie sighting, she cuts back across Ninth, poking her head into Kim's Video on Avenue A before working her way back down Second Avenue. She hits a Ukrainian diner where Sophie sometimes studies with friends, then the junk-filled thrift shop where she spends her babysitting money. Typical for a summer Saturday, the place is packed with teens who can't seem to decide whether to dress up as Times Square strippers or Wall Street bankers: lacy bustiers paired with baggy trousers. Bare, boyish chests paired with men's suspenders. Fishnets paired with oversized pinstriped blazers, the latter reinforced with military-worthy shoulder pads. But Sophie is not among them, and the plump transvestite working the register hasn't seen her. "I'd know, sweetheart," the latter confesses wearily, blowing a stream of smoke toward a small forest of candy-bright Pez dispensers. "I have to watch these kids like a hawk." She wiggles two hands stacked with rings, furred with hair. "Sticky fingers," she adds, with a grin that reveals two top teeth capped in gold.

Ava blinks, close to tears. "I'll come back later," she manages. "Thank you."

"Anytime," says the cashier kindly. "I'll keep an eye out."

And then, as Ava turns away: "Hey. What's your accent, baby?"

"Danish," Ava says. She doesn't turn back.

Outside she leans against the riotously painted wall. *This is pointless.* It's like trying to find a lost earring on the can-littered Coney Island beach. What she really wants to do is to sink down onto the sidewalk, next to the homeless girl parked there with her backpack and a pit bull that looks nearly as drugged out as its owner. Instead, Ava reaches into her bag for the granola bar she has remembered she has and has no interest in consuming herself. "Here," she says. "I'm sorry I don't have more."

The girl takes the green-wrapped square into a filthy-looking hand. She looks nonplussed.

"Thanks, *Mom*," she says, her tone implying that this is perhaps the worst insult she can think up at the moment. Ava stares down at the brat, torn between slapping and hugging her before forcing herself to resume her search.

Heading back down Second Avenue, she passes a piano shop, a nail salon, another vintage clothing store with windows showing faceless mannequins in fur-collared coats, blankly oblivious to the summerlike heat. At the corner of Third Street a man urinates against a graffiti-scrawled wall while his German shepherd shits behind him on the curb. A young woman in a headscarf pushes her stroller past them both quickly, her green eyes fixed resolutely ahead.

As the light deepens, the streets begin to feel not like Ava's beloved home city but a gauntlet lined by shadowy, sharp-edged edifices, structures whose sole purpose is to make her feel as small and worthless as she knows she is. She wends her way back toward Second, so tired she can barely see where she's going. *Stupid*, she thinks again. Stupid to even have tried to find her. But what else can she do? She has to find her. She has to fix this. *I'm sorry, baby*, she thinks. *I'm so sorry*. The thought brings her back to one of the many desperate pleas in Ilse's letters: *Perhaps one day*, she had written her former friend, *just perhaps, I might summon the courage to come and see you and Franz in New York. I have so many things I need to tell you. But really, in the end only one thing that matters:*

> *I am sorry.*
> *I am sorry.*
> *I am sorry.*

As her mother's words fill her head there's an overpowering urge to take the 1956 envelope out again, simply to prove to herself that she read its stunning contents correctly. Rummaging in her purse, Ava slows to a stop, frowning as she retrieves the yellowing missives. *1946. 1948. 1976. 1962* . . . she pulls the whole stack out, shuffling through it like a pack of cards. She's finally found the one she's looking for and is about to open it when something makes her glance at the building she's standing in front of, its title cheerfully pronounced in a hand-painted sign: *Eldridge Street Baptist Church*.

She peers up the block and then down it. Thinking: *How the hell did I get here?* Had her subconscious hijacked her as she stumbled along in her panicked daze? Because this is *it*: the very street where Renate Bauer lived, according to Ilse.

And for all Ava knows, she might still be here.

Feeling as though she's in a strange dream, Ava stares at the top envelope, then looks at the brass-plated numerals on the building across the street: *163 Eldridge*.

It's most definitely a match.

She is crossing the street without quite realizing she's decided to do so, drawn to the address like a fly to a flystrip. It strikes her suddenly that perhaps *this* is where Sophie came—after all, she'd read the address too. Is it possible that in her fury her daughter abandoned Erica and the park and went to find out for herself the truth Ava had denied her?

163 Eldridge is a cinder-block-style building of five floors and fifteen units. It is neat and well kept; through the window the tiled lobby

gleams, and the brass trim on the banister looks newly polished. There is nothing unusual or even vaguely eye-catching about it. In fact, Ava has probably walked by it hundreds of times, never once suspecting that one of its residents might hold the answer to every question she's ever had.

She tries the outer doorway to the vestibule, which is open. Inside it smells like floor wax and bleach. Spotting the building directory, Ava runs her finger down the list, her heart thudding so hard her vision vibrates. But not only is there no *R. Bauer*, none of the names listed look even remotely German. In fact, none—apart from a *C. Benedict*—even strike her as particularly Central European. There's an *L. Garcia* in 1C, a *J. Muhammed* in 3B. Two *Chans*—K. and S.—in apartments 2B and 5A. The original name on 5B—*I. Gruchowski*—has been crossed out with black marker. *W. Park* is written in small black letters beneath it.

Transfixed, Ava watches herself press 5B firmly. A woman's voice shrills from the speaker.

"Yeah?"

Static makes the voice sound an ocean away, and for a moment Ava's English seems to disintegrate. She can't think of a single phrase.

"Hello?" the woman repeats. "Who is it?"

Ava licks her lips. "Hello. I'm—I'm looking for Renate Bauer."

"Who?" In the background, a child wails and is silenced by a rapid-fire comment in an Asian-sounding language.

"Bauer," says Ava, articulating more clearly. "A German lady. I believe—I think that she used to live here."

"Oh, I dunno," the woman responds. "No, no. Not here."

Ava bites her lip. "Have you heard of her before? Do you know where she might perhaps have moved?"

"No, no," the woman repeats "Dunno. Not here."

Ava sifts through her scrambled thoughts for something to keep the woman on the line. "Wait—then have you heard from a girl named Sophie today by any chance?" Something is cutting into the palm of her right hand. Looking down, she realizes that she still has the '56 letter in her hand and is clenching it like an entrance ticket.

"No, no," the woman says. "Zupah. You try Zupah. Okay. Bye-bye."

"Zoo—what? Wait—please. Who should I try?"

But the speaker goes silent, and remains that way when Ava buzzes again, and then a third time. After the third ring she simply stands there, waiting; as though W. Park might return on her own or (even better) recall that she is not W. Park but R. Bauer after all.

This, of course, does not happen.

Carefully, Ava returns the letter to her purse and runs a trembling finger down the directory a second time. The closest thing to *Bauer* is *G. Babayev*. As she reaches the bottom this time, though, she spies a small-font listing that she hadn't noticed before:

SUPERINTENDENT: APARTMENT 1A.

Zupah. She wants to hit herself. She settles for pressing 1A for just slightly longer than she'd pressed 5B.

A few seconds later a man's voice answers: "Yeah?"

"Hello," says Ava. "I'm hoping that you can help me. I'm—ah—I'm trying to find someone. Two people, actually. But only one whom I believe has lived in this building."

"They all on the directory, miss." The voice is deep, limned with the faintly melodic inflections of the Caribbean or the West Indies.

"No—I mean she used to live here. Many years ago. Her name was Renate Bauer."

"Bowerrrrr," the man repeats. It sounds for a moment as though he's growling.

A pause follows. Ava feels herself holding her breath.

"Afraid it don't ring a bell," he says.

"Do you happen to know if a girl named Sophie tried to find her earlier today?"

"Not a clue." His voice is harder now, impatient.

"Do you—do you think anyone in the building might remember? Someone who has perhaps been here for a long time?"

An incredulous laugh. "What the hell you think I am? A goddamn private investigator?"

The speaker goes dead.

Ava wanders back toward the street, her self-berating chant resuming. *Stupid. Stupid.* What did she think, she'd just waltz into a strange building and reunite with her mother's long-lost best friend? In all likelihood, Renate Bauer isn't even Renate Bauer anymore. She's likely married and changed her name. Perhaps she is even dead.

Defeated, Ava begins slowly to make her way home—she will just have to wait for Sophie there. But when she passes the phone bank on the corner on Delancey and Essex she stops short again. Her first thought is to check messages, even though she's only a few minutes from home. But after she's tried two of the receivers (the first one is dead, the second coated in some sort of foul-smelling, greasy substance) and then called in to no voice mail, and then changed the answer message in case Sophie calls in (*"Sophie, it's Mom. I'm so sorry, sweetie. I'll tell you everything you want to know. Please just call me"*), an idea hits: an idea so improbable that it's almost certainly delusional. Ava acts on it anyway: after waiting for the tone again, she punches in three digits: 4-1-1.

"City and state, please," says the operator.

"New York, New York." Ava licks her lips. "I'm looking for a Renate Bauer."

"Can you spell the last name?"

"B-A-U-E-R. First name has an 'e' at the end."

"One moment."

As she waits for the results a new calm descends; as if her fate rests in this strange, polite woman's hands. *If she comes up with nothing, that is it. I will stop. I'll apologize to Sophie and answer all her questions. We'll put all of this nonsense behind us.*

"I have two Renate Bauers," the operator says.

Ava isn't certain she's heard the woman correctly. "Two?"

"Yes. One in Yonkers. The other's on the Upper East Side. Do you want both?"

"Ah—yes. Yes. Both, please."

Ava's hands are shaking so much that she nearly drops the phone as she rummages in her bag for a pen, pushing past sunglasses, a capless

ChapStick, two dirty-looking Wash'n Dri packets. For a heart-stopping moment she thinks she'll have to memorize the numbers before digging up a broken stub of artist's graphite. The only thing she has to write on are the envelopes: after hesitating, she pulls out the first one she finds and turns it over.

"Go ahead," she says.

Ten minutes later she's inside the graffiti-coated subway, which is packed for some reason (a concert? a game?) even though it's a weekend. The crowd writhes and twitches like a single living organism: passengers inhabiting a rainbow of skin tones press into one another like lovers. The fan seems to be broken, leaving the heat as unrelieved as the stultifying damp of a terrarium.

As the train lurches from the station Ava wills it to fly; to go as fast as her own blood races in her veins. *Renate Bauer.* The woman who knows the truth about Ilse's childhood past; who can answer the questions now swarming through Ava's jolted mind. *Renate Bauer!* Here in the city! It seems impossible; incredible to her. It's like discovering that the Blue Fairy is not only real but living on East 64th and Lexington.

As the car careens steamily through the city's glimmering tunnels, Ava's mind scrabbles for something to say, for some way to begin. *Begin at the beginning*, the White King had said. But where is that? *You and my mother were like sisters for years, before you became a Jew and she a Fascist.* But why should Renate Bauer want to hear something she already knows?

She tries again: *Hello. I know my mother betrayed your family. But she's dead now. And she's also very sorry.* But again, why would Renate Bauer care? Why wouldn't she simply slam the door in Ava's face, just as Sophie had done hours earlier? Given nearly everything that Ava knows now, the woman would have more than enough reason. For it wasn't just that Ilse joined the BDM and the Nazi Party. It wasn't just that she'd terrorized innocent Polish boys and destroyed Jewish property and physically attacked a man she'd once considered a friend. It wasn't just that she'd betrayed Renate and Franz. Incredibly—or so it had seemed to Ava as she read—there was still more. And still more after that.

After Renate and Franz left, Ilse was posted in Lodz, where she'd not only continued writing her poisonous propaganda but physically aided in the appropriation of Polish farms and homes, moving Poles out and into a brutal roulette of ghettoization, mass execution, and deportation. In her letters, she'd claimed to have had doubts at the time; to have felt pity for the people she so efficiently ejected; to be sickened by colleagues who physically abused them. But she didn't quit, or leave, or try secretly to help those who she herself noted were in desperate need of help. She told herself (she wrote) that her first loyalty was to her Party; that Party loyalty was what would save the nation. *Sacrifices have to be made.* She kept saying it until the Allies arrested her, convicting her of crimes against a civilian population and indoctrinating German youth into a Fascist ideology, and sentencing her to eighteen months of rigorous "reeducation." It was only when Ilse was able to establish that she had a fatherless daughter who needed her that they commuted her sentence on "humanitarian" grounds.

In other words, Ava had been Ilse's ticket to freedom.

At 34th Street the train judders to a halt, the conductor spewing an explanation that, between his Spanish accent and heavy static, is virtually incomprehensible. Ava finds herself groaning out loud while the West Indian nanny to her left hushes her wailing charge and a man in pinstripes snaps his *Wall Street Journal* in annoyance. The straphanger to her right curses stagnantly in Russian.

It seems they stay here, stalled, for hours, the agitation building within Ava like a hot inner balloon pressing against her lungs: *Jesus. Come on.* Then the lights go out and the panic descends, hotly crushing her in its suffocating fist. *We're all going to die.* Ava closes her eyes, but for some reason the soothing images she usually summons to defuse such moments (a sunny beach, an open field) fail to materialize. Instead of ebbing, the terror surges; instead of breathing she gasps, already feeling plaster dust in her lungs.

"Ma'am? You all right?"

The lights flash back on. Opening her eyes, Ava sees an almost shockingly lovely woman in bright blue scrubs, her skin the color of shining onyx. She is sitting directly below where Ava is standing, though Ava has no recollection of having noticed her there a moment earlier. Nevertheless here she is now, gazing up, her eyes velvet-dark and wide with concern.

"Do you need to sit?" the woman asks. Her voice is melodious, flute-like. Embarrassed, Ava shakes her head.

"I'm fine," she manages. "It's just the heat."

"Here. Sit." Standing, the woman nods firmly at the space she's opened up. "You need to rest. You don't look good."

Still struggling to breathe, Ava hesitates. Then she nods, sinking into the seat just as the train lurches back into motion. When she's composed herself a little she looks up again to thank the woman properly. But her benefactor has vanished into the close-packed flesh of the crowd.

Reaching Lexington Avenue is like surfacing on another planet. Ava has always thought of the Upper East Side as the Lower East Side's topsy-turvy opposite—shining town houses versus grimy tenements. Bowing doormen versus boozy derelicts. Purse-sized poodles versus homeless pit bulls. As she begins walking back downtown, however (*66th Street, 65th*), for the first time she finds herself thinking about their odd, invisible interdependence. For this is how New York has always functioned: immigrants from Delancey working their way up to Park Avenue; first the Germans, then the Irish and the Italians, then the Jews and now (gradually) the Indians, Chinese, Latinos. One swell following the next. Cycles of migrational chaos pounding the city's asphalt shore, each wave making the trip smoother for the next . . . As Ava pulls out the envelope upon which she'd scrawled Renate's address, she wonders how smooth

Franz and Renate Bauer's paths were after landing. Had they found safety and acceptance? New lovers? New pets? Had they ever seen their parents again?

The address the operator had given her is on a somewhat quiet pocket of street; a sleek, modern complex with a white-gloved doorman standing behind a security desk. Stepping inside, Ava feels acutely aware of her disheveled appearance.

"Can I help you?" the doorman asks, his expression opaque.

She clears her throat. "I'm looking for Renate Bauer."

"Is Dr. Bauer expecting you, Miss . . . ?"

Doctor? Ava's heart skips a beat. Had Renate followed in her mother's footsteps? "Ava," she says, not offering her last name, just in case. "And no. Or, not exactly. But I believe she'll want to see me. I have something of hers that I am trying to deliver."

"You can leave it here for her," he says, pointing to a pile of other correspondences and packages.

"I'd rather not," says Ava quickly. "It's personal. Private."

He looks her up and down, his lips tightening slightly. Then he nods. "Just a moment, then."

Picking up his phone, he punches in a short number and waits. Then he shakes his head and sets the phone back down on the receiver. "The doctor doesn't appear to be in right now."

The letdown feels like a physical drop. Ava steadies herself, swallows.

"Can you tell me if a young girl named Sophie has stopped by in the last hour?"

"Not on my watch. I've been here since nine."

"All right," she manages. "I'll guess I'll just wait, then."

And before he has a chance to say otherwise she has planted herself in a sumptuous leather armchair, beneath a chandelier that glimmers with a thousand rainbow-hued crystals shaped like tears.

She doesn't know how long she sits there, bag clasped tightly in her lap, legs crossed against the air-conditioned chill. Only that at some point her exhaustion catches up with her, and then she is nodding off. And then she's sitting on a train with Sophie. They're in the dining car, and Ava is trying to pour them coffee. But somehow it keeps missing both their cups. "I am sorry," she keeps saying. "I'm so sorry. I don't know what is wrong with me."

"I don't even know why you're pouring it," her daughter says, her voice sharply disdainful. "I don't want any of that anyway. It's disgusting."

Ava glances down at the table to see that she's been pouring not coffee, but dark red blood. It flows from the silver spout onto the white tablecloth, thick red stripes soaking into the fabric and dripping onto the floor.

"Oh my God," she says, sickened. "Where is this from?"

"It's from *him*." Sophie points to one of the other tables, and Ava sees Ulrich Bergen slumped over the surface, blood pouring from a bullet wound in his head.

"Don't you see," Sophie shouts, leaping up. "You *killed* him. Just like you killed Oma. And you lied about it. You lie about everything. Everything!"

And then she's turning and running off down the jolting aisle.

"Wait," Ava tries to call. "Wait, sweetheart. Wait . . ."

"It's too late." The voice is chill, familiar: turning around, she sees Ilse, sitting where Sophie had just been, her eyes silvery and smug.

"It's too late," she says triumphantly. "You've missed your chance, just like you always do. You've missed it. *Missed* it . . ."

"Miss!"

Ava wakes with a start. Standing before her is the doorman, looking embarrassed. Behind him is an old woman with silvered hair and bright pink lipstick. She is wearing a green spring coat and a black beret, holding a bag from Shakespeare and Co.

"Yes," says Ava, shaking her head groggily. "I'm so sorry."

"You said you had something for Dr. Bauer?" He nods toward the woman.

"Yes. Oh, yes." Stumbling to her feet, Ava clears her throat. "Dr. Bauer?" she asks.

"Yes." The woman smiles, looking politely puzzled. The lines in her face are deep and intricately intersecting, like the folds in a soft, often-folded map.

Ava finds herself laughing: with relief, with shock. With sheer joy. The woman looks alarmed.

"I'm sorry," she says. "Do I know you?"

"No." Ava takes a deep breath. "But I'm your niece."

19

Ava

1989

*U*pstairs, she sits on a miniaturized couch that is almost as overstuffed as the room's riotous bookshelves. Covering three walls, Renate Bauer's book collection looks like the setting for some antiquarian whodunit: weathered spines of varying hues, sizes, and degrees of wear packed and piled together so tightly that the effect is one of book-patterned wallpaper. Even the air smells bookish: like lavender and old paper, tinged by a faint hint of strong coffee.

"Do you want ice in your water?" calls Renate Bauer from her kitchen.

"Only if it's no bother," Ava calls back. And then: "I'm so sorry, really. I haven't eaten or really drunk much today—I suppose I'm dehydrated. I've been running around trying to find my daughter, who ran out rather angry with me . . ." She trails off, realizing she must seem even more of a lunatic than she had downstairs, even before she (quite literally) fainted.

"So, ice?" Renate clarifies.

"*Ja*, yes," says Ava, chagrined. "Thank you."

The collapse had happened with shocking swiftness: one moment Ava was making the most stunning statement of her life, to a woman she'd only just met. The next, someone seemed to be turning down the world's volume while white sparks looped and vanished before her eyes. She'd somehow landed back in the armchair, her head between her knees and her tote half-emptied on the lushly carpeted floor. And then the doorman was scooping it all up—keys, ChapStick, a few of the letters (*my God the letters*)—and Renate Bauer was bending over her, murmuring: "Oh, dear. Are you all right?" And to the doorman: "Let me take her upstairs until she gets her bearings."

Ava hadn't been able to make out the man's answer through the suddenly roaring silence. But she'd heard Renate Bauer's response: "Well, we can't very well send her on her way like this." And then, dryly: "Don't worry, Eugene. I'll call you if things get too desperate."

And so it was that Ava found herself shepherded into a wood-paneled elevator that smelled of lemon wax and Windex and whatever old-lady perfume (powdery and sweet) Renate Bauer happened to be wearing. The doctor had set Ava on the tastefully padded stool, patted her on the shoulder, and then thoughtfully watched the old-fashioned floor dial work its way from one to seven, seeming far less unsettled by the announcement Ava had just made than Ava still was herself.

Could it really be that easy? Ava had thought, as the polished box made its creaky trip up the building. *Is she really going to simply let me in?*

It wasn't just the cheerful reception that surprised her. As Ava had surreptitiously studied her mother's childhood confidante in the mirror, she saw little to match the image she'd formed in her head: that of a young girl with a gentle, bookish demeanor and a kindness Ilse described in one of her letters as *unmatched by any I have known since.*

Just on the cusp of seventy, Dr. Renate Bauer remains a striking woman, with high cheekbones, a pointed chin, and a small, well-shaped nose that sits perfectly symmetrically over her pink-painted lips. But it was the eyes that had struck Ava the most. Dark and wide behind their oversized plastic frames, Renate Bauer's eyes were at once solicitous and fiercely determined. They were thoughtful, and deep, and tinged with the life-weariness of one who has lived through trauma and remains trapped in its outer orbit.

They were also the eyes of a woman used to getting her own way. Not because she's been coddled, but because she's learned how to fight.

"I really don't want to cause trouble," Ava calls again now.

"No trouble for family!" Renate calls back. In the other room something rattles; something clinks.

Family, Ava thinks. It's like she's back in a dream.

Trying to ground herself, she surveys the small room. Like Renate herself, it exudes a bookish and slightly shabby elegance that seems untouched by the passage of decades. On the wall directly across from her hangs a framed document in Hebrew—a Jewish marriage contract, Ava guesses, remembering the small scroll-box she'd seen outside the door. On the walnut coffee table in front of her, a heavily annotated copy of Pearl Buck's *Peony* lies half open atop a fading copy of the *New York Review of Books*. A yellow legal pad lies next to it, covered with notes written in English (*filling loss with literature*, Ava reads; and beneath it *all extremist forms converge in the end*). Protruding from beneath the pad is a plain-looking green book, the cover of which is mostly obscured, though part of an illustration—a little black-and-white foot—seems familiar. When Ava gently slides it out she immediately sees why: the foot is part of Tenniel's iconic image of Alice, key in hand, pulling back the curtain to the door to Wonderland. Above the image is the book's title: *Alice's Evidence: The Absurd Across Language and Culture.*

The author is *Renate Sophia Bauer, PhD.*

Ah, Ava thinks. *That kind of doctor.*

From the kitchen comes the crash of shattering glass. "Oh, damn it," Renate calls out. "I'm sorry. One more minute . . ."

Despite herself, Ava smiles. Her mother had written frequently and fondly of Renate's clumsiness. Apparently her grace hasn't improved with age.

"Really, there's no hurry," she calls. She flips to the dedication and feels her heart leap in her chest:

For Franz.

Glancing furtively toward the kitchen, Ava pages forward to the introduction.

I first met Alice, she reads, *when I myself was a little girl, growing up in prewar Berlin. My brother, Franz, had an old copy of the original Antonie Zimmerman translation dating from 1869, and if I asked him very nicely, he would sometimes read to me from it. Like so many children all over the world, we were both charmed by Carroll's fantastical tale: the cheeky Cheshire Cat (or as I first met it, the "Grinsekatze"). The hookah-smoking caterpillar. The way Alice's very form could stretch and shrink with a bite of mushroom or cake. Visiting them soon became an almost weekly ritual; first as siblings and then, as I learned to read, alone. Over the years, I came almost to feel as though Alice were not a character but a friend. She was someone I could talk to, first as an imaginative child and then as a young Jewish woman whose world had quite suddenly been turned upside down in Nazi-era Berlin. I laughed at Alice's nonsense and was cheered by her resilience; I also took heart in her resolute pursuit of her goals, even in the face of the most unexpected changes to her landscape, her companions, and her own body. Throughout it all, though, it never even occurred to me that the pages I grew to know by heart contained anything other than Carroll's own imaginings.*

And yet the first time I sat down to read Alice in English—mere months after arriving in the wondrous new land of America—it felt like a different work altogether. For the first time, I realized how these gloriously absurd English phrases had been crammed into ill-fitting German idioms: Carroll's "little bat" who is "like a tea-tray in the sky" is twisted into a "little parrot" whose "feathers are so green." The fantastically funny Lobster Quadrille had been cruelly sedated into a far less hilarious "dance of aquatic beings." And the delightful play of "whitings" and shoe polish had been left out altogether.

But what was most stunning for me was my own response to Carroll's words, a kind of amazement that surpassed even what I'd felt as a child. In part, this was because Carroll's Alice seemed so much more wondrously

bewitched by his strange world, in a way that Zimmerman's Alice some-
how did not. I came to realize that this was because Zimmerman altered
or removed most of the comments that reflect the little girl's ongoing aston-
ishment: "how very strange" becomes a demurely appreciative "how won-
derful." And "curiouser and curiouser," that old favorite, is not to be found
at all.

The effect is that Alice, like any Little Red Riding Hood being chased
by a talking wolf, or a Dancing Princess attending nightly balls beneath
her bedroom, merely accepts the unexpected without apparent note or
comment. . . .

"Here we are."

As her hostess bustles back into the room, Ava quickly re-covers the little volume with the paper, just in time for Renate to briskly set down a plate of Fig Newtons and a glass of ice water before her. "Eat a biscuit, please," the older woman instructs, with all the authority of a certified medical doctor. "It will help get your blood sugar back up."

"Thank you," says Ava, dutifully picking up one of the soft, jam-filled squares.

"You're still quite pale, you know," the older woman observes. "Does this happen to you often? Fainting?"

Embarrassed, Ava shakes her head. "Not for years." The last time she recalls truly fainting was at Holy Mother, and then it was probably from hunger. Children had always been fainting from hunger there. It was just how things were.

"I just . . . this day has been difficult," she says. "On so many levels." She tries to laugh; it comes out more like a hiccup. "It started with my mother's ashes being delivered to me in a box."

"You mean Resl?" The older woman's whitened brows jerk toward her hairline. "You can't mean Resl, surely. I just saw her at Freda Goldblum's shiva. She seemed fine."

Ava hesitates, cookie halfway to her mouth. *Resl?* She thinks. *Freda? Shiva? Like the deity?*

"Actually," Renate Bauer goes on, "I'm ashamed to ask this, but whose daughter *are* you? I thought I knew all of Adam's relatives. Granted, there are quite a few of you." She smiles ruefully, a gentle tilt to her lips that somehow conveys as much sadness as mirth. "And of course my memory isn't quite what it was."

"Adam?" Ava repeats blankly.

"My husband, dear." Her voice is patient; as though Ava might have hit her head, or is perhaps just a little bit slow. "Adam Cooperman. Though I suppose I should start saying late husband."

She pauses, seeming to briefly fall into herself before briskly returning to the moment. "But that's neither here nor there, is it. The question is, how are you related to Adam?"

Renate Bauer places one mottled hand atop the other in her lap, waiting. *She doesn't know*, Ava realizes, stunned. *She doesn't know who I am.*

The air feels dense and pressing; as though she's entrapped in a solid glass cube. She sets the biscuit down on the plate slowly, deliberately.

"I'm not Adam's niece," she says carefully.

"But you said . . ." Renate frowns, her expression gently baffled. Then she shakes her head. "I'm sorry. I don't think I understand."

Ava takes a deep breath. "My name," she says, switching to German, "my full name, is Ava Fischer. Von Fischer, originally. My mother was Ilse von Fischer."

At the utterance of *von Fischer* the old woman's demeanor changes. Nothing about her actually moves. But there is a sudden sense of her pulling inward; a sense of a subtle tightening.

"I'm sorry if this is a surprise," Ava continues, tightening her clasp on her bag. "But you see, she passed away only a few weeks ago. Today I received her ashes. But also these . . ."

But before she even finishes the sentence, Renate Bauer, with surprising agility, is already back on her feet.

"You have to leave," she says. She says it in English, her voice suddenly high and shrill. "I'm sorry you aren't feeling well. But you must leave."

Ava swallows. "Please," she says. "I know—I know my mother hurt you. She hurt me as well."

"I'm sorry," Renate repeats crisply. "But that isn't my problem."

"But you see, she wrote you. She wrote you for years. I brought them all here. All her letters . . ." She starts rummaging in her bag.

"I don't *care* about the blasted letters," Renate Bauer interrupts. "I didn't want them when she brought them here, and I certainly don't now."

"She—she came here?" For a moment the room seems to shift, ever so slightly, as though readjusting its position.

"*Ja.*" The older woman's voice is shaking with outrage now. "We made it very clear she wasn't welcome."

"When?" Ava manages; but even before the question is out she realizes that she already knows the answer: *Of course.* That awful night of the blackout.

It rushes back; Ilse's wan face when Ava found her at the police precinct. Her inexplicable attachment to her purse: *Don't tell me what I have in it.* Ava glances quickly back down at her own tattered bag, the crumpled paper just visible in jumbled disarray.

"It doesn't matter when," Renate Bauer is saying curtly. "There is nothing more to discuss." With three tight strides of her vein-etched, stockinged legs she is at the door. Flinging it open, she steps aside. "Please go. I don't want to have to call the doorman."

"But you still don't understand—" Ava begins to say, but the other woman cuts her off.

"I'm under no obligation to understand anything for you," Renate says sharply. "Even if you are her daughter. *Especially* if you are her daughter." She indicates the hallway with her chin. *"Du musst gehen."*

"Frau Bauer," Ava pleads.

"Doktor Bauer," Renate snaps.

"Doktor Bauer," Ava repeats, dutifully, desperately. "Please, listen to me. Just for a minute." She takes a deep breath. "I'm not really here about my mother. I'm here about something she wrote you. In this letter." With shaking hands, she slips the page from its envelope. "Can I just . . ."

"How many times must I say it? *I don't care about her damn letters!*"

There's a wildness now to the old woman's voice, an unsteadiness that seems fully positioned to escalate into a scream. "I'd just as soon read *Mein Kampf*. It amounts to the same bloody thing."

"But if you didn't read them, then you don't know about Franz and my mother. . . ."

"She killed him!" This does come out close to a scream. For a moment the older woman seems as startled by its ferocity as is Ava.

"For God's sake," she adds, shakily. "What more is there to know?"

Beneath her cardigan, her narrow chest heaves. Ava blinks at her, speechless. "Wh-what?" she finally manages.

"She killed him." Renate takes a hoarse breath. "Ilse von Fischer murdered my brother."

"No," Ava says slowly, shaking her head. "No. That's not right. You both got out. You came to America together."

"Nein." The rebuttal is guttural, unchallengeable. "Franz was taken by the Gestapo in 1939. A day before he was to leave Germany."

"Taken?" Ava repeats blankly.

"Arrested." Renate shuts her eyes for a moment, her lips pressed together tightly, as though struggling to keep the words in. "He never came back."

It hits Ava like a force field, with such jolting abruptness that she actually feels herself rock in her seat. *Never came back.* She presses a hand to her forehead, as though she might somehow physically impose calm on the careening thoughts just behind the bone.

"She didn't know," she finally whispers. "My mother didn't know."

"Not at first." The old woman's voice is more level now, but still biting. "No. She showed up here all smiles and tears. With her *letters*. And her *need*. Her need to *talk to me*. Her need to *explain*. Her need to apologize to me and my brother. She said she'd gotten our address from Barnard." She shakes her head contemptuously. "She was always good in that way, able to put things together."

"She never missed a beat." It comes out barely a whisper.

"Adam didn't even want to let her in," the old woman continues, as though Ava hadn't spoken. "But I thought: *Why not, after all these years.*

What harm could it really do." She gives a rueful laugh. "She used to make fun of me for that. How gullible I was. People don't really change, in the end. Do they. My mother—she was a psychoanalyst—used to tell me that. They may defy expectations. But they don't *change*."

She is leaning against the door now, her eyes distant behind her glasses. "But of course, I thought there still was a chance. I brought her upstairs, all smiles and welcome. *Come to my arms, my beamish boy!*"

Ava blinks. "Boy?"

"Nothing." The thin lips twist bitterly. "Just my own gullibility. I gave her iced tea and a bit of lemon shortbread." She is staring not at Ava, but at the table between them. "When she first apologized, I thought it was simply over never having said good-bye to us. You see, she'd come to see me before I left. She brought me a book. And she'd promised to come back, but she never did." She shakes her head. "When she told me she'd really been spying on us, at first I didn't understand. I thought she was making some sort of horrid joke. But then she was crying, and saying how ashamed she was of her behavior, and how she wanted to apologize to Franz in person as well. And I finally put it together: the Gestapo took my brother away because she'd *given* him away to them. It was *her fault*."

She takes a sharp, shaking breath in. "I told her Franz was dead. That they'd come for him because of her." She locks eyes with Ava, unblinking. "I told her that she was a murderer."

Trembling, Ava drops her gaze to her hands. She can see it so clearly: her mother likely sitting right where she is sitting now, after years of convincing herself that she hadn't done that much harm. That there was a chance, still, for redemption. She sees Renate Bauer's expression transition from cautious to shocked, and then horrified. Feels her mother's heart tighten and plummet within the black well of her chest. Just as her own is doing now.

"And then what happened?" she whispers.

Renate shakes her head again. "I don't remember it all very clearly. I was so upset. I know I shouted. I think I might have become faint myself. That was when Adam told her she had to leave."

Ava shuts her eyes, and her mother's face that night comes back: the utter desolation and weariness. *I think I should not have come.* A wave of nausea descends, along with a profound sadness. So in two days, her mother had been ejected from the lives of the three people she truly cared for in the world—after learning she'd effectively killed the only man she'd ever loved.

It takes tremendous effort to force her eyes open, and even more effort to force them to meet Renate's. "She didn't want to spy on you," she says. "The Gestapo made her. As punishment for having helped your father on *Kristallnacht.*"

The older woman just looks at her blankly.

"It's in the letters," Ava continues, her heart thudding again in her ears. "The Gestapo made her betray you. She thought she'd stalled them—that she hadn't given them enough information to act on. She thought she'd bought you both time to leave the country."

Renate just continues staring, so utterly nonresponsive that Ava wonders whether she's actually even heard her. Then the other woman squeezes her eyes shut again. For a moment she seems not the hard-willed persona Ava had observed in the lift, but someone much older and frailer. When she reopens her eyes Ava sees that they are damp. But still, Renate Bauer says nothing. Wordlessly, she shuts the door. Wordlessly she leans against it, her face the color of talc.

Then, slowly, she makes her way back to where Ava is still sitting on the sofa. When she reaches the armchair she lowers herself into it, still very slowly, as though not fully sure of its solidity.

"I know it probably doesn't change anything," Ava says, in a small voice.

Renate just shakes her head. After what feels like an interminable silence she starts to speak again; dully, heavily. In German.

"We'd been packing. We'd been up to nearly midnight together, going over all the paperwork. The forms. Approvals. The lists. There were so many *lists.*" She shakes her head. "We'd been arguing about something. Something stupid. I think he'd run out of room for a book he wanted to bring, and wanted me to put it in my hand baggage. At that point, my books were my only friends, and I already was leaving so many of my favorite ones behind. I told him no. I accused him of thinking his books were more important because he was a boy and I was a girl." Reaching into her skirt pocket, she pulls out a handkerchief, her thin hand with its hot-pink manicure trembling. The spots on the backs of them are the color of light coffee. But as Ava studies her face, for the first time she thinks she glimpses the young girl described in her mother's letters: hopeful, thoughtful. Almost unbearably vulnerable.

"That was nonsense, of course," Renate continues. "Franz was remarkably progressive for the times. He could be condescending, but I always knew that was over our age difference, not my gender." Her eyes are distant and dark, gazing not at Ava but vaguely over her left shoulder, toward her wall of books. "But you see, I was just so tired. We both were. You can't imagine what things had been like for us at that point. We'd been eating poorly, sleeping poorly. I was so worried about my parents. I hadn't wanted to leave them, but my mother insisted that they would follow us." She pauses to lift her glasses, pressing the white cloth against first one eye, then the other.

"I was always the hot-tempered one," she continues. "Franz was generally so calm. When I picked fights he'd find a way to make me laugh— and that would be that. But that night he snapped. For the first time I could remember ever since we were both small, he actually shouted back at me. He told me I was spoiled, a child. That I thought the world revolved around me. That I was in for a rude awakening in America. I told him—" She breaks off, swallows. "I told him it would be less rude if I didn't have to go with him. I told him I wished he were staying in Germany." She shuts her eyes. "It was the last thing I ever said to him."

When she looks back up at Ava her eyes are welling again.

"I'm sorry," Ava whispers again, sickened by how useless a response it is, how completely vacuous.

"They came for him the next morning," the old woman continues, again as if Ava hasn't spoken. "Just before sunrise. That's when they usually came for people." Tears are rolling down her withered cheeks now, but she makes no effort to try to dry them. "There was a horrible pounding on the front door, and when my mother opened it they pushed past her and went straight upstairs to his room. They seemed to know exactly where it was." With thin, pale fingers she wrings the handkerchief in her lap, then smooths it out again over her knee. Dampness traces her jawline, her chin; drops plop unnoticed on her gray skirt, darkening the fabric. "They dragged him out without even giving him a chance to change out of his bedclothes. Or to get the cane he needed to walk. He had had polio, you see. . . ." She chokes slightly, swallows. "They dragged him down the stairs backward. When my father tried to stop them, one of the agents hit him in the face with his pistol so hard his nose broke. My mother tried to block the door, but they shoved her to the ground. Outside—I don't know why, he must have said something—they started beating him . . ."

She stops again, her eyes shut against the memory. "They beat him to a pulp right there, in front of our house. In front of my parents. In front of the neighbors who came to their windows and doorways to watch. They kicked his stomach over and over, in their heavy leather boots, until blood came out of his mouth and his nose. They kicked his teeth." She chokes slightly. "They kicked them so hard that broken parts of them were left on the sidewalk after they left. My mother . . . my mother collected them."

"No." Ava feels her hands fly to her mouth. "No. My mother wrote that she lied to them. About when you were leaving. About the meetings. She never told them anything. She was sure of it."

"It doesn't matter!" Renate's voice rises sharply again. "Do you think that mattered to my brother? To my parents, who saw him all but dead on the street before being dragged into one of those cars?" Gripping the sides of the armchair, she forces a jagged breath. "Do you know what we called them? Those black Mercedes the Gestapo drove? We called them *Leichenwagen*. Hearses. Because if you ended up in one, you were almost certainly dead."

Tot. The word seems to hang between them for a moment in the book-scented silence. Shivering, Ava hugs herself harder.

"My mother chased them," Renate resumes. "In bare feet and her nightgown. She chased them halfway down our street. Screaming:

Where are you taking him? When will he be back? For a few blocks, they drove just slowly enough to laugh at her from the windows. *He'll be back when he's back*, one of them shouted. That was all."

Ava gazes at her water glass, the ice melted to slim sheer chips, the condensation beading along the outside crystal. She wants to drink, but she can't seem to move.

"A day and a half later," Renate is continuing, more quietly now, "I left for America. On my own. With my own luggage, a bag full of my own books." She pauses, passes a thin hand across her forehead. "I tried so hard not to go. I argued and fought. I threatened to run away. But of course, in the end, I had no choice." Wearily, she shakes her head. "I remember watching from the deck as the ship left the Hamburg harbor. My parents were wild with worry and grief, of course. But they smiled and waved as though I were off on a pleasure cruise. They kept it up for as long as they thought I could see them. When I couldn't, I borrowed another passenger's binoculars. My last image was of my mother collapsing into my father's arms."

The tears have stopped for the moment. Behind her glasses, her reddened eyes seem unfocused; as though she's still gazing numbly at a fast-retreating shoreline, at the only two people left for her in the world. "I almost hurled myself over that rail. Even though I couldn't swim then; I would have drowned. I just kept repeating to myself: *They'll come soon. They'll come soon.*"

"And did they?" It comes out in a shaky whisper.

Renate shakes her head. "Mama wrote me later that she'd received notice of my brother's death. They told her he'd had a heart attack while in custody. That he'd been cremated 'for sanitary purposes.' And that she'd have to pay thirty *Reichsmark* for postage and handling for his ashes."

Ava thinks of Ilse's ash-filled plastic urn. She swallows back against another wave of nausea.

"A year or so after I left," Renate continues, "they were forced into a *Judenhaus* on Kurfürstendamm. Vati avoided deportation for a while because he was married to a non-Jew. But in 1942 he was sent to Auschwitz. He died there less than a year later."

"And your mother?"

"Killed by the Russians at the end of the war."

Raped and left in the snow, Ava thinks reflexively. For a moment she thinks she actually might vomit.

The older woman picks unseeingly at an invisible fray or thread on the handkerchief's edge. Ava stares at her own hands; grimy, sticky with cookie crumbs. The right is smudged slightly from Ilse's ink. Every fiber of her being seems to pulse with pain and shock. When she opens her mouth even her tongue feels broken.

"I'm truly so sorry," she murmurs, again achingly aware of just how hollow the term is.

The old woman continues staring at her lap.

"She didn't know either, then," Ava continues. "My mother. When she came here. She didn't know that he never made it out."

Renate shakes her head. "When I told her she seemed quite shaken. She tried to ask more questions, but Adam wouldn't let her. He took her arm. He walked her right out of the building."

Ava nods slowly. So on the day of the blackout Ilse, having somehow found this address, arrived with her decades-old letters and her dreams of friendship resurrected, of crimes absolved. Perhaps even of romance rekindled. Instead, she was given the full crushing weight of her crime, one she'd bear for the rest of her life.

She pictures her mother after being ejected from Renate's home, exiled back into the airless city. She sees her wandering dark streets blindly with her pocketbook of unread letters: Oedipus after his fall.

"It broke her too," she says slowly. "Discovering that she'd not only betrayed you, but was responsible for my father's death."

Renate looks up sharply. "Your father?"

"Franz. Your brother."

The old woman frowns. "Franz wasn't your father."

"Yes. Yes, he was."

The older woman shakes her head. "It's not possible. He would never . . . that would never have happened."

Ava starts to respond. Then, thinking the better of it, she reaches back into her bag.

"This," she says gently, "was written by my mother in June 1956. May I?"

When the old woman doesn't answer, Ava pulls the folded note from the envelope. Clearing her throat, she begins reading aloud.

Dear Reni:

It is a quiet Sunday evening here in Bremen, and I am at my kitchen table with a glass of sherry and my pen. Ava is in her room, loudly playing a record by that oddly popular American who gyrates his hips like a bellydancer. She is also crying into her pillow. The pillow and the music are intended for me: she doesn't want me to know what has happened. But I can guess. And while I'm sure a good mother would rush upstairs to offer sympathy and advice, there are several things that are keeping me from doing so.

You see, I suspect her heart is broken, and I suspect it has been broken by a Jewish boy whom she has known for years now. I tried to keep the attachment from forming, as it seemed inevitable to me that it couldn't last. Not because of his race—you of all people know that I'm certainly no anti-Semite. But because like you I understand, in a way she can't yet, that the barriers to happiness are always far too high when people come from such very different worlds. To be honest, I'm only glad that it happened sooner rather than later.

I would very much like to be able to say all this to Ava; even more so now that I've had some more sherry (!). But as I can't, I write you, as I have taken to writing you periodically over the past decade, just as I always did when we were girls.

Odd, the habits one keeps.

You and I spent a good deal of time considering romance, I remember. All those hours pondering potentially "dirty" bits of All Quiet on the Western Front *and* Anna Karenina. *All the juicy details you'd share about your moviehouse dates with Rudi Gerhardt. The long walks we'd take; talking and talking, stopping at Konditorei Schloss for our daily Mohnkuchen. To be honest, in all the years since, I have never had another friendship that was quite that close, quite that effortless.*

It makes me sad, sometimes, to think of how naïve we both were then. How we had no way of seeing the events that would roll over us both and change our lives. Though again, I suppose it's also more evidence for my theory: for as breathlessly as you loved Rudi for all those months, it could only have caused more heartbreak eventually. That is clear.

There is news on Rudi, by the way: He's still in prison, awaiting trial for some Aktion-related event in Russia or Hungary. I'm not sure when the date has been set for, but it will likely be quite some time yet. The backlog on these things is quite significant.

Pausing, Ava peers over the page, at Renate's face. But the old woman is staring at her books, her expression unreadable.

I wish I could send you a picture of Ava. Apart from an unfortunate haircut at the moment—I truly fail to understand the current fashions!— she's grown into a lovely young woman, though she seems to have absolutely no awareness of her own beauty. She's not unlike you in that way, I think. I always felt as though for you, your looks were like a complex gadget you'd been given and never quite deduced how to operate. And in fact, she looks not unlike you: dark hair, large dark eyes, lovely glowing skin. She's every bit as passionate about art as you were about books; when she begins to sketch or paint it's as though time ceases to exist. Sometimes she falls asleep with her sketchbook under her cheek. Ever the restless sleeper myself these days, I'll tiptoe in at three or four, cover her up and turn out her light.

At this point, I should add (and I've just had some more sherry to steel myself) that the likeness between her and you is almost certainly more than coincidental. Because the truth is that you are related.

The truth is that Franz is her father.

(There, I have finally written it.)

Ava pauses again, staring at the phrase—*Franz ist ihr Vater*—which had triggered such joyous shock earlier on in the day.

Swallowing again, she reads on.

I know you'd find this almost as shocking as I did, when I was finally faced with the truth. For months—years, really—I'd told myself that Ava's father was the editor I went with while working at the BDM publications office, even though beneath it all I'm sure that this wasn't even vaguely likely. Kai and I were still involved, yes. But he'd been away in Poland for weeks when Ava was conceived. Still, it was Kai I wrote with the news of the pregnancy, and Kai's name that I put on Ava's birth certificate and ration forms. Had he survived the war, I suppose that it would also have been Kai whom I ended up marrying, adding yet one more lie to the pile I'd built my life on.

But Kai died in the East, well before the end of the war. And the moment I picked Ava up at the orphanage I simply knew: the likeness I'd managed to overlook when she was a baby had become incontestable. It actually left me speechless at first.

I have no doubt that you'd be speechless too, were you to read these words. And yet I think you always suspected my feelings for your brother, even if I tried to hide them from you. Nor did I ever think that they'd be more than that: feelings. Certainly not after the race laws forced me away from your family. But fate has a way of playing pranks on us sometimes, and this was a particularly dark one.

Has Franz ever told you that I'd come to see him just a day or two before you left? I told him I'd come to see you, but I knew you wouldn't be home. So when he answered the door I got him to invite me inside with some excuse I can't remember, other than that it was something I was genuinely curious about.

But the truth was that I'd been sent there by the Gestapo.

I want to be clear that I did not do this willingly. I knew full well it was monstrous, and I loathed myself for it. But the Gestapo had pressured me in such a way that I could not refuse—or at least, that is how I saw it at the time. They sent me to determine whether Franz was still involved in his Socialist meetings, and to gather intelligence about when and where those meetings occurred, and the names of the other people who attended them. I did get some of this information, and my plan was originally to hold off delivering it until you were both out of the country. But they were waiting for me at our house the very night I returned from yours. I'd had no forewarning of the visit, and they obviously felt no need to share the reasoning behind it. But I must be as good a liar as you always said I was, because while they questioned me for hours, trying to trip me up, to trick me, to startle me with shouts and sudden stomps, I managed to stick to my story: that the next meeting was the following week, and that Franz would be in attendance and had agreed to bring me. I gave them the location, the time. When the time came, I reasoned, and he wasn't there, I'd simply say that I hadn't known he was leaving. That he'd lied.

Luckily, though, they never did follow up about it—perhaps because my Lodz posting came through less than a day later, and less than a week later I was out of the country. Or maybe they had too many other Socialists to process after the raid. Or perhaps (and this is what I'd like to think) the whole thing was just a test, set up to prove or disprove my loyalty. Either way, looking back, it remains in many ways both the best and the worst day of my life. The best, because it enabled me to spend one last moment not just with Franz, but with so many fond memories of and feelings for your home and your family. And worst because I came close to death at the hands of the Gestapo only hours later.

Did Franz ever tell you what happened between us that afternoon? For some reason I think he did not. I think that, like me, perhaps he's locked it away as something at once impossibly perfect and perfectly impossible. For my part, I have never told anyone. Not even Ava—or perhaps, especially not Ava. Not because I'm ashamed of her or her lineage, but because the story behind it is at once too personal and too painful. You see, for all your protestations that I was the brave one, I really am at heart a coward in the end.

But I am hoping that someday I'll be brave enough to tell her about it all: about Franz and you; about the good times we had as children and the harder times as young adults. Perhaps I'll even be brave enough to find you both. And if so, who knows what might follow? . . .

Ah. The hip-twitching American has been switched off; I just looked at the clock and saw the time. As usual I've gone on and on in a letter that most likely will never be read by anyone else. But also as usual, it leaves me with just a little less of that leaden, lonely feeling inside. As does the knowledge that even if you and Franz aren't yet aware of it, Ava and I do still have family.

Humbly yours,
Ilsi

Setting the letter in her lap, Ava closes her eyes for a moment. *The truth*, she repeats in silence, as she had earlier in her room, *is that Franz is my father.*

And: *The truth is that my mother killed him.*

For an instant there's again that disorienting sense of falling in place; the sort of motionless plummet one feels in dreamt tumbles which end with waking, shocked and gasping, in bed. Ava covers her face with her hands. When she looks up again, it's to find Renate Bauer staring at her. It's not the gaze she'd worn while sharing her heart-stopping story, when her eyes seemed trained not on Ava but on some invisible screen between them, upon which played out the cataclysm she was relating.

No, now she is actually *looking* at Ava; bluntly studying her through her glasses. Assessing each feature, each long dark eyelash while her mind works furiously to confirm or deny. Ava finds herself holding her breath; as though she were standing before a diminutive judge whose verdict will determine her very fate.

After concluding her survey, however, Renate Bauer doesn't immediately speak. She stands up. As Ava watches, twisting her hands in her lap, the old woman paces from the bookshelf to the window, her white hair illumined by pinkish, early-evening light. She seems agitated, almost angry. But for several sets of rapid strides—back and forth, back and forth—she neither looks at her newfound niece nor says a word.

"What is it?" Ava finally asks, aware of how tentative and nervous her voice sounds.

Stopping midway between door and bookshelf, Renate Bauer looks at her fiercely.

"It's your *mother*," she finally says, her tone caustic. "Even dead, she's turning everything to chaos."

Ava blinks.

"All these years," the old woman continues. "All this time, all I've had to do is *hate* her. And that was easy enough, after all. After all she did to me. To us." She flings an arm out, indicating Ava. "But now here you are, with her letters and your stories and you—your goddamn eyes. Your eyes that are *just* like Franz's."

"They are?" asks Ava, feeling them widen.

"Yes," Renate snaps, "Yes." And then, more softly: "You have his nose as well. She must have seen it every time she looked at you."

Every time she looked at me. Awed, Ava touches the outer corner of her eye, the very tip of her nose, as though she might be able to confirm the resemblance tactilely. She sees Ilse at her kitchen table again, the morning after the blackout. Staring at her with such bleakness, such utter despair that Ava hadn't been able to hold her gaze.

"And now here you are," the older woman is continuing. "And I have no idea what to do with you. None at all." She breaks off, glaring at Ava before looking away again.

"I'm sorry," Ava whispers, though she doesn't know what she's apologizing for.

Outside a siren blares, its tone rising and falling as its vehicle hurtles toward its unknown uptown destination. In a neighboring apartment, someone's dog breaks into howling accompaniment before falling abruptly back into silence. Renate remains motionless, eyes on her overstuffed bookshelves, thin fingers tugging absently at a salt-and-pepper strand of hair. Ava imagines drawing her like this; not out of the urge to create art, but for the opportunity to really ponder her features: the fine dark brows and softly etched lines in her forehead. The small nose. The distant look in the dark eyes. How many of those features, she wonders, did Franz share with his sister? Was it possible to find her father in her aunt's face? Does Renate have any pictures of him? She wants to ask her. Not just about that, but a thousand other things that Ava is just starting to know she doesn't know. Were there other artists in their family? Were there illnesses? Was she in touch with anyone else from the Bauer side of the family? Was anyone else even left?

"*So.*"

Looking up, she sees that Renate has sat back down, briskly placing her hands on her knees.

"What's next?" she asks, her dark eyes snapping and her head tilted in a way that reminds Ava of a bright-eyed little bird.

"I don't know." Ava hesitates, then adds: "I'd like to come back."

Renate bites her lip. "I'd have to think about it."

"I'd like Sophie to meet you," Ava says. "She never got a chance to know my mother." For a moment she sees her daughter again; the unfamiliar rage that had flashed on her face. *Sophie*, she thinks suddenly. She pulls herself to her feet. "Actually, can I use your phone?"

The older woman blinks first, then nods. "Around the corner. Next to the refrigerator."

The kitchen, Ava discovers, feels as cozily stuck in the past as the rest of the little apartment. Wood paneling on the cupboards and sink make the windowless space even darker, the effect brightened only slightly by the mint-green glint of the oven door and matching exhaust shield over the stove. Thankfully, though, the wall-mounted telephone—the color of Pepto-Bismol—is a punch-button model, not rotary. Ava dials in, cringing at her own slightly frantic-sounding voice before punching in her access code for the machine.

At first, all that follows is muffled movement and static. But then comes Sophie's bell-clear voice: "Hi, Mom." Her daughter's tone is tight-sounding, but the spitting rage of the morning seems to have faded. Sophie continues: "I'm okay. I'm just at Erica's watching music videos." She pauses. "And don't worry. We didn't go into the park." In the brief pause that follows, Ava's pulse leaps in time with the oversynthesized chorus in the background, a pulsing number she vaguely recognizes, something about blaming rain. "I was going to ask to sleep over," her daughter continues. "But if you really want, I guess . . . I guess I can come home, too. Leave a message letting me know."

An audible teenage snort in the background. Ava pictures both girls rolling their eyes in the eternal exasperation of the young. She's about to hang up when her daughter adds—almost curtly:

"I love you too."

Ava's knees seem to go weak. She leans against the Formica counter so washed with relief that she feels like she's drowning. She is tempted to call the machine again, just to hear those last three words (*I love you*, she said! *She said I love you!*). Instead, she hangs the phone up, redials, and leaves her own message after the tone:

"Hi, sweetie. Yes. Yes, please, come home. I have so much to tell you. I've had the most incredible day . . ." She pauses, wondering how she can possibly pack the past three hours into a thirty-second sound bite. In the end she just says: "We'll talk. We'll order in. I love you so much, *Liebling*."

Hanging up, she clenches the counter, briefly unsteady on her feet. Then she makes her way back to the living room.

"Is everything all right?" Renate asks, as Ava retakes her former seat.

"Yes. I was worried. But she's okay."

Renate just nods, as though she knows there is more.

"She was right to be angry with me," Ava says, dropping her gaze to her hands. "You see, I—I kept Ilse from her too. For thirteen years, I told her my mother was dead. She only found out this morning that I'd been lying."

"After the ashes arrived." Renate raises a brow. "Ilse always did have a way of showing up at crucial moments."

"She did." Despite herself, Ava laughs. Then she shuts her eyes. "I suppose I'm an awful mother."

A moment passes. Something dry and light touches her knee. Opening her eyes again, Ava sees Renate's weathered hand, tentatively hovering over the bare skin. "I'm sure you're a wonderful mother," the older woman says quietly. "And teenage girls can also be awful. I remember. I did my share of running out when I was one."

"Not in New York."

"True. But Berlin wasn't always so safe there in those days, either. Particularly for people like me." She smiles ruefully, returning her hand to her own lap.

"We never had children, Adam and I," she continues thoughtfully. "Between his medical school and my dissertation, and then his hospital shifts and my teaching, somehow the time never seemed right." She shrugs. "We waited too long, I suppose. Though sometimes I wonder if it wasn't because I was afraid."

"Afraid?"

"Of loving them too much." Her dark gaze seems to drift for a moment. "I couldn't have borne it, you see. Anything happening to them. Not after everything else. The truth was, I couldn't stand even having a pet. God knows Adam would have loved a dog."

She stares at the worn carpet, looks thoughtful again, a little wistful. Then she looks up.

"What is she like, your daughter?"

"Honestly?" Ava laughs again. "She's like a clone of my mother. Which is strange, because I've tried to raise her completely opposite, in every way, from the way my mother raised me. And yet in the end, Sophie is practically the spitting image. Not just in looks, but in the way she thinks and behaves."

"How so?"

Ava ponders. "She's very determined. Fearless. Focused. She has a memory like a steel trap."

"That does sound like Ilse."

"But she is also almost frighteningly honest," Ava adds quickly. "I don't think she has ever wittingly told a lie in her life."

Renate nods again. "Does she write?"

"Write?"

"As a hobby. Essays, stories, that sort of thing."

"Ah." Ava nods. "Yes. She's constantly writing something. Plays. Poems. Things like that. She rarely lets me read them." She suddenly remembers the letters. "Oh. Speaking of writing . . ." She reaches into her purse. "These belong to you."

But even as she is pulling the stack of worn envelopes from her bag, Renate is shaking her head. *"Nein."*

"No?" Ava looks up, confused.

"I don't want them," Renate says firmly.

"But . . . but what should I do with them, then?"

Renate Bauer just shrugs. "Perhaps give them to your daughter. After all, they're as much her story as they are mine."

Ava puts the letters back in her lap. They fall silent again, and Ava finds herself thinking about what the other woman had said earlier, about her last sight of her parents. She pictures them herself: two small, stark figures on a receding dock. Which was worse, she wonders—knowing and losing both? Or never knowing them at all?

The question seems to usher an endless flood of others. Why *had* the Gestapo shown up at Ilse's house that night? Had her mother really thrown them off as firmly as she claimed she had? Or was that just another falsehood she'd told herself to avoid taking blame, the same way she'd lied to herself by imagining that—despite all the exhaustive paperwork the Bauers must have filed—the Gestapo wouldn't have known of Franz's and Renate's travel plans? Or that in talking so glibly with those agents that night, she'd been saving anyone other than herself? For in the end, Ava realizes, it was *these* untruths—the ones she told herself—that had been her undoing.

The things we tell ourselves, she thinks. *The things we lie about to make our crimes bearable.*

In another room a clock starts to chime softly. Ava counts along absently in her mind: *One. Two. Three* . . . After the sixth tone she hears Renate catch her breath. "Oh dear. Is it really six o'clock? I'm afraid that I have to leave soon. I've opera tickets tonight. *The Magic Flute.* I almost forgot about it completely."

She stands up, smoothing her skirt. Realizing she's being dismissed, Ava feels a wave of something approaching panic. What if this is it? What if Renate Bauer has had enough of her already, and never wants to see her again?

"I'm sorry. I've kept you," she says, trying to keep her voice steady as she climbs to her own feet again. "I didn't realize it had gotten so late either."

"It's fine," says the other woman. "It's just that I must change." She smiles wryly. "I'm still old enough to believe in dressing up for these things."

Slinging her bag over her shoulder, Ava straightens the canvas straps, her mind racing. "Can I call you, at least? I mean, in a couple of days or so. After you've had time to let all of this . . . settle somewhat." She indicates the space between them. "I have so many things I want to ask you about. . . ."

Renate appears lost in thought a moment. Then she nods. "Yes. Yes, you may call. And then we can make a plan. Perhaps dinner somewhere. You, myself, and your daughter."

"That would be wonderful," says Ava. "Just wonderful." She's been following Renate to the door now, and as the other woman pulls it open Ava turns to face her, once again at a loss. How does one part with a sole surviving relative that she didn't even know had existed before today? With the one person who can tell her everything she's never known about the father and grandparents she never knew?

Tentatively, she extends her hand. Renate studies it for a moment. At first she makes no move to do the same, and Ava bites her lip, unsure of herself again. Then, to her complete surprise, the older woman bridges the distance between them to give Ava a short but surprisingly strong hug. Startled, Ava has just enough time to return the embrace, her heart skittering, before stepping back awkwardly.

As Ava struggles to recompose herself Renate studies her again, one pink-tipped finger pressed thoughtfully to her cheek. "It's so strange," she says.

"What is?"

"You." Reaching out, the older woman traces a light line from the corner of Ava's eye to her chin. "You are," she says, slowly, "a mixture of everything I have ever loved, and everything I have ever hated in my life."

As Ava gazes back at her, something inside her chest seems to ineffably unknot, the way a muscle that has been cramping releases. In its wake, for the first time since learning of her mother's death—actually, the first time in what seems like years—comes a lightness. Almost a giddiness.

"I think that makes me family," she says.

Acknowledgments

Many people helped me to grow, shape, and hone this novel as it evolved. Thanks to Michael Epstein for spying—in a *New Yorker* piece about a somewhat obscure German memoir—the seed of an interesting narrative, and then brainstorming, cheerleading, and workshopping along as I coaxed that seed into a book. Amelia Atlas at ICM rescued me from representational wilderness and helped me sharpen and tighten the *Wunderland* manuscript, and Hilary Rubin Teeman offered it an extraordinary and enthusiastic home at Crown, along with narrative and stylistic suggestions that made it so much better. Thanks to Jillian Buckley for expertly shepherding me through the production process, and to Amy Schneider for her invaluable copyediting expertise. Thanks to Dr. Catherine Epstein of Amherst College for her close reading for historical and cultural context of an earlier draft, and to Endre M. Holeczy, Daniel Brandl-Beck, Dr. Aine Zimmerman, and David Kay for further essential insights into German culture and language usage. All errors that remain despite their heroic efforts are mine and mine alone. Thanks to Renate Olsen for sharing recollections of her childhood in wartime and postwar Germany, and to Johannes Beilharz for granting me the use of his lovely translation of Else Lasker-Schüler's poem "To the Prince of the Grail."

Heartfelt thanks to Jennifer Egan for providing sage professional advice and direction when I direly needed it.

Many historical sources were consulted for this project, but a few stand out as uniquely informative and of possible interest to *Wunderland* readers. First and foremost is Melita Maschmann's confessional memoir *Account Rendered,* which provided emotional and historical insight into one woman's incremental journey from youthful idealism to full-on Nazi fanaticism, and from intimate friendship to brutal betrayal. Victor Klemperer's *I Will Bear Witness: A Diary of the Nazi Years, 1933–1941* depicted the horrific deterioration of Jewish daily life under Nazi rule, while Joachim Fest's *Not I: Memoirs of a German Childhood* explored the same period from a non-Jewish/Catholic perspective. Erica Fischer's *Aimee and Jaguar* was both a breathless read and a treasure-trove of period detail, particularly regarding the onerous bureaucratic gauntlet faced by German Jews trying to flee the country. Elizabeth Harvey's *Women and the Nazi East* shed fascinating light on daily life in Nazi Germany's Labor Service programs abroad. Jonathan Mahler's *Ladies and Gentlemen, the Bronx Is Burning: 1977, Baseball, Politics, and the Battle for the Soul of a City* painted a richly vivid portrait of the 1977 New York blackout, while Jillian Becker's *Hitler's Children: The Story of the Baader-Meinhof Terrorist Gang* provided compelling background for understanding the rise of Germany's 1968 protest movement.

Novels worth their salt require smart readers along the way, and *Wunderland* has had so many: Hillary Jordan and Joanna Hershon provided—as always—inspiration, encouragement, and astute feedback, as did my Brooklyn writing coven (Alison Lowenstein, Julia Lichtblau, Courtney Zoffness, Maura Sheehy, Michelle Brandt, and the late and deeply missed Sarah Coleman). Joan Cody, Tom Cody, Dina McGuinn, Rozanne and Steve Epstein, Andrea Lafleur, and Amy Simon Hopwood all offered perspective and encouragement throughout various drafts, while my trusted BOCOCA mom posse (especially Amy Sirot, Julie Beglin, Virginia Terry, and Laura Sweet) weighed in dutifully and thoughtfully when called upon. Thanks too to Pam Loring for the peace and austere tranquillity of the Salty Quill Women's Writing Retreat, and to

Scott Adkins and Erin Courtney of the Brooklyn Writers Space for providing an oasis of quiet and literary camaraderie.

Last but never ever least: thanks to my amazing daughters, Katie and Hannah, for inspiring me daily and believing in me and my work (even when I don't), and once more to Michael—as always my muse, hausfrau, and partner in creative mischief.

Wunderland

JENNIFER CODY EPSTEIN

A Reader's Guide

RANDOM HOUSE READER'S CIRCLE

Wunderland

1. The various points of view in the novel give us insight into a character's thinking and help us understand why they made certain decisions. Did any character make a decision that you felt was unforgiveable?

2. Which character did you most relate to in the novel? Which character did you find the most difficult to understand?

3. We first enter the story through Ava's point of view as she reads Ilse's letters for the first time. What is the benefit of using this structure? Why does the author choose to write in multiple time periods? Would the story have been different had it been written chronologically?

4. Renate's sense of identity is turned upside down at a pivotal point in her adolescence. What impact do you think this had on Renate's life? Can you relate to her experience?

5. As the novel progresses, we see Ilse remain silent as drastic changes take place in her city, many of which ultimately impact Renate. Why do you think Ilse doesn't speak up?

6. Despite butting heads at every turn, Ava and her mother are similar in many ways—they're both headstrong, determined, and protec-

tive. What more do you think they have in common? Why is their relationship so strained?

7. Why do you think Ilse keeps so many secrets from Ava? Do you think Ava would have fared better had she known the truth from the start? Why or why not?

8. Did you find Ilse to be a sympathetic character? When did you begin to understand her point of view, or when did you lose touch with her?

9. *Wunderland* opens with an epigraph from *Alice's Adventures in Wonderland* and Renate returns to this children's story several times in the novel. What is the significance of this to the novel and to Renate in particular?

10. Were you surprised by the ending? What did you think of Renate's decisions in the last chapter?

11. Ultimately, Ilse and Renate's story is a fictionalized account of what truly happened to millions of people in Europe during WWII. What is the benefit of reading a fictionalized novel about this time period? How is it different from reading nonfiction about the same events?

12. Do you feel that any of the themes explored in *Wunderland* are applicable in today's world?

Author of *Wunderland*

Q. Could you tell us more about the actual WWII memoir that inspired *Wunderland,* and the research you conducted while writing the novel?

A. I first learned about *Account Rendered*, Melita Maschmann's extraordinary memoir, in a 2013 *New Yorker* piece my husband happened upon. The article recounted how Maschmann, a former Hitler Youth enthusiast, wrote an intimate account of her rise and fall as a national socialist that was about to be published in English here. Her confession takes the shape of a long letter to Maschmann's childhood best friend, a girl who found herself classified as a *Mischling* (person of mixed race) under Hitler's race laws at roughly the same time Maschmann joined the Bund Deutscher Mädel, which is the girl's branch of the Hitler Youth. Reading the article, I felt a flash of recognition. I'd known for years that I wanted to write about the Holocaust—not about the monstrous mechanics of the Final Solution, but something that would help me better understand the individual choices people made at that time, choices that might have seemed logical or mundane in the moment, but which could have had a devastating impact. How could people who thought of themselves as good citizens, as ethical human beings, have knowingly contributed to such an inhumane and unforgivable event?

At that point I hadn't really read any historical accounts that shed light on that question. But in both the *New Yorker* piece and *Account Rendered* I spotted the seeds of the kind of story I wanted to tell, and the rough trajectories that my book's two central characters might take in order to explore those themes. From there sprang Ilse and Renate: two German girls caught up in the madness of Hitler's Germany, but in very different ways, as Renate has her life destroyed by the Nuremburg laws, while Ilse rises to the Hitler Youth's highest ranks. Since I was interested in understanding the impact of those kinds of choices on the next generation, I created a third character: Ava, Ilse's estranged daughter who has fled Germany to live in New York and uncovers the secret of her mother's history after Ilse's death.

To help flesh out Ilse's world, I read works including Alison Owings' collection of oral histories, *Frauen: German Women Recall the Third Reich,* and Wendy Lower's *Hitler's Furies: German Women in the Nazi Killing Fields.* For Renate's perspective I read works that included Victor Klemperer's marvelously detailed two-volume diary, *I Will Bear Witness,* as well as *Aimée & Jaguar: A Love Story, Berlin 1943* by Erica Fischer and *The Nazi Officer's Wife: How One Jewish Woman Survived the Holocaust* by Edith Hahn Beer.

Q. In *Wunderland,* stories from WWII Germany are interwoven with 1980s New York City. Can you talk about how the two juxtaposed settings lend themselves to an exploration of the characters' relationships?

A. In *Wunderland,* Ava flees to New York because she needs to escape both her dysfunctional relationship with her mother and (relatedly) the Holocaust's catastrophic legacy. Like many Germans of that generation, Ava grew up hearing next-to-nothing about the war. The revelation of Germany's Hitler-era sins is crushing for her (as it seems to have been for many Germans) and New York becomes a place where she not only can pursue her dreams as an artist but quite literally escape her nationality; she even at one point tells a sales clerk that her accent is Danish. As for so many of us who end up in New York, the city offers Ava a chance at re-invention—at least, until Ilse arrives, with the full weight of her own damning history in tow.

The glorious grit and creative chaos of New York—especially the East Village in the 70's and 80's—also stand in powerful contrast to the tightly regimented polish and repressive order of Nazi-era Berlin, something that is reflected in Ava and Ilse's fraught and ultimately doomed relationship.

Q. Did you know how the story would unfold when you began the novel, or did you learn where it was headed along the way, like Ilse, Renate, and Ava?

A. When I sat down to write, I had a rough sense of the general storyline— e.g., a best friendship is shattered when one friend becomes a Nazi and the other discovers she's Jewish. I knew there had to be some sort of enormous betrayal that would later haunt the character who became Ilse. I wasn't initially sure what that betrayal would be, though I think I had an inkling when I decided to give Renate—the Jewish character— an older brother (though at the time it felt less like a decision on my part than on Franz's—he sauntered into the narrative on his own). I knew that there had to be a third character in the current day who discovers the betrayal, though as a character Ava initially started based in Germany, not New York. The mystery of Ava's paternity was another thing I hadn't solved at the start; it was rather something I sort of stumbled toward through what felt like an endless series of rewrites and much helpful input from my reading friends and husband.

Q. The novel is told from various perspectives. Did any challenges arise writing the different characters' voices?

A. I didn't find the voices for Ilse and Renate as difficult as I might have, I think because I read a lot of memoir and fiction and watched movies from the period, which gave me a sense of how they might have spoken and interacted. Interestingly, I had a lot of trouble with Ava, both as a character and as a voice. I knew I wanted her to be kind of a mess, but finding the right balance—e.g., "messy" enough to engender empathy, but not so screwed up as to alienate readers—was a challenge. She was definitely the character I rewrote the most; she started out as a frazzled fashion writer, graduated into being an adulterous wife and had a somewhat distasteful phase as a punk rock groupie at CBGB's before I found (I hope) a kind of balance for her as a struggling artist. Even then, though, trying to capture the nuances of someone who is almost entirely fluent in English but still thinks and speaks with a slight German inflection was tricky.

Q. *Alice's Adventures in Wonderland* is referenced several times throughout the novel. Can you tell us more about how the classic children's story connects to your characters?

A. I've always loved Lewis Carroll; there is something at once so beguiling and silly and yet also intriguingly dark about his work. I didn't initially expect to build a beloved children's book into a Holocaust novel, but I kept finding myself using the term "rabbit hole" as I tried to explain the project, both to myself and to others. And the more I thought about it, the more parallels I found. Like Alice, both Berlin characters start out as normal, happy, slightly smart-mouthed girls who chase their own versions of the white rabbit—BDM membership, romance, social acceptance. This leads them to surreal if oppositional worlds: Ilse in the dystopic construct of Hitler's "pure" Germany, where propaganda is fact and hate is patriotic; Renate in a world where she has—almost overnight—gone from happy citizen to persecuted outsider, caricatured in newspapers, ostracized at school, and stripped of even the most basic of rights. Ava has her own chase—though in her case, it's the truth about her mother and her paternity that turns her sense of herself on its head.

Upon researching the way Carroll's work was translated and published outside of England, I was intrigued to learn that the original German version of it was radically different from what I'd grown up with, in large part because some of Carroll's famous absurdisms simply baffled the books' initial German translator, who turned his twinkling tea tray–like bat into a far more boring green-feathered parrot.

Q. *Wunderland* delves deep in its exploration of the darkest potential of humanity. Do you feel that any of the themes explored in *Wunderland* are applicable in today's world?

A. One thing I love about writing historical fiction is that I am continually discovering unexpected connections between the worlds I'm exploring fictively and the real world around us. It drives home the commonality of the human experience; the fact that the issues we struggle with today tend to be the same ones human beings struggled with in generations past, all over the world. That said, when I started *Wunderland* in 2013 the themes I was interested in exploring—how ostensibly "good" people get swept into the toxic current of a national hate movement, and how that movement manifests itself in the daily flow of life—felt pretty comfortably removed. Donald Trump was a reality TV star known for beauty pageants and gilded toilets. America had just re-elected our first black president. We were legalizing gay marriage, having tough talks about race and privilege, even embarking on a national health plan. As I began to write, though, that landscape changed chillingly: within three years Trump had ridden a toxic swell of voter partisanship and xenophobia into the White House. At times the comparisons were unnerving: I'd come home from writing about the Nuremberg rallies and there Trump would be on CNN, surrounded by a sea of red hats, calling Mexicans rapists, referencing "global finance," and dismissing the independent media as "fake news," his own spin on what Hitler called the *Lügenpresse* or "the lying press." Then came Charlottesville and other horrifying manifestations of the anti-immigrant and anti-Semitic backlash we are now experiencing, not just here in the US but across Europe as well. Obviously, there are marked differences too—and Trump is certainly no Hitler. But the similarities were striking enough that reading the news or Twitter sometimes felt like an uncomfortable extension of my research for the novel.

Q. What do you hope readers will take away from *Wunderland*?

A. Reading for me is such an intensely personal experience, so I'm a little reluctant to distill the spectrum of possible reader reactions and emotions to my work into a single desirable "message." But I guess I hope that in reading *Wunderland*, they'll engage some of the tough questions I engaged with myself while writing it: How do the lessons of the past translate into the present? How you recognize evil amid the everydayness of life—and perhaps even in yourself? And once you recognize it, what do you do about it?

JENNIFER CODY EPSTEIN is the author of the international bestseller *The Painter from Shanghai* and of *The Gods of Heavenly Punishment*, winner of the 2013–14 Asian Pacific American Librarians Association Honor award for outstanding fiction. She has written for the *Wall Street Journal, Vogue, Self, Mademoiselle,* and many others. She has an MFA in fiction from Columbia University and a Master of Arts in International Affairs from the Johns Hopkins School of Advanced International Studies. She lives in Brooklyn with her husband and two daughters.